Divorce and the Holy Puck

Divorce and the Holy Puck

By

Richard L. Becker

iUniverse, Inc.
Bloomington

Divorce and the Holy Puck

This is a work of fiction. All of the characters, names, incidents, organizations, and dialogue in this novel are either the products of the author's imagination or are used fictitiously.

iUniverse books may be ordered through booksellers or by contacting:

iUniverse
1663 Liberty Drive
Bloomington, IN 47403
www.iuniverse.com
1-800-Authors (1-800-288-4677)

ISBN: 978-1-4759-4599-7 (sc)
ISBN: 978-1-4759-4601-7 (hc)
ISBN: 978-1-4759-4600-0 (ebk)

Library of Congress Control Number: 2012915864

Printed in the United States of America

iUniverse rev. date: 09/07/2012

Divorce And The Holy Puck

in which *Sly* lives his life to the fullest,
Sam contemplates suicide,
and they both pursue *The Holy Puck*

Table of Contents

Period One

THE FEEL

They Call Me Sam

- 1 -

After ten years I had become immune to their suffering. Any divorce lawyer who failed to develop this immunity was destined to suffer a serious drug addiction or a nervous breakdown, with a suicide attempt thrown into the mix at one point or another.

Besides, I had enough suffering of my own. I didn't need any of *theirs*.

On a Thursday morning in September I had forced myself out of bed, showered and shaved and then stood on my apartment's balcony with a shot of whiskey, smoking a cigar as the sun broke free of the horizon. In fourteen hours, I told myself, I will be back on this balcony, the cell phone off, the world quiet, another cigar in my hand and a bottle of whiskey by my side. It was not that far away. I could make it.

The good part of being a divorce lawyer was that my clients were usually depressed and miserable. It was nice spending time with people who felt as hopeless as me.

At the law firm's office I met my newest client in one of the firm's smaller conference rooms, a twenty-by-twenty foot square with a circular table and windows overlooking the parking lot. I hated the room because the leather chairs had no wheels so I couldn't lean back and rock across the carpet.

"I'm Samuel Oliver," I said, closing the door.

"George Tolliver."

We shook hands.

"Hey, our names rhyme," I noted.

He didn't smile.

I sat down.

George pushed the divorce pleadings towards me in disgust. "I was served yesterday by the sheriff's deputy at my office, in front of several subordinates. The papers say she's filed for divorce and I have three days to vacate our house, and I'm supposed to pay her $15,000 a month in spousal maintenance."

Every client in a divorce case existed somewhere within the five stages of grief: denial, anger, bargaining, depression and acceptance. It made no difference whether the client was male or female. The emotions were the same.

It was important to be in control when dealing with clients in such situations.

"I am sorry. Did you see this coming?"

"No. I thought I was the one who wanted the divorce. The bitch beat me to the courthouse."

Not denial, I thought.

I started our meeting by obtaining basic information from him, supposedly for his case but really for use in the event our law firm sued him for unpaid fees.

"Where do you live?"

He gave a residential address.

"Impressive. That's an incredible neighborhood. A gated community, right?"

"The house cost close to three million dollars."

"How much do you owe the bank?"

"About half of it."

"Where do you work?"

He named a telecommunications company. "I'm the Vice President of Marketing for the cellular division."

"Your income?"

"Last year, with bonuses, about a million and a half."

I could see he would be a lucrative but problematic client. George Tolliver oozed importance like liquid flowing from a crushed grape. It was doubtful people ever said 'no' to him. He wore a Patek Philippe watch worth four years income to the average American worker, a Hugo Boss suit with a perfectly pressed white shirt and dark blue tie. He was a middle aged George Bush, Jr. clone with striking blue eyes and pepper gray hair.

A less experienced lawyer might get bowled over by him, following whatever ridiculous orders he gave, taking insane legal positions to try and please him. Out of fear. Out of the blind hope George would recommend more wealthy clients to his lawyer.

I was past all of that. I would do my job based on his reasonable requests and the law. If George didn't like it he could find another lawyer to represent him. There were plenty of ass-kissing lawyers in town for him to boss around.

If there was one thing I had learned from my alter ego, Sly, it was that no law forced me to work for narcissistic assholes.

"So what happened?" I asked. "What brought you here?"

"We met in college," George began. He sat straight in the chair, perfect posture, one hand on his lap and the other resting on the table. "We dated our freshman year, broke up and saw little of each other until a few years after graduation. We ran into each other at a bar and started talking. We ended up getting married. She couldn't have children and I didn't want to adopt. That nearly ended the marriage but we struggled and got past it. We focused on our careers. She's a psychologist with a good practice, specializing in family counseling. We've been married for twenty-seven years. Twenty-seven years."

He paused and rubbed his eyes. I waited, trying to look empathetic. I used that expression with every client as he or she told the story of the marriage, even if the client was a serial killer and the divorce was due to the spouse finding body parts in the flower garden.

"So what happened?" I prompted.

"Nothing," he said. He looked me in the eye. "We moved into our house on our twenty-fifth wedding anniversary. It was our dream house. I thought we were doing well. We served on the board of a number of charities and did volunteer work in the community. Once a week we went out on a date as if we had just met. Twice a year we went on a romantic vacation. Except for not having children, all of our friends and family believed we had the perfect marriage. I think a lot of people envied us, how we acted together. I bought her everything. Gifts. Jewelry. Everything and anything."

George wasn't being honest, I knew. Clients always ignored their own flaws and the problems they caused the marriage. The other party was always to blame.

"Then what made her file for divorce?" I asked.

George reached to the floor for his shiny metal briefcase, opened it and dumped the contents onto the conference table.

By reflex I kicked out and since the chair had no wheels it toppled backward, spilling me onto the floor. I rolled into a crouch, desperately wishing I had a 'conceal and carry permit' and a loaded Glock handgun.

"What the fuck are they!" I yelled.

"A few of our pets," George said.

There were five of them, all lying still.

"I used half a can of pest spray on them this morning," George said. "I think it did the trick."

"Are you sure?"

"Actually no, I'm not. They are hardy bastards. I set one on fire a few weeks ago and the damn thing writhed on the lawn and put the fire out. I think it's still living. My wife went nuts, called me a sadist and threatened to file a police report."

George explained they were South American Stinging Beetles, natives of the Amazon rain forest. I listened, pressed against the door, my eyes locked onto their bodies. The best way to describe them was to consider a very large cockroach—two inches long and half an inch thick—with multiple antennas protruding from each side of its head. The insects were jet black and their antennas were almost as long as their bodies. The three-jointed body ended in what appeared to be a scorpion's tail.

"Those things live with you?" I asked. "In a three million dollar house?"

"Now you understand," George said. He sat back down and gestured to my chair.

I am in control, I told myself, sitting but staying a few feet from the table.

"You said a few of her pets," I said. "How many others does she have?"

George shrugged. "Five or six hundred. Unless they're breeding quicker than she can count them."

"There must be zoning laws . . . . animal ordinances . . . . something."

"Could be."

I felt a tremor in my gut and wanted to vomit.

"It started with six of them," George Tolliver said. "She made some connection over the Internet and the insects were smuggled into the country. That was two years ago. Four were females and they bred. They bred fast. My wife had a sealed room built in the basement with four glass walls, special lighting and heat lamps, simulated rain and fauna from South America. The room is basically a huge rectangle in the middle of the basement and one wall has slots to add food and water, and a door. They live in that room but one or two sometimes escape when a slot is opened."

"Who knows about them?"

"Just the two of us. And now you."

"You sleep in a house with five or six hundred of these things in the basement and a few get loose every now and then?"

"Yes."

"And you have guests come over for dinner parties and the like?"

"Yes."

"I'm going to throw up."

"You are looking a little pale."

"How can you live there?"

"I can't. It was the bugs or me. I told her that so she filed for divorce."

"How are you ever going to sell the house?"

Tolliver smiled. "I have an idea."

I shook my head, staring at the creatures. They were bigger than a baby's fist.

My client sat across from me, gazing at the bugs, his facial expression mostly calm but his eyes were filled with fire and hate.

Finally, "Why?" I asked.

"According to certain entomologists, the South American Stinging Beetle may have a family structure similar to primates and people. It fascinated my wife. She thought she could discover some universal truth by studying them and it would lead to a breakthrough in the way she treated her patients. She thought she'd have ten or fifteen of them. She never expected so many but they kept breeding and she wouldn't let any of them be killed. I think she considers them her children."

Stay in control, I thought.

Something clicked.

"Oh shit," George said. "I used half a can of pest spray, too."

"What?"

The antennas on one of the bugs twitched and the insect suddenly launched itself towards me.

Screaming I dove for the floor, rolling, swatting at the air.

"By the way," George said as he removed a huge can of pest spray from his briefcase. "They can fly."

Sly's World

- 2 -

Deep in the heart of Sly's World, Fay Blondeshell comes to work in a bright blue bikini. Sly watches her walk out of the elevator into the law firm's reception area, her skin shaded bronze with sweat glistening on her chest and thighs.

"Have we ruined anyone's life today?" she asks in her throaty voice.

"Not yet," Sly replies, "but it's only nine in the morning. It's going to be a long day."

Fay brushes back her hair. "Then let's start it with a bang."

Sly drops his aluminum briefcase and holds out his arms. She slips into them as if she is putting on a nightgown and they waltz slowly across the marble floor, bodies pressed against one another, listening to a slow rock ballad no other human can hear. She nips at his ear; his hands slide down the skin of her back, cupping her round bottom. The air shimmers. A discothèque ball floats near the ceiling spraying a rainbow of colors into the room. Four small blue birds with yellow beaks flutter about their heads, wings keeping time with the music's beat and their tiny heads bobbing to and fro. Sly hugs her tightly and her body melts into his business suit, cloth disappearing, her sweat against his skin. They kiss deeply, wet and slow.

"The couch," she whispers. "You can have me on the couch."

"We're in public," Sly grins. "What about her?"

The receptionist watches them, a fifty-year-old woman wearing a blue hospital gown who has been addicted to cigarettes for two dozen years and living with cancer for seven. She sits at her desk behind a ledge of granite, blowing smoke into the air.

9

"Maybe she'll learn something," Fay breathes into Sly's ear.

"The only thing she'll learn," Sly replies, "is how it feels to suffer a heart attack."

"You are no fun in the morning."

She pushes him away, the music fades, the birds fly off and the discothèque ball recedes into the ceiling. They stand apart.

Fay serves as Sly's paralegal at the law firm. Occasionally after work they hit the town. Together they make a formidable and impressive team, during the day at the office or in court, at the local hot spots in the late hours of the night, and between the sheets of any bed in town, at any time.

"You have a new client in conference room three," the receptionist gasps at Sly between bursts of smoke.

"Am I going to like this one?"

"He's wearing a very expensive watch."

Money, Sly thinks. I'll like him.

"Don't get too excited," the Blondeshell purrs over her shoulder as she strides from the lobby towards her office on the other side of the skyscraper's floor. She pauses, looking over her shoulder. "You can buy fancy looking watches on the Internet that are just cheap knockoffs of the real thing. The watch face may appear authentic but you can't tell if the watch is real until you see what's ticking inside the case." She sways down the hall.

"Don't bring me down!" Sly calls after her.

But he knows she's right.

He heads to the conference room to meet his new client.

Sam

- 3 -

I made it back to my office alive.

I stood by my desk until the trembling passed and then swallowed half a bottle of Pepto Bismol. I hated insects. As a kid I would run into the house anytime a bee or wasp headed my way. I pulled Kleenex out of a tissue box and wiped the sweat from my face. It had taken George a good ten minutes to subdue the ones that were still alive with the pest spray and then he cut all of the insects in half with a bowie knife he kept sheathed to his calf.

Amazingly, George hired me and handed over a retainer check for $5,000. George figured revulsion to insects would work in his case and didn't feel supreme cowardice in the face of an insect attack equated to being a loser in a courtroom. Things might have been different if one of the bugs had managed to crawl inside my shirt. I was sure I would have pissed on myself if an insect's exoskeleton brushed against my skin.

A knock on the door and Brandy stuck her head into the office.

"Are you alright?"

"Sure. Why?"

"Some people didn't know why you were shaking so much as you walked down the hall."

"A new form of exercise," I lied. "Contracting and relaxing the muscles. I feel great. What's new?"

Brandy was my paralegal, a nice grandmother-type who was sixty years old and on her fourth husband. She only worked for me. My partner, Arnie, had a male paralegal. Arnie and I were the attorneys who practiced family law at the law firm. Arnie was the reason the firm hired me ten years ago. The firm was looking for a male to work with Arnie, given allegations of sexual misconduct after Arnie met with a comely young client alone in a conference room. Arnie now had a male paralegal and a male secretary and me, a male junior partner. Arnie never met with female clients by himself. In addition, no one at the firm was allowed to use Arnie's computer; the rule implemented to avoid a sexual harassment lawsuit by any male or female employee who viewed the contents of his hard drive.

Arnie's clients paid fees to our firm each year in excess of one million dollars.

Brandy said, "Arnie is really excited. He has a special client this afternoon. The quarterback for the Mohawks has filing for divorce and his wife wants to retain Arnie."

The Mohawks were our town's Professional Football League team, winners of the World Championship a few years ago. Arnie was one of their biggest fans. He wore war paint and dressed like an Indian for home games and had owned season tickets for three decades. When the Mohawks lost on a Sunday, no one wanted to be near Arnie the following Monday.

"He's going to sue his favorite football player?" I asked.

Brandy shrugged. "That's technically the plan. I'm betting he turns traitor and helps the quarterback get a good deal in the divorce. He'll parlay it into locker room passes for next season."

Don't tell the legal ethics board, I thought.

"You have a new client in an hour," Brandy said. "One of those hockey parents, I'm told."

"The mom or the dad?"

"The mom," Brandy answered.

The crazy one, I thought. Sometimes a dad would go way overboard but it was usually the moms. It was not uncommon for hockey moms to fight, scratch and claw to get their child ahead in the sport, and in every hockey association there would be at least one mom offering sexual favors to a coach in exchange for special treatment for her child.

I had played ice hockey in town as a child and coached a travel team for the local youth hockey association after graduating from law school. I stopped because it was taking too much of my time and some of the parents were getting on my nerves. When people found out I was a family law attorney, referrals began coming my way. During the years I coached, I represented a few parents whose children played for the association and I became known as the lawyer for hockey parents in need. The association became a valuable referral source for me. Some lawyers depended on men's clubs or charitable groups or churches for clients—I attracted clients from the ice rink.

"Okay," I said. I sat down behind my desk, leaned into the high-backed leather executive chair and began rolling it back and forth between the desk and credenza.

"You sure you're okay?" Brandy asked with the same look of concern on her face that immediately preceded the death of her three prior husbands.

"I'm feeling peachy," I replied.

Frowning, she left my office, closing the door behind her.

- 4 -

She was absolutely adorable.

She was not a young clothing model nor did she have the features of a classic beauty. She was not the type who I could imagine posing in a skin magazine, like Fay Blondeshell.

But I looked at her and fully understood how Arnie found trouble in that conference room years ago.

And I felt sad. Did she notice me wince or my teeth grind together? The feeling was momentary and I forced it away, at least for the time being. I was sad because I would never hold a woman like her. She was beyond me, as were most of the women who drew me into fantasies and dreams. I envied Arnie, a fairly unattractive older man who managed to have a lovely woman at his side on most occasions. How did he do it? He would find a way to spend an evening with a woman like Rebecca; gazing at her over candlelight at a private dinner, stars in the sky and the surf trickling up sand, a warm bed awaiting them, tenderness and animal lust erupting at the same instance, the next morning feeling her breath against his skin. Why did I seem forever to be on the outside of some party, watching the pretty people inside, never figuring out how to gain entry?

"I'm Rebecca Warren," she said, extending her left hand since the right clutched a Blackberry device. Her hand was small and soft, her fingernails all light pink with white trim at the ends and I barely touched her as we shook.

I sat at the head of the fifty foot long oval table and she sat to my immediate right. Twenty four empty chairs surrounded the rest of the table. The wall on my right was comprised of floor to ceiling glass overlooking massive trees and another tower in the office park.

"I have to divorce my husband," she said.

"Okay," I replied, wanting to be helpful to her. "Would you like me to describe the process of divorce to you?"

"No."

"Excuse me?"

"You're the fifth lawyer I've seen. I probably know more about the divorce process than most third year law school students."

"Who did you meet with?"

She rattled off the names of four prominent lawyers, all very experienced and very aggressive family law practitioners.

"Are you still considering hiring any of them?"

"No. Hold on." Her Blackberry had vibrated and she pressed buttons, probably reviewing and responding to an email or text message.

"Work issues?"

"No."

I gathered her initial information. She worked for an accounting firm as a business consultant, earning about $150,000 a year. Her husband was an engineer, designing power plants and making about the same annual income. They had lived in Florida until this last summer when a promotion led to the husband's transfer from a satellite office in Miami to the company's main headquarters in town. There was one child: Donnie. There were minimal assets and close to thirty thousand dollars in credit card debt.

"How did you come to our firm?" I asked.

"From talking to people at the ice rink," she replied. "I didn't want to. I was hoping to do this far away from any connections with the Kansas City Shooters. But none of the other lawyers understood me or the temporary orders we needed, and the final parenting plan that is necessary. They all thought we would ultimately lose at trial. I'm hoping you will fight for us."

"Us?"

"Me and Donnie."

It was fairly common for one parent to be aligned with a child and see the divorce as a struggle between them and the other parent.

"What are we fighting about?"

"Donnie has special needs and my husband refuses to understand them. He did for awhile in Florida but he won't anymore."

That explained the credit card debt, I figured. There must be some sort of a medical problem and a dispute between the parents on the course of treatment. I had handled these types of cases before. Sometimes the case involved a fairly common disease such as a type of aggressive cancer and the need by one parent to attempt radical and untested treatments. Other times the case involved an issue as to whether the child even suffered from a diagnosable condition and arguments as to whether any medical treatment should be undertaken. The cases were very sad. Both parents believed they were right. Neither parent acted, in his or her own mind, to the child's detriment nor was there any question both parents loved the child dearly. It was an unfortunate and very sad situation with no solution to satisfy everyone, least of all the child.

"And what are Donnie's special needs?" I asked slowly, looking into her large, brown eyes and experiencing something much closer to desire than empathy.

"Donnie is special," Rebecca said. "He's the next Great One—the dominant hockey player of his generation. He's the next Sidney Crosby; the next Mario Lemieux; the next Wayne Gretzky."

I looked down on the intake sheet. Yep, I thought, she's going to be in my thoughts tonight but she's just another crazy hockey mom. Lovely for sure, but another crazy hockey mom.

Donnie was ten years old.

- 5 -

I agreed to represent Rebecca although she thought the case had more to do with Donnie than her. Not an uncommon belief, I knew, misguided as it was. I dropped her retainer check off with the accounting department and headed back to my office, somewhat annoyed I had agreed to watch Donnie play a hockey game on Saturday. The kid likely was only an above-average player and I'd have to lie about his abilities to please Rebecca. It had been a number of years since I entered the ice rink and for some reason the thought was unsettling. But then again, I reasoned, maybe Rebecca would be wearing tight, faded blue jeans at the game.

When asked to describe my partner and boss, Arnie, I would suggest one consider a giant beach ball with stumpy legs and short arms, wearing an expensive dark suit. He slouched in one of the guest chairs in my office, having taken off his dark shirt and tie to reveal a sweat stained t-shirt adorned with the Mohawks logo. Arnie balanced a smartphone on his gut and held it with both hands. His bifocals had slid to the end of a bulbous nose and the fluorescent light shined off the smooth skin of his skull.

I took my seat and began rolling between the desk and credenza.

"Don't you have a meeting with a new client?"

"Damn right," Arnie said. "I'm just trying to get pumped for it by watching some videos."

He always had the country's most technologically sophisticated smartphone, upgrading to the newest model every few months. He could afford it—he was one of the highest paid lawyers at the firm. The current model had a huge screen and tremendous resolution and operated at the highest speeds possible with current technology.

"Watching clips of the Mohawks?"

"Hell, no," Arnie said. "Pornography on the Internet. That's why I'm in here. I don't want anyone seeing me do this in my own office."

I tried to understand the logic but gave up.

"Think about it," Arnie said. "Joey Balton led the Mohawks to a World Championship and was twice voted the league's most valuable player. He's one of the most popular men in town. He could have married anyone in the world and he married the woman who will be walking into our offices in an hour or so. I'm hoping I don't come in my pants when I shake her hand."

"Remember, the client is going to be the wife. Not the quarterback. You can't screw her by taking the husband's side in the case. And you can't screw her, physically. Either instance is a breach of legal ethics. You would be disbarred."

"I'm going to demand his World Championship ring as part of the divorce settlement and then I'm going to convince her to pay part of my fees by giving me the ring."

"To sell on eBay?"

"Sacrilege. It's going on my right hand and when I watch a good porno video . . ."

"STOP!" I glanced at my computer's screen and my Outlook program held lots of incoming emails. "Get dressed and get out of here."

Arnie nodded, put down the smartphone and dressed. "Tell you what," he said. "I'll get you involved in the case. You can value the Professional Football League's pension plans and stuff. It will be fun. Maybe we'll get to tour the team's locker room before and after a game."

I tried to ignore him. He laughed, farted and left my office.

- 6 -

There was one more work assignment for the day.

I drove out to the courthouse for the final hearing in a divorce case. We represented the wife; it was a 12-year marriage and the husband did not have an attorney. The parties had signed an agreement settling all issues in the matter and just needed to go through the routine of having the agreement approved by the judge and the Decree of Divorce signed.

My client and I sat at a table facing the judge and the husband sat at another table, alone. Other than the court reporter, no one else was present. I called my client to the witness stand. As was the custom, I asked questions that resulted in her responding either 'yes' or 'no.' I quickly obtained the answers needed so the judge could determine he should grant the divorce and issue the requested orders concerning the parties and their two young children. We went over the terms of the settlement agreement and parenting plan so the judge could determine they were fair and equitable. They were in fact fair and equitable—the wife wanted a divorce but was not looking to financially castrate the husband. I finished quickly. The judge asked if the husband had any questions for the wife; he did not. The judge asked whether the husband wanted to present any testimony of his own; he did not.

We sat waiting as the judge skimmed the settlement agreement, parenting plan and Decree of Divorce.

After the second child was born the husband had a brief affair with a co-worker. The wife found out. They worked hard to repair the damage and save the marriage, going to several different counselors. Ultimately she could not forgive him.

They had made a handsome couple. They were both good parents. Except for the affair, they had a very good marriage.

When I asked the wife, while she was on the witness stand, whether the marriage was irretrievably broken she began to cry.

At one point during her testimony, the husband cried as well.

I'm sorry, I wanted to tell him. But you made a mistake and some mistakes cannot be corrected.

Every day we wake and join the world. On the drive to work there could be a car accident, of no fault of our own. We could end up on a slab in the morgue or sitting in a wheelchair for life or walk away from the wreck unharmed.

The husband had an affair, moments when he soared. He came back to the ground and found the world scorched and devastated.

I wanted to soar. No, I wanted to soar based on my own doing; my own creation. I would hear a certain song in which the lyrics and music formed a seamless sonic wave, each syllable fitting perfectly with each beat, each word efficiently telling a beautiful tale, the whole a melodic poem flowing through the air and I would be in awe, my heart at peace, my mind still, my flesh and bones without pain. To be able to create such beauty, such perfection . . .

To be in love and be loved back in return.

The judge granted the divorce and signed the paperwork. I took it to file with the clerk. Neither my client nor the ex-husband wished to wait. They left with the understanding I would mail copies of the filed documents to them later. They walked to their cars, legally different than when they entered the building thirty minutes ago, no longer husband and wife.

Twelve years ago, they had stood at an altar before a priest and professed they would love, honor and cherish each other until the day they died. Those promises had turned to dust.

I left the courthouse for my car and the drive to my ranch house many miles to the southwest, out in the country. On the drive home, I started to cry.

Sly's World

- 7 -

Sly saunters down the courthouse steps dressed as The Executioner: black shoes, black suit, black thin tie and a dark, gray button down shirt. His courtroom briefcase is clad in black leather with silver studs. Another great day, he thinks. His client only deserved $4,000 a month in maintenance but he had gotten her $8,000. When the husband took the witness stand at the hearing, Sly had shoved the husband's heart right up his ass and when he pulled it out gold coins spewed to his client. Another day, Sly thinks, another case with justice done.

Fay's band plays in the parking lot by his Ferrari. She holds the microphone so tightly her knuckles turn blue as she rages through "Goodbye To You," her face a snarl of fury and revenge. Sly sometimes plays lead guitar, other times he watches from the mosh pit, his body writhing to the music. Fay points a finger at him, hair flying across her face, body twisting and barely contained in the leather miniskirt and mesh halter. The band would be banned in most countries but the local cops dig the sound and they lean against their squad cars at the back of the crowd, letting the song take them to their own revenge fantasies.

As usual, the band attracts an eclectic crowd. Straggly haired prisoners in orange jumpsuits, legs shackled and hands cuffed to belt chains, sway to the music beside men and women in business attire, an elderly judge still wearing his black robe, teenagers adorned in shorts and t-shirts with numerous body piercings, and three toddlers in diapers and sequined vests shaking their booties to the beat. Fay's band is now called "Angry Bitch And Her Minions." They used to be called "The Sexy Bitches" when they were an all-girl ensemble, but the other females were replaced by men due to a pregnancy, a marriage and a sex change operation.

Sly falls out of his suit coat and tosses away his tie and during the guitar riff Fay jumps off the stage and rips open his shirt, buttons flying like bullets to punch holes into the sheet metal of parked cars and she takes a deep bite out of his muscular chest.

"Did you do well at the hearing?" she whispers, spitting out chest hairs.

"Kicked ass and took no prisoners."

"See," she says. "I was right this morning. We did ruin a life today."

"Perhaps we should celebrate."

"And how should we do that?"

"I have a few minutes," Sly says. "Anyone on the bus?"

A flash of concern on her face tells it all. Sly turns his head as the enraged husband from the hearing raises a sledgehammer for a death blow.

"Not my fault," Sly explains. "Blame your lawyer. He sucked."

The comment produces no change in attitude.

Sly jumps and spins, right leg kicking out and knocking the sledgehammer from the husband's hands. As Sly lands, he reaches out and finds the nerve beside the husband's neck. The man freezes and crumples but Sly catches him before he smashes against the asphalt of the parking lot.

Can't let him get hurt, Sly knows. I don't want to diminish his capacity to earn income and pay maintenance to my client.

Fay Blondeshell whirls back to the stage. "Goodbye to you!" she sings, "Goodbye to you!"

She gestures at the bus, mouths 'later' and smiles.

The drummer paints houses as a day job and at night when he isn't banging his instruments he indulges in his second passion as a tagger. According to various web sites he is the best graffiti artist west of New York City. His only legitimate canvas is the band's vehicle, an old school bus bought from a local school district suffering from severe budget problems. During his homoerotic period the drummer styled it as a penis on wheels but the highway patrol frowned on that incarnation and he quickly found other inspirations. Currently in a 1960's phase, the bus has become a multi-colored psychedelic joint and pedestrians claim to get stoned as it rolls past them, spewing exhaust into the air.

More relevant, the seats have been ripped out of the bus and the windows painted black. One of the installed couches converts to a queen size bed and Fay always needs to unwind after a performance.

She points again but not at Sly.

It is his client, the wife from the hearing. The wife picks up one of the toddlers and from his viewing angle Sly can't tell if he is watching a motherly kiss or some serious tonguing action.

To each his own, Sly thinks. $8,000 a month will keep that lil' fella in premium diapers for quite awhile.

He wonders if the BabySuperStore sells condoms for toddlers.

Sam

- 8 -

I lived in two residences. During the work week I stayed in a sparsely furnished apartment less than a mile from the office. On weekends and holidays, my home was a ranch inherited from my father some thirty miles to the south on forty acres consisting of a pond, grazing land and woods. The driveway snaked five hundred feet through the woods to reach my house from the rural road.

Jenny sat on the porch waiting for me. I stowed the Porsche SUV in the barn behind the ranch and joined her. She had a cigar for me and three fingers of single malt scotch.

"You ever been attacked by a three inch long cockroach with a stinger?" I asked her.

She sipped her whiskey and coke. "On bad days," she said.

Jenny suffered from borderline personality disorder with depression and anxiety attacks as side effects. She took medications for the latter two issues. There was no treatment for the disorder.

"I never understood your aversion to insects," she said. "Hell, you live in the country. Who knows what crawls around your house late at night."

"That's why I have you: to protect me from them."

"Forget it," Jenny said. "I'm rooting for the bugs."

"Really?"

"No," she said. "Well, maybe. Depends on the day."

Jenny owned two wardrobes. At times she played Happy Girl, a rambunctious bachelorette in brightly colored blouses and skirts, her nails painted pastel colors, her lips pink and inviting. Other times, she transformed into The Satanist, a relic from medieval times. She skulked through the world dressed entirely in black, sometimes sporting vampire fangs, especially for late night supermarket runs or a fast food drive thru.

Initially, the local police were not happy about The Satanist, with or without the vampire fangs. Jenny developed a close relationship with several of the patrol units and reached an understanding with them. She agreed to text them when The Satanist would be making an appearance. For Jenny, this led to a decrease in whole body frisks and wasted hours at the police station and for the police it led to less time spent having to deal with her. As a bonus, both The Satanist and Happy Girl routinely bought police officers coffee and donuts during their shifts.

Tonight she seemed caught between worlds. Her fingernails and toenails were painted black and little silver skulls dangled from her ears. But she wore a blue leather coat with pink running shoes and black sweatpants and her eyes were clear.

I leaned over and kissed her cheek. "Fifteen more years," she murmured. "That was our deal. If we both reach fifty and neither of us is married then we marry each other."

We stole the idea from a movie, or perhaps it was a television show. We had been drunk. Who remembered?

"And then we get to have sex," I said.

Jenny giggled. "Yes. But not with each other."

Marriage was sacred to Jenny. That point was made clear to me after her last boyfriend broke off their year-long engagement. Jenny believed their marriage was guaranteed; however, like most men who dated her the violent and sudden mood swings eventually overcame the lust for her beach volleyball player's body and beautiful face, framed by flowing, golden hair.

The day after the relationship ended Jenny had driven to all of the toy stores in town, buying Ken and Barbie dolls, dressed for upcoming nuptials. She laid them down on her living room floor, holding hands, twenty three perfect couples, and smashed them to bits with a hammer. Pieces lay scattered on the hard wood floor for months and the holes in the wood still remained.

"We should be mute," Jenny said.

"Who?"

"Lovers," Jenny said. "When people fall in love, they should become mute. Just touching and holding. No talk. The world would be an easier place if that was the way things worked."

- 9 -

We had met three years or so ago at a liquor store I frequented because it also had a cigar humidor room the size of a small closet. Open boxes of cigars sat on shelves along three walls of the room. I had grabbed five Padron cigars, each close to eight inches long and as thick as my thumb and in the main room grabbed a couple of bottles of whiskey. I held the bottles to my chest with my arm and the cigars in my other hand.

The cash register was by the front door and I stood in sunlight streaking through the windows, waiting my turn. An elderly woman was fishing through her purse looking for forty-four cents worth of change. The clerk at the register waited patiently.

Something bumped into me from behind.

"Sorry," she said.

"Okay," I replied, turning my head slightly.

"So should I hit you again?" she asked. "Harder, this time?"

I turned around fully.

She was taller than me with hair almost white flowing like a wave about her face.

"Move!" she snarled.

I stepped aside and she easily lifted two cases of beer, one held in each hand, onto the counter, pushing aside the elderly woman who dropped change onto the floor.

"Good afternoon," the woman said. She smiled and giggled at the clerk.

"Afternoon, Jenny," the clerk said.

The elderly woman glared at her and bent to retrieve her coins.

Jenny walked back to her spot in line behind me.

She tapped me on the back.

"You live around here?"

I turned around and started to respond and froze.

She smiled at me. Her eyes were bright blue and her skin as clear as her hair and she had high cheekbones and a lovely smile.

"I'm Jenny," she said.

I held out the cigars. She giggled and shook my closed hand. "Sam."

"I smoked cigars for awhile. Cigarettes too, but I stopped smoking them. It was too expensive a habit."

"So you just drink lots of beer?"

"Yep," she answered, giggling.

I guessed she was in her early thirties, wearing faded jeans and a collared shirt from Target or a similar store. She could have been a swimmer, tall and lean and appearing to be in great shape.

"I don't mind smoking a cigar now and then if it's free," she said.

She stared at my clenched hand.

The elderly woman took her purchase from the store and I put my items on the counter.

"There's a park near here," Jenny said. "It has a lake and benches and people go fishing. It's nice to sit on a bench and look out over the lake. I have a cooler in my car and some plastic cups. We can keep the beer cold and drink from the cups and smoke cigars."

"Today?"

"Are you asking me?" Jenny giggled. "Okay, let's go. Or do you have anything better to do than me?"

"Huh?"

Ten minutes later, not knowing why, I was following her black Lincoln sedan, heading to the lake.

We parked and Jenny transferred some of the beer into a cooler in the trunk of her car, already filled with ice. She offered me a can of beer. I declined, choosing instead to pour several shots of whiskey into a plastic cup she gave me.

A walking path circled the lake and we found a bench far from the docks where several people were fishing. I lit both cigars and handed one to her.

"Cool," she said. She inhaled to an extent that was unlikely to draw any measurable smoke from the burning tobacco leaves.

"Do you really like smoking cigars?"

"I like the thought of smoking a cigar," she said. "I like holding it."

"The key word was smoking."

"It's burning," she said. "It is smoking." She waved the cigar and wisps of smoke drifted from the glowing end into the clear, warm air.

"But you're not smoking."

She smiled at me. "I'm not smoking?" She giggled. "Maybe I'm smoking in a different way?"

"Huh?"

"Smoking hot?" She gulped down some beer, her eyes focused on my reaction.

I sipped from the cup.

"So what do you do?" she asked.

"I'm a lawyer."

"I work part time for a mortgage company, doing closings. I've been there for years and I get off early every afternoon."

"You like it?"

She shrugged. "I have my own office and I really just talk a lot on the phone and go over paperwork. I don't have to see anyone except when there's actually a closing and people come to sign the papers."

"You like not having to see people at work all day?"

"It's easier on me," she said.

She finished her beer, looked around and then fished another can out of the small cooler. After she poured the beer into the cup she tossed the empty can back into the cooler. "Sure you don't want a beer?"

"Yes."

After awhile, I asked, "So why did you ask me here?"

"What do you mean?"

"If you don't like seeing people at work, it sounds like you like being alone. So why didn't you come here by yourself?"

"I don't know," she said. "I saw you and wanted to ask. Why did you come with me?"

I thought about it for a moment. If I hadn't met Jenny, I would have driven back to The Ranch Retreat and sat on the porch or in the living room, drinking and smoking by myself, seeking quiet and those moments when my mind would go empty and I could just sit by myself in peace. Those were the moments I enjoyed the most—when I could sit alone, my heart quiet, my mind empty, no frightening or depressing thoughts running scattershot through my head, just alone by myself, in peace.

"I don't know," I finally said.

"You have a girlfriend?"

"No. Not for awhile."

"That's not good," Jenny said. She leaned over and gave me a quick kiss on the cheek. "I have a fiancé. We've been engaged for months. He wants to marry me."

"That's good."

"I want to be married."

"That's good."

"I'm not going to cheat on him. I'm not looking for another boyfriend. But he doesn't like to smoke cigars."

"Okay," I said.

"Good," she replied. We had sat on the bench by the lake for a few hours, smoking and drinking, just letting the rest of the afternoon pass us by.

- 10 -

I called them sadness bubbles. They started in my gut, a pinpoint of emptiness that rapidly expanded until it filled my entire chest and I wanted to burst into tears. They came without much warning; I could be enjoying a cigar or watching a good movie or spending time with Jenny laughing and drinking. The bubble would form. The world would turn dark.

The only escape was unconsciousness. The bubbles formed one after another, without respite, and life became hopeless.

They had been with me for as long as I could remember. They dissipated in strength the first few months of my marriage but when the fighting started they returned in full force.

I had tried medications, going through a series of them. Either each one would fail to work after a time or the side effects of the medication became as dehabilitating as the depression the pills sought to cure. The psychiatrist said it was not uncommon for one's body chemistry to ultimately reject a drug or for the side effects to be pronounced. After the fourth kind failed I gave up.

I knew of only one real solution to the bubbles.

Years ago I visited a high school friend who lived in Montana, shortly after my divorce was finalized. My friend had purchased a Colt .380 after relocating and we spent a few hours at a firing range, shooting at paper targets. I remembered being nervous as I watched my friend load the clip and hand the gun to me. It was a small weapon, silver steel with a textured grip. Surprisingly I relaxed when I took hold of the gun. It felt solid and comfortable in my hand. In moments I was clustering holes about the center of the target, fifty feet away.

"You're a natural shot," my friend said.

After my return home, every so often I thought about applying for a license and buying a handgun. Sometimes I would wander through a gun store near my apartment, checking out the prices and talking to the owner about the pros and cons of various pistols.

I never bought one.

I knew that if I did, I would put a bullet into my brain.

I woke, my neck aching. I normally woke with either a backache or a neck ache when Jenny spent the night. In the kitchen I made a pot of coffee, put on a leather jacket and stepped outside. A half-finished cigar was in the ashtray and I lit it up. The smoke mixed with my breath in the crisp air. I had slept in the clothes I changed into after getting to the ranch, not even taking off my sneakers. A faded sweater, white socks and blue jeans. My normal attire this time of year.

I probably should dress better. It would help with my appearance. As a male, I was not good looking. That wasn't false modesty; unfortunately it was the truth. I stood five foot six and barely weighed 140 pounds. My hair was brown and thinning although I was just thirty-five years old and I had been told I had something of a rat's face, thin and all angles with a somewhat long nose and narrow eyes.

I met my ex-wife at a bar frequented by lawyers. She was short and plump and liked to party and thought I was amusing and liked my paycheck. Ultimately, her like for my paycheck was overshadowed by her like for some muscular construction worker who fell for her eyes and smile while she waited on him at a local bar. During the weeks before our separation it seemed she spent more time fucking him than being in the same room with me. She ended up with a year of alimony, twenty thousand dollars of my retirement assets, a fully paid off BMW and another thirty thousand in cash. Last time I heard about her, she was going through another divorce because the construction worker found someone with prettier eyes and a prettier smile and a much better body. The construction worker traded up, in the lingo of the divorce lawyer. The thought wasn't comforting because when she left me for him, I knew she was trading up, too.

"Bullshit," Jenny said when I told her the story. "The bitch was trading down when she left you. She gave up a lifetime of someone caring for her in exchange for what? A few good orgasms?"

The thing about Jenny was that when she tried to make you feel better she usually ended up making you feel worse.

"I wasn't good enough for her," I said. "And she's a tramp. What does that say about me?"

"You're not so bad," and she kissed me on the cheek but said nothing more.

In a legal setting I had built-in power, whether in court or at a deposition or just meeting with a client. I had my law license. Almost everywhere else, I was a ghost. People looked right though me. I almost did not exist.

Only the ice rink had been different.

Jenny popped her head out the front door. "Hungry?"

"Sure. We can go out."

"I want to cook," Jenny said.

"Are you sure?"

She nodded and went back into the house.

Jenny didn't need to work or even cook for herself. She had wealthy parents who paid for most of her living expenses so long as she lived more than twelve hours driving distance from their home.

"They had a GPS unit installed in my car," she once told me. "The unit alerts them whenever I'm driving within two hundred miles of their cell phones, which they always carry. It gives them time to clear out of town to avoid me if they want to do so."

"You can drive a rental car and fool them."

"No," Jenny said. "I know I can be a horrendous problem for them, when I'm off. Besides, they'd stop making my car payments and I like my new car." She should like it—she had traded in the Lincoln for a brand new top-of-the line 2010 Jaguar sedan, loaded with every feature imaginable. She lived better than most of the partners at my law firm.

I smoked, enjoying the silence of the morning until the screaming and sounds of metal against wood and breaking objects forced me back into the house.

She stood amidst the wreckage of breakfast.

Scrambled eggs, pancakes and syrup, all sprayed across the counter and floor and the window above the sink. The pan lay on the floor but its handle was still in Jenny's hand. Somehow a sausage link got stuck to the ceiling.

"I burnt the pancakes," Jenny explained, giggling. "It made me mad."

Well, I thought, she could be giggling because she knew she lost it and had to apologize. On the other hand, she might have become insane. If the latter, it could last for minutes or hours or days.

I had represented the wife of the owner of 'The Golden Waffle House' some time ago and could never prove the husband was lying about his restaurant's income, and thus could not get my client the monthly maintenance she clearly deserved.

"Let's go out to eat," I suggested. "I know the perfect place."

Jenny nodded and giggled.

- 11 -

Rebecca retained our law firm only after I promised to watch her son play his first game of the season. Jenny and I said our goodbyes at the restaurant after breakfast. The restaurant's owner agreed not to press charges against her so long as she promised never to return.

The Ice Kingdom was next to a baseball complex and a bar. Train tracks and a steep wooded hill separated the rink from the city's main landfill. For a short time the youth hockey association was named The Gulls in honor of the birds that regularly flew overhead. After a few visiting teams inquired as to the reason for the name the association changed its name to the Shooters.

The parking lot was crowded. Rebecca's son played for the Shooters' 10U AA Travel Team, the best team in town for nine and ten year old boys. The team was hosting a tournament and the license plates of the parked cars proclaimed the attributes of Kansas, Missouri, Iowa, Nebraska, Illinois and South Dakota. The tournament ran Friday to Sunday; when taking into account team entry fees, hotel rooms, meals and auto fuel, each player's family was probably spending over $500 for the glory of watching their child play in four games. At this age, the games consisted of three 12-minute periods. When one took the happening of a hockey game into account, most of these kids would be playing for about 12 minutes each game [or 48 minutes total] and during that time each player might have the puck on his stick for about 8 minutes total. It was a great way to spend $500.

I coached for a few years after law school, for the Gulls/Shooters. Coaching the kids was great fun; coaching some of the parents was a horror show.

It felt a little funny walking into the rink. I had timed it to arrive just as the game was about to start so the lobby was filled with the parents involved with the game that just ended. Based on the paraphernalia it had been the Omaha Tornadoes against the Fargo Felons. It appeared as if every parent and sibling in the place, about sixty in all, were wearing something that showed their allegiance to one of the two teams. I walked through part of the milling crowd, past the trophy cases and message boards into the rink's main lobby. Ahead was the concession stand and unfortunately it appeared the rink still served beer. There was nothing like a whole bunch of parents of competing teams drinking lots of beer and then 'discussing' the finer aspects of play after the game was over. To the right was the pro shop and meeting room, to the left a few video games lined the wall and a door led to the back offices.

I headed right and pushed open the double doors into the ice rink. Cold air assaulted my skin. Tall bleachers lined one side of the rink and across the ice surface the team benches were separated by the penalty boxes and scorekeeper's station. Banners proclaiming tournament and league championships hung from rafters above the benches.

Two of the banners proclaimed league titles for teams I had coached and my name was listed on the bottom as 'Head Coach.'

I timed it right. The warm-ups were ending and the players clustered by their coaches at each bench for final instructions.

Donnie's first game was against the Iowa rivals of the Shooters, the Des Moines Pumpers. Sponsored by the city's fire department, the logo of the Pumpers was a muscular fireman resembling a young Arnold Schwarzenegger, shirtless with a fireman's hat and suspenders, holding a thick fire hose in both hands. The hose was shaped like a hockey stick with the nozzle being the stick's blade, spewing droplets of flames.

Sometimes when I was bored I would log onto youth hockey websites and read the forums and blogger reports. Friday night, after Jenny went to bed I checked the on-line information on The Pumpers. The consensus seemed to be that the team was going to be big and fast and unlike most 10U AA Travel Teams, they were practicing every day of the week and would be traveling as far away for tournaments as Florida and Montreal. The Pumpers hockey association had placed seven players in the NHL and the parents in the stands had cowbells which they rang furiously each time their team scored or their goalie made a great save. They expected to have one of the best teams in the Midwest.

Surprisingly, there was little to no talk on the forums about the 10U AA Travel Team of the Shooters.

The five Pumper players skated to the center ice face-off circle while their goalie headed to the net. They wore red uniforms with their logo in a whitish color resembling semen on the front of their jerseys. The coaches on the bench wore fireman helmets and black rain slickers. I spotted Rebecca standing in a corner of the rink, her face almost pressed against the Plexiglas. She wore black sweatpants and a red hoodie adorned with the Shooters' logo. She had her hands in the front pocket of the hoodie, staring intently at the Shooter players. A few feet to her left stood a tall man, bearded and balding with thick glasses and wearing a full length grey trench coat. Her husband? I wondered. Maybe. She was ignoring him.

I found a seat with the Pumper parents and glanced over to the other side of the bleachers where most of the Shooter parents had gathered. Most of the fathers stood together, clutching video cameras or notebooks, preparing for the game. The moms sat in a bunch. There were two types of moms: the ones who dressed up as if they were going on a date and the ones who dressed in tight jeans or tight workout clothes. MILFs, I thought.

I would have sat amongst the Shooter parents but none of them knew me. I would have driven them crazy, a stranger in their midst. He must be a rival coach, they would think, coming to watch our team, to devise strategies so *his* team could beat us in the future. Or better yet, he's a scout, even from the NHL, who heard about *my* son, the Next Great One, ready to offer scholarships or playing time.

Out of all of the types of sports parents, hockey parents were the worst. They were, for the most part, all nuts.

Rebecca said Donnie wore #10.

The referee blew his whistle and the starting Shooter players skated to center ice. Donnie was playing center and would take the face off. He was average height for a ten year old but his skates astounded me. They were huge. How big were his feet? I wondered. He seemed to be of average build. His two wingers were smaller and the two defensemen on the ice with him were about the same size. He skated slowly, like an old man suffering from arthritis. Like all of the players he wore a helmet and an iron cage that covered his face, almost like a birdcage, to protect him from injury. I couldn't see his expression at all.

I'll get out of here between the second and third periods, I thought. That should be enough. Damn, it's cold in here.

Be nice when you talk to Rebecca, when she calls on Monday morning, I thought. Don't crush her dreams.

The referee dropped the puck and the game started.

For the next hour I barely moved.

The Shooters won, 14 to 1. Donnie scored nine goals, six of them unassisted. No one on the ice could skate with him so most of the time he was flying down the ice with the puck by himself. Checking was not allowed at the 10U level and the Pumpers' defensemen just waved their sticks at him as he flew by. Each time he would bear down on the goaltender alone and the goalie would wait and wait, trying not to be faked out, but Donnie would move the puck and his shoulders and the goalie would lunge to one side of the net and Donnie would slide the puck into the other side.

After the fourth goal, when the score was 5-0, the Pumper players deflated. They could not stop Donnie, they knew. They could never catch up.

"Looks like your hoses ran out of water!" a Shooter parent yelled from the stands.

"Looks like you shot your load before the game!" another Shooter father joined in.

The Pumper parents didn't bother to respond to the catcalls. They sat quietly, in awe. After Donnie's seventh goal even the loudmouth Shooter parents stopped cheering.

Rebecca stood by herself in a corner of the rink, clapping each time her son scored.

He skated effortlessly, long graceful strides and yet he was going twice as fast as everyone else. The puck stuck to his stick like magic and he moved it around as if he was holding it in his hand instead of at the end of a four-foot long hockey stick.

He wasn't just good. He was the best youth player I had ever seen.

He would have scored more but his coach put him on defense after goal number nine, apparently with orders to only pass the puck. Somehow, just by passing the puck from his own end of the ice, he tallied four more assists.

Towards the end of the game, Donnie was standing at center ice as his teammates fought for a loose puck. A Pumper player skated behind him and slashed at the back of his legs with his stick. Donnie went down onto the ice like a rock falling from the sky.

Play was halted and his coach opened the bench door to step on the ice but Donnie looked at him and shook his head. He got up slowly, ignoring the outstretched hand of the referee.

Everyone turned as Rebecca began slamming on the Plexiglas with both of her hands, screaming, "You fucking losers! That was my son! Call a fucking penalty! What is your motherfucking problem! Do you want someone to get killed out there! Open your motherfucking eyes!"

The boards began shaking about the rink. The tall man slowly backed away from her.

Eventually the local police escorted her into the parking lot, the Shooters were assessed a two minute bench penalty for fan misbehavior and the game was allowed to end peacefully.

Rebecca gave both officials the finger as she was led out of the rink.

There was an exchange between Donnie and the referee.

Later I learned:

"Your mom?" the referee asked Donnie before restarting the game.

"Yes," Donnie had replied. "She's awfully mad. Hope you're wearing a disguise when you walk to your car."

The referee had started to chuckle but looked at the boy. Donnie was being serious.

Fuck, the referee probably thought.

- 12 -

In the parking lot Rebecca waited by her car, puffing on a cigarette and I noticed the way the fabric of the black sweats clung to her thighs and hips.

"I may have gotten carried away," she said. "But that was a really cheap shot."

"Donnie looked like he was going to be okay."

She shrugged. "I'll find out tonight. He never shows pain on the ice. Once when he was six he got tripped and a teammate's skate slashed his leg in a space between his hockey pants and shin guards. Donnie kept playing, leaving a trail of blood on the ice wherever he skated. After he scored a few more goals and the game was clearly won the coach sent him off the ice for stitches."

I had no idea how to respond. Should I compliment the child's perseverance or report Rebecca to Family Services for child abuse?

She was so adorable.

"He is very good," I said.

"Tell me the truth," she said. "I'm a big girl. I can take it. What did you think?"

You're an adorable five foot two inch beauty in love with your son, I thought. You don't want to hear the truth.

"Tell me."

She was asking me to return to being The Coach. I hadn't been The Coach in years. Like The Lawyer, The Coach had power in the world.

"He is an amazing player but he holds onto the puck too much," I said. "Just because he can skate around everyone doesn't mean he should always do it. Some opposing coach is going to figure out the way to beat the Shooters is to knock Donnie out of the game.

The players may only be ten years old but someone is going to try to break his legs or use a hockey stick to decapitate him. You know that: hockey parents and hockey coaches are all nuts. The kid who slashed Donnie today did it out of frustration. Next time it will happen at the beginning of the game as the other team's strategy. Some parent or coach will clearly be telling a player to do that. Donnie needs to make his teammates better and more a part of the game so the other teams don't just focus on him. Plus, you can't get too carried away with the way he plays now. He's only ten. He may have peaked. He may stop growing. It doesn't matter how good he is when he's ten, it matters how good he is when he's seventeen."

Her face turned pale, she sucked in cigarette smoke and blew it towards my face.

"Okay," she said quietly.

"You asked."

"I know."

I had made negative comments about her son's future. Even if I weren't her divorce lawyer, even if she didn't see me as an unattractive man, I knew my chance of tasting her lips was forever gone.

"So what would you do?"

I was The Coach. Fuck it, I thought. "In case he doesn't respond to growth hormones?"

A flash of anger crossed her face. "For this season."

"Put the meanest and biggest players the Shooters have on Donnie's line and have those players take an illegal hit on any opponent who cheap shots Donnie, immediately. Then, every time that kid touches the puck during the game I'd make sure somebody on the Shooters slams him to the ice."

"There's no checking at the 10U level. Checking starts at the 12U level when the players are eleven and twelve year olds."

"Don't care. The word will get out that any player who cheap shots Donnie is going to be targeted. My team would protect its own players."

"Interesting. I like it. I like it a lot."

I shrugged. "It's just the way the game is supposed to be played."

"Your teams won a lot of games when you coached, didn't they?"

"We did okay," I replied. Her Blackberry vibrated and she glanced at the screen "You get a lot of messages on that thing. Work or fun?"

She began typing a return message.

"Neither. It's from a coach for St. Mary's Preparatory School. People from that school have been calling us for the last two years. They want Donnie to enroll when he's fourteen."

St. Mary's was the #1 hockey factory in the country. They enrolled players from all over the world and regularly won high school national championships. Their players went on to major colleges and the National Hockey League.

Donnie was ten years old.

"Minnesota gets awfully cold in the winter," I said.

"That's what the coach from Boston College told us. He wants Donnie to enroll in a private high school by their campus."

Boston College had one of the best college hockey programs in the nation.

"Seems like you're going to have some decisions to make," I said.

"We haven't even talked about the Canadian junior team that's offered to pay us $250,000 immediately if Donnie will agree to play for them when he reaches age 16."

"Is Donnie really being recruited by all of these schools and teams?"

Rebecca nodded. "A lot of people want a part of him. I had a call from a hockey stick manufacturer. *Training For Excellence*, a private firm that works with athlete to unleash their potential, has been in contact. They want to offer him free lessons. All these people see great things ahead for him."

"Amazing."

"Not really. Everyone wants a piece of the next great athlete. Kids that are Donnie's age are being recruited in every sport."

I was speechless.

"I didn't tell you at our meeting," Rebecca said. "I wanted to wait until you saw Donnie play. Now you can understand my problem."

"What? How to find an honest financial advisor?"

"No. Donnie's father wants him to quit playing ice hockey."

Sly's World

- 13 -

The Blondeshell exists within an inverted cone of sunshine, a temperate zone between seventy and eight-five degrees depending on her whim. Sly didn't so limit the weather, though he's prone to wearing blue jeans and a black leather jacket.

The Mountain Palace looms above them.

"We haven't been here for some time," The Blondeshell says. "I thought we were done with these memories." She listens to her iPod in tight white cotton shorts and an orange halter. Sly gazes at her body, knowing they have journeyed to the northern reaches of Canada instead of spending the weekend in his bed.

"We need to be here," he states without further explanation.

The Hockey Gods are on the frozen pond.

"There's been talk of an impending alien invasion," The Blondeshell says absently. "Maybe from a wormhole. The Joint Chiefs want your input."

"Not now."

Sighing, she turns up the volume of her iPod, her head, breasts and hips bopping to the Ramones. Notwithstanding her name, today The Blondeshell sports short reddish brown hair.

They stand on the edge of the frozen pond, the mountain above them, watching an impossible game on an ice surface that is just too flat, too clear and too smooth to be real.

Awe: Sly watches in awe. His breath floats before him but he is not the least bit cold.

The flakes collect about the rink in mounds like cotton candy but the ice surface remains clean and pure. Sly steps onto the ice, looks down at his feet and the world shifts; he tips backwards, almost losing his balance. Vertigo strikes as if he stands atop the world's tallest building and looks down. Sunlight pierces the water's depths, seemingly falling into an abyss, falling forever.

The Blondeshell bops to the music.

The players wear warm-up suits with hockey gloves of matching color. One team wears white and the other midnight blue. No one wears helmets or any other equipment besides skates, sticks and gloves, except for the two goaltenders playing in full hockey gear.

The white team takes possession of the puck, two men and three women and the goaltender, the latter's gender hidden behind a mask.

At the edge of the rink, behind the goal the white team defends, looms a mountain of bluish-grey rock sprinkled with a frosting of snow. The mountain towers into the sky and from the distant peak snow blows into the air like smoke spiraling from a chimney. Somewhere near the summit, built of rock and ice, is The Mountain Palace.

Beyond the blue team's net, a plain of snow stretches away as far as the eye can see, broken by crests like waves reaching towards shore.

The teams play. It is unlike the games Sly played as a child, when players would skate up and down imaginary lanes on the ice. Back then, the left wing would stay on the left side of the ice, the right wing on the right side, the center would patrol the middle section. Back then they had played as if they were bowling balls rolling on assigned lanes and straying too far either way would lead to disaster and a ball falling into a gutter. Now, the white team's players circle and crisscross, skating to open areas of the ice, the puck spinning perfectly from one player to another, hitting the center of each stick blade as it passes between teammates. Each player moves like a pinball ricocheting about an arcade game surface and yet the five teammates somehow move together as if they are skating some coordinated pattern or dance only they know, avoiding collisions, always finding open ice for themselves and the puck.

They are beautiful, Sly thinks. He watches more than a game. Art, he realizes, I am watching beautiful art.

The blue team skates a dance as well, four men and a woman. The white team maintains possession of the puck but the blue team shifts and whirls with them, somehow always in place to prevent a pass that would allow a white team player to breakaway for an easy shot on net, somehow always forcing the white team from gaining access to ice near the blue goaltender.

The speed of the game increases.

After many minutes, much longer than any team should ever possess a puck during a game, the white team fires a shot on net and the blue goaltender's hand is a blur, moving faster than seems normal, catching the puck before it finds the top left corner of the net. The white team retreats, allowing the blue team to take possession of the puck and the dance begins again, this time the blue team circling, the puck flying from stick to stick, the white team defending.

Sly wants to skate with them but each team already has enough players and they ignore him. Although they sprint from place to place faster than any of his teammates ever skated, they never seem to tire.

Can I play like that? Sly wonders. Can I be one of them?

The ice surface expands, the nets at each end of the pond recede into the distance and even the bluish-grey mountain loses its towering presence as it touches the horizon.

The game continues without him.

Sly stands on the edge of the pond feeling as if he stands on the very edge of the world and no one knows he is there and he cries.

"Need a blow job?" The Blondeshell asks.

Sam

- 14 -

Monday morning.

As usual, I forced myself out of bed, smoked a cigar, drank three cups of coffee and two shots of whiskey to steady myself for the day and headed to our offices.

The receptionist intercepted me in the main lobby. "Mr. Prickles wants to see you," she told me in a stern voice. "Now."

I nodded with a glare, suggesting she did not have the authority to address me with such a tone. It was an act. I was a non-equity partner. I didn't have an ownership interest in the firm or a vote at partnership meetings. I was a glorified employee, capable of being fired at any moment without any severance pay or a buyout of a partnership interest. The label of 'partner' was supposed to keep me happy and calling me a partner was supposed to impress clients. But the actual position held little power and the receptionist knew it.

I took the stairs two at a time to the top floor leased by the firm. Prickles had the firm's most desired office occupying the northeastern corner of the building and overlooking the downtown skyline a few miles away. It was more of a hearth room than an office with a gas fireplace, heavy leather chairs, couches, wood paneling and portraits of the three other lawyers who held the position of managing partner during the firm's eighty-seven year history. Surprisingly, all bore the surname of Prickles. A circular conference table of glass was positioned in the corner by the windows. Prickles didn't have a desk. It was rumored his billable hours per year could be counted using the fingers of one hand. He was twenty-four years old.

"Come in," he said in a squeaky voice when I knocked. He sat on one of the leather chairs smoking a pipe and reading the *Wall Street Journal*. Probably checking on the investments in his trust, I thought. Assuming, of course, that the son-of-a-bitch knows how to interpret the financial pages. I took a seat on the couch across from him as he folded the paper and tossed it onto the marble coffee table.

"Terrible thing," he said. He had bright red hair and freckles and could have passed for a ventriloquist's dummy. "Just terrible."

"I'm sorry," I said. "I'm not following you. What happened?"

"Arnie."

"Yes?"

"Didn't you hear? He had a heart attack Friday afternoon."

"What?"

"It happened during a meeting with a client. That quarterback's wife. He's in intensive care."

A sadness bubble rose in my chest. "Nobody told me," I said.

"Oh," he shrugged. "They'll be a firm-wide email sent out later this morning. We wanted to take certain steps before the word got too far out and rumors spread all over town. We even covered his face with a towel when he was wheeled out of the building on a stretcher. Not sure how that worked, given the size of his stomach. But it did. There was nothing in the newspapers the last few days."

"Will he be okay?"

"Unclear. But we think we have everything under control."

"Of course," I said. I was listening to the kid sitting across from me but I knew I was really listening to his father who retired from the firm at the relatively young age of sixty but still controlled the firm via his son. How he was able to do that was a mystery to all but the most senior equity partners of the firm. I really wanted to peak behind Prickles's chair and see if his father was behind him, pulling some invisible string, causing Prickles to talk. Nah, I thought. We were in the techno-age. The midget probably had a device in his ear and was repeating his father's instructions while the bastard played golf and sipped a Bloody Mary. To be retired in good health, I thought. To have years of enjoyment ahead, instead of work and suffering.

I answered confidently, "Our firm's Family Law section has a good number of cases but the two paralegals and I should be able to keep things afloat until Arnie gets back on his feet. We may need occasional help from one of the litigation associates but only for a few simple hearings."

"I doubt that," Prickles said.

"Excuse me?"

"We've been thinking about adding another lawyer to your section for months. With Arnie's health problem the time appears right."

"You want me to train a young lawyer at this time? That could be difficult given I have to handle all of Arnie's cases."

The twenty-four year old kid lawyer smiled and I wondered if he kept his teeth clean with *SpongeBob Squarepants Sparkling Toothpaste*. "You won't have to train a new lawyer. In fact, the reverse might be true."

"Excuse me?"

"We offered an equity partnership interest in the firm to James Landscuda yesterday and he accepted. He's probably moving his files into his new office even as we speak."

In my office my paralegal was waiting for me. "When did you find out?" I asked.

"This morning," Brandy said. "By the way, call him Jaime. He thinks it helps with morale."

"Whose morale?"

"His," Brandy said.

I briefly wondered if she could work the magic on Landscuda that resulted in the death of her three prior husbands. I fell into my chair and rolled between my desk and credenza.

Landscuda, I thought. Fuck.

I had opposed him on a number of cases and found his reputation to be only half-true. He resembled a middle-aged Robert Redford though he liked to tell people he was better looking. He would use every dirty trick in the book during a case, was as demeaning as possible to the opposing lawyer and in his spare time liked to climb Mount Everest or win triathlons. He ran the New York City marathon with little training and won the amateur division. He had never married, knowing both the horrors of an acrimonious divorce and that he couldn't keep his hands off any pretty lady that wandered within his view. He was everything that I wasn't.

He also showed up in court or at settlement negotiations unprepared. After his initial meeting with a client, his legal secretary and paralegal did all the work. He barely looked at the client's file until the morning he had to do something with it. He was a business generator without equal. As a divorce lawyer he was all show and little substance but he was such a good salesman his clients never seemed to care.

"Jaime wants to have a staff meeting at ten."

"Tell me what happens during it."

"Don't you understand anything?"

"What?"

"You're staff, too."

"Staff?" I said.

"And he wants you to bring the coffee," Brandy said.

Fuck.

- 15 -

I had graduated near the top of my class at a local law school. With a multitude of job offers after graduation I chose to work with Arnie at the firm.

He was the ultimate rainmaker, bringing in more business than any lawyer could handle by himself. The associate that used to work for him—a very good female attorney—left the firm with a large severance package after being subjected to one too many comments and touching that clearly would have led to a successful claim for sexual harassment. The firm needed a smart worker bee that could handle Arnie's personality. I had graduated with few friends and no social skills. The odds of my attracting clients of my own were slim but that was a skill unneeded at the firm. It was a perfect relationship.

I worked the cases given to me with good results. Clients rarely developed any strong relationship with me but were, by and large, content with the outcome of their cases. Arnie's ability to generate clients remained the same. The firm made lots of money. I accepted Arnie's quirks and his need to confess his increasingly odd sexual fantasies. All was well.

Without Arnie, I was expendable.

I didn't care. I lived each day just trying to make it to the next.

I was polite and respectful and a good soldier.

Each day, the sadness bubbles attacked.

Each day, I managed to survive.

- 16 -

We met in the firm's largest conference room. Cowboy Jake slouched in one of the leather chairs eating a pastry and I sat next to him. Across from us sat two tiny identical twin blondes wearing black cocktail dresses they seemed to consider business attire. Mia and Mai, they introduced themselves. One was a legal secretary, the other a paralegal. I wondered if either of them was actually old enough to have graduated from high school. They grasped expensive pens held inches from legal pads, ready for action.

Cowboy Jake passed me a note under the table.

Landsluts, it read.

Brandy took a seat on the other side of Cowboy Jake, leaving the seat at the head of the table empty. Jaime strode into the room wearing a thousand dollar suit, using his looks the way most salesmen used their business cards. He slapped my shoulder with the palm of his hand.

"Good to see you," he said. He spoke in a confident and deep voice that somehow made me want to puke. "A non-equity partner, right? And you've been here ten years. Amazing. So where's my coffee?"

I smiled, standing and reaching out a hand. "Glad to have you aboard our firm. It's going to be good finally working with you, instead of against you."

His eyes were a deep blue and rivaled those of The Blondeshell.

"My coffee?" he asked.

We spent the next three hours reviewing every case that either our firm or Landscuda had going at the time. I kept my cases. Arnie's cases and Landscuda's cases were basically combined and he 'asked' me to handle those cases which appeared to be the losers of the bunch. Except for the Quarterback's Wife case he took the cases that appeared to be the ones that would generate the most profits for the firm.

Afterwards, Brandy was going to meet with George Tolliver and Rebecca Warren to have them sign their pleadings. Cowboy Jake and I drove to the hospital to visit Arnie.

"Should we tell him about Landscuda?" I asked in my Porsche. "We don't want to give him another heart attack."

"Maybe not today," Cowboy Jake said.

"You met with Arnie and the quarterback's wife, right? I never heard how that turned out."

"I guess I can tell you now. It's your case, according to Landsucker."

"What happened?"

"She told Arnie some confidential facts and he grabbed his chest and collapsed."

"What facts?"

"The quarterback has been throwing games."

- 17 -

Cowboy Jake worked on a bison ranch until he injured his back breaking up a fight between wild horses and pigs and had to find more sedentary work. He never forgot his days on the plains, however, dressing each day in worn boots and a cowboy hat. Unless he was due in court, he kept his trusty six shooters holstered at his sides. Once I asked him if they were loaded. "What kind of a man ain't always ready to unload at a suitable target?" he replied with a forced Texas drawl. Arnie liked to joke that Cowboy Jake had to find a new line of work because too many days out on the plains with the bison had made them his normal, suitable target. The firm thought Cowboy Jake would keep Arnie in line as Arnie's paralegal and for the last decade the arrangement had worked out fine.

"I'm going to be toast," Cowboy Jake said. "Ain't no way Landsucker is going to keep me on the payroll."

"Jaime isn't going to be able to overrule Arnie, and Arnie likes you a lot."

Cowboy Jake adjusted his black hat and let his hands drop to the handles of his guns. "Arnie? He won't know what hit him. You check out Jaime's paralegal and secretary? I clearly ain't Landsucker's type."

"I'll stick up for you with the other partners."

Cowboy Jake chuckled. "Hell boy, I'm betting I outlast you."

In the hospital Arnie lay quietly in his bed, his breath shallow, watching pornography on his smartphone. "Found a good bison movie," he told Cowboy Jake. "Rated four out of five stars."

"Movies ain't real life."

"Well, it will have to do. Been years since a bison was seen wandering around our town. You want me to email you the website?"

"Did your memory go to hell along with your heart? I sent you the web site, remember?"

"Just checking," Arnie said. He turned to me. "And how's Landscuda?"

It took me several seconds to respond. "How did you find out?

Arnie gestured to Cowboy Jake. "Can you go lasso a pretty nurse or something? I need a few minutes with Sam."

"Sure thing, boss."

Arnie waited until Jake left the room, closing the door behind him. Arnie sagged in the bed. He looked old, I thought, lying there. He seemed to have lost weight in his face in the few days he'd been in the hospital, his cheeks hollowing, his eyes sinking into his face.

"Sit down," Arnie said.

I pulled a chair up to the bed. Arnie had a private room; with the television off we could hear sounds from the hallway. The machines hooked up to Arnie were silent.

"We've been negotiating with Landscuda for over a year," Arnie said. "It's been kept very quiet."

"But why not tell me?"

Arnie sighed. "It was decided you didn't need to know."

"Someone could have asked me what I thought."

He was blunt. "No one cared what you thought."

I'm expendable, I thought. Arnie's getting old and nearing retirement age; he generated most of the revenue in our section of the law firm. The firm needed to replace him with another superstar rainmaker, another super magnet for clients.

I was hard working and honest and very good at my job. But I was not a client magnet. I was just a part of the machine. The firm could order a replacement part and send me out the door.

"You've been very loyal to me," Arnie said. "I felt bad about it."

"Sure," I said. "Okay."

"I'm supposed to get out of here soon and then rest at home for a few weeks. But I'll be back at the office. I'll make sure it all works out for you."

"Thanks." I reached over and gave his arm a pat. "The place isn't the same without you."

"It will all work out."

"Okay."

There was a knock on the door. Cowboy Jake stuck his head inside the room. "Done?"

"Sure," I said.

He had three paper cups and a flask of whiskey.

Jake poured.

We all drank.

- 18 -

Landscuda sauntered into my office with a big smile on his face.

"So how's the Rebecca Warren case going?" he asked, standing before my desk.

I stopped sipping my coffee. "Fine. Brandy had the client sign the paperwork and one of the litigation associates brought it to Court yesterday. She should be very happy—the judge granted her request for temporary orders, which included a provision that she stays in the house and her son keeps playing hockey. We also filed our responsive pleadings in the case with the telecommunications executive. We should generate good fees in both cases."

"Really?" Landscuda asked with an even broader smile on his face.

"Yes. Why?"

"Rebecca Warren just fired us."

Landscuda let the paper he was holding fall out of his hand and it floated in the air to land neatly before me on the desk.

"Way to go: you managed to get fired before we really did something wrong. You're going to have to work on your client-relationship skills, I think. Talk to you later."

I stared at the paper as he left my office.

> To The Firm, it read. I have decided to obtain new counsel for my divorce case. By this letter, I am terminating the services of Sam Oliver and your firm, effective immediately. Please have my file ready for pick-up later today.

What the hell? Maybe I shouldn't have been so honest when Rebecca asked me what I thought about Donnie. What the hell did I do wrong?

I was preparing to call her when my phone rang. It was the President of the Shooters Youth Hockey Association. Ten minutes later, over several protests, I was appointed head hockey coach of Donnie's team.

"So let me understand this," Landscuda said a few minutes later. "Rebecca Warren fired you so you'd be her son's hockey coach?"

"Apparently," I said. "She didn't consult or ask me but that's apparently what happened."

"Does our firm get paid for you being the hockey coach?"

"No, but when I coach part of my marketing monies goes to buying an advertisement in the Shooters Association's annual yearbook. That could lead to some business."

"Could? So this will end up costing the firm money?"

"Well . . . . , yes."

"And not necessarily lead to the firm making money?"

"Well . . . ., probably, yes."

"Wonderful," Landscuda said. "Just wonderful."

- 19 -

Fay Blondeshell asks, 'What makes you want to breathe?'

I walked into the Ice Kingdom an hour before practice to meet the team's assistant coach. The night before, I spoke at length with the President of the Shooters Youth Hockey Association, who gave me a very detailed rundown of the players and parents of my new team.

The assistant coach sat at one of the tables by the concession stand staring intently at a laptop computer's screen. He looked about a foot taller than me and about fifty pounds heavier, more fat than muscle, and he wore glasses with thick lenses and black plastic frames. I tossed a plastic garbage bag by his feet and took a seat across from him.

We introduced ourselves.

"Herb Rooks," he said as we shook hands over the screen. "So how did you end up coaching the team?"

"Divine intervention," I replied with a smile.

At the ice rink I was The Coach and I didn't mess around. Parents were an annoyance I tolerated. Assistant coaches were there to move pucks and cones during practices and open the bench doors during games so players could get on and off the ice. Preferably both parents and assistant coaches would suffer from muteness ninety-nine percent of the time. Temporary blindness during games also would be acceptable.

"Huh?" Rooks asked. "Do you want me to tell you about my hockey background? I never played ice hockey myself, but . . ."

Each year, I was later told, Herb began the season with a new outfit of coaching gear, coming to the rink in a matching sweat jacket and pants outfit with his name and title (Assistant Coach) stitched on the jacket and sporting a white Shooters ball cap on his head.

"Very sharp looking outfit," I told him. Herb took it as a compliment. I wore my typical coaching attire: a stained blue hoodie proclaiming the name of my alma mata and black sweat pants and I was fairly certain my garb would be older than all of my current players.

"I watch a lot of ice hockey on television," Herb was saying. "I've bought a lot of instructional videos and really know how to teach skills to the boys. Do you want me to go over the practice plan I did for today?"

"We can about it talk later," I said. "And I'll tell the parents how I came to coach the team at the parents meeting in twenty minutes."

"Hey, you want to me to give you a rundown on the players? My son played on this team last year, for instance, when he was only 9. He led the team in scoring last season."

"That's great. You can tell me about the players later. But I've already watched them play a game and have some idea of what we have on the team."

"I have all of the statistics from last year up on the computer. I keep the team's statistics and have spreadsheets covering a lot of different areas of the game."

"Great," I lied. "Please print them out and I'll look at them later."

I had bought mesh practice jerseys at a local sports store. Usually, a team had six players on the ice during a game: a unit consisting of a goalie, two defensemen, and a forward line of a center and two wingers. Hockey was a read and react game—even though teams had systems for offense and defense at any moment players would be changing their positions on the ice based on the location of their teammates, the opposing players and the puck. Decisions needed to be made in split seconds; therefore, it was good to keep a unit together so each player knew the tendencies of the other players on the unit, making it easier to anticipate passes, shots, and where a player would be during any particular moment.

I had printed off the team's roster from the team's web site and then assigned each player a number. All the defensemen would wear black practice jerseys; each of the three forward lines would wear a different color jersey. I didn't care what the goalies wore and didn't bother to buy them anything.

"The new practice jerseys are in the garbage bag," I told Herb and gave him the list. "Make sure each player wears the jersey I assigned him."

"Yea, okay." Herb studied the list.

"It will be good coaching with you," I said.

"Yea, uh, these aren't the forward lines we've been using."

"I know," I said.

"My son plays with Sean Manyard and Steele Williams. They were a very potent line last year."

"Okay," I said. "Let's talk later."

The ice rink had a meeting room with a whiteboard hanging on a wall behind a long table, and facing the table were forty folding chairs.

'Breath,' Fay Blondeshell says.

At the parents meeting I introduced myself and went over the team rules for the parents. "Have the players here thirty minutes before practice and an hour before games. No parents can be in the locker room fifteen minutes before a game and fifteen minutes after a game."

I explained my background. "I played here in town on travel teams from the time I was six through eighteen. I played for intramural teams in college and law school. After law school I coached travel teams for a few years for the Shooters, winning 80% of the tournaments we entered and two league titles. I've kept my coaching card current and am ready to go.

"I'm very excited to be coaching this team. It's unfortunate your prior coach had family issues but I was available and when the President of the Shooters called I jumped at the chance to get back on the ice."

I looked over the parents. They sat staring at me. Most sat as couples, husband and wife and dressed alike—either business casual or jeans and shirts. The women who sat without husbands wore either tight sweat suits or tight jeans. The men who sat without wives dressed either in impeccable business suits or as if they just got off work at the nearby landfill.

'Which of the women do you want to fuck?' Fay Blondeshell asks me.

Rebecca wasn't in the room.

"Any questions?" I asked quickly. Before anyone had time to answer I said, "Okay, thanks, see everyone around the rink," and strode from the room.

One of the dads caught up with me as I passed through the double doors and entered the ice rink.

"On the way here I was listening to the radio and the radio guy said there's a tornado warning right now," he told me. "Tornadoes are pretty dangerous, right?"

"If one lands on top of you or you live in a trailer park, sure."

"My son is Billy, he's a defenseman. We just moved here from New Jersey. We didn't have tornado warnings in New Jersey. Just hurricanes."

"We don't have hurricanes in the Midwest," I replied. "We have tornadoes. Occasionally we have a serial killer operating in the area. No hurricanes though."

"I hear there are warning systems in place for tornadoes."

"Very true," I said. "The local government takes tornadoes pretty seriously. If there's a chance of one forming sirens will go off and people will be asked to head for cover or go to a shelter."

"Does the rink have a shelter?"

"No," I said.

Outside in the distance a siren began to blare.

"Is that the kind of siren you were talking about?"

"Yea."

"Should we do anything?"

Ice time was very valuable. If the boys huddled in a locker room for thirty minutes during a tornado warning that was thirty minutes of ice time that would be lost forever.

"Only if you don't want your son to attend a very important practice," I replied.

Billy's father stood still for a moment, nodded and walked away.

I sat on the first row of bleacher seats and put on my skates, donned my gloves, grabbed my stick and clipboard and walked to the team's locker room.

Rebecca Warren stood outside the door to the locker room, watching.

"Are you going to run practice better than that?" she asked, pointing to the team on the ice.

The Shooters 8U AA Travel Team [the players were seven or eight years old] was on the ice and the coaches were having the players sprint up and down the ice again and again as punishment for a loss to an inferior team last weekend. A bunch of the team's parents seemed happy with the practice, smiling and talking about how this would teach the kids a good lesson.

What bullshit, I thought, but I shrugged at Rebecca, not wanting to comment on the nonsense going on. "You missed the parents meeting," I said.

"Parent meetings suck," she replied.

"Okay."

Inside the narrow locker room the boys sat on wooden benches lining each wall, fully dressed, wearing their helmets and holding onto their sticks with gloved hands. They were in their assigned practice jerseys. Herb Rooks stood to the back of the room, looking pained and fondling his whistle.

I introduced myself and explained the team's new rules, the ones that had led to much success in my past.

"Four things," I said. "First, you guys can talk to me. If you have any questions or are unhappy about anything, just talk to me in private. No one will get punished for talking to me. Let's just talk in private. Not in the locker room, not during games or on the ice. We'll talk in private in a corner of the rink and no one will know what we talk about. But it has to be about hockey. Don't talk to me about your girlfriends, or your recent arrests, or where to buy drugs, okay?"

They looked at me, mostly confused, but Donnie was smiling.

"Second, during games and practice you do exactly what I say without argument or comment. If you think I have the forward lines wrong or hate the drills we're doing we can talk about it in private. But on the ice and during games no one questions me. Just do what I say.

"Third, no one worries about failing. In every game and during every practice, every player in this room will fail at least two times. Every player will make at least two mistakes. That's the game. I don't care about mistakes or failure. Just try and do your best. Skate hard and try. That's all I ask."

Herb was wincing. The players stared at me, wide-eyed and a few more of them were smiling.

I had placed Donnie as the center for Steele Williams and Sean Manyard on the first line. From what I had seen the prior weekend, they were the two most aggressive and biggest wingers on the team. I had placed Andy Rooks on a line with two talented but less physical wingers.

"Last rule," I began. "We have to protect ourselves on the ice. We can't let anyone on the other team bully our teammates. If one of our teammates gets a cheap shot, then we have to retaliate. Understand?"

The two big boys got it, I saw.

I took Donnie aside as the other players headed to the ice surface. "They'll protect you during games," I told Donnie. "Reward them. Set 'em up for lots of easy goals."

"Sure thing, coach," Donnie said with a smile.

I planned each minute of the team's practice, keeping the boys on a tight schedule while on the ice, moving them from drill to drill. I told them to forget everything they had been taught since the season began and installed simple offensive and defensive systems we would run for the rest of the year. The boys were nine and ten years old; I wanted them to be creative on the ice but simple systems were necessary so the boys had a general idea where to be during the game.

The parents clustered in groups, either in the bleachers or standing by the boards. Most of the parents were either holding a cup of coffee or a can of beer purchased from the rink's concession stand. One parent was responsible for keeping the water bottles filled on the bench. I saw Rebecca standing by herself in a corner of the rink. She watched Donnie move effortlessly, scoring goals at will, making passes to teammates that one wouldn't expect from a ten year old. He was first in line for every drill; the most attentive when the team gathered by the benches to listen to me; the best player no matter what skill was showcased in the drill.

Afterwards, I dressed and carried my stick and bag into the lobby. I left Herb to deal with the team's water bottles, pucks and dry eraser board.

"Good practice, coach," one parent said.

"You got them sweating real good," said another.

"Keep working them hard," said a third.

Rebecca wasn't in the lobby.

"Coach, can I talk to you for a second?" a parent asked.

"Yea, sure."

Michael Williams was thin and short, sporting a Rolex Submariner watch, Italian loafers that matched his tan slacks and a blue, button down shirt. According to the President of the Shooters he was an investment banker and played in each of the three adult hockey leagues at the rink. In each league he had the most expensive gear and was the worst player on the ice. His wife, like her husband, was short and thin and she was standing with another group of moms, not wanting to miss out on any of the team gossip. Most of the moms were holding a cup of coffee.

I doubted the moms were drinking coffee. It was a rite of passage for the sisters of the players to join the moms in the parking lot before practices and games. There, they would be shown how much brandy to pour into a cup of coffee, depending on the size of the cup, the type of coffee, and the place where the coffee was purchased. I figured college credits eventually would be given to the sisters who learned the correct serving proportions.

Michael Williams and I walked away from the other parents.

"I was wondering why you changed the forward lines," Michael said. "Is my kid going to play with the Warren kid?"

Steele Williams, Michael's son, was almost as tall as his five foot six inch father. I figured it was an early growth spurt and in the end Steele would be about the same size as his parents. The kid was fast for a ten year old because of his long legs and stride, but just like Sean Manyard his speed would disappear when the other boys caught up to his height. Steele would go from being an effective player to a scrub by the time he was sixteen but for now he did well on the ice and his parents had dreams of NHL glory.

Fucking morons, I thought.

Michael's wife walked over.

"Hi," I said, not wanting anything to do with her.

"That new boy is fast," Sharon replied. "Is he from Florida?"

"Yea."

"He must have gotten more practice time down there then our boys get up here. That must be why he's so fast."

As she spoke I could smell the alcohol on her breath. "I guess they develop quicker there, given the long and cold Florida winters," I replied.

"Has anyone checked his birth certificate?" she asked. "He seems really fast for someone who's only ten years old."

"The President checked," I lied. "Donnie's ten. And a very young ten at that."

"Does he pass the puck in games? I'd hate for him not to pass the puck to his teammates."

"Donnie and Steele are going to be on the same line," her husband said.

"Only if he passes the puck," she replied and there was a glint of fury in her eyes directed at Michael. "Last season, Andy Rooks almost never passed Steele the puck. I hope the Warren kid will be different."

Her full name was Sharon Suzette Williams. She liked to be called Shari but behind her back most of the other parents called her S.S. They joked that at home she donned a black Nazi Waffen-SS uniform, complete with full length black high heeled boots and demanded Michael obey all of her household cleaning commands.

"Excuse me," I said.

"Another thing," Michael said, taking a quick hold of my arm. "My investment firm would be happy to contribute to the team. Say, ten thousand dollars?"

"Really," I said.

"Sure. You can figure out what to do with it. I trust you. None of the other parents have to be told about it. And let me know if you're ever thinking of changing Steele's linemates."

"Absolutely."

Rebecca was standing outside, smoking a cigarette.

"You always smoke after a game or practice?" I asked.

"It gives me an excuse to get away from the other parents."

"I don't blame you."

April Rooks was waiting in her car and she gave me a dirty look from a hundred feet away.

"What's that about?" Rebecca asked.

"Donnie scored more goals in practice than her son," I replied. "And her son lost his two wingers from last season."

Rebecca dropped the cigarette onto the pavement and stubbed it out with her sneaker. "Am I going to have trouble with these people?"

"Some of them will be jealous of Donnie and consider him a threat to their son's future NHL career. But as long as the team is winning and Donnie is a team player, they'll probably keep it to themselves."

"And if they don't?"

I was The Coach and I was in control. "We'll poison their fucking coffee," I replied with a smile.

- 20 -

It was mid-week so I drove to my apartment by the law firm's offices to spend the night. I took my skates from the bag and made sure the blades were dry—I didn't want any rust forming on them—and was about to enter the shower when the doorbell rang.

Sean Maynard was a huge kid for his age. He just turned ten and already stood five feet six inches tall and weighed 147 pounds.

His parents owned a sporting goods store and considered Sean to be the premier athlete in the area. According to the President of the Shooters, last season Sean played on a line with Andy Rooks and scored twenty-six goals. The President knew the goal total because Herb Rooks had emailed the team statistics to the entire Board of Directors. Andy Rooks would normally have the puck on his stick and rather than pass he would skate with it for while and then shoot it at the net. Sean would just stand in front of the other team's goalie and he was so big and strong that no one on the other team could push him out of the way. If Andy didn't score Sean would tap in the rebound.

Sean played football, basketball, hockey and baseball. It was widely opined throughout the city's coaches that he was a mediocre talent in all of them. But he had size and sometimes that was enough.

Sean's mother stood outside my front door holding a large cardboard box, slightly out of breath. "I've got some stuff that might be good for the boys but I didn't want to show it to you at the rink," she said. "It was just delivered to our sporting goods store. We can give everyone on the team a huge price discount. Can I show them to you?"

I looked about. "You followed me here?"

"No," she said. "I Googled your address. I came after dropping Sean off at home."

"Oh."

"Can I come in and show you?"

"Uh, okay, sure."

"I didn't want the other parents to see this," she said and then forced a laugh. "They'll think it's a bribe to give Sean lots of ice time and let him play with Donnie this year."

"I already put Sean on Donnie's line."

"Where's the bathroom?"

I pointed and she carried the box to the bathroom and closed the door behind her.

Amazing, I thought, debating between using The Lawyer persona, the hockey coach persona, or my typical, real self. The hockey coach persona seemed to fit.

She came out of the bathroom and walked towards me.

"What do you think?" Mrs. Maynard asked.

If pressed, I would say she slightly resembled Jennifer Aniston except for her rear end, of which she could be a body double for Kim Kardashian. Her stomach was fairly flat and her thighs and calves appeared sculpted from granite. All of this was obvious because at the moment she was wearing some type of red bodysuit that flowed from the nape of her neck to her toes. The silky material clung to her skin so tightly I thought it must be restricting the flow of blood to her arms and legs. I stepped back towards the center of the living room.

"It's the newest sports fabric," she said. "Professional hockey players will be wearing it. It keeps the body warm, collects sweat but stays dry against the skin. It's amazing and works whether the boys are playing on an outdoor ice rink in February or sitting in a sweltering locker room in August."

She walked towards me, hefty breasts jiggling as she spoke. She touched my chest, dirty blonde hair tickling my nose, turned and walked away. Her bottom rolled with each step as if it was constructed of ball bearings and the red fabric dug into her like miners searching for gold.

"What do you think?" she asked, looking over her shoulder, hands on her hips, smiling. She smelled sweet and fresh and clean.

"I can talk my husband into giving the team a huge discount if we order a bodysuit for everyone on the team," she said. "My husband really wants to help out, given the new store in St. Joseph."

St. Joseph was a town over an hour away.

"New store?" I asked.

"We're opening a new sports store there. He's going to have to work most weekends, for months, all winter long. He won't be traveling with our team this season. It will just be Sean and me. My husband will want the coaches to be looking out for us on the road. He can be talked into a huge discount for that."

She smiled again.

They had a name for women like Teri Manyard: MILFs. Mothers I'd Like to Fuck.

Since my divorce, I had spent each night in bed or on the couch at The Ranch Retreat, alone. In all my life I had never slept with a woman most men would deem attractive. In social situations I fumbled for words and my appearance could not make up for my lack of charisma. I had no close relatives. Except for Jenny, I had no close friends. I wasn't good at anything besides practicing law or coaching young hockey players. When the sadness bubbles struck, there was no future hope to fend them off.

I faced the world alone.

She was the mother of one of my hockey players and she stood before me willing to trade the pleasures of her body for some unspoken agreement to treat her son well.

I knew it would be entirely wrong and inappropriate to peel off her clothes and tongue her salty, soft skin and then drive into her body repeatedly with reckless abandon, without any need to worry if she was satisfied and happy.

But it had been a long time since I had been with a woman and tonight I was The Coach so what the hell, I did it anyway.

"This is going to be great," George said. "I'm going to start talking about the beetles and my wife's attorney isn't going to know what hit her."

We waited in the lobby of Susan Henderson's law offices as the receptionist went to fetch us coffee.

"Why wouldn't your wife have told her attorney about the beetles?"

"Are you kidding?" George sneered. "If a few of those damn things escaped they'd infest this entire country, destroy the ecosystem, causing who knows how much economic harm. Forget attorney-client privilege, my wife believes her attorney would have to report her to the authorities because importing those bugs into the country is a crime."

"I don't think that's right," I said. "I think your wife's communication to her attorney about the beetles would be protected by the attorney-client privilege."

"My wife will believe it's not protected. Trust me."

"How do you know?"

"Because my wife and I talked about this very topic several times in the past and I told her that she couldn't even talk about the beetles with an attorney. My wife trusts me. It was one of the strong points of our marriage. This attorney won't know a damn thing about the beetles until I tell her. This will be great."

We had arrived for George's deposition. Some attorneys liked to depose the other spouse at the start of a divorce case, mainly as a method of gaining as much information as possible early in the case. Other attorneys, such as me and Arnie, conducted the deposition towards the end of the case after information had been gathered by other discovery methods and from third parties.

"Remember," I told George again. "Only answer the question that's asked. If she asks you for the time, don't tell her how to build a watch. Don't volunteer information. And don't guess if you don't know an answer."

"Yea," he replied.

The receptionist brought us Styrofoam cups of coffee and led us to the conference room. The law offices were on the first floor of an old building and the rooms carried the smell of must and dust particles were visible in the air. Old legal books lined the conference room walls, probably unused for years with the advent of computer research. The carpet was frayed and stained. I sat in one of the chairs at the rectangular table, happy for its wheels. The court reporter sat at the table's head, fiddling with her stenographer's machine and laptop computer. I knew her, introduced her to George and out of habit handed her a business card. She was middle aged and well dressed and had been taking depositions in divorce cases for a decade.

George's wife and Susan Henderson entered the cramped room. Susan took a seat across from George, with the court reporter 'between' them. George's wife sat across from me.

"How are you, Sam?" Susan asked.

"Doing well. How are you and the kids?"

"I'm either a lawyer for my clients or a taxi driver for my children," Susan said with a laugh. "I spend more time seeing them in the car than I do seeing them at home."

"Both almost teenagers?"

"Yes and way too active."

"Keeps 'em out of trouble."

"You're right about that," Susan said.

Susan and I had been opposing counsel on quite a few divorce cases over the years. She was not a 'killer.' She did a good job for her clients, was very professional, did not antagonize a situation and tried to reach an amicable settlement. She was a good opponent; not too tough and easy to work with. She also was easy to look at, with a lithe figure and a pretty face.

George sat with his hands folded on the table, smirking. He wore his usual attire: an expensive dark business suit. I was in kakis and a blue button down shirt; Susan wore a blouse and jeans. We both knew depositions, unless videotaped, were usually very informal.

George's wife also dressed in jeans and a blouse and yet she carried the clothing as if she was wearing an evening gown. She was approaching fifty-five and yet she didn't look like she was growing old; she had a maturing beauty with just touches of gray in her hair and a calmness in her eyes.

The plan according to George was to start mentioning the bugs in an offhand manner, drawing the other attorney into the subject. When Susan learned the extent of the bug issue, George was sure she would be speaking to her client about a quick settlement. Susan would not want to go to court with a client who had knowingly and intentionally violated Federal laws on animal importation.

I had pleaded with him during our deposition preparation session to not say anything about the bugs; to leave that issue to me so that I could raise it with opposing counsel at an appropriate time. However, George was insistent and I could only advise him. I couldn't control what he would say.

"Ready?" George asked with a wry smile.

"In a moment," Susan said. She was looking through her file and glancing at her deposition notes which were on her lap. Her client sat quietly, refusing to make eye contact with anyone.

"Okay," Susan said.

The court reporter had George raise his hand and swear under oath that he would tell the truth.

"What's your name?" Susan asked, starting the deposition.

"George Tolliver."

"Are you married to Marjorie Tolliver?"

"Yes."

"You understand you need to tell the truth during this deposition?"

"Yes."

"You understand you can be charged with perjury if you lie?"

"Yes. Yes."

"Okay," Susan said. "I'm going to hand you a photograph that I've marked on the back as Exhibit "1.""

In the photograph George lay on a king-size bed in what appeared to be the master bedroom of his house, his suit trousers and boxers down at his knees and his dress shirt and undershirt pulled up to his nipples. A South American Stinging Beetle clung to the underside of George's blood engorged penis.

"We have videos, too," Susan Henderson said. "Wonderful resolution. Individual drops of white liquid are clearly visible shooting into the air."

The court reporter vomited onto her stenographer's machine.

"Seems like a good time for a bathroom break," I said, grabbing George's arm. I pulled him from the conference room, the law offices and the building and kept pulling him until we were standing by my Porsche in the parking lot. I need a smoke, I thought, a smoke and a drink. More than one drink. I opened the hatchback and grabbed the travel humidor and then thoughts of the cigar's cylindrical shape and George's penis flashed into my imagination and I tossed the humidor aside.

"What the fuck was that?" I asked.

"The bitch must have installed surveillance cameras in the house," George said bitterly. "Hell, I work for a telecommunications company. Everyone's cell phone nowadays has a camera; everyone's camera is really a small surveillance unit. I should have thought of that possibility."

"Great, she had cameras in the house. But what the fuck was that?"

"They molt," George explained. "In the Amazon they would attach themselves to a tree and rub against it to help break off their exoskeleton. When they grow their skeleton doesn't grow with them. A new one forms and when it's time they break out of the old one like a butterfly breaking out of a cocoon."

"Great, they molt. But what the fuck was that?"

"I'm a creative guy." He shrugged. "I had fallen asleep one afternoon in sweats, taking a nap and I woke to have one of the damn things nosing around my crotch. You know how lots of guys wake up with an erection? Well, the bug was interested. They don't bite and they're harmless when you remove their stinger."

"What the fuck was that!" I yelled.

"My wife and I stopped having sex a few years ago."

"You said you had the perfect marriage!"

"It was perfect," George said. "I no longer wanted to have sex with her."

I paced by the vehicle, shaking my head, trying to figure out what the hell to do and how this affected the case.

I stopped in front of him. He stood with his hands in his pocket, frowning and mumbling to himself.

"How come she never walked in on you when you were . . . . experimenting with the bugs?"

"I thought I was being very careful. I only . . . . studied the bugs when I knew she'd be gone for a few hours. Besides, there never was any evidence. They drink down all of the semen, seems to be part of their new American diet. A few would watch and actually fly into the air, trying to catch the droplets before they'd hit my chest. Remarkable creatures," George said.

It was my turn. I vomited all over my shoes.

Sly's World

- 22 -

They sit in the conference room and Sly asks the question again.

"And where did you put the million dollar bonus payment?"

"I told you," the husband of Sly's client says with a big grin on his face. "There was no bonus payment this year."

Sly frowns and glances to the left at his client, a nineteen year old child-bride imported from the Philippines. "He lies," she whispers furiously.

They sit in the firm's conference room and Fay Blondeshell enters with Sly's martini, placing it on the table and taking a seat to his right.

Sly sips from the glass and directs his gaze to opposing counsel, sitting next to the husband across the table from him. "He's lying. One is not supposed to lie during a deposition."

The other lawyer, a former world champion bodybuilder and movie star, wears a skimpy bathing suit and an outlaw biker's vest. The vest's pockets are stuffed with Montblanc pens. He pounds his massive hands on the table, throwing a tantrum. "You can't prove it! You can't! You cannot do it!"

"He is a liar and you know it."

"That's enough!" the attorney shouts, standing, posing with his biceps bulging and abdominal muscles quivering. "You will not impugn the integrity of my client!"

Sly draws the Magnum .44 from the shoulder holster and points it at the lawyer.

"Down Fido," Sly says. With the revolver still pointed, Sly nods to Fay who takes a file stamped document from the folder besides her and slides it across the table.

"*I knew this deposition was going to be a problem,*" *Sly explains.* "*So I obtained an Emergency Order For A Truth Serum Injection from the Court. It's all perfectly legal.*"

On cue, the court reporter picks up a syringe and rubber strap and begins pulling up the husband's shirt sleeve.

"*This is outrageous!*" *the other lawyer growls.* "*You will not get away with this!*"

Sly shoots him in the forehead and puts away the gun. "*Guess you won't be coming back this time.*"

The needle slides into the husband's vein.

Sly opens a law book and peruses the statutes.

"*Keeping the crime of statutory rape in mind, which carries a mandatory ten year prison sentence, can you tell me when you first had sex with my client?*"

An hour later they reach a final settlement. Sly's child-bride client receives the million dollar bonus payment, the mansion, all of the personal property, a Rolls Royce convertible and ten thousand dollars a month of maintenance, for life.

"*Good doing business with you,*" *Sly says as more drool drips from the husband's mouth. He finishes his martini and smiles at Fay.* "*Can you clean this mess up?*" *he asks.*

"*Of course,*" *Fay replies.*

In the lobby, the receptionist coughs up a piece of her lung. "*Done for the day?*"

"*Seems that way,*" *Sly responds.*

"*Perhaps one last assignment before the weekend starts?*"

The fifty-one year old woman puts down her cigarette, walks around the granite ledge and shrugs out of her hospital gown.

"*Well . . . .*"

The air shifts, she stands before him naked, short and adorable, reddish hair and big, brown eyes. "*Well,*" *she says.*

She wears a thin gold chain with a charm of crossed hockey sticks.

He reaches out and envelopes her.

"*Thank The Hockey Gods,*" *Rebecca says.*

They fall entangled onto the couch.

Sam

- 23 -

Landscuda knocked on my office door. "I was walking through the lobby," he said, sticking his head inside. "And found you have a visitor. It's waiting for you."

"It?"

"A vampire, I believe. Funny it's out during the daytime, but then again I'm not surprised about anything that has to do with you. Do you want me to call for the police or an ambulance, or perhaps the firm should hire a priest?"

"I'll handle it."

"Do it quickly," Landscuda said. "It's scaring away potential clients and probably staff, too."

The Satanist flashed fangs at me in the lobby. "I'm hungry," she said. "Feed me."

We drove to a sports bar at a strip mall a few miles from the office. We'd been there before. The owner brought Jenny a huge Bloody Mary and a plate of super hot and spicy chicken wings. She spat her fangs onto the table and dug in.

"You eating?" she asked.

"Not hungry."

"You need to eat. You look like a walking twig."

"Thanks."

Juices from a chicken wing ran down her chin, smearing the white face paint.

"What's the matter?" she asked.

"I screwed up. Literally."

"How?"

"I had sex with one of the hockey moms. Her son is on my team."

"Donnie's mother?"

A sadness bubble expanded and burst and I reached out and took a gulp of her Bloody Mary. "No, some other mom. She came to my apartment after practice and I let her seduce me."

"Why did she do that?"

"She probably wants to make sure I treat her son well."

"Maybe she just wanted you."

"Think so?"

"No," Jenny said. "Not really." She cracked a chicken bone with her teeth and sucked on the marrow. "But it doesn't matter. You needed to use that little thing of yours or it was going to be repossessed and given to the truly needy."

"Funny," I said, not sure if I should be more pissed about the comment on the size of my manhood or the comment on my lack of sexual encounters since the marriage failed, or both. I gave up thinking about it, took another sip from the Bloody Mary and looked at the vampire ghoul sitting across from me.

Damn, I thought, even in that outlandish Goth get-up she still looked good.

What appeared to be blood dripped from her front teeth.

Her eyes freaked me out just a bit; to complete the costume, she wore contacts that made her pupils a bright shade of red.

"My ex-fiancé is dating," Jenny said. "She's a tall brunette and a human resource director at some computer company. I saw them out last night at a steak house. They were drinking Jackson Kendall Merlot with their meat. That had been our wine. We drank it when we went to that steakhouse."

"I'm sorry."

"When I lay in bed last night, I fantasized he called me, needing to talk, and we went to that restaurant and ordered filets and a bottle of Jackson Kendall Merlot. And I imagined that in the middle of his meal I told him that the piece of meat he was eating was the cooked thigh muscle of that brunette."

"Charitable," I said. "What were you eating?"

She grinned. "The same thing he probably ate last night when they got back to his place."

"Do you mean . . . ."

She grinned at me, water in her eyes making her pupils appear to be on fire.

"Be right back," she announced suddenly, standing and grabbing her huge purse. She pushed the half-full plate of chicken wings at me. "Eat that. You need to and I'm done."

I sat alone, taking a few small bites out of a chicken wing. Teri Manyard walked by the table in the red bodysuit and pushed out her hip to tap me on the shoulder.

"Keep it coming, big boy," she purred.

Keep it coming, big boy? Even my fantasies were beginning to suck.

Just stay away from her, I thought. It was just once and no one knew about it. It won't happen again. It was a mistake but no one died or got hurt. It would be okay.

The Happy Girl returned to the table, wearing a white cotton blouse and skirt, both adorned with big, bright polka dots, purple and yellow. Her blue eyes sparkled beneath the yellow straw hat and her skin was clean and wet.

"Afternoon," Jenny said to me, smiling. The waiter returned. "A garden salad and a glass of chardonnay, please." He nodded and walked away.

"Can't decide on your mood today?"

"My mood is fine. It's always the same. I just haven't decided who I want the world to see."

She leaned across the table and kissed me on the cheek.

"Enjoy the hockey mom," she said. "Just don't get caught. As long as you don't get caught, it doesn't mean a thing."

I thought of George Tolliver and the surveillance cameras in his house.

"But someone's always watching," I said.

She wriggled her nose. "Not true. They may be looking in the right direction, but few people really see anything at all."

She drove us back to the corporate park in her Jaguar.

When I got back to my office, I noticed Landscuda had left me a present. On my desk was a box filled with dead cockroaches.

'Way to prepare our client for his deposition,' his note read.

Fuck.

- 24 -

I met my newest client in the small conference room. Jason Storm was in his thirties, with short hair parted on the side. He dressed in tan slacks and a long sleeve Polo shirt and took a seat across from me at the table. I smiled, taking down the basic information and out of the corner of my eye I thought I saw a South American Stinging Beetle crawling along the floor.

Calm down, I thought. Different client.

"My wife and I are going to get a divorce," Jason Storm said matter of factly, with almost no emotion in his voice.

"I'm sorry."

He shrugged. "That's the way things seem to be."

"Can you tell me what's going on?"

"We're getting a divorce. She's going to file. The other lawyer will send the paperwork to you."

"So you want to retain me? Do you want to talk about my fees?"

"No," he said. He took from his pants pocket a folded check and gave it to me. It was made out to the firm for ten thousand dollars.

"We've met before," he told me.

I looked closely at him and looked at the information I had written down on the client intake sheet.

"I'm sorry, I guess my memory is failing as I get older. I don't remember meeting."

"We've all met before," he said. "You've met my wife and her lawyer and everyone in this city."

"Excuse me? If our firm has represented your wife in another legal matter, there may be a conflict of interest. We may not be able to represent you."

"In your present form, you haven't met my wife."

"Excuse me?"

His expression hadn't changed since I entered the room. He continued to look at me with blank eyes and a dead face. He could be lying in a coffin, I thought.

He asked, "Do you understand the Big Bang theory concerning the creation of our universe?"

"I remember it briefly, from high school."

"Okay," he said. "It's very simple, really. At the beginning of time all of the matter and energy of the universe was compressed into a space much, much smaller than the tip of a needle. It then exploded, becoming a primordial fireball that expanded and formed the entire universe as it exists today. Okay, get it?"

"I got it."

"So, you see, we are the same."

I sighed. "You lost me."

"Everything, all of the matter and energy in the universe, every single atom that makes up our bodies and the air and all of the objects in this world were all once connected, squeezed into an infinitesimally small space at the very instant time began. The Big Bang broke us apart but we all began together, as one thing. Understand? We all began as a piece of the same thing."

I glanced down at my notes. "You never went to college, right? And you work in a warehouse, loading trucks?"

"Einstein was just a patent clerk."

"Actually, I think he did really well in school in math and the sciences."

"No matter." He finally showed a glimmer of a smile. "Matter," he said. "That could be a pun."

"Okay. Can you tell me about the history of your marriage and let me know a little about the assets and debts? Are there any children?"

"We can talk later. Who do I see about making my next appointment?"

"Uh, usually people call my paralegal, Brandy, to schedule appointments."

"Good," he said, suddenly standing. "I will call her. I would like to meet with you once a week during the case."

"That can be expensive. I usually only meet with clients when something in the case requires it."

"I like meetings," he said. "I'll see you in a few days."

"I don't understand," I said, confused.

"You will," he replied. "Remember, we're all the same. That means I can always find you."

"What?"

He left the conference room. I looked at the check and shrugged.

Some people just liked to have a lawyer, I reasoned. Made them feel important. Maybe he inherited ten thousand dollars. Maybe it was a gift from his parents or lottery winnings. Anyway, what the hell did I care. It was his life.

- 25 -

That weekend my team was playing in a tournament near St. Louis against U10 AA teams from Affton, Chesterfield and Meramec [townships outside of St. Louis]. My team's initial game wasn't until mid-Saturday afternoon; I didn't have to leave town until nine that morning.

I remembered what it felt like years ago when I coached, before tournament games. Before my obligatory shot of whiskey and morning cigar, I spent several minutes in the bathroom, dry retching into the toilet.

Great, I thought. All for a kid's game.

I smoked two cigars on the drive towards St. Louis and at a rest stop downed another shot and ate a pack of breath mints.

Our first game of the tournament was against the host team, the Affton Anvils, who played in an old barn off the beltway surrounding St. Louis. Rebecca was helping Donnie get his equipment bag and sticks from her Lincoln MKZ's hatchback. A few of the other boys were dragging their hockey bags into the rink and Donnie rushed ahead to join them.

I parked my Porsche besides her.

"Have fun!" Rebecca called.

Donnie looked back and waved his sticks at her and hurried into the rink.

"You drive alone?" she asked as I got out of the Porsche and was retrieving my coaching bag from the rear seat. "I'm surprised you didn't get a ride with Rooks or another player's family."

I shook my head. "Then I'd have to talk to parents," I said. "Imagine listening during a four hour trip to their opinions about the team, their kid, other kids, and worse, about the times they played lousy hockey when they were kids. I'd rather pay for my own gas."

Rebecca grimaced. "I was a good hockey player when I was little."

"Uh . . ."

"Gotch ya!" she said, laughing.

"You played?" I asked.

"You're kidding."

I changed the subject. "How's Donnie?"

"He's very excited and ready to go. He loves to play."

"Does he have car leg problems?" I asked. Sometimes, a player cooped up in a car for hours skated as if his legs were worn out. To combat the situation, I would run the team through a dryland routine prior to the game to get their legs going.

Rebecca smiled and pulled up her sweatpants, revealing shapely calves.

"Do I have car legs?" she asked. "Maybe car legs run in my family."

I stared open mouthed and she laughed and turned away. Ms. Manyard pulled into the parking lot in a black BMW sedan and frowned at me.

"I'd better go see the boys," I said, heading to the rink.

"Good luck!" Rebecca called. "Have fun!"

I looked back at her. "Your son is playing youth travel ice hockey and you're a travel ice hockey parent. What does fun have to do with any of this?"

The Shooters would play each other team in this tournament once; after round robin play the two teams with the best records would play for the tournament championship.

An hour before the game I ran the team through stretching exercises and light running and then gave them the game strategy during a locker room chalk talk. The boys dressed as I stood outside the locker room, drinking a cup of coffee. Parents were allowed in the locker only to tie skates. On the ice, Chesterfield was beating Meramec 3-0.

The rink's coffee, as usual with ice rinks, sucked.

Herb Rooks joined me after tying Andy's skates. "He's in a real good mood," Herb said. "He remembers last year. Andy really wants to stick it to those fuckers from Affton."

"They're just kids," I said. My assistant coach clearly was not in a good mood.

"He's been working on his stickhandling a lot," Herb said.

"Good. I'm sure he'll play well."

"Any more thought on the forward lines?"

"Not really," I said.

The rink had a huge arched wood roof and steel bleachers circling the ice surface. The place smelled of Freon and unwashed jockstraps and I could see my breath floating from my mouth. The white boards were marred by countless black streaks from pucks and there were numerous scratches on the Plexiglas panels. The ice was very hard and the faceoff markings and lines painted beneath the thin layer of ice shone brightly.

I loved the place. It was a good, old fashioned hockey rink. It felt like home.

My team took the ice. The parents gathered in the stands, mostly sitting or standing in groups across the ice from their respective team's bench. I shook hands with the refs while watching Affton warm-up. The Affton coaches weren't paying any attention to my team as their kids took shots on their goaltender. That meant the other coaches hadn't heard about Donnie.

They learned in a hurry. Affton's defensemen were small and slow. Donnie scored two goals in fifteen seconds, taking the puck right off the faceoff and skating between the defensemen for breakaways.

The Affton parents watched open mouthed. One man screamed down at a defenseman to get his head in the game. The Affton coaches were frantically scribbling on their game boards, trying to figure a response.

The Shooter parents politely applauded. It was becoming old hat.

The Affton coaches called for a timeout. They had one in the game. I had never seen a timeout called less than a minute into the first period of a hockey game.

"The Hockey Gods must love me."

"What?" Herb Rooks asked.

"Huh?" I asked.

Herb was looking at me.

"Everything okay?" Herb asked.

"Sure," I said. "All's well."

I sipped coffee.

The game restarted. On the faceoff, the Affton defensemen charged forward.

Donnie cleanly won the puck at the faceoff, danced around the opposing center and drove through the Affton defensemen like a knife slicing butter. He scored again.

"Maybe we should change lines," Herb said.

"But Donnie's line has only been out there for twenty two seconds," I replied but changed the lines anyway. Three goals in twenty two seconds was more than enough to start the game; there still needed to be some sportsmanship in the world.

Andy and his two linemates rushed onto the ice. I patted Donnie on the helmet as the boy sat down. "Remember to pass the puck to Sean and Steele," I whispered into Donnie's ear.

"I'll have to skate a lot slower," Donnie whispered back. "I'm not trying to ignore them but they just can't keep up with me."

"It would be good to conserve your energy," I replied. "The season's just beginning."

By the third period, Donnie had scored another two goals and assisted on four more. I had moved him to defense at the end of the first period, with instructions not to score anymore. The game was lopsided enough. The Affton players were skating head-down, dejected. Our players all had smiling faces, except for Andy. I felt sorry for the kid. He was skating hard and trying but luck wasn't with him to begin the season. Opposing goaltenders were making great saves on his shots and his wingers were missing easy passes that should have resulted in goals. Andy kept looking at the bench to his father after every unlucky break, as if somehow his father knew some magical word or trick that would fix everything.

What made it worse for Andy was that his father clearly was an asshole.

With a few minutes left in the game, Andy ended up on the ice with Steele Williams and Sean Maynard and Donnie was playing defense. An Affton player took a shot; our goaltender made the save and the rebound came to Donnie near our net. Andy circled for a pass as Donnie retrieved the puck but Steele broke out of the zone, skating up ice. The puck spun off Donnie's stick like a flying saucer, whizzing past the Affton defensemen to fall flat on the ice just a foot before it struck Steele's stick who was skating alone, crossing the far blue line on a breakaway. Steele faked left on the goalie and went right and pushed the puck into an open net. It was his third goal of the game. He jumped in the air, smashing shoulder first into the boards, arms and stick raised in celebration.

Andy skated slowly to the bench. He did not have a goal or an assist in the game.

Herb walked to the other side of the bench, ignoring him.

The horn sounded; the teams lined up to shake hands. When I reached the other coach I said, "Good game. Good luck during the rest of the tournament."

The Affton coach replied with a wistful look on his face. "Yea. You got a helluva player there. Can we trade for him? I'll talk to my parents—we probably can throw in a few new cars and a gym bag full of cash."

"I think some colleges already offered him more," I replied. "Seriously."

The Affton coach nodded. "No doubt but that kid will never wear a college uniform. He's going to be playing pro before he hits nineteen."

I met Rebecca outside the rink, still The Coach, not yet me. "If you have money problems after the divorce, I think the Affton parents will pay for you to relocate, find you a job and throw in some expense money, too."

"Really? The Affton coach is young and fairly good lucking."

"He's married with a newborn," I lied.

"All of the good ones are taken."

I shrugged. "There's always Chesterfield," I said. "I hear their coach just went through a divorce. And he has two daughters.

Maybe he can set one up with Donnie and you can double-date. Although I hear leprosy runs in his family."

She didn't even bother to smile.

The next game was in the early evening against Chesterfield. As the boys dressed in the locker room the Chesterfield coach approached me, an older man with gray hair and a face lined with age. "Hate to do this," he said. "But we need to check birth certificates. I'm sure that kid is 10 and all but I'm going to catch hell from my parents if I don't check."

"No problem," I said. "I probably need to get used to it."

I went to the rink's coffee shop and told our team manager, Michael Williams, that he needed the Book.

"They think Steele is really 12, right?" Michael asked, putting the cap on his bottle of Gatorade. "It's because he scored three goals and had a few assists this afternoon and because after Sean Manyard he's the biggest kid at this tournament. They probably hope we forgot his birth certificate and want to try and ban him from the tournament! Amazing!"

"Yea," I said. "Amazing. Can you get it?"

Williams retrieved The Book from his car and he and Shari brought it down to the hallway outside the locker rooms. The Book was really a photo album with two pages devoted to each player, showing a photograph of the player, a copy of the player's birth certificate and a copy of the player's USA Hockey registration.

He opened the Book to Steele's page. The Chesterfield coach looked at Michael. "Your son, right?"

"Yes and he's really just ten. Steele just keeps on growing," Michael said.

"He played for the Shooters U10 AA team last season, right? Our teams played against each other four or five times. He was nine last year, right?"

"Yes, he was."

"Then I guess it makes sense he's ten now. May I?"

"Uh, sure." Michael handed over The Book and the Chesterfield coach turned to Donnie's pages. He studied them for a minute and then gave The Book back to Michael. "Looks legitimate to me. Too bad. Thanks."

"Uh, sure."

I slapped Michael on the back. "Great job."

Shari Williams pursed her lips and followed her husband back to the coffee shop.

"She still called SS behind her back?" the Chesterfield coach asked me.

"Think so."

"I think the Nazis would be insulted. They weren't as bad as that bitch and her husband."

"A little overboard on that comment, don't you think?" I asked.

"You know, I think coaching would be a lot more pleasant and the kids would have a lot more fun if we just banned all parents from the rink during games and practices. You ever think that?"

"Ever since I was six years old," I replied and the Chesterfield coach laughed.

Chesterfield was a smart, well coached team. Their players all could handle the puck, passed it unselfishly and they were good skaters. Usually, the Chesterfield hockey association fielded some of the best youth hockey teams in this part of the Midwest.

Chesterfield assigned not one but two of their best players to shadow Donnie. They bracketed him all over the ice, trying to deny him the puck and when he got it, they just tried to slap it away from his stick. At times they would even send a third player after him. They played clean, not throwing checks or taking penalties, but they were relentless and they did not want Donnie to score.

"Don't get frustrated," I told him on the bench. "Remember, if they have two or three players on you, then either Steele or Sean have to be wide open. Trust them."

"Okay," Donnie said. He looked at me through the bars of his face mask. "Don't worry coach. I got it. They tried this sort of stuff in Florida."

"What did your coach do?"

"I skated towards our own goalie and my team passed the puck back to me so I could get it."

"A back pass system?"

"Yep," Donnie said. "Like the Russians used to do."

Donnie's line took to the ice again.

Herb walked over to me from his usual spot working the door for the defensemen. "This is what's going to happen," Herb said. "They'll lock Donnie down. We're going to need Andy to come through and pick up the scoring slack."

The faceoff was outside of our offensive zone. Donnie was talking to the defensemen and to Sean and Steele and the boys were all nodding.

The referee blew his whistle, demanding that everyone line up.

The puck dropped. Donnie knocked it to the side to Sean who passed it back towards his own goal to one of the Shooter defenseman. The Shooter defenseman, in turn, passed it cross ice to his partner as Donnie skated behind both of his defensemen and then circled back, building speed. He skated past the defenseman with the puck who gave Donnie an easy pass as Donnie raced up-ice. At full speed, it didn't matter who Chesterfield sent after him. They were powerless. Donnie burst over the offensive blue line, a bullet aimed at the net and the goalie prepared himself for the fake but Donnie didn't even bother, firing a wrist shot into the top right corner of the net from fifteen feet away.

"Nice," I said.

When the other team managed to trap Donnie he would hold the puck long enough to find Sean or Steele with a pass that seemed to always lead to a shot on net. A few times he simply stickhandled around the defenders surrounding him, breaking into empty ice and heading for the ten year old Chesterfield goaltender who was developing nervous ticks under both eyes and acted as if he really needed to go to the bathroom. Other times the Shooters would pass the puck backwards to our defensemen to allow Donnie to break free of his pursuers and catch an easy pass as he turned up ice, speeding towards the opposing net.

Chesterfield did a god job. Donnie was held to four goals and three assists. We won, 8-2.

- 26 -

Past midnight. I left the hotel, restless and my knees aching. I felt as if I needed to jump out of my own skin to feel better. The hotel was located next to an office complex. I wore jeans and a light leather jacket and walked through the parking lots among the office towers. One bore the name of *Microsoft*; another advertised *T-Mobile*. Heavy hitters, I thought. But on this Saturday night the buildings were all dark and the parking lots empty.

I took a short and thick cigar from my jacket pocket, clipped off the end and lit it. The smoke tasted of nuts and I sighed deeply.

My head ached, joining my knees. The ache in my knees was from the years on the ice. The headache I could not explain and aspirin had not helped.

I kept walking.

Once or twice I took my cell phone out of my pocket and looked at it. Make a call, a voice said to me. Call her.

Call who?

Call her, the voice said again.

Who?

I stood alone in the parking lot before the *Microsoft* building. It was fifteen stories tall and shaped like a rectangle but curved, as if it had been bent around half of a ball. What am I doing out here?

Call her, the voice said again and I was actually holding the cell phone in my hand.

"Fucking call who?" I said aloud.

I put the phone back in my pocket and inhaled deeply on the cigar, holding in the smoke and then breathing it out my nostrils like a dragon. I closed my eyes and tried to will the headache away. I blew more smoke out of my nose and tried to let everything fall away, to let my physical existence separate from my mind so I could be calm but the pain in my knees and head would not lessen and the restlessness continued to assault my body and mind.

"Damn it," I muttered.

A face in a window on an upper floor, looking down at me. I opened my eyes and for a moment saw her standing in the black square of the window, long blonde hair and fair skin, a white gown billowing about her tall and lithe figure.

I closed my eyes again, opened them and stared back at the window.

The phone was back in my hand and I looked at it, perplexed.

Above, the window was dark. I pulled smoke into my mouth and tried to shake the feeling that someone was watching me from the building, a woman, who wanted me to call . . .

My phone buzzed as a text message was received.

'How about a nightcap?' The text was sent by Teri Manyard. I erased the message and remembered our time in my apartment and how she looked in the red bodysuit.

Her husband had not made the trip to St. Louis, I knew.

I looked up to the empty window.

Fay?

Back at the hotel. I stood by the lobby entrance and finished my cigar. A nightcap, I thought. I am The Coach now. Why not?

I walked into the lobby with a smile on my face.

Rebecca had finally changed out of her sweats. She sat in the breakfast area reading *People* magazine and sipping from a cup of Chardonnay. None of the other parents were around; at this time they were either in their rooms or, in the case of Herb Rooks and some of the fathers, still adding to their tab at a nearby tavern.

She gazed at me, waiting. She wore black slacks and a dark blue satin blouse and sat with her legs crossed, twisting her body towards me.

"Evening," I said.

I walked over to her table, forgetting about Teri Manyard. Rebecca looked up at me, a tilt to her head and her eyes soft and warm.

"Out drinking with the guys?" she asked.

"I went out for a walk."

"Worried about tomorrow's games?" There was a slight smile on her face and I noticed traces of make-up, turning her lips fuller and drawing me into her eyes.

"Just couldn't sleep, I guess."

"I see."

"Well . . ." I looked around. The desk clerk was playing a game on a computer and the rest of the lobby and breakfast room was empty.

She motioned with her head and I sat beside her. Her left ring finger gripped her cup, naked.

"Is Donnie asleep?"

"Yes." Rebecca reached to the floor and put the wine bottle on the table along with another plastic cup. "Drink?"

"Sure."

She poured a generous amount into the cup.

"How's the divorce going?"

"There's a hearing scheduled on Monday, but maybe it would be better if we left that to my new lawyer."

"No, of course. I meant how is the divorce affecting Donnie?"

"Oh." She drank wine. "It's for the best, for him."

"Is he close to his dad?"

"Do you ask that of all of your players?"

She wants me to be The Coach, I thought, and not The Lawyer or just myself. But I just wanted to be myself and be sitting with her, with nothing connecting us except a mutual desire to be together.

It would never happen. If she didn't believe I was of some benefit to her son she would dismiss me the way an investment banker looking for a client would dismiss a janitor.

"No," I replied to her question.

"Then why ask me?"

Because I want you. Because I am so fucking alone.

"Sometimes kids need someone to talk to," I answered. "If you want, if you think he needs it, I could refer to you to a few good counselors."

"He doesn't need a counselor," she replied. "He just needs to be on the ice."

The automatic doors of the hotel opened and the Affton U10 AA coach walked into the lobby, wearing dark blue jeans, cowboy boots and a blue sweater.

"Hey coach," he said, reaching out his hand. I stood and we shook. The Affton coach and Rebecca exchanged a look and a smile.

"Well," I said.

"Our teams might play in the championship game tomorrow."

"Good, okay."

Rebecca put the cork into the wine bottle.

"I'd better get back to my room," I said. "I probably should start planning for the games tomorrow."

"Good night," Rebecca said.

I left them in the lobby.

Dejected, I went to my hotel room.

- 27 -

The hotel room's telephone rang loud and repeatedly. I rolled over, reached out and grabbed the receiver. I was greeted by silence.

"Hello?"

The other party hung up.

Fuck. I replaced the receiver, rubbed my eyes and looked about. *Sportscenter* on the television, the room lights off, my body lying atop the covers with my head propped up by a pillow.

What time was it? Two forty-five.

Probably a Meramec parent, I thought. We played them tomorrow at 10 a.m. They were probably trying to mess with me, ruin my sleep and keep me tired. These hockey parents were all nuts.

There was a soft knock on the door.

I looked down: yes, I was dressed in boxers and a t-shirt.

I opened the door.

Teri Manyard was in the hallway wearing a full-length pink robe.

"Evening," I said.

She smiled and without an invitation walked into the room. The robe fell to the carpet and she was wearing that red bodysuit.

"Are you busy?" she asked me.

Rebecca would be giving her body to that Affton coach. A sadness bubble came into being and engulfed me. Teri waited as the depression overwhelmed my heart and mind.

The hotel floor tilted.

Why am I always so alone?

If I had purchased that handgun bits of my brain and skull would be sticking to these hotel walls.

If only . . .

I reached out, touching the sides of her waist and her perfume smelled of wild flowers and her eyes seemed so bright and true.

She was an afterthought.

I took her to bed.

Period Two

STICK HANDLING

Sam

- 1 -

I checked out of the hotel early Sunday morning. Teri Manyard had gone back to her room before dawn so she would be there when Sean woke. I left the hotel shortly thereafter because I didn't want to run into either her or Rebecca in the lobby that morning.

Did Rebecca sleep with the Affton coach? Did they rent a separate room for a few hours so as not to disturb Donnie?

I remembered the Affton coach wore a wedding ring on his finger. What the hell did he tell his wife to get out of the house at midnight?

What if either Donnie or Sean woke in the middle of the night to discover mom gone? What would the kid think? What would his mother say when the kid asked about her absence?

Would either boy tell his dad about her absence?

I drove to the rink, stood by my Porsche, drank coffee and smoked a cigar until the players began to arrive for the morning's round robin tournament games.

In our game, we crushed Meramec by twelve goals. Chesterfield defeated Affton and so we would play Chesterfield in the championship game that afternoon.

After our game most of the team families left the rink for an early lunch and to check-out of the hotel. I stayed at the rink, returning back to my usual position by my Porsche with a lit cigar in my hand, wearing my black leather jacket, trying to look composed.

Teri Manyard and her son left the rink with the Williams family. Steele Williams and Sean Manyard had enjoyed big games that morning against Meramec—rather than try to score himself, Donnie spent the entire game passing the puck to his linemates. They each scored four goals.

Teri didn't look at me, nor did Shari Williams. Michal Williams waved, beaming.

"They had good games on the score sheet," Herb Rooks said. He walked towards me, hands in the pockets of his coaching jacket, frowning. "But Donnie did all the work."

I shrugged. "Okay," I said. "So?"

"It's just annoying, that's all. Mike Williams and his wife were walking around the rink like their son just set the season scoring record in the National Hockey League. But Donnie did all the work."

I drew smoke from the cigar, held it and then breathed through my nose, tasting the spices, smelling the chocolate and nut flavors.

"Donnie's a good player."

"So is Andy." Herb looked at me with disapproval. "His mom took him to breakfast; I told them I'd wait here. I don't know what to tell my son. Last season he led our team in scoring. Our team did well. This year, what does he have? A couple of goals and a few assists? It's frustrating. I want to give him a hug and tell him it's okay. I want to kick him in the ass and get him jump started, playing better. If this keeps up, he may not even want to keep playing hockey."

"Why not?"

"Huh?"

"Why would he not want to play hockey?"

"He's getting frustrated."

"He's getting lots of ice time, as much as Donnie's line. He has the puck a lot when he's on the ice. He's skating hard. He looks fine when he's playing."

"But I see him on the way home from games and practice. He's not the same."

I smoked my cigar, nodding.

"This season," Herb said. "It's not the same."

- 2 -

The championship game began. Donnie bent over, his feet more than shoulder width apart, his stick blade inches off the ice. The opposing center at the face-off was a very big kid. The referee dropped the puck. Donnie's stick flashed out, making contact with the puck and slapping it back towards our team's defensemen. The opposing center ignored the puck completely. As soon as the puck left the referee's hand he was straightening up, moving forward and smashing the shaft of his stick violently into Donnie's facemask. Donnie fell backward. From the bench I could hear the impact of his helmet crashing onto the ice.

The referee raised his hand, signaling a penalty, his whistle rising to his mouth. Before he could stop play both Sean Manyard and Steele Williams had flown towards the opposing center as if they were wearing jet packs. I glanced at Donnie and through his facemask could see him smile as the opposing center lay crumpled beside him.

Donnie waved me off, stood, stretched his neck and was ready to play. Sean and Steele each received two minute penalties for unnecessary roughness. They likely would have received more but no one knew the opposing center's ribs and clavicle were broken until his parents got him to the hospital.

Donnie didn't worry about passing that game and no one blamed him. He scored nine goals. We won 10-0.

In the handshake line he pulled his hand back when the Chesterfield coach tried to shake it. "That kid should learn some manners," the Chesterfield coach told me a few seconds later when we reached each other in the line.

I pulled my hand back, too. "You ever try to hurt one of my players again," I said, "And I'm going to take a hockey stick and ram it up your ass. And if I were you, I'd walk out of this place with my head on a swivel. You wouldn't want to get accidentally hit by a car in the parking lot or anything."

"Are you threatening me?"

"Damn right," I said. "You fucking jackass."

As was customary in tournaments, after the handshakes each team lined up on the blue line closest to their bench. A tournament official announced each player's name over the public address system, starting with the players on the losing team. Each player skated to the center ice area to receive his individual medal; afterwards, the championship trophy was presented to the winning team. It was considered an honor for a player to be selected by his coach to accept the championship trophy, hoist it into the air and carry it back to his team.

My cell phone buzzed as the official began announcing the names of our players.

"Hello?"

"He's thrown three fucking interceptions!" a woman screamed.

"Uh, who is this?"

"Three! The last one he just aimed it right at the other team's player! None of our receivers were anywhere in sight! That motherfucker is going to ruin me!"

"I'm sorry, but . . . ."

His name called, Donnie skated to get his medal, gloves and helmet off, stick lying on the ice, the crowd applauding.

"It's Meredith Balton! The quarterback's wife! Your paralegal, Jake, gave me your number, said you would be handling my case."

"Yes."

"Then fucking do something!" she screamed. "He's thrown three fucking interceptions!"

The tournament official raised the championship trophy, looking at me. I met Donnie's eyes and nodded. But he shook his head 'no' and grabbed the jerseys of Steele and Sean and gave them a quick push. I nodded again. Steele and Sean skated to the official and with one hand each raised the championship trophy high, beaming.

Herb Rooks looked like he was going to cry.

- 3 -

Monday morning. A cigar on the front porch of The Ranch Retreat and a shot of whiskey to go with it. The morning air was brisk like a dry cold shower and I was alone. I looked at the surrounding trees and the driveway winding towards the hidden road. Quiet. Not even the sound of a passing car. Alone.

I wondered how Rebecca felt after years of marriage, waking up in bed this morning, Donnie asleep in his room and no one beside her in bed.

I wondered if the Manyards slept together. If so, I wondered how Teri could face her husband when he awoke.

Does she wear that red bodysuit for him?

I realized I didn't care about the answer.

When I got to work the receptionist at the law firm had a message for me. A call from my amateur physicist client—he wanted to meet later that day. Wonderful.

The elevator doors opened and she walked into the lobby. Tall, long black hair, slender, a blue dress hugging her frame.

Fay?

She walked straight to me.

"Mr. Oliver?"

"Yes."

"I recognize you from a photograph," she said. Her skin was smooth and unblemished, her dark eyes glistening, her lips wet.

"What photograph?"

I have a stalker, I thought, happily. She reached out a hand towards me *we danced beneath strobe lights as the band played we walked our feet sinking into beach sand as the sun slipped beneath ocean waves we kissed* and she handed me the papers.

"You've been served," she said, turning and walking away. Her beautiful body disappeared behind elevator doors.

- 4 -

"Lovely, wasn't she?" Landscuda said. "Don't tell anyone but it's one of the requirements for the position. I call it the 'fuckability' factor. We have our gals serve men and our guys serve women. To be hired, a potential process server has to be sexually desirable to the greatest extent possible to the opposite sex."

It turned out Landscuda owned the company hired by the attorney for Rebecca's husband to serve the subpoena on me.

Serving Your Needs, Inc., Landscuda named it. There were rumors the company also was involved with bachelor and bachelorette parties and a knowledgeable person could alleviate the pain of being served by obtaining a private massage from the process server, at premium prices.

"Excellent idea," Prickles, our infant managing partner replied. "We need more of your type of thinking at this firm."

We were in Prickles's office and I felt like I was being interrogated by the enemy. The managing partner and I sat at the glass conference table while Landscuda lounged in one of the leather chairs by the fireplace.

"So which party served you with the subpoena?" Prickles asked.

"Rebecca Warren's husband," I answered. "He wants me in Court this afternoon to testify at a hearing."

"A hearing on what?"

"To modify temporary orders."

Before being fired, our firm had filed Rebecca's divorce case and obtained temporary orders. Pursuant to law, the husband was allowed to request a hearing and challenge the orders.

"Anything unusual about the temporary orders?" Landscuda asked.

"Anything unethical done to obtain them?" Prickles added after adjusting something in his ear.

"No. And no," I said. "They were standard. We gave Rebecca the house and she received primary residential placement of the child and reasonable child support. The husband got a parenting time schedule that didn't interfere with the child's hockey schedule."

"Hockey schedule?" Prickles asked.

"Didn't you know?" Landscuda explained. "Sammy is the kid's hockey coach."

"What!" Prickles said with outrage on his face. "You had temporary orders entered to deal with one of your hockey players? To benefit yourself?"

"After I was fired," I explained. "I only became the kid's hockey coach after I was fired."

"So this has nothing to do with our firm's work on the temporary orders?" Prickles asked.

"They were obtained legally and ethically."

"Then did you have sex with her?"

My turn for outrage. "What!"

"Did you fool around with the client?"

"No," I replied. "Never." And I felt dejected for having to admit it.

I wanted to sleep with her, I thought. I wanted her in my arms, if only for awhile.

"Then why does the husband want you to testify at this hearing?"

"I really don't know."

Prickles frowned. "Jaime, can you call the husband's lawyer and find out what's going on? We can't have our attorneys wasting time showing up in Court for nonsense."

"Gladly."

"Good." Prickles looked at me. "You're going to need a lawyer to go with you in case they try to ask you questions involving your conduct as her attorney. We don't want to find ourselves in a malpractice case or having to deal with an ethics complaint with the state's bar association."

"The firm has nothing to worry about," I said. "We did nothing inappropriate in this matter."

"So you say," Prickles said. "I hope you're right."

"I'll go with him," Landscuda volunteered, flashing a Robert Redford smile. "Be glad to do so. It should be fun."

I wondered who I should be more wary of: the husband's lawyer or mine.

- 5 -

Landscuda insisted we travel to the courthouse together in his car. He owned a Rolls Royce Ghost which rested at the edge of the parking lot away from all of the other cars, except for two Toyota Prius hybrids parked on either side of the Rolls.

"That's our cars," Mia said. "Jaime parks between us every day so he knows some moron won't open a door and dent his vehicle."

"What if one of you is sick or on vacation?"

"Then he hires someone to drive our car to work so his vehicle stays protected."

Mia, or at least I thought it was Mia, said the word 'vehicle' in a tone that implied reverence. It had to be an act, I thought. She and her sister couldn't be that full of hero worship for him.

The pretty young blonde opened the back door of the Rolls Royce for Jaime, who slipped inside. I went around to the other side of the car, opened the door for myself and sat beside him. Mia, her head barely sticking above the steering wheel, drove the car from the parking lot.

Landscuda began instructing me on the nuances of testifying. I pretended to listen, nodding occasionally, enjoying the comfort of the sculptured leather seat and occasionally feeling the wood trim of the door. My Porsche cost close to seventy thousand dollars. This Rolls Royce made it seem to be worth the price of an economy car. How much does one of these go for? Three hundred thousand dollars? Somehow, in the great business of the practice of law, I clearly had fucked up.

Landscuda began droning on about the fine line between perjury and avoiding a question. I focused on Mia's head. She and her twin sister followed Landscuda around the office like lap dogs, fetching him coffee or paper or pens, dialing telephone numbers for him, picking up his dry cleaning, drafting his pleadings, preparing his files for Court appearances. They always seemed eager and happy. I doubted the guy could get through the morning without them.

And she was a damn good driver, I thought. The car accelerated and slowed and yet from the back it felt as if the car had been motionless, as if I had entered it and then it just magically transported itself to the courthouse, as if it hadn't really moved at all.

She would wait with the car, parking far away until summoned by Landscuda, making sure no one came close to laying a hand on its perfect paint. We walked up the courthouse steps and through the phalanx of security guards and metal detectors at the courthouse entrance and then headed for the elevators.

Landscuda had called the husband's attorney to try and find out why I was being required to testify. The lawyer never returned his calls.

"You can never lie," Landscuda was telling me. "Act as if you're stoned, feign a heart attack, or claim you're drunk. All would be forgiven. Just do not lie."

I wanted to bash him with my briefcase and watch him 'lie' bleeding on the ground.

The elevator doors opened and Susan Henderson stepped into the hallway. Landscuda went inside amongst a group of people but I stayed back, motioning to Susan with my eyes.

"Be right up," I told him.

He looked to protest but the doors closed in his face.

Susan and I stepped away from the other people waiting to board the next elevator and spoke quietly.

As usual, I looked frumpy. I bought suits off the rack and even with tailoring they never seemed to fit me. Susan did not have that problem. Like Jenny, she could wear anything off the rack and looked just fine.

"Do you really work with that jerk?" she asked me.

"I'm not sure he works," I replied. "I think he just orders his twin servants around."

"Mia and Mai? I like them. They're always very nice to me when I see them."

I didn't want to talk about pretty people.

"Listen," I said, getting down to business. "I've been thinking about those photographs from the deposition. This is a no fault divorce state. The conduct depicted in those photos is irrelevant and will never be seen by the judge."

"Would they be irrelevant to the business community?" she asked.

"That's blackmail."

Susan shrugged. "My client is very mad. It's one thing for her husband to have an affair with a co-worker or a family friend or even a prostitute. It's something else for him to be sleeping with insects."

"No need to remember anniversaries," I said. She didn't laugh. "Okay, some sort of confidentiality agreement needs to be part of the deal."

"That's going to cost your guy some money."

"What about the fact your client illegally brought the bugs into the country? There might be a criminal prosecution for that. It seems like she needs a confidentiality agreement from my guy, too, which will cost your gal some money."

Susan smiled. "Prove the bugs were brought into the U.S. for my client and not by your client to satisfy his obscene sexual urges."

Fuck, I thought.

"My guy is going to be very reasonable about all of this," I said. "I can make him be very reasonable about all of this."

"We're way past being reasonable," Susan replied. "He'd better be prepared to pay her an awful lot of money."

"Good talking to you."

"Have a nice day," Susan said.

- 6 -

The hearing was on the seventh floor in Division Nineteen. The elevator doors deposited me into a narrow hallway with three doors spaced far apart on the opposite wall leading to three different courtrooms. Division Nineteen was on the right. Landscuda stood next to Rebecca and her attorney, Randolph Pudsworth.

"You're in good hands," Landscuda was saying with but a trace of sarcasm. "Randolph here is one of the best family law attorneys in town."

Pudsworth beamed when he said it, vigorously nodding his bald head in agreement. Thick gray facial hair surrounded his mouth and covered his cheeks and I could discern lips and a chin lurking beneath the whiskers.

I nodded to Rebecca, feeling light in the chest for a moment, hoping an erection did not stir.

"Do you know why I'm here?" I asked Pudsworth.

"Not a clue, have I," Pudsworth said. "No one told you of your reason to be here? Damnations. We'll have to see what Evelyn's got up her sleeve. Could be anything. Devious, that she is."

Is he speaking English? I wondered.

Rebecca looked at me with a flash of horror and I shrugged. Maybe you shouldn't have fired me, I thought.

Landscuda and Pudsworth began talking about their vacation homes. Rather than speak to Rebecca I wandered over to the courtroom door and peered inside through a small window. The judge sat on the bench as a lawyer spoke from a podium. The judge seemed to be turning the pages of a magazine.

Hope it's a trial exhibit, I thought, but I knew better.

Evelyn Baum and her client stepped from the elevator. As always, Evelyn dressed as if she was going out for the evening, in a long black dress with pearls about her neck and wrists. She oozed elegance, using it the way some predators used camouflage to sneak up on their prey.

Mr. Henry Warren was not much taller than Rebecca. He wore a conservative gray suit with a blue tie, with short brown hair neatly parted and a pleasant if unremarkable face. He gave a half-nod to Rebecca and walked towards the courtroom doors, keeping away from the rest of us. Evelyn and Landscuda were exchanging hugs while Pudsworth stood fuming, apparently annoyed that Evelyn didn't greet him first.

Rebecca came to stand beside me.

"What are you and your husband arguing about?" I whispered to her.

"Donnie."

"Where he lives?"

"No. What he does."

Evelyn shook my hand and as usual I was struck by her eyes, which unlike the exuberance of her body language seemed to belong to the dead.

"Glad you could make it," she said.

"I think you had something to do with that," I replied, holding up the subpoena. "Why am I here?"

"You'll see." Her black eyes showed nothing.

The doors to the courtroom opened as the litigants and attorneys stepped into the hall. Both lawyers were men, the clients a man and a woman. The man was weeping. The woman laughed at him.

"Serves you right, you bastard," the woman spat at the man.

Pudsworth stopped the man's lawyer. "What happened in there?"

"It was a hearing in a divorce case. The fucking judge was heartless."

"How so?"

"He awarded temporary custody of the couple's dog to the wife. And it was really the husband's dog. He was the one who walked and played with it, took it to the vet, treated it better than the wife, actually. That dog was his best friend for the last nine years."

114

The husband had taken a seat in a chair in the hallway and buried his face in his hands as his wife and her lawyer boarded an elevator.

"No visitation rights for the husband with the dog?" Pudsworth asked.

"Won't matter," the other attorney said. "As soon as she gets that dog she's going to kill it. Probably run it over with her car. Several times."

"That's funny," Pudsworth said, chuckling.

"I'm not kidding."

"Did the judge know that?"

"Yep. That's why he did it."

"I don't understand."

"A dog bit the judge when he was a child and he never got over it."

"So what?"

"The judge hates dogs."

Evelyn held the doors open for us.

"We're up," she said sweetly.

There were two long tables before the Court's bench and a railing separated the tables from two rows of pews in the back. It was a fairly small courtroom, without windows and with a low ceiling. A podium separated the tables. The judge glared at us from the bench, an elderly man, somewhat sickly looking who had served in his position for the last twenty years. The court reporter sat perched above her machine in front of the judge's bench, waiting.

Landscuda and I took seats in the back and the parties and their attorneys each appropriated a table. A man with a gaunt frame and thick beard also sat in the back, his hands folded on his lap, looking bored.

It's the guy from the rink, I realized. The one standing next to Rebecca when I first saw Donnie play.

"So why are you all here today?" the judge growled, his voice booming along the walls. I had practiced in front of Judge Frailly many times and knew that first time litigants were always amazed that such a powerful voice could emanate from his frame.

"We're here on a motion to modify temporary orders," Evelyn said.

"What are y'all arguing about? A house? Amount of child support?"

"Extracurricular activities of a child," Evelyn replied.

The judge grimaced, looked down at his magazine and turned a page. "Wish I was fishing," he mumbled. "The Court calls Case No. 2009DM03467, In The Matter Of The Marriage Of Rebecca Warren and Henry Warren!" the judge bellowed. "State your appearances please!"

Each lawyer stood and stated his or her name and the name of the client.

"Why hello, Evelyn," the judge said. "So nice to see you."

"It's a pleasure to see you again, your honor."

The judge glared at Rebecca's lawyer.

"Pud," the judge said.

"Good afternoon," Pudsworth replied.

"Let's get on with it," the judge demanded.

"I'd like to present testimony," Evelyn said.

"Be quick about it. I have a sentencing hearing in an hour. Got to make sure some convict makes his prison date in a shower with his fellow cellmates."

The court reporter skipped those words.

"I call Master Ginskofsky to the witness stand."

"Who the hell is that?" Landscuda whispered to me.

I shrugged but saw Rebecca glare across the room at her husband who sat passively, hands folded on his lap, erect in his chair.

The gaunt bearded man took the witness chair to the left of the judge and was sworn in.

"Please state your name," Evelyn said.

"Karl Ginskofsky."

"Where do you live?"

"Miami, Florida."

"And what is your profession?"

"I teach chess."

"And do you know the Warrens?"

"Yes."

"And their son, Donnie?"

The man took a handkerchief from a coat pocket and dabbed an eye. "Yes, of course."

"And how do you know Donnie?"

"He was my student for three years. He is one of the finest chess players for his age in this chess-impoverished nation."

Chess?

Rebecca flinched at the word.

"When did you last work with Donnie?"

"A year ago when his mother made him quit to play with boys on ice."

For the next twenty minutes we listened to Ginskofsky's tale of woe: orphaned during the Hungary uprising in 1956, living on his own, scrounging for food from garbage bins and cooking dead dogs until one day he was noticed by the men playing chess in a park. They took him in, sheltered him, nurturing the talent within. He became a Grandmaster. Chess saved his life. Chess held the answers to all of life's questions. It was the Redeemer. How he emigrated to America to bring the nuances of the game to the New World. How he came across Donnie while giving a talk at a school; how he saw in Donnie his own self, trapped but just waiting to break free and rule the world from the sixty-four squares of a chessboard. How Donnie already moved the pieces like a master; how he was destined for greatness; how his mind was being destroyed because he wasn't able to labor hours over the chessboard every day, becoming one with the pieces and the great chess players of lore.

Landscuda looked at me. "I think I'm going to cry."

"He needs to practice every day," Ginskofsky said. "He could be the best. But he is wasting his God given talents. He is wasting his life by spending too much time on the ice."

Evelyn smiled. "That's all for this witness."

"Cross examination?" the judge inquired.

Pudsworth stood and waddled to the podium.

"You know Bobby Fisher?" Pudsworth asked.

"I met him once. Strange fellow."

"I saw a movie named after him," Pudsworth said. "You see it?"

"Yes. Good film."

"You remember how the dad in that film encouraged his chess prodigy son to play other sports and have other interests?"

"I did. Big mistake."

"A mistake." Pudsworth looked to the ceiling. "A mistake to be an All American boy and play real sports with real kids in real places. You say you met Bobby Fisher. Well, Bobby Fisher was a great American. He learned chess on his own. Donnie could learn chess on his own. Donnie does not need you. Bobby Fisher did not need you. Bobby Fisher was a great American and you sir are no Bobby Fisher!"

Pudsworth sat down.

"Rebecca fired you for that idiot?" Landscuda asked me.

The chess grandmaster left the witness stand and Evelyn retook the podium.

"It is very simple," she said to the judge. "Hockey parents are obsessed and crazy. For the last few years, the life of this family has been hijacked by Ms. Warren and her obsession with Donnie playing hockey. They spend hours at the rink on school nights. Donnie misses at least seven or eight days of school a year to travel to hockey games. Mrs. Warren received a reprimand from her employer for missing work to take Donnie to hockey games. The family's finances are tied up in skates and sticks and equipment and ice fees and coaching fees and travel expenses. It is not normal. Mr. Warren isn't even sure Donnie likes to play that much. If he stopped playing today, by next week it probably would all be forgotten and he'd be dribbling a basketball or playing computer games or actually spending time with classmates. Does Mrs. Warren even know the names of Donnie's classmates or teachers? Or what grade he is in? I doubt it. All she cares about is Donnie playing that sport. Do you know the family's basement was dedicated to Donnie's career? Trophies and old jerseys and photos line the walls and cover every flat surface. It is unreal. It is crazy.

"Hockey ruined this marriage. It is ruining Donnie's life. It is crippling them financially. It has to stop. There has to be sanity. It does not make sense to spend one thousand dollars every weekend for road trips so Donnie can play four games. So he can be with teammates and not his family and relatives. And his beloved Mr. Ginskofsky. It is nuts.

"Donnie can be at home, playing chess, a truly intellectual game. Instead, he travels the country with hockey thugs."

"So that's your case?" the judge asked. "Chess good, hockey bad?"

"We have another witness," Evelyn said. She called my name and pointed to the witness stand.

Fuck.

I took the stand, swore I'd tell the truth and waited.

"I thought Sam and Landshark were here to observe," the judge said.

"Mr. Oliver is here pursuant to my subpoena," Evelyn informed him.

I shrugged.

"This just gets better," the judge muttered.

Evelyn and I began our dance.

"Your name?"

"Sam Oliver."

"And you are a divorce attorney?"

"Yes."

"You in fact represented Ms. Warren?"

"Yes."

"She fired you?"

"Yes."

"So you could coach her son's hockey team?"

"You'd have to ask her."

"So Ms. Warren fired one of the very best family law attorneys in our county because it was more important for her to have a hockey coach for her son?"

"Again, you'd have to ask her."

It felt strange sitting in the witness chair, answering questions. I had always been the one at the podium; the interrogator. Here I wasn't The Lawyer. I didn't feel like The Coach. I felt vulnerable, like someone caught by a hotel maid stepping out of the shower or as if I was dressing in my bedroom and spotted an old woman across the street, peering too intently through a bedroom window at me.

"So you are Donnie's hockey coach?"

"I think I already said that."

"You listened to Mr. Ginskofsky testify?"

"It was very moving."

"He has quite a resume as a chess teacher, doesn't he?"

"He talks a good game."

"Yes, he does," Evelyn said. "But I want to talk about you. Did you play professional hockey?"

"No."

"Try out for any professional team?"

"No."

"Play Division I hockey?"

"No."

"High level of junior hockey?"

"No."

"Coach professionally?"

"No."

"Coach in college?"

"No."

"You have never even carried a water bottle to a hockey player who made it to the professional level or played at a major college, have you?"

"Never saw such a position being advertised."

Landscuda chuckled.

"And you haven't coached in years, right?"

"Yes."

"And you have only about four years of coaching experience, right?"

"Sounds about right."

"And you coached kids ten or younger."

"Pretty much."

Evelyn smirked as if she had just won some debate tournament. The judge looked bored.

"Most of the time on the away trips, on weekends, the boys aren't playing, right?"

"Correct."

"In fact, if the boys are gone from Friday afternoon to Sunday evening, they're probably only playing four games?"

"Yes."

"Four hours of ice time?"

"Yes."

"Over a forty-eight hour period?"

"Something like that."

"A lot of time on the road but not playing hockey. And this costs a lot of money, right?"

"I guess."

Evelyn nodded. "A lot of time for these boys to get into trouble."

"They're ten years old."

"Running around unsupervised in hotels?"

"Parents watch them. I'm usually at the hotel watching out for the kids."

"And Mrs. Warren is always watching Donnie?"

The Affton coach. Donnie asleep in his hotel room. Someone having sex with Rebecca and it wasn't me.

Fuck.

A thin line between perjury and avoiding the question.

"I don't spend every minute of a road trip with Donnie and Ms. Warren. I couldn't say."

"Has she ever left Donnie alone?"

I kept my eyes aimed at Evelyn as I thought of Rebecca and the Affton hockey coach. I didn't want to look at Rebecca. I didn't want her to think badly of me.

"Not that I know of," I lied.

Evelyn turned her gaze towards the judge. I stayed on the witness stand. No one told me to leave it.

"It's clear," Evelyn told the judge. "Hockey takes a huge amount of time, costs the family huge amounts of money and it's for but a few hours of playing time, and Donnie's being coached by someone with no real expertise or experience. This is not like he's playing for Team USA or being coached by a hockey legend. This is all a phenomenal waste of time and money and it needs to be stopped. Donnie could be spending time with his father and Mr. Ginskofsky. Instead, he travels around the country with Ms. Warren."

"You done?" the judge interrupted.

"I have a few more points."

"You're done," the judge said. "Next."

"Thank you." Pudsworth stood and took a deep breath. "Your Honor, Donnie Warren is a fantastic hockey player. He has been playing ice hockey since he was four years old—for the last six years. He practices twice a week during the school year with his team, spends countless hours in his basement shooting and stickhandling and plays close to sixty games a season. And that's just in the fall and winter. He plays for a team based out of Minnesota in the spring and summer. He attends four weeks of hockey camp every summer. The sport is his life."

"I take it Mrs. Warren goes to all of the games and practices?" the judge asked.

"Absolutely."

"Figures," the judge mumbled.

"May I continue?"

"No," the judge said. "I've heard enough. Sit down."

The judge looked over at me in the witness chair, still under oath. "Is Donnie a good player?"

"Yes."

"He's having fun?"

"He's probably the happiest kid on the team."

"You mean it?"

"Yes."

"Okay. Go join the Landshark in the back."

The judge fiddled with his magazine for a few minutes. The parties and attorneys waited.

"Okay," the judge finally said. "This one's easy. The kid was playing hockey when the divorce was filed. Unless the kid wants to quit, he'll finish the season. Whatever parent has him during practices or games will make arrangements to get him there. Ms. Warren will pay all the costs for the sport, including travel costs. When the season's over the parties can evaluate whether the kid keeps playing or he goes back to chess or whatever. If you all can't decide, I will. For now though, we keep things going as they are and according to the coach, the kid seems happy playing hockey and he's good at it so that's what he'll keep doing, for now. No chess lessons for now except for when he's with his dad. If there's a conflict between hockey and Mr. Warren's parenting time, hockey wins, just for now. Anything else?"

Each attorney shook their head to the negative.

"Good. And Ms. Warren, to keep things fair and square and to make sure the kid is playing hockey for himself and not for your social agenda or whatever agenda you got, it seems only right that you can't watch any of the kid's games or practices. Understand?"

"What!" Rebecca cried.

"That's unfair!" Pudsworth exclaimed.

"Relax," the judge laughed at Rebecca. "I'm just pulling your pud."

- 7 -

I listened to sports talk radio in my Porsche when I drove to and from work. According to league insiders, Milton Farmers was football's most ruthless agent. Several Professional Football League teams would rather lose a talented player then enter into negotiations against Farmers. If sports agents were snakes, Farmers would be a giant Anaconda, happily squeezing his opponents to mush before devouring them.

He sat in our firm's conference room with Meredith Balton, a former Miss Alabama and wife of the World Championship winning quarterback.

"We want the Court to order him to play better," Farmers said.

"Excuse me?"

"Am I not speaking English?" Farmers demanded. "I am fluent in several languages. Would you prefer I speak in another tongue?"

"English is fine."

"Then don't make me repeat myself."

Farmers played on the defensive line for twelve seasons in the Professional Football League before retiring and going into the sports representation business. He stayed in shape. The person sitting across from me carried three hundred pounds of flesh and muscle, mostly muscle, on a six foot eight inch frame. Truthfully, even as I played The Lawyer, he scared the hell out of me.

"What are you going to do?" Meredith spat at me.

"About . . . ."

"Making him play better!" she screamed. "Now!"

They stared at me, waiting.

The decline in the play of the town's quarterback had been radio fodder for the past two seasons. Joey Balton led the team to the playoffs during the two seasons after the Professional Football Championship. Last season, however, had been a debacle with a last place finish. This season, the last year of Balton's contract, he had led the team to zero wins and four losses and Balton was rated as one of the worst quarterbacks in the league.

"Is it the divorce?" I asked. "I've seen a divorce case lead to serious problems at work."

"So it's my fault!" Meredith screeched. "You idiot, don't you know anything?"

Farmers leaned forward in his seat and I wondered if the chair had been made to support such a huge body. "I don't think you are grasping the ramifications of this situation. That's why Ms. Balton asked me to attend this meeting."

"Okay. You have my attention."

His chair creaked. He folded hands big as baseball gloves on the table, resting on forearms as thick as a house's central steel beam.

"Joey is in the final year of his contract. If he continues his current level of play, no team will offer him much more than a two year contract for a few million dollars. He's only thirty-two, however. If during these last twelve games he returns to his prior greatness, he will double the length of the contract and quadruple the money. Understand?"

"Yes," I said. Alimony and child support, I thought. The more money he makes the more alimony and child support the ex-wife will get.

"So what are you going to do about it?" Meredith asked. "Or do I need to find another attorney to help me?"

"This is where I take my leave," Farmers said, standing. His head came perilously close to the ceiling. He walked out of the conference room, ducking his head to clear the doorway.

"Does Milton Farmers represent your husband?" I asked, thinking the agent's goal also involved maximizing earnings by getting Balton a bigger payday.

"No," she said. "He's a friend. He looks out for me."

I let it go. "So what is it that Farmers doesn't want to hear? A story about gambling?"

"What did Arnie tell you?"

"Not much. Tell me all of it."

Meredith and the quarterback had married during his senior season at Alabama. They moved to the city after he was selected in the fifth round of the Professional Football League draft, and they had a family of two children before he became the team's starter. Two more children and a World Championship later, his legacy seemed secure. Until the last season and a quarter, when unexplainable interceptions and inaccurate passes led to a career spiraling towards mediocrity.

Team doctors checked his eyes and his arm; fans questioned his motivation and his heart. No one, however, dared contemplate the point spread of the team's games.

"He's losing games on purpose," she said.

"Why?"

"I don't know."

"Arnie said something about a gambling problem."

"Joey? Are you kidding me? Joey doesn't gamble. We spent a week in Las Vegas and it took him six days before he was willing to put a quarter in a slot machine. We live in a four hundred thousand dollar house and he makes seven million dollars a year. He spends every off day during the season monitoring our investments online and yelling at our stockbroker if we lost more than a hundred dollars in a day. He was suicidal when the market crashed in 2008. Joey does not gamble."

"Well someone is making a ton of money when he loses on purpose."

"Doubtful. The Professional Football League is incredibly vigilant. If there was an unusual amount of money bet against Joey's team and the team lost based on bad throws by Joey, the Professional Football League's private security forces, the FBI and God knows who else would be barging into our house at night."

"Then what?"

"I don't know. That's what you need to find out."

- 8 -

Brandy sat in one of my office's guest chairs facing me. "She has no idea?"

"She claims not but I don't believe her. She knows, she just isn't ready to tell me."

"How do you know she's lying?"

I wanted to throw up.

I had lied on the witness stand. It was a single question and a single answer but the answer was a lie.

"Gut instinct," I said slowly. "After you've done this job long enough, you get an idea when a client isn't telling the truth."

"True," Brandy said. "So true." She pointed to a few files she had placed on my desk. "You have two quick hearings on Monday. I prepped the cases."

"Thanks."

"Well, I think I'm done for the day. You?"

I glanced at my Omega watch. "I have a late meeting with that client who paid us $10,000 but wants us to do nothing."

"That's my favorite kind of client," Brandy said.

For some reason I didn't think she was right.

I headed to the conference room with a pad and pen. It was six o'clock, most of the office staff was leaving and only a few attorneys remained in the building.

He was waiting for me, sipping from a cup of coffee, courtesy of the firm.

We shook hands and sat down.

"So how's it going?" I asked.

"So far, so good," he replied. He wore tan slacks and a yellow sweater.

We sat and stared at one another for awhile.

"Did your wife file for divorce yet?"

"No."

"Do you want to file for divorce?"

"No,"

"Do you want to talk about the eventual divorce case and some pre-divorce planning you can do?"

"No."

"Good."

We sat and stared some more.

"I charge two hundred and fifty dollars an hour, you know."

"Should I pay more now?"

"No, that's okay. We can sit here for another forty hours or so before you'll use up the retainer."

"Great."

I put my pen on the blank pages of the notepad. The items rested on the table before me, orphaned.

"Physics, huh?"

The man's face brightened. I noticed he still had a very good tan from the summer.

"Have you been considering the ramifications of our talk the last time?"

"I've been somewhat busy."

"We're all the same stuff, remember? We were all squeezed together so tightly at time's beginning that we are all related. Our very atoms know one another. I believe the basic particles of matter can communicate with one another, due to that initial closeness."

"Right."

He reached into his pants pocket and retrieved a business card holder and placed his card on the table.

UNITED WASTE MANAGEMENT
"For Disposing The Trash Of Life."

"Catchy," I said.

"Very appropriate, actually."

"So you work in the garbage removal industry?" I asked.

"We have a piece of that."

"A piece? But we are all one thing, right? We all have a piece of it."

"Exactly!" The Physics Guy exclaimed. "You get it! And so you'll understand how much it hurts then, too."

"Hurts?"

"To harm oneself."

"Huh?"

"If you hurt someone or something you end up hurting yourself."

He stared at me, not blinking, his face suddenly made of stone.

"Who is getting hurt again, exactly?"

"My wife hired Gerald & Gerald as her attorneys for the divorce. You heard of them?"

"Husband and wife team. Very experienced."

"They are very successful," he said. "They represent a lot of successful people in town. Even football players."

He spoke slowly and calmly but his face remained impassive and he wasn't blinking.

"Football players," I said.

He reached out and placed another business card on the table.

The garbage industry, I thought.

"What exactly do you do for United Waste Management?" I asked.

"Nothing," he said. "Unless there are labor problems, or a town isn't willing to pay the offered rates of service."

"Oh."

"Then my associates and I help out the business. We help the employees or community leaders understand the perspectives of the business. You might say I work in the area of resolving disputes."

"Resolving."

He smiled. "We get rid of the trash of life." The Physics Guy glanced at his watch. "I think I've spent enough money today. Let's say we meet again next Tuesday around six in the evening? I usually sleep late. I usually do most of my work at night."

"Sure." We stood and shook hands. "By the way, does your wife work for your company, too?"

"You could say that," he said. "Though, of course, there are no paychecks for her."

"Do you get a paycheck?"

He smiled. "For the tax returns, sure." He paused at the door. "I hear the football player's divorce is going to be put on hold for awhile."

"From who?"

"From me. So are you going to walk me to the elevator?"

"Gladly."

"We are going to be good friends. And I'd hate for anything to happen to a friend. It would hurt me."

"Because we are all the same."

"Exactly," he said.

- 9 -

The Physics Guy boarded the elevator and the doors closed. I stood alone in the lobby.

So he's with the mafia, I thought. Maybe I'll finally be able to find a good Italian restaurant in town.

I stood in the lobby feeling cold, unmotivated and tired.

The trembling started.

I lied on the witness stand, I thought. I lied.

Pain crushed my chest and I staggered, reaching out to grasp a chair for balance. I pictured Jaime Landscuda, having discovered the lie, laughing as I sat chained to my office chair, a blade gleaming in his hand, approaching me and grinning with sharpened teeth.

"I own you now," he said to me. "And I'm going to take what's left of your soul."

The Physics Guy followed close behind.

Where would I be, if this job was gone?

Fuck.

Sweat dampened my underarms and the crack of my ass.

Why did I do it? For Rebecca? What the hell did I owe her?

The hallways separated the outer offices from the floor's interior offices: secretarial and paralegal stations, kitchens, copier rooms, elevators and machinery. I left the lobby still trembling, barely considering The Physics Guy's threats, instead hearing my voice repeat the lie, over and over again.

Have you ever watched *The Shining*?

Jenny and I watched it one night at The Ranch Retreat and she came prepared in full Satanic dress with blood dripping off her lips and chin to splatter onto black robes. The only time we screamed aloud during the movie was when there was a close-up of Shelly Duval's face.

I turned a corner of the hallway.

"Do you want to play?" they chimed at me.

I froze.

Mia and Mai smiled, thirty feet down the hallway, their bodies seemingly exposed to me, every curve and fold of skin outlined by skin hugging red bodysuits.

They looked like teenage girls, naked and painted in blood.

"Do you want to play with us?"

Drawing in a deep breath, sweat now sliding down my forehead, "Excuse me?"

"Do you like our outfits?" Mia—or Mai—asked.

"They were gifts," the other said. "Do you want to play with us?"

"Gifts from who?"

"Jaime's new client. He owns a few sporting good stores."

"Oh."

"His wife's a slut. She sleeps around when she travels out-of-town with her son. He's a hockey player. Jaime thinks you might know them."

"Oh."

They faced me, two perfect creatures, beckoning.

"Do you want to play with us?" they chimed.

"Play what?"

They giggled, turned and walked away. I watched their bodies sway with each step, transfixed.

If I had any balls, I thought, I would have said yes to them.

Landscuda hunched over me clenching a knife, the twins in their red bodysuits in the background, chanting.

I vomited onto the hallway carpet.

- 10 -

"You seem to be making a habit of vomiting," Jenny said. "Do you want me to steal some air sickness bags for you?"

"Funny."

"Just trying to be helpful."

We were talking on the phone. I arrived at The Ranch Retreat the next Friday evening expecting her to be there but instead she left a message on the landline's answering machine, asking me to call her.

She told me she couldn't make it for the weekend. She didn't say why.

"So does that mean you're traveling by airplane somewhere?"

"Are you jealous?"

"Curious."

"But there's a reason for the curiosity."

"Could be but I'm not really in touch with my feelings to figure it out."

"It doesn't sound like you'll be in touch with anything this weekend other than Vaseline and your hands."

"Hey, that's very unkind. It sounds like locker room talk. You're a girl, remember?"

"I am aware of my gender, but it's nice of you to notice. Sometimes I wonder."

"Why? What do you want me to do?"

"Bite me," she said laughing and hung up.

I spent the night watching a high school football game on television, drinking lots of whiskey and smoking a few cigars. I left the lights out in the living room, letting the television screen provide the only illumination and dressed in just thermal underwear and a frayed blue bathrobe. At some point I dozed off and woke with a start as whiskey splashed onto the robe. Damn it, I thought, putting the whiskey glass on the coffee table. At least the cigar was out and I didn't burn the house down. I considered getting up and going to bed but the thought depressed me so I slouched deep into the couch and closed my eyes and let the world slip away.

I skated on an ice rink, wearing just my long black thermals. The bleachers and player benches were empty. I skated fast, the cool air striking my face. "Hey!" someone shouted. Rebecca stood outside one of the rink's corners banging on the Plexiglas with open palms, trying to get my attention. I waved, skating over to her. She was smiling when I reached her and she pressed her lips against the Plexiglas. I leaned down and kissed her through the glass.

"Be wary," she said.

"Huh?"

She pointed to my left.

The Zamboni barreled towards me with Teri Manyard at the wheel wearing a red bodysuit and laughing hysterically. I dove out of the way, the machine's horn blaring throughout the rink, Teri grinning at me as she spun the Zamboni around three hundred and sixty degrees for another strike, smoke spitting out its exhaust pipes, its headlights seemingly aimed at my groin . . .

Light. My eyes opened. Something had brought me back to the world. I rubbed my eyes, wishing I was still asleep, finally standing and smelling whiskey on my breath and bath robe. I found a cigar, lit it, slipped on sneakers and stepped onto the porch for a typical Saturday morning awakening.

A huge black limousine was parked in front of the porch. Its windows were darkly tinted and I could not see inside it.

The front passenger door opened and a huge man dressed in a dark business suit walked around the front of the car towards me.

"Good evening," he said.

I looked about. "It's morning."

The man laughed. He was at the driver's side rear door and he opened it for me.

"We'd like you to come with us."

"Come with who? Forget it."

The man opened his suit jacket to reveal a gun handle sticking out of a shoulder holster.

"You're coming with us. Okay?'

"Who are you?"

He reached for the gun and I almost ran into the house, planning on sprinting into the backyard and then into the woods, hopefully losing whoever the hell was chasing after me. But I thought of a lesson I always taught my hockey players. I would have a player skate as fast as he could away from me and then I would shoot the puck past him. See, I would tell my players, the puck moves faster than you can skate, so pass it to a teammate!

I reckoned the same general philosophy held true for a bullet.

Resigned, I climbed into the back of the limousine, still holding the cigar.

The man sat behind the front passenger seat, large and heavyset with a bald spot surrounded by thin dark hair and a five o'clock shadow covering his face. The man wore a black suit with a white shirt and blue tie; there was a wedding ring on one hand and two diamond encrusted rings on the other. His brown eyes locked onto mine.

"Last stop of the night," he said, his jowls shaking as he spoke, his eyes still staring at me.

"Uh, night?"

"Until I go to bed it's night."

"Okay."

The burly button man got back into the car, sitting beside the driver who was just as big. The limousine rolled down my driveway onto the county road but instead of heading towards civilization the driver went south, traveling deeper into the country.

They can easily hide a body out here, I thought. The police would never find it.

"You can smoke. I usually do."

The cigar had gone out. I lit it, my hands trembling.

"Epilepsy? Tourette's syndrome?"

"No. Just fear."

"Nothing to be scared about. I wouldn't be here if we were going to do anything but talk."

"Talk about what?" although I already knew. Mobsters; the quarterback and his wife; bad passes and games being thrown away, gambling debts. "You know I am bound by attorney-client privilege."

He looked at me and laughed. "You think, with me?"

"Technically, yes."

"You're a funny guy."

I puffed anxiously, waiting.

"You know who I am?" he asked. His voice was deep but gravely.

"No."

"You ever see *The Godfather*?"

"Yes."

"Then you know who I am. Here, we're not like our associates in New York City. We stay out of the newspapers and off the television. It's better for business, here. I never wanted to be a rock star. I like going places and having most people not recognize me. I'm just a businessman trying to make a living."

"Great. Really, no problem, fine by me."

"Business is good. It's important that it stays good."

"Everyone likes money," I said.

"We don't want you to hurt our business arrangements."

"I don't know anything about your business arrangements."

"That's why we're talking now. Scotch?"

"It's kind of early."

He looked at me and laughed again. "The way you look and smell I bet you drink all the time. Besides, it's still night. People drink at night."

The limousine's interior was black leather and dark wood. The man opened the console between us and retrieved two tumblers and a bottle of Johnny Walker Black. He poured us each a generous amount and held out his glass. I tapped my glass with his and we drank.

"Good scotch?"

"Exceptional."

"Cigar good?"

136

"Yes."

"You know you wouldn't be able to enjoy either the cigar or the whiskey if someone put a blowtorch into your mouth and turned it on."

What did he say? I looked at him, suddenly dazed.

"Our business," he prompted.

"I'm listening."

"We don't want it ruined."

"How can I help you?" I asked meekly before downing the rest of the alcohol in the glass.

"Don't mess with Donnie."

The limousine slowed, turning down a dirt road, branches scratching the windows, the sun momentarily hidden.

"Donnie?"

"The kid. The hockey player. Don't fuck with him."

I tried to say something but ended up just opening my mouth and shaking my head a few times.

"What?" he asked calmly.

"You're making the quarterback throw interceptions because he owes you money from gambling debts," I blurted. "What the hell does Rebecca have to do with that?"

The mobster smiled. "Slip of the tongue? She is pretty, isn't she? Then again, so are some rattlesnakes."

I sighed deeply. "I don't understand what you're talking about."

"We do not mess with professional football," he said. "Whoever put that idea into your head is a fucking idiot. Sure, every now and then some small-timer with a family may try to mess with a particular game, football or basketball or baseball, but we deal with him pretty harshly once we find out. We make a lot of money handling bets on pro football and the other sports. We'd poison the well if our customers thought we were also trying to influence the outcome and basically fuck them over with their bets. They wouldn't bet if they thought it was a rigged game."

"The quarterback isn't indebted to the mob?"

"The mob." He laughed. "Maybe he just got old or scared of getting hit. But neither I nor my associates have anything to do with it."

"You mentioned Donnie Warren."

"Yes. Donnie."

He poured us each another glass of scotch. "You were on the right track. Betting."

"On kid hockey games?"

"Kid everything games. Think about it. How many kid games are played in every town in this country every Saturday and Sunday afternoon? One of our guys takes a particular sporting venue, say that rink you play in, and handles the action. Don't have to be lots of bets, maybe a thousand dollars total but it adds up."

"Point spreads?"

"There's always an expert for every sports league. He gets a cut to set 'em."

"No offense but are you kidding?"

"Do I look like I want to spend the end of my night dealing with some fucking lawyer in the middle of the damn country?"

"Not really."

"It's simple," he said. "Be consistent. If you're going to keep the score down, do it all the time. If you're going to burn other teams by a lot of goals, try and do that. Just be consistent. You could really fuck with the spread if you aren't using Donnie the same way in every game."

"We're talking about ten year olds playing hockey in the Midwest. This isn't Detroit or Chicago or New England."

"Money here is the same. And he's going to keep playing, right?"

"You hear about the court case?"

"Is he going to keep playing?" The mobster locked onto my eyes, no longer smiling and his face hardening.

"Sure. Why not?"

"Exactly. Why not."

We finished our drinks as the limousine took me back to The Ranch Retreat. I was dropped off, no one saying anything else. I found myself back on my front porch, holding the cigar and the tumbler still half-full with scotch.

I downed it quickly, went inside and began drinking a lot more.

- 11 -

I stopped at *Starbucks* on the drive to work.

"Excellent," Landscuda said, taking the cup from me after I got to the office.

"Thought you might like it."

"Have a seat."

Mia and Mai sat on a black leather couch, dressed in dark slacks and blouses. Landscuda's office, twice the size of mine, was sparsely furnished and had little decorative touches, which surprised me. I had expected the walls adorned with photographs of Landscuda and celebrities; framed newspapers and plaques proclaiming his legal accomplishments; a trophy case filled with the memorabilia of triathlon wins and other athletic achievements. Instead the room had an empty bookcase, the firm's standard desk and credenza, two guest chairs and the couch.

I sat in a guest chair, the twins behind me.

"So you've heard about the Manyard case," Landscuda said.

"They told me."

Landscuda smiled. "They also said you wouldn't play with them."

"I figured they were joking."

"They weren't. Those bodysuits are damn hard to peel off."

One of the twins giggled.

"Mr. Manyard retained us," Landscuda said. "He knows you coach his son but he wanted me to represent him anyway. I need to ask you a question, however."

I should have poisoned Landscuda's coffee, I thought. Rat poison or lye. I should have played with the twins on Friday night and then fled to South America.

"Okay," I said.

"You've spoken to Ms. Manyard, right?"

Between orgasms, I almost said. "Sure."

"Did you ever give her any legal advice?"

"Uh, no."

"Did you ever give her the slightest impression that you would represent her in a divorce or for any legal matter?"

"Nope. Never came up."

Landscuda smiled and drank his coffee. "Good. So there's no legal conflict of interest."

"Right," I said.

"However, I don't want to recreate that Warren fiasco with you being dragged into Court as a witness. So I made Manyard sign a paper saying that under no circumstances would he involve you in the case or have you called as a witness."

"Good," I said, knowing that such a piece of paper was legally worthless. "I appreciate it."

"We're going to have fun with Mrs. Manyard," one of the twins said.

I looked behind me.

"She sleeps around on hockey trips," Mia—or Mai—said. "Can you believe it? She's traveling with her son and she's slutting it up."

"Really?"

"You know anything about that?" Landscuda asked.

"Ha, ha. No."

"Good. Let's keep you out of this. Stay away from her, okay?"

"Yes, sir."

"Hey," Landscuda said. "Let's all go out to lunch today. The four of us."

"What's the occasion?" I asked.

"I won a hundred dollars betting on a kid's softball game this past weekend. Free money basically and I feel like spending it. Lunch is on me."

I smiled and wondered if Jenny had managed to get me any of those airline sickness bags.

- 12 -

Of course I should have told Landscuda about my relationship with Teri Manyard. I sat in my office when the work day was over, staring at a hockey blog on the computer, lost in thought. After the divorce, I had been alone. Sometimes I would go to a sports bar on a weekend towards the dinner hour and either have a few drinks at the counter or sit at a table with a newspaper or magazine. Every so often there would be a woman who would catch my eye, a waitress or bartender or another patron, but nothing ever happened. If she were an employee, a few casual words might be exchanged, but nothing more. I was not handsome; was not witty or charming; had no natural charisma that brought a crowd around me. I was quiet and shy. Even during my days coaching, before the marriage, I mostly kept to myself at the rink, joking with the kids, ignoring the parents. There had been no Teri Manyard showing up unannounced, offering herself.

If one didn't count Jenny, I probably had not said more than a thousand words to women in general outside of the workplace after my divorce.

I went to work. I drank. I smoked cigars, to kill time. I breathed but I did not live, other than through Sly.

I should have told Landscuda but in my heart and head, I was hoping the divorce action did not change anything. I was hoping that Teri would still knock on my hotel door, late at night, for whatever reason. The reason didn't matter. With her, for a few hours, I was not alone.

When I got to The White Apartment that evening I locked the door, stripped off my suit and shirt and lay on the floor in my socks and underwear, staring at the ceiling. I shouldn't get hammered tonight, I thought. I have work tomorrow. Maybe I'll take a bath. Maybe I should just slit my wrists and relax in the hot water.

A sadness bubble erupted. There was an unopened bottle of whiskey in the kitchen.

A knock on the door.

I did not get visitors at The White Apartment. Teri Manyard probably had been the first person to be in the apartment with me in years; even Jenny didn't visit me here. This was a place to decompress after work, to wallow in my depression, to watch the minute hand slowly advance on my Omega watch. I didn't even speak to my neighbors. I didn't even remember their names.

More knocking.

Fuck.

Through the peephole, Rebecca Warren, impatient, knocking on the door again.

Teri Manyard, appearing unannounced, offering her body to me.

No. It was not possible.

I remembered my ex-wife, early in the marriage, seeking me out like a guided missile, warm to the touch, so alive, filled with want.

Through the peephole, Rebecca waited.

The apartment wore my clothes. I stood still, confused.

She was beautiful to me.

What could she possibly want?

"Give me a minute!" I called.

"It's cold out here!"

Okay. What the hell. I opened the door.

"Expecting company?" she asked. She walked about the living room, gazing at clothes scattered over furniture and the floor.

I closed the door.

In my mind that perfect song began to play, lyrics and music together, a seamless love song.

To me she was the perfect song I could never write or perform.

"Where's Donnie?" I asked.

"With his father for the night. Let's not talk about Donnie or hockey, okay?"

"Sure. No problem."

Rebecca stood facing me, just an arm's reach away.

"Did we have an appointment tonight?"

Her eyes twinkled. "Not officially." She took off her coat. Faded blue jeans hugged her lower body.

"Give me a minute. I need to get dressed."

"No," she said. Smoothly she pulled the sweater over her head. She was not wearing a bra. My penis immediately pointed towards the North Star. "Let me get undressed instead."

This never happened in my life. I slept with my ex-wife and a hockey mom coming to me with an ulterior motive. Rebecca did not need anything from me. Her kid was a superstar. I would kill to have him on my team.

She reached out her hands.

It happened.

- 13 -

This morning she would wake next to me.

I lay on my side watching her breathe. She rested on her stomach, hands clasped in prayer beneath the pillow, air gently flowing through her mouth. Her face was small, her reddish hair tussled. Beneath the sheets her naked body was still. I faced her watching her breathe.

We had talked little. Small jokes, words of warmth, happy sounds. She had been so soft to hold. I had lived for such softness.

I waited. She had never indicated a time she needed to leave. I had no pressing matters on my desk for the day. The legal system could do without me for awhile.

What would Jenny say? I wondered. A second hockey mom from my hockey team. You are becoming a male gigolo, she would say with a laugh.

No. Maybe it's just my time. It had been so long.

Did it matter? I lay next to her.

Eyes fluttered.

"Morning," I whispered.

She smiled. "Morning."

Still beneath the covers but getting up on hands and knees, back arching, stretching like a cat. She kissed me on the forehead.

"Breakfast?" she asked.

"I can make something. Eggs."

"I left an overnight bag in my car. Can you get it? I parked near your SUV."

"Sure."

"My keys are in my coat, somewhere in the living room."

A thin layer of frost covered car windshields and windows on this October morning. Her gym bag was on the passenger side floor. I locked her car and went back to The White Apartment, cold in my bathrobe, sweats and sneakers.

"Got it!" I called to a closed bathroom door.

She came out, water dripping off skin, no towel in sight. I dropped the gym bag. She opened my bathrobe and we lowered ourselves to the carpet and I licked the water from her body as she gazed at the ceiling, moaning a quiet song.

- 14 -

As we ate scrambled eggs, both of us showered and dressed, I finally asked, "Why?"

She looked up from her plate. "My lawyer says this is a no fault state. As long as I don't waste any money the Court can't punish me for having an affair."

Gently because I had to know, "That's not an answer."

"I have needs," she said. "I like you. You're honest and fair and we'll be spending a lot of time together on the road."

"Honest." I moved eggs around my plate. "I lied on the witness stand."

"Did you?"

"I said you didn't leave Donnie alone at the hotel. But I saw you. I saw you with the Affton coach."

"How do you know I left Donnie alone?" She blinked her eyes, smiling. "You don't know really, do you? Maybe I had the hotel find me a babysitter to wait in the room with him. Did you really lie?"

"Are you trying to become a lawyer?"

"No," she said quietly. "But I'm trying to be with you."

"Why?"

"I just told you."

"So I'm just available," I said. "And I'm convenient and you have needs."

A pinprick of a sadness bubble formed in my gut.

"You're not convenient," she answered, standing and stepping around the table to be next to me. "Convenient is a stranger I'd meet in a bar. Donnie really likes you. So do I."

Bending down, our lips together, her hands on the cheeks of my face. The world tilted and the sadness bubble evaporated. My heart burst through my chest, seeking hers. She hugged me and I nuzzled her neck and lightly bit her skin. She moaned softly. I stood.

Locked together, her body against mine, no resistance felt.

I wanted to believe her.

I wanted her.

- 15 -

She left for work. I went onto the balcony in a suit and tie smoking a cigar. I didn't bother with a tumbler of whiskey. This morning, it wasn't necessary.

- 16 -

My paralegal, Brandy, had prepared a settlement agreement for one of my divorce clients. I sat slouched in my chair, feet on my desk and the agreement on my lap, reading slowly, making a few corrections with a red pen.

She came into my office.

"Everything okay?" Brandy asked.

"Sure. But cancel everything I have this afternoon. Lunch will be my last appointment of the day."

"What should I tell Mr. Landscuda if he asks about your whereabouts?"

I wrote 'Rebecca' in the margins of the settlement agreement and then scribbled over it.

"Tell him I'm feverish."

"Are you?"

"Maybe," I replied. "Maybe I am."

- 17 -

I had expected to see Rebecca outside the Ice Kingdom, smoking a cigarette and waiting for me. She wasn't there nor was she in the lobby. The usual crowd milled about, purchasing beer and spiking coffee. Teri Manyard stood off by herself and raised her hand when she saw me. I nodded with a smile and hurried away.

Inside the rink, Herb and Andy were by the team's locker room. Herb was demonstrating something to Andy regarding his hockey stick. On the ice the coach of the U8 AA travel team was yelling at the top of his lungs at his seven and eight year old players.

Herb released Andy and the boy went into the locker room to join his teammates.

"Evening coach," Herb said.

"What's going on?"

"I found a fatal flaw with Andy that if not corrected was going to doom his days as a hockey player."

"Is he sick?" I asked.

"No. Why would he be sick?"

I shrugged. "No reason. What's the problem?"

"He's holding the stick incorrectly. His top hand needs to rotate about a quarter of an inch to really have control of the stick. That's probably why he's not scoring a lot of goals this year. I showed him what to do and we'll work on it at home. I think it can be fixed with lots of repetition and effort."

"Great news," I said. "Good job. Way to spot the problem."

"Just glad to help," Herb replied.

Fucking idiot, I thought.

Talking about Donnie was a sore subject for Rooks but I didn't care. "Is Donnie here? I didn't see Rebecca anywhere."

"He's here. The nanny brought him."

"Nanny?"

"A college exchange student from Sweden. My wife spoke to her. She's absolutely gorgeous. She dropped him off to run some errands. She'll be back when it's time for him to leave."

"Where's Rebecca then?"

Rooks shrugged. "Don't know. Why?"

I thought of the Affton coach. Had that been a one night stand? Did she make a habit of such encounters or did she and the coach have a past together?

And what about me? Regardless of what she said, was I just a one night stand?

Frustrated, wanting to jump out of my skin or, in the alternative, beat the hell out of anybody, I looked away from Rooks to the ice surface.

Was she with someone else tonight?

On the ice, the seven and eight year old hockey players were doing sit-ups and pushups as the coach continued to yell at them. The management of the Ice Kingdom rented out the ice surface at $350 an hour, and the U8 AA coach was using expensive ice for training exercises that could be done in the locker room for free. Unbelievable.

"Do you need to talk to her about Donnie?"

"Huh? No, I was just curious. She's always been here since I took over the team. It was just strange not to see her at the rink."

"Could be because of her divorce," Rooks said. "Did you hear about the Manyards? He filed for divorce, too."

"You're kidding."

"No. It's not much of a surprise. We all expected it, eventually."

"We?"

"Us parents. Teri's been sleeping around for years. There was a night during a tournament in Chicago when I couldn't sleep before a big game and I ran into her in the hallway. She was scurrying back to her room and her robe was loose and she was wearing some kind of a mesh bodysuit beneath it. Weird."

"Who was she sleeping with?"

"That season? I never found out."

"And her husband never knew?"

"He didn't go on the road trips. His store was the excuse. I brushed against her once by accident and the next day I went and got myself tested for sexually transmitted diseases."

Everyone's crazy, I thought. And then there was Jenny, alternating between The Satanist and Happy Girl. She might be more sane than the rest of us. At the very least you always knew who she was. There was no need to guess. She didn't play the same games as everyone else.

Where was Rebecca?

"So what's the plan for tonight's practice?" Rooks asked.

"Pushups and sit-ups," I replied.

We worked on passing and shooting drills and I spent most of practice working individually with some of the players, helping them with their accuracy and power. Passing and shooting were learned skills. Anyone could become good at them. It was all technique and repetition.

The boys skated hard, were attentive and didn't mess around. As a reward I let them scrimmage for the last fifteen minutes, breaking them up into two teams. In the stands S.S. Williams aimed a digital camera at the ice and taped the impromptu game.

I let Rooks be the referee, telling him to only stop play if it was necessary. I wanted the boys to have fun, as if they were on a frozen pond with no parents in sight, just playing.

I stood leaning on the boards near center ice. Donnie skated with the puck up ice, crossing the offensive blue line, taking a defenseman with him into the corner. He put on the brakes, faked left and right, skated around the defenseman and headed to the net. The other defenseman reacted, moving towards him. Donnie faked with his head and then the puck was spinning off his stick into the air, seemingly heading nowhere but Steele Williams had been slow behind the play and as he crossed the offensive blue line the puck gently dropped to the ice onto his stick. He fired at the net, scoring.

Donnie's playing chess, I realized. He's playing two or three moves ahead of everyone else on the ice. I skated over to the bench when it was his line's turn to rest.

"Nice passing," I told Donnie as he spat out his mouth guard and gulped from a water bottle.

"Thanks, coach."

Where's your mom? I wanted to ask. Did she give the Affton coach a blow job?

Instead, "Your mom and I spoke the other day. I bet chess really helps you play hockey, right?"

He looked at me, confused.

"In chess you always have to think about what the opponent is going to do and what you are going to do in the next three moves or so. That's kind of how you play hockey, always anticipating what everyone else is going to do."

"I play chess," Steele Williams said.

"Chess is for pussies," Sean Manyard muttered.

"Right?" I asked Donnie.

He shrugged at me. "I don't think chess is for pussies."

"No, not that. Did you and Mr. Ginskofsky ever talk about hockey and how it relates to chess?"

"Who?"

"The chess teacher."

"Did one of the moms put something in your coffee?" Donnie asked.

"What?"

"Who is Ginskofsky?"

"Ginskofsky. Your chess teacher."

"Maybe my mom put something in her coffee before she talked to you," Donnie said. "Never heard of that guy. And I never took chess lessons. I don't play chess."

Sly's World

- 18 -

They begin as specks on the horizon, black dots on a sea of white snow.

Sly and The Blondeshell wait as do the two players remaining on the ice. They had stopped the game and most of The Hockey Gods left the pond, climbing the stairs carved into the mountain towards the palace above.

"Who are they?" The Blondeshell asks.

"Wait," Sly says.

They trudge onward, approaching. One is tall, the other short. The short one carries a stick.

The Hockey Gods skate to the edge of the ice, a man and woman, both blonde haired, trim and powerful, blue eyes and high cheek bones. One wears white, the other blue. Snow blows in swirls off the mountain top. The sky is clear of clouds. The ice surface, unmarked, smooth and pure as if the game had never been played.

They are closer now. It is a man and a boy, no more than ten years old.

"We've been expecting you," the woman says as they reach the frozen pond.

Sly and The Blondeshell stand back, watching.

The boy sits in the snow and his father helps him lace and tie the hockey skates. The boy takes the hockey gloves from the bag that had been slung over his father's shoulder, in which the skates had been stored.

"Are you ready?" the woman asks.

The boy nods. He shrugs out of his coat and pulls off his snow pants and he is wearing the same type of skin hugging suit as The Hockey Gods, but his is gray.

The boy gingerly puts one skate and then the other onto the ice. Slowly, he begins skating towards the puck that has been left at the center of the pond. His father steps forward but the man places his palm on the father's chest.

"No," the Hockey God says. "Only him."

The father watches as the two figures skate towards his son.

"Where are you from?" Sly asks.

"Indiana," the father says.

"Where's the boy's mother?" The Blondeshell asks.

"They wouldn't let her come."

The boy reaches out with the hockey stick and the blade latches onto the puck. He pivots, skating backwards, the puck still on his stick, twirls now going forward, crossing to the left and the right, the puck circling about him like a planet orbiting a star. The Hockey Gods watch. Approaching one of the nets, the boy raising the stick behind his body and then exploding it downward, the shaft bending, the blade impacting ice a quarter of an inch behind the puck and then the rubber disc fires into the cold air. It hits the cross bar and ricochets into a snow drift.

"Damn," the father mutters.

The woman has another puck in her hand and she tosses it to the boy. He skates with it for a few more minutes, stopping and starting and the puck like magic follows him wherever he goes. He takes several more shots, each finding the net inside the goal.

"Better," the father says.

The Hockey Gods skate to him. They are smiling.

"You have a lovely boy," the woman says. "You should be very proud of him."

"I am," the father says. "He loves the game. It's his life. Every day he shoots and practices. Every day."

"Yes," the woman says.

"But it is not enough," says her male companion. "We are sorry, but it is not to be."

They skate to the boy, who has stopped playing and stands alone on the ice holding the stick with both hands, watching them. The woman bends down and speaks in his ear. He nods and keeps his lips pressed tightly together. He looks as if he is about to cry. The man and woman both hug him and then they skate to join their companions in The Mountain Palace.

The boy slowly approaches his father.

"I'm sorry," he whispers.

The father says nothing. He helps the boy take off the skates and put the gloves and skates in the bag as the boy gets back into the snow pants and coat. There are tears in the father's eyes.

Sly and The Blondeshell watch as they trudge away from the pond. Soon they are just black specks on the sea of white snow.

"What happened?" The Blondeshell asks.

"He was not The Next One," Sly responds. "He was not destined to carry The Holy Puck."

Sam

- 19 -

Arnie supposedly died in his sleep. He had been released from the hospital and his doctors expected him to make a full recovery. He lived alone and his body was not discovered until a cleaning lady came to his home a week after he passed. The coroner listed the cause of death as 'total organ failure.' It seemed suspect.

Everyone attended the funeral: the entire firm. From late night escapades with Arnie I also recognized employees of several strip clubs, all tastefully attired, as well as the owners of an adult bookstore.

Rain drizzled from dark skies. I stood near the casket beside Brandy, avoiding her umbrella, letting the drops fall into my hair and soak into the fabric of my dark business suit. My leather shoes sank into mud and grass. A priest conducted a brief graveside service which seemed absurd since I had never known Arnie to espouse any religious beliefs in the ten years we worked together. His relatives clustered at the head of the closed casket, consisting of a few aunts and uncles, all elderly. His parents were long since dead, he had no siblings and he never married, leaving no children in the world. His genes would be forever lost, buried beneath six feet of dirt, entombed in wood that eventually would rot away.

The rain plastered hair to my scalp.

Sighing I looked away and saw him standing on the path leading to the cemetery's parking lot, a hundred yards away. The Physics Guy, wearing a full length dark Australian coat and matching cowboy's hat. Rain would slide off that coat, I thought, like Holy

Water repelled by a demon's skin. He stood with his hands in coat pockets facing the graveside service, seemingly staring at me.

The priest continued reading from his book of prayers. I couldn't leave. Did anyone else see him? Rubbing my eyes, shaking water from eyebrows, looking back and he was still there, motionless, looking at me.

The service eventually ended. I tried to hurry, didn't want to break out into a full run but it probably would not have mattered. He began moving before the priest finished. He was in his car and already gone.

What the fuck?

I was dragged along by the crowd. Attorneys at the firm had prepared Arnie's estate documents. A few of us were called to the main conference room to hear the reading of Arnie's will. I was bequeathed his entire pornography collection of books, magazines, tapes and DVDs.

Cowboy Jake received Arnie's home computers. That's where Arnie probably stored the material of the most interest to the FBI, I thought, bison movies and the like.

We snuck out of the office and spent a few hours after the reading of the will at a bar and grill by the office, sitting in a booth in the back, drying off from the rain and matching each other shot for shot.

"You ever end a life?" I asked him.

Cowboy Jake looked annoyed. "I worked on a ranch. What do you think?"

"I mean a person's life."

He still looked annoyed. "What do you think?" he asked.

Another round of shots downed quickly. I was never going to make it out of the bar.

"What is it like?" I asked.

"You thinking of Arnie?" he asked. "You thinking about the quarterback's wife and all?" I didn't answer. Cowboy Jake motioned to our waitress for another round. "Well, I am, too. He was doing better; then he just dies. Alone. And I saw that guy standing at the cemetery. One of your clients, right? He's the one who pays lots of money to just sit and talk to you?"

"Yea." I had told him about The Physics Guy as well as my Saturday morning visit from the stars of *The Sopranos*.

"Killing is both power and failure," Cowboy Jake said. "You can't control a person any more than by killing him. But it also means everything else you did to get your way with him failed."

"If only that was always true," I said, clearly drunk. The room tilted, my eyeballs fell out of my head, bounced off the table and popped back into their sockets. I was about to pass out.

"Huh?"

"You're talking about having a motive, like killing for money or sex or something tangible. That isn't what I'm talking about. I think people kill mostly because they want to. The person killed isn't real to them. The person's just a prop for the act."

Cowboy Jake might have replied but my body was already falling sideways, in the process of incurring bruises that would bother me for days.

- 20 -

The purge began immediately.

I returned to work the next day and found Brandy's cubicle empty, devoid of all personal effects. All of her photographs of children and grandchildren and husbands; her diploma; the knickknacks that cluttered her desk and which she knocked over each time she opened a file or reached for the telephone. Even her computer had been taken away. It was as if she had never been there at all.

Stalin would be proud, I thought.

- 21 -

My U10 AA team had a home game on Saturday night against a weak opponent. Even if Donnie broke his leg that afternoon we would still win by several goals. I had most of the day to kill so I agreed to spend time with her.

She took me to the city's largest indoor shopping mall, recently renovated and home to upscale shops and several anchor department stores. We bought large lattes at a coffee shop and wandered about until we found two empty leather chairs. Throughout the mall four chairs were set in pairs facing each other, fifteen feet apart with each pair separated by a small table. I figured the chairs were for husbands and boyfriends as their partners refused to quit shopping. We sat in the middle of a concourse near escalators and clothing boutiques for the young and fashionable. Rap music pounded from one of the stores whose entrance resembled the opening to a cave with fog seeping along the stone floor and scantily clad mannequins beckoning customers inside. Jenny crossed her legs sipping from her cup, a version of Happy Girl with a white leather jacket and form hugging black slacks. She leaned towards me smiling, her eyes bright and clear.

"Let's play a game," she said.

"What game?"

"It's simple," she said. "I want you to imagine you're a senior in high school and I want you to pick out ten teenage girls you would like to fuck."

"Huh?"

"Pick them out and tell me. We'll stop at ten. And don't point or make any overt gesture at them because we don't want to end up listed as sexual predators on the Internet."

"You want me to ogle teenage girls?"

"Just find ten that make you really hot," Jenny said.

"Why?"

"Just humor me, okay?"

Teenage girls either shopped alone, in pairs or in packs. I watched them, trying not to stare, becoming embarrassed because a part of me was becoming excited. I must have been fairly picky in high school because it took almost fifteen minutes for me to reach the magic number.

Jenny smiled. "Very interesting," she said.

"Why?"

"Game's not over. Same idea but now act your age. Pick ten women you can see yourself asking out on a date, today."

"Are we going to hit all of the demographics? I saw a gray haired lady with a walker that likely would appeal to eighty year old invalids."

"Your own age. Begin."

Okay. I held my cooling latte with both hands, leaning deep into the brown leather, glancing about. A woman with short black hair approached with speed skater's thighs in tight jeans and a slim waist. She laughed. I looked away and then glanced back at her face; pleasant and somehow comforting. She held a man's hand.

"One," I said. "Two o'clock. Black hair."

"Interesting," Jenny said.

This time it would take thirty minutes. Several times I almost pointed out a woman to Jenny but held back, unsure. Would I really want to date her?

I finally pointed out number ten.

"Game over," Jenny said.

"Did I win?"

"What do you think?"

"I don't know. Was there a time limit or something?"

"No time limit," Jenny said. She pulled her legs beneath her body. "When I'm lonely during the day or night I sometimes play this game. Choosing men, of course. Do you know what it means?"

"No."

"There are so many people in the world," Jenny answered. "So many people that can catch our eyes. Whenever I think it's hopeless and that I'll never find anyone I play this game. Sometimes at a mall, other times at a park or at a concert or a ballpark or just walking city streets over the lunch hour when people leave their cubicles for fresh air. There are so many people to choose from. We don't have to be alone. We just have to walk up to one of the chosen and say hello."

Women continued to walk by our chairs, many alone, many without a ring on that possessive finger. So many people.

"Do you realize something else?" Jenny asked.

"What?"

"When you were picking women to date who were your own age, when you could have picked anyone in the mall, anyone at all. You disappointed me."

"Why?"

"You didn't pick me."

- 22 -

Rebecca smoked in front of the Ice Kingdom, Donnie standing next to her. He shivered in the evening breeze in his team warm-up suit.

"Is Donnie having a pre-game smoke, too?" I asked.

She laughed but it seemed forced.

"Donnie?" she nudged.

"Coach, I need to apologize," he said slowly.

"For what?"

"Lying."

"You lied to me?"

"About chess." He looked to the ground, hands in his pocket, long hair blowing in the wind. "I didn't want to talk about it in front of the other guys. Sorry."

Both he and Rebecca kept glancing between me and the ground.

"No problem," I said. "I get it. It's fine."

He nodded and mumbled "Thanks," and headed into the building.

"He is sorry," Rebecca said, tossing away her cigarette.

I nodded, staring at her. She suddenly looked so small.

"It's cold out here," she said.

"He was at Donnie's game."

"Who?"

"The chess guy. He was standing next to you."

She nodded and shrugged.

"How come?"

"To talk to me about Donnie and chess. I didn't want to deal with him."

"Is Donnie that good at chess?"

She shrugged again. "Not really."

"Then . . ."

She cut me off. "This had nothing to do with chess or Donnie! My husband is angry and he's waging war every way he can, including using that chess teacher! He wants to hurt me! He doesn't care if he ends up hurting Donnie, too! Okay?"

"Yea, sure."

Rebecca stared at me with her large brown eyes.

"Sure," I said. "Okay."

- 23 -

Mr. Williams gestured to me as I walked through the lobby. "Coach!" he called. "A minute of your time?" He had a cup of coffee in his hand and offered it to me. I looked at it for a moment. "It's clean," he assured me. "No alcohol."

"Okay. Thanks."

"The team we're playing isn't very good," Williams said.

"I know."

Williams gave a tilt of his head to the left. "See the guy in the overcoat with the big guy next to him?"

"Yea."

"He and I were talking. We talk before every game here at the Ice Kingdom. He says you met his boss."

I didn't respond.

"I told him that our team should win by at least twelve goals and that Donnie would go full tilt until sometime in the third period. I'm right, aren't I? About all of it?"

"That guy wants to know the likely margin of victory of our game?" I asked.

"We should win by at least twelve goals," Williams repeated. "Right?"

"Twelve?"

"At least."

"That doesn't seem very sporting."

"Twelve," Williams said.

I wished there was alcohol in my coffee.

- 24 -

We led by ten goals after the second period even with Donnie, on his own, spending more time setting up his teammates for goals than trying to score himself. Before the third period began I glanced over at the other team's bench. The coach was glaring at me. His boys slumped on their bench, heads down. The coach clapped his hands and the team looked at him. In a few second, some of his players were laughing, and others stood and banged their sticks against the boards.

An off-color joke? I wondered. It didn't matter. He was a good coach. His team responded to him. They were losing badly but they were just kids playing a sport and he had them laughing. It was enough.

I let Donnie continue to generate offense in the third period.

We won by fourteen goals.

Williams shook my hand in the lobby after the game. "Good job, coach," he said gratefully. "Way to go."

I nodded and walked away.

Rebecca waited by my car. "It's my husband's weekend with Donnie. I have to drive Donnie to his house now."

"Okay."

"I'm free until six on Sunday evening. No child to watch. No special place to be."

"Freedom is good."

She tossed her cigarette on the ground. "Damn right it is," she said. "Freedom is damn good. So after I drop Donnie off at his dad's house I'm going to follow you home."

- 25 -

I couldn't sleep. In the kitchen I lit a cigar, cracking open the back door to draw out the smoke. There was a half-full bottle of whiskey on the counter along with a clean tumbler. The Ranch Retreat was quiet as my watch's hands approached 3:00 a.m. Rebecca slept in my bed. The whiskey bottle was an arm's reach away. Quiet.

I drew in smoke and then exhaled it through my nose in the direction of the door, wisps spiraling into the cold air of the night. It was quiet, I thought. My head was quiet.

I was used to hearing my mind constantly thinking or daydreaming, worrying or planning, critiquing the world around me, including myself. But now I felt as if someone or something had fastened a muzzle on my mind's voice, shutting down the movie projectors and turning off the sound. The objects in the kitchen, lit only by the moon and stars through the window seemed distinct and clear. I ran my fingers over the scars of the wooden table, the hairs on my wrist dipping into the furrows like a rake in loose dirt, the tip of the cigar a cluster of individual burning points constantly flaming out as others sparkled to life.

I don't want the whiskey right now, I realized. I just didn't need it.

"Hey," she said, pulling a chair close and sitting beside me. Somehow, even after sleeping her hair remained neat, her eyes bright and her skin so smooth. "Is this a private party?"

"I guess I just wasn't tired."

"Should I be insulted?" she giggled. "Not strenuous enough for you?"

"You are more than enough for me," I said and then felt somewhat off balance for saying it aloud.

She smiled but said nothing.

We sat.

I leaned over, rubbed her arm and kissed her lightly on her cheek. Her skin was warm against my lips.

"Thank you," she said.

"For what?"

"For being nice to me."

"That should be a given."

"You're a divorce lawyer. You know it's not a given."

The cigar tasted of chocolate and nuts. Smoke floated out the door. Neither of us spoke, the only movement involved the cigar glowing in the room. Peace and quiet, I thought. This was it. This was what those words meant. All was calm.

She stood and grasped the whiskey bottle and poured a generous amount in the tumbler. "Let's share," she said. "It will help us sleep." She handed me the glass.

Disappointed, although not sure why, I drank with her for awhile and then we went back to bed.

- 26 -

I awoke, Rebecca pushing on my shoulder, eyes wide and worry on her face. "You need to call the police," she whispered.

"Police?"

"There's someone in your house," she whispered.

Rubbing my eyes, checking my Omega watch. 6:37 a.m.

"Listen," she demanded.

I sat up. The bedroom door was open, dust floating in the light's rays. Floorboards creaked as someone walked in the kitchen or living room. Water from the sink, a cabinet opening.

I lay back down and rolled onto my stomach.

Rebecca hit me in the back. "Wake up and call the police!" in a fierce whisper.

"It's okay. It's just a vampire."

"What?"

"Nothing to worry about. It's daylight. Vampires are only dangerous at night."

"Are you still drunk?"

"No," I replied. "Just tired."

"Do something!"

"I am," I said. "I'm going back to sleep."

She punched me in the back again with her small hand.

"Okay." I started to rise but rolled to my left, taking her in my arms, rolling almost off the bed but ending up with Rebecca lying on my chest. She was light and soft and I kissed her, morning breath and all. I let my hands slide to the sides of her hips and rubbed small circles on her body.

"It's okay," I whispered. "It's a friend. She probably figured I'd be alone."

"She?"

"A friend."

"Breaking into your house at dawn?"

"The front door's left open. I'm usually alone or on the porch by now smoking a cigar. She'll make us coffee."

"You have a female vampire friend that cooks for you?"

"Doesn't everyone?"

Jenny walked into the bedroom in pink sweats, her hair tied in a long ponytail holding two mugs. "I don't mind you having an overnight guest," Jenny said. "But you can't spend all day in bed."

"This is Rebecca."

"Hi," Rebecca said.

"Go Shooters," Jenny replied. "I take it there was some scoring last night?"

"My team won," I said.

"I was speaking about your bed," Jenny replied. "I'll be in the kitchen. Don't keep me waiting."

We sat up, taking the mugs and Jenny left the room.

"She's pretty," Rebecca said.

"I guess."

She took a deep breath. "You ever have sex with her?"

"No."

"Okay." She took a sip and wrinkled her nose. "This coffee is terrible."

"It usually is."

"How do you mess up coffee?"

"You forget to put in the brandy."

I put on my bathrobe and joined Jenny at the kitchen table. She was sipping from a quarter full tumbler of whiskey and had taken one of my better cigars from the humidor. She cut off the end, lit it and handed it to me. "Good morning."

"Thanks."

"Maybe we should have a signal," Jenny said. "You can send me a text message or maybe hang a photograph of an erect penis on the front door."

Smoke filled my mouth.

"You were able to get it erect, right?"

171

I blew smoke at her. "Funny."

"She go back to sleep?"

I shrugged.

"Maybe she's waiting for me to leave," Jenny said.

"You don't have to go anywhere."

"You sure?"

"Yea."

"In that case . . ." She retrieved another cigar from the humidor, clipped and lit.

"You screw up the coffee on purpose?"

"Well, yes. I only used half the amount of Folgers for the pot. I was pissed. I saw her lying in bed with you and was pissed. I figured my morning was ruined."

"Are you doing okay?"

"I'm not wearing fangs."

Rebecca joined us. She had put on her jeans and sweater from last night. I leaned back into my chair, enjoying the cigar, wondering if I should play host or let them get to know each other by themselves. For a moment a sadness bubble flowered in my gut but I gritted my teeth and refused to accept it and it burst before it reached my throat.

Rebecca went to the sink, poured the coffee from her mug down the drain and began making a fresh pot. Jenny sipped whiskey. I cracked open the back door again.

When the coffee was done Rebecca poured herself a cup and sat at the table between us. "So you're a vampire, I hear," she said.

Jenny laughed. "Sometimes."

"How come?"

"I'm emotionally needy. And most of my boyfriends have said that I suck the life out of them."

Rebecca glanced at me.

"No, not Sam," Jenny said. "You've seen more of him than me. The best I ever did was see him in sweats."

"Waiting for the wedding day to consummate the relationship?" Rebecca asked over the lip of the mug.

"Let's not talk about marriage," Jenny said. "Or Barbie dolls and hammers."

I laughed.

Rebecca looked at me, perplexed.

"It's a private joke," I explained.

"No, it's okay," Jenny said and explained the story of the Barbie and Ken dolls and her smashing them to plastic bits.

"I'm sorry," Rebecca said.

"Sam told me a little about you. He said your son is a hockey star. And I'm sorry to hear about the divorce."

"It's for the best. My husband is a scumbag."

"All men are scumbags."

"All men have scumbags," I corrected.

"Same thing," Jenny replied. "That and your penis are the only parts a girl really needs anyway."

"I'm in too good a mood to take offense."

"No," Jenny said. "It's because you know I'm right."

"You guys should be a comedy team," Rebecca said. "You should post videos on the Internet."

"Sam's already started on that project."

"Huh?"

"Haven't you seen his creation?" Jenny asked.

"Seen what?"

"Follow me."

Sly's World

- 27 -

They stand by the frozen lake again, waiting. This time, both teams wait with them, blue and white. In the distance, as before, two smudges on the sea of snow, approaching.

"Another one?" Fay asks.

"They come all the time, from everywhere on the globe. They all have the same hope. They all live for the same dream."

Fay decides to make the best of the situation and wears just snippets of cloth on certain areas of her body, letting bright sunshine tan smooth, unblemished skin. Sly dresses in a warm-up suit, red and black. He longs to put on skates and join the players on the ice but he does not even bother to ask them. He knows he will never be invited.

It seems to take forever.

They all wait.

Finally, the pair reach the frozen lake. The boy has carried his equipment bag and stick and he sits in the snow, tossing off shoes, putting on skates and tying the laces. The adult watches him, saying nothing, doing nothing. Satisfied with the feel of the skates on his feet the boy stands, donning hockey gloves and helmet and looks to the other players.

The blonde haired woman on the white team nods.

The boy steps onto the ice, skates a few strides and then stops, stretching muscles, loosening up. After a few minutes he skates to the puck waiting for him at the center of the ice surface. Both nets are empty, the goaltenders waiting with the other players. The boy cradles the puck with his stick blade, moving it back and forth a few times, feeling its weight through the shaft of the hockey stick. He looks to the other players.

"Well?" he asks. "Are we going to play?"

One of the male players on the blue team skates up to him and touches his shoulder. The air shimmers and the boy now wears a blue uniform and the Hockey God is dressed in the white and black stripes of a referee.

"Go," *the referee says.*

The boy waits until all of the other players take their positions on the ice, his blue teammates behind him, between him and his team's goaltender.

The boy nods and passes back to one of his teammates.

The blue team begins its dance with the white team shadowing them. The boy watches for a few moments as a white player skates up to him, preparing to play defense. The boy nods his head, shaking it to some silent beat and then begins skating. He moves slowly at first and then picks up his pace, skating faster and faster, seemingly darting to open ice and crying out for a pass and he collides with a blue teammate and goes sprawling to the ice.

Blood oozes from a cut on his neck.

"Start again," *the blonde haired woman in white says.*

The boy goes back to center ice, takes the puck and passes back to a teammate. He moves tentatively at first, getting a pass, sending it safely to a teammate, letting them flow around him and then he picks up his speed, flowing in the choreographed pattern of the others and the puck comes to him and he turns and spins and fires a pass that is intercepted by the other team.

"Again," *the blonde haired woman says.*

The boy stands with the puck at center ice, eyes closed, mumbling to himself. He seems to be praying. His head bobs up and down, his eyes tightly closed.

Everyone watches him.

He starts but this time he moves differently. He doesn't hesitate. He doesn't look all about him. He moves quickly and firmly, as if by instinct. The puck comes to him; he stickhandles smoothly around a white defender and fires a pass to a waiting teammate. The blue team circles back into their defensive zone and he moves with his team, one piece of the machine, no different than any of the others. The referee is smiling. The boy could be one of them.

And then the boy breaks the pattern, suddenly stopping, darting apparently into the path of his own teammate but at the last moment veering away, up ice and he has shaken all of the defenders and he is alone and the puck is passed to him as he flies up the ice undefended and the white goalie readies, preparing for a blistering shot but the boy fakes with his head and shoots what resembles an off-speed baseball pitch, the puck seemingly moving in slow motion and the goalie overreacts and can't adjust and the puck flutters into the net.

His blue teammates surround him, congratulating him, patting him on his head.

The white team stands, slapping the blades of their sticks on the ice in praise.

"What happened?" Fay asks.

"He went beyond The Hockey Gods," Sly whispers in awe.

The blonde haired woman in white skates to the edge of the frozen lake, smiling at the boy's parent.

"He has been chosen to carry The Holy Puck," she says.

"Thank you," Rebecca replies. "Thank you so much."

Sam

- 28 -

The women came back into the kitchen, Rebecca in a new change of clothes. They were giggling and Rebecca tussled my hair.

"An artist," she said.

Jenny poured a finger of whiskey into two clean glasses and they drank.

"See you later," Jenny said.

"What?"

"We've decided to have a 'girls only' morning," Jenny said. "We'll be back later."

"What? Did I do something wrong?"

"I haven't done this in so long," Rebecca said, smiling. "See you in awhile."

They left the house, giggling.

Wonderful.

For Rebecca's sake, I hoped The Satanist didn't make an appearance.

I sat in the kitchen until I finished my cigar and then poured the rest of the whiskey into a glass and carried it into the living room. A James Bond movie was on cable. I sipped and watched and soon fell asleep.

- 29 -

Jenny once told me that on a good day her focus fought like a boat plowing through seas covered by a layer of ice. On bad days her focus struggled against massive waves, typhoons blasting from the ocean floor to smash air and clouds above, hurricanes colliding and annihilating life forms.

The medicines allowed her to have more good days than bad.

For me, I went through four different medicines and two different psychiatrists. Each medicine either failed to work after awhile or had a side effect I could not live with. Eventually I gave up. I decided to go forward without any pills.

I awoke with sunshine splashing about the living room and the glass of whiskey empty.

A quick shower, teeth brushed, face shaved, a fresh pot of coffee brewed and another cigar lit. My Omega watch indicated a time of twelve thirty-five. Rebecca and Jenny had not returned.

I went into the living room.

There was nothing much to do.

I could clean, I thought.

A boat on rough seas.

The sadness bubble began as a pinprick on my heart, barely noticeable, then it suddenly expanded like the universe in the first moments of the Big Bang and devoured me.

There would be images and emotions and voices: Inner Voices I called them; voices created by my mind, assaulting me.

It's all a joke, an Inner Voice said. Everything. She is playing with you.

I saw Rebecca walking into my apartment and undressing. Rebecca sat at the table in the courtroom, staring at me. Landscuda crept up behind her, leaned over her shoulder and his mouth found hers greedily.

Arnie's casket was lowered into the ground.

She will be gone at season's end, The Inner Voice told me. She'll be divorced and taking her superstar child to Minnesota or Boston or Canada. You are an attorney licensed to practice law in a flat and temperate Midwestern state far from the frozen heart lands of hockey. She won't stay for you. You won't even have the nerve to ask her to stay.

I found myself in a hotel bedroom with Teri Manyard as this season's diversion from her married life. Then I stood naked in my apartment with Rebecca knocking on the front door.

For what? The Inner Voice asked. Why is she with you? You have no looks and little personality; you offer no future for her. You are alone, like Jenny.

The bubble turned inward, becoming a black hole, sucking away hopes and dreams. The Inner Voice continued, Landscuda will have you fired for lying on the witness stand or because of Teri Manyard. You'll have nothing. Nothing.

Fear gripped me and squeezed my chest until I could barely breathe. I felt like weeping. I felt like screaming. I wanted to die.

Banging on the door.

Hope?

Rebecca?

No. A big guy, close to three hundred pounds, wearing a black Harley Davidson jacket sporting leather frills and silver studs. A tattoo of a spider web adorned his round, bald head. The man's eyes were small, his face decorated with a dark mustache and goatee and what seemed to be a perpetual snarl featuring yellowing teeth. A pick-up truck with orange flames painted on its side was parked beside Rebecca's sedan.

Unexpected visitors were becoming a bad habit, I thought.

He stared at me after I opened the front door. "Sir, are you alright? You look like shit."

I should have bought that gun years ago, I thought.

"Excuse me, but can I help you?" I asked.

His voice sounded like that of a three year old girl, high pitched and whiney. "Are you Mr. Oliver?"

"Yes. What of it?"

"Mr. Landscuda sent me. I'm one of his private investigators. Max Huber." He handed me his business card. *Serving Your Needs, Inc.* "Mr. Landscuda suggested I speak with you. May I come in?"

His black motorcycle boots left traces of dirt on the living room floor.

"Coffee?" I asked, struggling to focus and ignore the sobbing in my chest.

Max pulled a leather clad flask from his jacket. "I'm good," he said. "You?"

"No. No, thanks."

"You look like you need it, friend."

I shook my head. "How did you find the house?"

"A GPS navigator. The law firm had both of your addresses. I tried the apartment then drove out here."

Max seemed to be sitting on the entire length of the couch so I took a seat on the recliner across from him.

"So you work for Landscuda's company? I was served by one of his employees."

"Darla, my wife."

"Your wife? Really?"

"She talked me into joining the company. We met while working at a construction job but she thought we needed to change fields. Landscuda's company offered better benefits and the job was safer for her."

"Safer? How so?"

"She was bolting beams on a skyscraper a couple of hundred feet off the ground. I worked in the office, answering the telephone and doing the bookkeeping."

"Okay," I said.

"We have a lot in common. Mr. Landscuda keeps saying he won't know who to represent in our divorce but that ain't going to happen. We have too much in common."

"Do you?"

"Country music. We like to go line dancing. We both like stupid comedies."

I tried to picture the gorgeous woman who served me with the subpoena and the hulking Neanderthal sitting in my living room together, waking on a Sunday morning to read the newspaper and enjoy morning sex but I got frustrated and disgusted and gave up.

This is too fucked up, I thought. How much of that whiskey did I drink?

"So what can I do for you?" I finally asked.

"I'm doing background work on the Manyard case. Mr. Landscuda wants to find out what Mrs. Manyard has been doing during hockey road trips. You're the coach, right?"

I nodded.

"Has she been sleeping around?"

"I wouldn't know," I lied.

"Hear any of the other parents talking about her?"

"My assistant coach, Herb Rooks, told me that she has a reputation for having a good time on the road trips. But this is my first year with the team. I'm new to all of this."

"So have you seen her spending a lot of time with any of the hockey fathers?"

"Not really. She mostly hangs out with the hockey moms."

"Really?"

"Hey, you ever think maybe she's not sleeping around with a man? Maybe it's one of the other moms."

"That didn't cross my mind," Max admitted. "I'll have to consider that angle."

"Either way, I don't think I can help you much."

Max drank from his flask. "Well, if you see or hear anything, will you give me a call?"

There was the sound of a vehicle pulling up the driveway.

"Expecting anyone?" Max asked.

Rebecca, I thought. He's seen her car. Casually, I took my smartphone from my pocket.

"Got an email," I lied.

I texted Jenny a quick message. 'Keep Rebecca away from the house and car,' I typed quickly. 'Trouble here.'

Max stood and walked to the front door. I followed him and we watched the Jaguar make a U-turn.

"Must be the wrong house," I said. "Kids."

"In a hundred grand car?"

I shrugged.

Max took another shot from the flask.

"Okay," he said. "Call me if you notice anything."

"Sure."

We shook hands and he left.

You are so fucked, The Inner Voice said. You are going to lose your job. You are going to lose everything.

Another sadness bubble burst open.

"Leave me alone!" I shouted into the air.

On a bad day, my mind was an endless scream.

- 30 -

Rebecca didn't stay. "I need to do some things at my house," she explained. "I'll see you soon."

"Sure."

She kissed me on the cheek and was gone.

She never said what she and Jenny had been doing for the last five hours. I tried calling Jenny but she never answered her phone.

- 31 -

On Monday morning Cowboy Jake and I met in one of our law firm's small conference rooms. Jake had spread out on the table the discovery responses we had received from Joey Balton. They included questions he had answered under oath and copies of the documents we demanded he provide us. In a few minutes we would be talking by telephone to the experts retained on behalf of Meredith Balton for the case.

I sat down with my cup of coffee across from Cowboy Jake. The telephone was surrounded by stacks of bank statements, tax returns, credit card statements and pounds of other papers that recorded the financial life of the Baltons.

"Well, what did you find out?" I asked.

"I looked at all of the financial papers we got from the quarterback as well as the documents that Meredith got us. Nothing seems out of place. These people save more money than they spend and Meredith does most of the spending. She likes fancy clothing and jewelry. Females."

"Kind of stereotypical to say that."

"Maybe but it's what they do. He's the thrifty one. He's maxing out his retirement plans and also set up IRAs for himself and Meredith. They also got some hefty education funds for the kids."

I asked, "Any unexplained receipt of monies into the accounts?"

"Nope," Cowboy Jake said. "Just his pay from the football team and from off-the-field stuff he does, like his radio program and being a spokesman for companies. There's really nothing unusual here."

"So what do you think is going on?"

Cowboy Jake shrugged. "He ain't playing well. He's either doing it on purpose or he's just not that good anymore."

"Other than for gambling purposes why would he play bad on purpose?"

"You want me to be cynical?" Cowboy Jake asked.

"Sure."

"Well, his contract is up this year. If he plays bad he'll only get a one or two year deal from the Mohawks or some other team for a much lower salary. The trial court will use that lower salary to determine his maintenance obligation to Meredith. If he suddenly starts playing great again after those one or two years are up, he'll be in line for one more huge contract. If his salary increases Meredith will be able to go back to the trial court and get more child support but the trial court can't increase her maintenance. He'll be locked into paying her at a lower amount."

I nodded. Under the laws of our state, once the trial court set a monthly amount of maintenance, Meredith could not go back to the trial court to get the monthly amount increased. It could be reduced but not increased.

"I did think of that," I said. "But that doesn't really make sense. Even if Balton has to pay more in maintenance, if he played well and signed a new, huge contract, he'd still end up putting more money into his bank account with each paycheck. He'd still, in the end, be better off. There's no financial reason for him to play badly."

"You're the lawyer," Cowboy Jake said.

He dialed the first telephone number. This expert was involved in sports betting and had been recommended to us by Milton Farmers, the agent who accompanied Meredith to our previous meeting.

"Sonny Hendricks here," a suave voice answered.

I introduced myself.

"I have been looking at the data," the betting expert said. "I've been taking a hard look at the betting on the Mohawk games for this season and the past season. There's nothing unusual."

"Are you sure?"

"The amount of money bet on the games in Las Vegas seems about normal. I've spoken to friends involved with offshore gambling and Internet gambling and they tell me the same thing."

"What about the game results as compared to the points spread?"

"Nothing unusual there either. The Mohawks are not supposed to have a good year. Their defense is getting very old and they lost a few offensive playmakers. They were only supposed to win about six or seven games this year."

"But what about the point spread?"

"Nothing unusual there, either. They haven't deviated from the point spread more than most teams. They're covering the spread at about the same rate as in past years. Looking at the numbers, I can't say anything unusual is going on."

"What about the point spread itself? Does it look like the number is out of whack?"

"I know what you guys are thinking. You think the quarterback is throwing games away. The point spread looks fine, too. It seems to be taking into account that the quarterback is not playing well. So his bad play is built into the spread. There's just nothing unusual there."

We talked for a few more minutes but gained no new information.

I thanked him and hung up.

"Maybe he's just getting old and he sucks," Cowboy Jake suggested. "If it's on purpose and it's not for gambling then what the hell is going on?"

"There could still be gambling but there's just not a lot of money being bet on the thrown games."

"If there ain't a lot of money being bet then it ain't a gambling issue."

"So then what the hell is it?" I asked.

"Maybe he is just getting old."

Cowboy Jake placed the second call. This expert also came to us from the sports agent. He had been a 'quarterback guru' for the past thirty years, coaching only quarterbacks for professional and college teams.

"I've looked at the team's game films," the quarterback coach told us. "I spoke to contacts around the league and managed to get the films for all of the team's games during the last two seasons and this season. Balton had missed two games over that time span but that's still thirty five games to look at."

"What are the team's game films?" I asked.

"Those are the films that each home team makes of each game. They aren't part of the television network feeds. The team's game film shows the entire football field and the coaches can see the position of every single player during each play. These are the films exchanged between teams during the season."

"So what did you find out?" Cowboy Jake asked.

"There is something strange going on. I'm just not sure what it is. Balton's mechanics seem fine. They haven't changed since two seasons ago and his velocity on the football seems fine, too. But I analyzed plays from this year and the past two years and one can say that his accuracy is off."

"What do you mean?"

"Well, for example, there's one play the Mohawks like to run where a receiver on Balton's right will run ten yards and then cut hard to the near sideline. Two seasons ago, Balton would throw the ball in the exact same spot for each play. If the receiver got there when he was supposed to, the ball would strike the receiver right in the chest. Last season and this season, however, Balton's off. The Mohawks have run the play 15 times this year. Each time Balton has thrown the ball, he's off. The ball is either a foot or two in front of the receiver or a foot or two behind him. Balton's not throwing it in the same place."

"Is it on purpose?"

"His footwork and throwing mechanics and the velocity on the ball have not changed. There does not seem to be any physical reason why the ball isn't being thrown accurately."

"So he's intentionally missing?"

"I'd say by a foot or two. It's not blatant but he's got some young receivers and they are having trouble adjusting to the throws. If the throws aren't perfect they aren't catching them. Plus, when Balton throws a foot or two behind the receiver the ball can be intercepted."

"So Balton actually is being accurate. He's missing on purpose."

"I'd have to say so."

"But why?"

"I don't have a clue."

I felt like I had received all the information the expert could provide.

"We made need to explain all of this to a judge at trial," I said. "And the judge may not grasp the finer aspects of quarterback play. Is there some kind of visual presentation you can do beside your testimony?"

"Sure," the expert said. "I can prepare a computer video comparing the same play from the World Championship season and this season, and that will show the difference in where the quarterback is throwing the ball."

"That would be good," I said. "And can you do that for a number of plays so the judge can clearly see what's going on?"

"I can do better than that. I can do that video and then do another video where I can telestrate the differences in the throws. I can even juxtapose one play from last season over one play from this season so the judge can clearly see the difference in ball placement. I have software that lets me do it. It's the same software Professional Football League teams use to instruct their players during team meetings."

"That would be very helpful to our case. Can you do that and send them to me to review?"

"Absolutely. Apple or PC computers?

"The courthouse uses PC computers."

"Okay."

The conversation ended. I looked over the stacks of financial statements, telephone bills and other documents. "Are you sure there's nothing else in here that can help us?" I asked Cowboy Jake.

"I'm happy to look at it again. Hell, our client can afford for me to look at it three or four more times. However, I don't think I'm going to find anything."

"Do it anyway. If you see anything that looks strange, mark-it and we'll talk about it with Meredith. Also, send her a copy of all of this. Let her look at it, too."

"Sure thing," Cowboy Jake said.

Offhand, I remarked, "So have you brought in any empty boxes in case Landscuda decides to treat you like he treated Brandy?"

Cowboy Jake shook his head to the negative. "I'm feeling a little more comfortable in my employment position," he said.

"Why's that?"

He looked at me. "Didn't you know about the Landsluts?"

"What about them?"

"They've been going to law school at night. I hear they will be taking the bar exam next fall. Once they pass it they won't be working as Landsucker's secretary and paralegal anymore. I imagine they'll be looking for jobs as attorneys."

"Attorneys?"

Cowboy Jake nodded. "No offense, but maybe you should be the one looking for boxes."

- 32 -

It's cold, I told myself. She wouldn't be smoking outside tonight even if bundled up in winter clothing. She's inside. I entered the lobby of the Ice Kingdom on Tuesday night. Rebecca was nowhere in sight.

She doesn't want to see you, an Inner Voice said to me. She would be here if she wanted to see you.

I paused for a moment in the lobby, looking about. Teri Manyard was talking to a tall brunette and they both turned in my direction. She's talking to Darla, I realized, the woman who served me with the subpoena. Max's spouse. Teri waved and they walked up to me.

So Max is checking out the girl-on-girl angle, I thought.

"Good evening, coach," Teri said.

"Hey."

"I want to introduce you to Darla Wright. She and her family are moving here from Wisconsin and her son is a hockey player. She came to the rink and was hoping to talk to someone about our program."

Teri told Darla my name and that I was doing a great job coaching the boys this season.

I smiled at Darla, nodded and took a quick look at my watch. "I need to be on the ice soon and I need to talk to the players beforehand. Maybe we can talk later, after practice?"

"I'm going to stay and watch practice," Darla said. "Afterward sounds great."

"Sure thing."

I walked away.

Inside the arena Herb waited for me outside the team's locker room.

"Can we talk?" he asked.

Where was Rebecca? I wondered.

She doesn't want to be with you, an Inner Voice repeated.

"Coach, can we talk?" Herb asked again.

I wanted to say 'no.' I did not want to deal with Herb at the moment.

Where was Rebecca?

"About what?" I asked.

"I really need to talk to you about Andy. I'm really concerned. This season is not going well. My wife is concerned, too."

"Look, what if we talk after practice? Does that sound okay?"

"Sure."

"Is Rebecca here?" I asked.

Herb looked at me. "No. She had the nanny bring Donnie again. Why, do you need to tell her something today?"

"No. Just asking."

He looked at me strangely, shrugged and we walked into the locker room.

During practice I saw Teri and Darla in the stands talking. She can't possibly be telling Darla about her extramarital affairs, I thought. There's just no way she would do that.

Hell, an Inner Voice said. Maybe that's a good selling point. Maybe Teri is telling her that if your son joins this team you'll get to score off the ice as often as your son scores on the ice.

During practice I tried to spend as much time as possible working with Andy and his linemates. Donnie and his linemates didn't need my attention at the moment; they were scoring plenty of goals without any instruction from me at all. Andy looked good at practice and I made sure to give him pointers on shooting and passing. The problem wasn't Andy, however. The problem was the expectations of Andy's parents, especially his father. Andy was a good player. He just was not exhibiting the skills, talent and determination necessary for a college scholarship or a pro career. Those qualities, especially the talent, were either inside the player or not. No coach could create them. The Hockey Gods would either bless Andy and he would be a late bloomer or they wouldn't. Based on the odds it likely was not going to happen.

Practice ended. Herb and I stood outside the locker room while the boys entered to change.

"Can we talk now?" Herb asked.

"Sure," I said.

I looked around and saw Michael Williams talking to a group of men. I waved him over. "Can you go into the locker and watch the boys and make sure everyone stays calm in there?" I asked him. "Herb and I need to talk."

"Sure thing, coach," Michael said. "Anything going on?"

"No, we're just discussing some strategy for this weekend's games."

"We're going to crush them this weekend, right?" Michael asked.

"Sure hope so."

"By more than twelve goals?"

"Right," I said. "Twelve goals."

"Good," Michael said. "Twelve."

I walked with Herb and checked the locker room assignment board. Locker room #2 at the other end of the rink was empty. We wandered down to that locker room where we could talk privately, without anyone else around.

I opened the door and we stepped inside. Herb turned on the light as the door swung shut behind us.

Teri and Darla lay on the floor, most of their clothes off, their mouths locked together and their hands roaming over various body parts. Human music filled the room, a song coming from the throats of both women, a rhythmic moaning, together.

Herb and I stood there, speechless.

The women broke apart quickly, looked at one another and then at us and then about the room as if to determine if there were any other intruders. Darla made a half hearted gesture to put on her bra but gave up and tossed it on the floor.

"Excuse me," I said. "Sorry. We'll go elsewhere."

"No, wait a minute," Teri said.

"No, it's okay. We'll go elsewhere. I'll talk to Darla about our hockey program later."

Darla stepped forward.

"You didn't see anything, alright?" she asked me.

"Absolutely not," I responded.

Herb looked at Teri and Darla and slowly said, "I guess not."

Darla walked up to Herb. She wore only her red thong panties. "You didn't see anything, right?"

Herb looked about. "I understand there is a divorce going on and I don't want to get involved. I won't tell anyone, okay?"

Darla said, "You're not going to tell anyone even if you are asked on a witness stand, right?"

Herb looked at me. "He's the lawyer. Ask him, but I don't think I can promise that."

Darla reached behind Herb and locked the door.

"Yes," Darla said. "You can."

She kneeled down before Herb and grabbed onto his sweatpants.

"Hey!" Herb said.

Darla looked up at him. "This is just between us, okay? No one needs to know what you saw or what we're going to do together now."

"My kid needs a ride home."

"This will just take a moment," Darla said. "But it will be a moment you will never forget."

"What about them?"

Teri walked over to me. She was wearing her bra and panties. She got on her knees as well and pulled down my sweatpants.

"See," Teri said to Herb. "Everyone is in the same position."

"Same position?" Herb asked.

"Yes. No one is going to say anything at all."

You're going to be disbarred, The Inner Voice told me. You're going to be disbarred. And worse, what if Rebecca finds out?

- 33 -

The next day I received a telephone call at the office from Hugo Gerald of Gerald & Gerald. Hugo and his spouse were the lead partners at their firm, and they only handled divorces involving very wealthy people. I had dealt with Hugo on a number of divorce cases. He always had been forthright and honest with me.

"I understand you represent Jason Storm," he said.

The Physics Guy, I thought. "Yes, we do."

"We represent his wife."

"Okay."

"I'm calling to see if Mr. Storm plans on filing his petition for divorce anytime soon."

"We have not prepared a petition and at present we don't plan on filing one anytime soon," I replied.

"That's interesting because our client also has instructed us not to file a petition. It looks like we have two clients who like to speak to their divorce attorneys but neither is making any effort to get a divorce."

"That seems to be the case."

"Your firm represents Meredith Balton, the quarterback's wife, right? I know you do. It's a matter of public record."

"We do," I said. "From the public record I know your firm represents the quarterback."

"Yes, we do," the other lawyer replied. After a pause, "I know you can't tell me, but does Mr. Storm talk to you about the quarterback's case?

"That would be protected by attorney-client privilege. I couldn't tell you one way or the other."

"Enough said. For the quarterback's case we are hoping to get you a comprehensive settlement proposal within the next few weeks."

"That would be good. I think the case might be easier to settle if Meredith received the first offer as opposed to Meredith having to make the first one."

"Agreed. In terms of the children have you heard of any problems?"

"No. It seems the Baltons are trying to keep the kids out of the divorce. From what I understand they are co-parenting very well."

"That's what I've heard," the other lawyer said.

"Well, we look forward to receiving a settlement proposal. We'll discuss it with Meredith."

"Sounds good. And if anything comes up in regard to Mr. Storm's case, please let us know."

He hung up.

He's worried, I thought. He's worried about something having to do with The Physics Guy's wife and the handling of the quarterback's divorce case. He was getting the same message from The Physics Guy's wife that I was getting from The Physics Guy.

What the hell was going on here?

It was time to find out.

- 34 -

I met them at the sports bar by the office. Darla wore a black cocktail dress with a pearl necklace. Max was outfitted in his studded Harley gear. We sat down at a booth and ordered iced tea and coffee from the waitress.

They sat beside each other, looking as different as two people could be.

What did Teri tell Darla? I wondered. What did the two women do after Herb and I left the locker room, both of us embarrassed yet extremely satisfied? Did Teri tell Darla about her affair with me?

"I'm glad you could meet me," I told them.

"We're always looking for someone to do," Darla told me with a smile.

"Excuse me?"

"What?" Max asked.

"Someone to do?" I said.

Darla laughed. "I meant something to do," she replied. "Something to do."

Max put his beefy arm around her shoulders, small black eyes locked onto my face.

"Oh," I said. "Okay."

Max continued to stare at me and hug his wife.

"So what did you think of our locker room escapade?" Darla asked.

"What escapade?"

"It's okay," Max said slowly. "I know all about it. Darla told me."

"Do you? You know all about it?"

"Who looks better in their underwear: Darla or Teri Manyard?" Max asked.

"Darla, of course."

"That's what I thought," Max said.

I opened my mouth to ask a question but Max shook his head, baring yellow teeth at me. "You don't want to ask me anything," he said.

"Okay."

I handed them each a contract and explained the situation. I told them about the Balton divorce case and the quarterback's recent accuracy troubles, about The Physics Guy and his implied threats, and about the visit to The Ranch Retreat by the mafia and our talk of sports betting.

"We need to find out why the quarterback is intentionally playing badly," I said. "Are you guys willing to take this case?"

"I assume you've looked into the betting angle," Darla said.

"We have. Betting on football games does not appear to be the reason for his play."

"Interesting," Max said. "And you don't know anything about The Physics Guy or his connection to the quarterback?"

"Just the little he's told me," I said.

Darla and Max exchanged looks. "Maybe Darla could do some checking up on this Physics Guy," Max suggested.

"Is he good looking?" Darla asked.

Max shot me an evil glare.

"I hope he's good looking," Darla said.

- 35 -

My hockey team had three games in St. Louis that weekend. On the four hour drive to the first game I pondered my own financial situation. The Ranch Retreat was paid for and The White Apartment only had a one year lease. I had been maximizing my retirement plan contributions during my time with the law firm and also had built up somewhat of a nest egg. Even though I lost money as a result of my divorce I probably still had enough liquid assets to get me through a couple of years if I lived frugally.

If need be, I thought, I could even open up my own shop. I didn't generate a lot of business each year but I probably could pay myself a salary of about sixty thousand dollars if I opened up a small office on my own, after paying a part-time assistant, malpractice insurance, office rent and supplies. It clearly would have to be a pretty low budget operation.

But I was used to the fancy law firm life and all of the assistance and perks it provided. I was used to a steady and hefty income. I didn't want to lose that.

Do you really want to be completely on your own? an Inner Voice asked. At least with the law firm there are other people around and a fairly stable environment in which you worked. What would you do if you had to create your own environment? Could you do it? Would you be able to make it or would your inner demons finally take control, if you had to spend so many hours alone?

My thoughts were interrupted by my cell phone.

"Hello," I said.

"Hi. I was hoping you'd have a few minutes to speak with me."

"Who is this?"

"Henry Warren. I'm Donnie's dad."

I didn't respond.

"Your firm no longer represents Rebecca so I thought it would be okay if we talked."

"Even though Rebecca fired us there's still attorney-client privilege," I told him. "I can't tell you anything about your case or anything that she told me."

"I don't want to talk about the divorce and I don't want to talk about her. I want to talk about my son and hockey."

"Are you going to be at the games this weekend?" I asked, hoping the answer was no. I had been looking forward to spending some time alone with Rebecca.

"No," he said. "What if I met you at your office?"

"My office? That might be a little awkward since we represented Rebecca."

"I know. That's why I want to meet there. You can have one of your assistants join us for the meeting. That way it will be clear that nothing unethical is happening."

I thought about it.

"That's fine. I think I have some time this Monday in the afternoon. Why don't you call the offices on Monday morning and ask for my paralegal, Jake. He'll schedule the meeting and probably join us for it."

"Okay. Thanks. I appreciate it." He hung up.

Put the call out of your mind, I thought as I tossed the cell phone on the passenger seat. Forget about him. Don't let him spoil your weekend with Rebecca.

- 36 -

The team's first game was at a new complex built as a partnership between the local township and a Fortune 500 corporation headquartered in St. Louis. As a result, the complex was the finest in the city. Two rinks were housed within the complex, one of which had stadium seating for 5,000 people and which could be the home for a minor league professional hockey team. The other rink, not as lavish, still seated several hundred.

The complex also managed to make a deal with a large mail order hockey equipment supplier. Via the Internet and telephone sales, the hockey supplier sold equipment throughout the United States and Europe. The supplier made the pro shop within the complex its main brick and mortar store and it became the flagship of its business. If someone wanted to buy hockey equipment hands-on and obtain the advice of knowledgeable staff, that pro shop was the place to go. The store itself featured ten thousand square feet of showroom space and was connected to the stadium arena though the main complex lobby.

Inside the cavernous lobby, the usual groups clustered. The hockey moms stood to one side drinking from their travel mugs. A good number of hockey dads were either talking in small groups or walking through the pro shop, studying the merchandise.

I noticed Herb and April Rooks near the store's entrance, talking heatedly but trying to keep their voices low. Herb had a beseeching look on his face while April fumed like a volcano ready to erupt.

They saw me. April scowled, said a few more words to Herb and began stalking towards me. Herb gave me a pitiful glance and ducked into the pro shop.

"Are you happy?" April asked me. Her eyes were red.

"Depends on the day," I answered.

She pointed to the pro shop. "We were saving money to go to Hawaii; a second honeymoon, this summer."

"I hear Hawaii is beautiful although I've yet to go there."

"That makes two of us," she snarled. "And it's not going to change anytime soon, thanks to you."

She stomped away.

Andy and his father came out of the pro shop laden with new hockey gloves, new shoulder pads, new top-of-the line Bauer skates and two new graphite hockey sticks.

"Afternoon coach," Herb said.

"Hi," Andy said. He looked sad even though he would soon be wearing and holding over a thousand dollars of new gear.

It's never the player's fault, I thought. Always blame the equipment.

- 37 -

I had an idea.

Rebecca wore her usual game day attire: black sweatpants, running shoes and a hoodie. She sat by herself near the concessions stand sipping from what was supposed to be a cup of coffee.

I hadn't seen her since the time we spent together at The Ranch Retreat. I wanted to lean down and kiss her but knew I could not. I wanted to devour her.

I sat down beside her.

"Hey," she said, smiling.

I tried to ignore the churning of my heart. This was business. I was The Coach.

"Donnie's sick," I told her.

"What!"

"In the locker room before the game, he's going to tell me that he feels nauseous. He may need to sit out for awhile."

"How do you know he's sick? You haven't even been to the locker room yet!"

"Call it ESP."

"Explain."

"The team we are about to play has won just two games all year. Their coach put them in the wrong division. I called around this week. They should be playing in the 'A' division but their coach had dreams of grandeur and put them in the 'AA' division. This is going to be a massacre."

"Another one of your coaching ideas?" she asked after a few moments of thought.

"Trust me."

"Okay. I trust you."

I stood to leave.

"Tonight?" she asked.

I soared.

"Of course."

I walked away from the table, gestured to Michael Williams and pointed towards the rink doors. He followed me inside.

"The game doesn't start for another forty-five minutes," I said. "That should be plenty of time."

"For what?" he asked.

"Think three goals, not twelve or so."

"Three?"

"Donnie isn't going to play."

"Shit."

"Hurry," I told him. "You're going to have to adjust the spread. Oh, and I need a cup of coffee. Have someone bring it to the bench just before the game starts."

In the locker room Herb was lacing up Andy's new skates. I took the skates from him and put them to the side. "Never wear new skates for a game," I said. "He'll need to break them in at practice over the next few weeks."

Both he and Andy looked stunned.

"Trust me," I said. I fished around Andy's hockey bag and pulled out the old skates. Old, I thought. Not really. They were probably bought just a few months ago, but they weren't 'top-of-the-line' anymore.

Donnie was already dressed. I caught his eye.

Outside the locker room, he looked up at me through the steel bars of his facemask. I bent down so our eyes were level.

"Remember how we put those two big kids on your line, for protection? Remember how that worked so well?"

"Yes, coach."

"Well, let's talk about what we're going to do for this game."

The Zamboni cleaned the ice and my team stood by the ice surface's entry door, waiting for the referees to grant the players permission to skate. I stood at the bench, sipping from a cup of coffee that S.S. had brought me.

After skating for a minute or so Donnie came to the bench. I nodded and he sat down, bending over so that his head almost touched his knees. I wondered if Mr. Warren would hear about this and want to sign him up for acting classes.

Herb Rooks moved to talk to Donnie but I waved him away. "Watch our goalie," I told him. "Tell me if he looks ready to play."

I watched the other team during warm-ups. They were small and slow and shot like the puck weighed a ton. Their goalie moved as if he suffered from arthritis. His head barely reached the crossbar, only four feet off the ice. The other coach was yelling at his team, exhorting them to skate harder. He was large and fat and wore a suit. Maybe after the game he was going to attend a funeral. In reality, that's what had been happening all season for him. But the decedent wasn't a relative or an old friend but his team.

The buzzer sounded, the referees checked the nets for loose pucks and the teams gathered near their coaches at their respective benches.

"We have a problem," I told my team. "Donnie is sick: stomach flu or something. We're playing this game without him."

Donnie brought his head up from his knees, faked a cough, grasped his helmet with both gloves and slumped back down.

Acting lessons for sure, I thought.

"Andy, we need you. You'll play with your line and with Manyard and Williams. Are you up for it?"

Andy looked to his father who suddenly was beaming.

"Yes, coach!"

"Okay. Let's do it!"

"Our goalie looks like he's in the zone," Herb confided in me. "We should be golden."

"Thanks, Herb. I really needed to hear that."

Andy skated towards center ice with Manyard and Williams.

The referee dropped the puck.

The game began.

I thought the coffee was spiked. I drank it anyway.

"Your husband called me," I said. "He wants to meet at my offices on Monday."

"About what?"

"He didn't say."

Donnie's health had improved for our game that evening. We won, 13 to 3. Michael Williams gave me a thumbs-up sign when I left the rink.

"Are you going to meet him?"

I handed her a glass of wine. She sat in the plush guest chair in a corner by the window, and I turned the desk chair to face her. Our feet shared the hotel room's ottoman.

The bed, still made with pillows arranged neatly against the headboard, took up much of the room. "Sure," I replied. "Why not?" She wore the Shooters' hoodie and dark sweat pants. Donnie slept alone in their hotel room.

"I don't think it's about you. I think it's just about Donnie."

"Maybe he wants you to become a chess coach."

I laughed. "Only if he doesn't want Donnie to ever win another game."

We finished our glasses and I poured more Merlot.

"You might be getting an offer," Rebecca said.

"About what?"

"That Minnesota high school coach found out that Donnie likes playing for you. There might be an offer to keep coaching him as an assistant if he goes to high school there."

"What does that pay?"

"Not much."

"I'm not licensed to practice law in Minnesota."

"I've been promised a very good job near the school. Maybe you'll just live with me as my sex slave."

"What does that pay?"

She slowly licked the rim of the wine glass.

"Okay," I said.

She laughed. "Besides, maybe you could be Donnie's agent. You'd get ten percent of his contract."

"Hey, I know he's good, more than good. But an NHL player? There's no way to tell. He's ten."

"We can dream."

"Everyone can dream."

"Which brings us to Sly."

"Who?"

"Let me freshen up." She put down the glass and walked into the bathroom, my eyes tracking every step.

I stood, paced, drank more wine and turned out the lights except for the lamp on the desk.

"My dad really wanted that for me," I called to the bathroom door.

"So do most dads," she called back.

"Except for your husband."

"Except for him."

She stepped out of the bathroom wearing one of the world's skimpiest blue bikinis and a blonde wig. "Call me Fay," she said in a throaty voice.

I walked to her.

"Call me Sly," I replied.

- 39 -

"Are you and Mr. Prickles becoming buddies?" the receptionist asked me as I entered the law firm lobby on Monday morning.

"Not that I know of," I answered. "Why?"

"He and Mr. Lanscuda want to see you. Now."

Wonderful, I thought.

Landscuda and Prickles were up in Prickles's office, smoking cigars on the couch. They both looked at me.

"Morning," I said.

"What?" Landscuda said. "You didn't bring me coffee?"

"I didn't know we were meeting."

Prickles said, "Are you sure about that?"

"Excuse me?"

"You didn't know we'd be meeting this morning?"

"No. Why?"

"I take it you don't read the local newspaper."

"Usually not. The newspaper doesn't deliver out where I live in the country."

"What about the local news on television or the Internet?" Prickles asked. "Hell, don't you make any effort to keep informed? That's how a lawyer attracts business—by always knowing what's going on in town!"

"What's this about?"

Prickles gestured to Landscuda.

My immediate supervisor blew smoke into the air.

"You might want to sit down," Landscuda said. "It's been in the newspaper and on television this morning and I already received a call from the sheriff's office. They want to talk to you."

"Why?"

"Henry Warren, the husband of your former client. A neighbor found his body last night. He's been murdered."

Period Three

FULL CONTACT

Sam

- 1 -

The voicemail light on my office phone blinked rapidly, signifying a number of messages.

During the day while I was at work I forwarded my cell phone calls to the office phone. It made it easier to take personal calls from Jenny at work; if I was on the office phone no one could tell if I was speaking to a client or someone else.

I listened to the messages.

Jenny wanted to know if I needed to retain a criminal defense lawyer.

Hope the cops don't ever talk to her, I thought.

Michael Williams wanted to know Donnie's status for the upcoming games as soon as possible.

Herb Rooks wanted to know the same and whether he should keep Andy home from school for the rest of the season in case Donnie wasn't emotionally ready to play, so Andy would be able to log the extra ice time and lead our team to victory.

A deputy sheriff asked for a return call, saying it was important.

There was no message from Rebecca, either on the office phone or my cell phone. That made sense, I thought. She was dealing with a child who just lost his father and even though they were divorcing he had been her husband for many years. There would be the five stages of grief starting all over again for her, not for the loss of a marriage but for the loss of a human being.

The telephone rang.

"Hello, Sam Oliver," I said.

"Morning," Rebecca replied, sounding bright and chipper. "How are you doing?"

"Well, uh, I guess fine. How are you and Donnie holding up?"

"We'll be okay. I'm going to need to find a twenty-four hour nanny, though. Henry won't be available anymore to watch Donnie when I want to spend the night away from home."

"That's true," I replied slowly. "Have the police found out anything yet?"

"Don't know. Hey, I bet some of your clients who become single moms need overnight help. Do you know how I can find a nanny who will stay overnight?"

"I can check with our paralegal," I replied.

"That would be great."

I'm talking to her about babysitting arrangements because her husband was murdered, I thought.

"Listen, the reason I called is I don't want anything to change," she said.

"Anything to change?"

"Henry's parents are flying into town in a few hours. They'll be spending the week here, packing up the belongings I give them, stuff like that. Donnie will be out of school and will stay with them at their hotel tonight."

I didn't respond.

"I hope it's okay but he'll probably miss a few practices. Henry's parents will go apeshit if Donnie's on the ice this week. It's crazy. They should be thrilled for the opportunity to watch him skate."

Thrilled.

"That's okay," I said. "Do whatever you think is best for him."

"So I'll see you tonight at your apartment? Say, eight o'clock?"

"Rebecca, your husband was murdered. How will it look?"

"We slept together before he died. We'll sleep together after he died. I don't care how it looks."

"Well . . . ."

"Don't you want to comfort me during these difficult times?" she asked.

Not much to think about there. "I'll see you tonight," I said.

She hung up.

Fuck.

- 2 -

The Physics Guy called and demanded a morning appointment.

"I can shoot him," Cowboy Jake offered, holding his pistols in both hands and twirling them around like batons. "We can make it look like self-defense."

"We haven't spent his entire retainer yet," I reasoned. "Let's wait until he owes the firm money and stops paying his bill. Then you can shoot him."

"Spoil sport."

He was standing in one of the conference rooms, sipping coffee, dressed in tan slacks and a button down shirt. "Have you ever seen the *Saw* movies?" The Physics Guy asked.

"No."

"They are about this serial killer who puts people into complicated torture devices. For example, the device may give the victim the choice of say, cutting off his arm to escape or being doused with gasoline and lit on fire. The victim has only so many minutes to decide or the choice will be made for him. The gasoline will be poured. The flame will be lit."

"And your point?"

"Just making conversation," he said.

I sat down. He continued to stand.

"Have you read the morning newspaper?" he asked. "There was a murder last night. I think you knew the victim. Your law firm used to represent his wife, correct?"

"Are you threatening me?"

The Physics Guy acted insulted. "Of course not."

"So what's your point? Why are we having these stupid meetings? Why did you have to see me this morning?"

"Are you feeling alright?" he asked. "You seem upset."

"Who the fuck are you and what do you want from me?"

"Don't be upset," he said. "If you're upset then I'm upset. Then everyone is upset. Remember, we're all one."

"So we were all murdered last night?"

He didn't miss a beat. "A part of us changed form. We changed from animate matter to inanimate matter. To us and the universe in general, nothing more happened."

"So that's it?" I asked testily. "Death is no big deal? It's just a change in the classification of matter?"

The Physics Guy finished his coffee and heading for the door. "We all die, one day," he said. "The important question is: what do we achieve while we are here?"

- 3 -

The sheriff's department was across the street from the courthouse. I agreed to meet one of the deputies during the lunch hour.

The deputies of the sheriff's department all had one thing in common: they were bulky and huge. Even the women deputies looked like power lifters. I was sure the deputy I met had to get his socks custom fitted to pull over his calf muscles.

We sat down in one of the interrogation rooms. It was the only room available, he told me. He introduced himself as J. Wales. Flat top hair cut on a square head, he could have been either a Professional Football League lineman or a strong man in a circus.

"Terrible thing," Deputy Wales said. "What did you think of the condition of the body?"

"What condition?"

"The way we found Mr. Warren."

"I don't know how you found Mr. Warren."

"He was in a terrible condition," Wales said.

"If you say so."

"You ever meet him?"

"I met him at a hearing in the Warren divorce case. I had been subpoenaed to testify as the hockey coach for his son."

"Donnie, right?"

"Yes."

"He's supposed to be a very good player."

"He's a great player," I said.

"Is that the only time you ever dealt with Mr. Warren?"

"Well, not exactly. This weekend, on Saturday he called wanting to meet with me to discuss Donnie."

"You mean to discuss Rebecca Warren and the divorce case."

"He said he wanted to talk about Donnie."

"What about Donnie?"

"I don't know. We were going to meet today at my law offices."

"Why at your offices?"

"That's where he wanted to meet."

"To talk about Donnie?"

"That's what he said."

"You believed him?"

I shrugged. "I did."

"Pretty nasty divorce case, isn't it?"

"I wouldn't know. Our firm was fired at the beginning of the case. And you know attorney-client privilege prevents me from telling you anything that our former client said about the divorce."

"I'm not going to ask you to breach attorney-client privilege," Wales said. "Yet."

He had a manila folder in front of him containing what appeared to be a hand written police report and several yellow pages of notes.

"Why did you want to speak with me?" I asked.

"Your name came up."

"From who?"

He smiled at me. "From someone." He looked over his notes. "And your relationship with Ms. Warren?"

Fuck, I thought. I knew this was coming.

"When?"

He glanced up at me, a brief look of surprise on his face. "When?" he asked.

"Well," I said. "I met her when she came to our law firm to retain me in the divorce. However, she fired our firm a few days later and I became the coach for Donnie's hockey team."

"How did that happen?"

"I met her at the rink while I was still her attorney to watch Donnie play. I guess I said some things about Donnie and the hockey team that she liked. Apparently, she pulled some strings and got me appointed as the head coach."

"You know hockey?"

"I played when I was a boy. I played a couple of years for my college. I coached for a few years after law school. I know the people who run the local hockey association."

"That is very interesting," he said. "So she fired you?"

"Yes."

"And so you basically know her as Donnie's hockey coach?"

"That's correct."

"Do you talk a lot with her at the rink?"

"We don't talk very much at the rink," I said. "We talk elsewhere."

"You talk elsewhere?" Wales asked.

"It was a travel hockey team. We talked on some road trips when the team played away games."

"Oh, of course."

"And at my apartment," I admitted.

"You talked at your apartment?"

"She showed up one night, uninvited."

"Why?"

"I never got around to asking her."

"Why not?"

"We ended up sleeping together."

Now he really looked surprised. "You slept with Rebecca Warren?"

"Yes."

"At your apartment. She spent the night?"

"Yes."

"Where was Donnie?"

"I guess with his dad."

He was frowning. "Do you want to keep going?"

"We had a game a week ago on a Saturday. After the game Donnie went to his dad's house and Rebecca came to my house out in the country. She spent the night."

"You're having an affair with Rebecca Warren?"

"I'm not sure it's an affair."

"You slept with her twice?"

"Three times," I said. "We also spent time together this Saturday afternoon at the hotel in St Louis."

"St. Louis?"

"The team had games in St. Louis on Saturday and Sunday. On Saturday night we were together in my hotel room."

"You're having an affair with Rebecca Warren."

"I don't know what to call it."

"You're sleeping with her."

"Yes."

"You're having an affair."

"She's getting divorced and I'm not married."

"You're having an affair."

"Fine. Sure. Yes."

He began writing on a new sheet of yellow paper.

"Maybe I should hire myself a lawyer," I chuckled.

He did not chuckle back.

"You make a habit of sleeping with moms on your hockey team?" Wales asked.

I tapped my fingers on the table. "How do you define habit?" I asked.

He didn't look surprised anymore. He looked angry. "More than once."

"Once? Do you mean more than once with the same woman or with more than one woman?"

"I think we already established the former."

"I slept with Teri Manyard."

"Who?"

"Sean Manyard is one of Donnie's line mates. They play together during the game."

"Teri Manyard plays with Donnie?"

"No. Donnie plays with her son. Teri is the mom."

"And you sleep with Teri Manyard during the games?"

"No. I'm coaching during the games. I slept with Teri at the team hotel or at my apartment."

"Your apartment and these hotels seem to get a lot of action."

"I guess."

"Who else knows about this?" Wales asked.

"I don't know," I replied. "Hopefully, no one."

"Does Rebecca know you're sleeping with Teri Manyard?"

219

"Was sleeping with her. Not anymore."

"Are you sure?"

"Well, not exactly."

"What do you mean—not exactly?"

"Well, in the locker room this past Tuesday we had oral sex."

"You both had oral sex?"

"Teri did the oral part. I guess I had the sex."

"In the locker room with your hockey team watching?"

"We had oral sex in another locker room."

"Does anybody else know about this?"

"My assistant coach for the hockey team."

"Your assistant coach knows about this?"

"He was having oral sex, too."

"What? With Teri Manyard?"

"No. With a private investigator our firm hired."

"A private investigator your firm hired to have oral sex with your assistant coach?"

"No. She was hired for another case not having anything to do with Rebecca. You realize this is all protected by attorney-client privilege."

"But regardless, your firm paid a private investigator to have oral sex with your assistant hockey coach?"

"No. Well, I'm not sure if she's going to bill us for the time she spent giving oral sex to my assistant coach. I can check on that, if you'd like."

"We'll see about that," Wales said. "I suppose Mr. Manyard is alive and well or should I check with homicide?"

"He's alive. Our firm is representing him in his divorce."

"The divorce from who?"

"From his wife: Teri Manyard."

"You're getting a blow job from Teri Manyard while your firm is representing Mr. Manyard in their divorce?

"Something like that."

Wales closed the manila folder. "Maybe you should talk to a lawyer."

"I don't need one. Other than being a complete fool, I haven't done anything wrong."

"What about this weekend? You said there was a game on Sunday."

"Yes."

"Was Rebecca there?"

"Yes."

"What time did the game end?"

"About eleven o'clock."

"And this was in St. Louis?"

"Yes."

"When did Rebecca leave St. Louis?"

"I'm not sure."

"You didn't ride together?"

"No. I drove myself."

"You don't know when she left?"

"Well, I'm the head coach. I stay around the rink until all of the boys are out of the locker room and all of the parents and boys leave the rink complex, to make sure nothing crazy happens."

"How old are the boys? Ten right? Donnie is ten. What kind of crazy thing could happen?"

"Not the boys. Sometimes the parents get a little agitated."

"With their children?"

I thought about Herb Rooks. "Sometimes but mostly with the parents of the other team. They sell beer at some of these rinks."

"So you're the head coach of a hockey team and during games parents of both teams drink beer and get into fights after the game."

"Sometimes they get into fights during the game. On a few occasions, they get into fights before the game."

Wales just stared at me.

"So when did you leave the rink?" he asked.

"I'd say I was on the road by eleven forty-five or so."

"Where did you go?"

"I drove straight to my ranch out in the country."

"How long did it take?"

"It's about a four hour drive."

"Did you stop anywhere?"

"Just for gas."

"When did you get to your house?"

"Probably about four-thirty."

"Anybody there at the house with you?"

"No."

"Anybody see you that night?"

"No."

"When was the next time someone saw you?"

"I guess people saw me drive to the office this morning."

"You have any of their names and phone numbers?"

"No."

"When was the first time someone saw you?" Wales asked with an edge to his voice.

"Our receptionist saw me when I walked into our offices."

"When?"

"It was probably sometime between nine and nine-thirty."

"So there's no one to account for your whereabouts between eleven forty-five yesterday morning and nine o'clock this morning?"

"Well, I mean I drove my car. I didn't fly. So if you want to be accurate and assume I drove straight home, probably between four-thirty yesterday afternoon and nine o'clock this morning. That's probably right."

"What about Rebecca?"

"I have no idea."

"Did you talk to her?"

"Not after the game."

"Where did she go after the game?"

"I don't know. I know what kind of car she owns. It was gone when I drove out of the rink parking lot in St. Louis. I don't know where she went or when, or even if, she got back to town. I don't know."

"I think we probably should stop talking now," Wales said. "You'll be available if I have more questions?"

"Sure," I said. "And, well, the people at my law firm don't know about my relationship with either Rebecca or Teri. Unless it's important for your investigation, maybe it would be okay if you didn't tell anyone at my law firm about this?"

"I can't help you there," Wales said. "You made your own bed. You're going to have to lie in it. And it sounds like you've been lying in it a lot."

- 4 -

"I saw this in a movie once," Jenny began as we spoke on our cell phones. I sat in my Porsche in the law firm's parking lot, stalling, not wanting to go back to work. She continued, "The gal got her boyfriend to kill her husband so she would inherit all of the husband's money. The gal ended up on a beach in the Pacific. The guy ended up in jail for murder."

"And your point is?"

"Kathleen Turner and William Hurt starred. It was a really good movie. I get hot every time I watch it. When I'm alone I end up playing with myself."

I ignored the latter remark. Jenny was just being Jenny. "You think I'm being set up?"

"So that you'll watch that movie alone and masturbate?"

"I don't need to do that. I am sleeping with Rebecca."

"So she fills all of your needs?" between giggles.

I didn't take the bait.

Jenny said, "I guess the bigger question is whether you're filling all of her needs. Filling them adequately, that is."

Again, I ignored the bait and the reference to the size of my manhood. "Am I in trouble?"

"If you put a video camera in your bedroom I can give you an informed opinion."

"Seriously."

She stopped giggling. "Sounds like it to me."

"Then I guess I have to solve the murder of Mr. Warren and clear my name."

It began as a giggle but evolved into cascades of laughter. She laughed so hard she dropped her phone and I winced as it banged off the wood floor of her living room.

I waited until the cell phone was back in her hand and I could hear the laughter clearly though my phone's speakers.

"Thanks," I said. "Love the support."

"Sorry," Jenny gasped. "I was just picturing you as a detective. Sam Oliver: Man of Action."

She burst out again into hysterical laughter to the point where I worried about the onset of a convulsion.

I kept quiet but her laughter drenched me like acid.

- 5 -

Sly spent little time contemplating the past. In *Sly's World* the past did not hinder actions in the present.

What would that be like? I wondered. How would one's outlook on life change if one wasn't haunted by the mistakes and lost opportunities of the past?

I did love her, I thought. On the computer screen flashed images of my ex-wife. She had not been a beauty. She had not sported a body built for a bikini or a face destined to grace magazine covers. But she was fun. She made people laugh. She made people want to be around her. She acted as if she wanted to be with me.

I sipped scotch, sitting at my desk in The Ranch Retreat's spare bedroom. Computer print-outs and photographs hung from corkboards lining the walls. Binders filled with *Sly's World* were stacked beside the desk on the dusty floor.

My ex-wife did want to be with me, I knew, but only for awhile. And then it was over. She left, never looking back. It was as if I never existed.

Old news, I thought. I'm just plowing ground until the soil won't hold a single root.

Had Rebecca used me?

I shook my head. That wouldn't make sense. Donnie was a superstar. Rebecca didn't need to bribe me or any other coach with sexual favors. Every coach dreamed of having the next Wayne Gretzky on his team. We all prayed to The Hockey Gods for such luck. Rebecca didn't have to sleep with me in order to help Donnie's hockey career.

His hockey career. This was nuts. He was ten years old.

And his father was dead.

How would he react to his father's death at the rink, in the locker room, or on the ice?

I hadn't turned on the heater and cold air seeped up the legs of my sweatpants and down my neck and I shivered.

My mother died in a car accident when I was four. My father raised me by himself. He had been born in rural Canada, met my mother in a Detroit factory and they ended up in Kansas, my father working on machines that molded plastic for poker chips and boat parts. I learned the concept of two homes from my father. He loved The Ranch Retreat because the property reminded him of the place where he grew up and because of the pond and its icy surface during winter days. During the school week we lived in a tiny one-bedroom apartment in town. He slept on the couch and my hockey equipment covered the dirty rug between the couch and the television. When he awoke he had to step through shoulder pads and skates to get to the kitchen. The place always smelled like a locker room. My father, a large and broad shouldered man, filled up the bathroom when he stood before the mirror to shave. But we lived there for thirteen years as I grew from a 6 year-old kindergarten student to a high school graduate because it was close to the schools and my father's job site and it also was only three miles from the ice rink. When I left for college he went to The Ranch Retreat to live. He died there in his sleep while I was at college. The doctors were never able to tell me why. Organ failure, they said with a shrug. He just gave out. He was fifty two years old.

Did Rebecca care about me?

Next year she and Donnie would be in another state. Minnesota probably with Donnie stashed away at a middle school until he was ready to attend that high school hockey factory. Rebecca was not going to live in this town for me, watching Donnie play inferior opponents and be surrounded by inferior teammates. No, that would not do for Rebecca. She was like my father: for her son, she pursued The Holy Puck.

And an inferior coach, I thought. She would not want Donnie playing for an inferior coach.

If not for Rebecca I wouldn't be coaching the team. I wouldn't have been questioned by the police. I wouldn't have met Teri Manyard. I wouldn't be in serious jeopardy of being fired from the law firm. If not for Rebecca . . .

I thought of my ex-wife and the years since I had held her in my arms.

If not for Rebecca, I realized, I wouldn't be happy today.

- 6 -

Donnie didn't come to practice that week or the following week. None of the parents had discovered our affair nor had word of it leaked to the press. The parents asked me if I had spoken to Rebecca and how she and Donnie were doing and that was it. No one gazed at me like Deputy Wales. At the rink I was not yet a suspect.

Herb Rooks beamed at everyone, higher than an addict with a free supply of heroin. Andy took Donnie's place on the first line during the practices and the kid seemed to have gained a great deal confidence from the four goals he scored last weekend. He flew up and down the ice, the puck glued to his stick, scoring from all angles.

At one point, Herb shouted, "He's back!"

Even April Rooks seemed giddy. She actually smiled at me when she said, 'hello.'

I should call Deputy Wales, I thought. He should place the Rooks on his suspect list.

The team had an off weekend and a number of families were going to attend the funeral on Saturday. A closed casket affair, I was later told. I was going to avoid it.

The night before, Rebecca left Donnie with a nanny for a few hours and drove out to The Ranch Retreat.

"Are you crazy?" I asked as she walked into my living room.

"You talking to me?" Jenny asked.

"No! Her!"

"You sure you're not talking to me?"

"He's sure," Rebecca said.

Jenny went to the kitchen for another beer, barefoot, in tight jeans and a white sweater. Rebecca sat next to me on the couch. She wore loose blue sweats and sneakers and looked like she was ready to go for a light workout at the gym.

"The funeral is tomorrow," I noted.

"Really? I didn't know," she replied.

"The killing's still in the newspaper. What if someone followed you here?"

"'It was on page five of the metropolitan section today. It's no longer on the front page. Besides, who reads anything in that newspaper other than sports scores and movie reviews?"

"I read celebrity gossip and funeral announcements," Jenny answered, returning with three open beer bottles. We each took one. "Sometimes they're the same thing."

"Must be good fodder for The Satanist." Rebecca said.

"Interesting," Jenny said, looking at me. "Actually, it's for Happy Girl. Other people's misfortune makes her world a little brighter."

"Then she would love being around me," Rebecca said. "My husband was murdered during my divorce and I'm now both a single mom and a suspect in his death."

"Thank you," Jenny replied. "I'm feeling much better already."

"Then let me go on," Rebecca continued. She began to complain about her dead husband's family, many of whom had flown into town for the funeral. His elderly parents told her repeatedly they wanted his body returned to Florida for burial and the sentiment was echoed by various aunts and uncles. Forget it, Rebecca told them. He wanted to come here and he dragged me and Donnie here. He can stay here. As soon as the body was released by the district attorney, Rebecca sent it to a funeral home where heat and flame reduced it to fine powder. No need to pay for expensive reconstruction and make-up. The bludgeoned and beaten corpse would no longer offer its wounds for inspection. Fire cleansed, purified and reduced deformity to uniformity. He'll be buried here, Rebecca told us. If they want to see him in Florida they could go to the beach. For all practical purposes he had been turned into Florida sand.

She sat on the couch, her hands folded together in her lap, her feet dangling at least eight inches above the floor. She was tiny, I thought. She could be a doll.

"You saw the body?" I asked.

She nodded.

"You said bludgeoned. Is that how he died?"

"His skull had been cracked open and his brains bashed in," Rebecca replied matter of factly. "He also had two broken arms, a broken hand and several splintered ribs. Someone beat the hell out of him."

"Gruesome," Jenny said. "And the police think you did it?"

"Or paid someone to do it, I guess," Rebecca answered. "But I'm clearly a suspect although they haven't read me my Miranda rights or anything."

"How do you know?"

"The police took all of the hockey sticks in my house to a lab for testing."

"Donnie's hockey sticks?" I asked.

"They think my husband was beaten to death with a hockey stick. I guess they were looking for traces of his blood or skin on a stick's blade."

Always The Coach, I asked, "Did they return Donnie's sticks? We have games next weekend, you know."

"Yes. Donnie has his sticks back."

I sighed with relief.

The Rooks, I thought. The Rooks family owned lots of hockey sticks. Maybe one of the Rooks killed him in order to mess with Donnie's mind. I considered the idea for a few moments and then disregarded it. Herb or April Rooks wouldn't do that, I decided. There would be no guarantee the father's murder would have a negative impact on Donnie's play. If it had been Herb or April Rooks, he or she would have murdered Donnie instead.

"Maybe Donnie needs police protection," I said aloud.

"What?" Rebecca asked.

"Oh, sorry. Nothing, nothing, really."

I hoped.

Rebecca frowned, shrugged and then continued. "And death is so damn burdensome," she said. She spoke of having to deal with Henry's landlord about the breaking of his lease so that there was no claim by the landlord against his estate; of the amount of money she would have to pay the moving company to take his stuff from the apartment and to cart his personal belongings to the nearest landfill; of the drudgery of presenting death certificates to insurers; of the many calls she would need to make to retirement plan administrators and bankers so all of his assets would be transferred to her.

"There is way too much paperwork," Rebecca whined.

Jenny's smile just grew brighter. She put her bottle of beer on the coffee table and went around the couch to stand behind Rebecca.

Rebecca turned her head and looked up at Jenny. "This should make you even happier. I'm having sex with your best friend and as a result he's probably a murder suspect, too."

Rebecca glanced at me and for a moment I wasn't sure if I should kiss her or toss her out of my house.

"You poor dear," Jenny said. "You must be so tense. Let me help you relax." She began massaging Rebecca, thumbs digging into the muscles below the back of her neck, fingertips gently pressing above collarbones. Rebecca closed her eyes and leaned back so the top of her head touched Jenny's stomach. After a few moments Rebecca began to purr.

"You've had such a rough time," Jenny whispered into Rebecca's ear, bending over so her breasts nestled against Rebecca's head. "You've had a really rough time." Her thumbs climbed up back muscles and joined fingers on Rebecca's chest and all together hands slid down to Rebecca's abdomen and then back up to her collarbones. Rebecca moaned. Jenny's palms began moving in a pattern, forming circles that grew smaller with each rotation, spiraling towards Rebecca's nipples. Rebecca shifted in her seat, slightly opening her legs, hands clenching in her lap, mouth open, breathing deeply. When nipples were reached Jenny let the heel of her hands trace circles around the tips of stiffening stubs and then raised her hands in the air, waiting until Rebecca opened her eyes.

Jenny slid her hands beneath the collar of Rebecca's sweatshirt and bra and began kneading her nipples as if she were thirsty and seeking milk.

What the hell was happening here? I stared, aroused and upset and unsure. Did I want to watch or join in? Is Jenny trying to piss me off or am I going to have to compete with Jenny for Rebecca's affections?

Oh, fuck it, what the hell does any of this matter, anyway?

I knelt on the floor and squeezed Rebecca's thighs. Her legs opened wider, her hands separating into fists resting at her sides. I tugged and she arched her back, raising her hips and I pulled sweatpants and underwear down to delicate ankles.

"Tell me of another misfortune," Jenny whispered into Rebecca's ear. "Tell me something that will make me even happier. You see what I am willing to do for you, when I'm happy."

She was warm and wet and I tasted her and she squirmed, groaning, my hands beneath her bottom lifting her and her hands atop my head, rubbing and scratching my skull.

"Score," Rebecca managed to gasp.

Jenny grabbed hold of each nipple and twisted and pulled roughly and Rebecca's body arched and convulsed and fluids of release spread over my tongue and lips and chin and spread into the creases of the leather of the couch.

Her body dissolved into the furniture. I stood, glancing at Jenny and then at Rebecca.

"Nice," Rebecca sighed. "Which one of you is next?"

"No," Jenny replied. "Not tonight. This was all for you." She retrieved her beer and sat down on the recliner facing the couch. I nodded, took a cigar from the humidor and lit it up as Rebecca dressed.

"I should be getting back," she said.

She kissed me on the lips and gave Jenny a hug and was gone.

"What was that about?" I asked.

"Do I ever need a reason to do something strange?" Jenny asked me.

"I guess not." I puffed on the cigar. "So does that count as our first, mutual sexual experience?"

"You are pathetic," Jenny sneered at me. "You acted like a dog licking its master awake in the morning. I'm surprised you didn't start humping her leg."

"What? I was just following your lead!"

"Really? My lead?"

"Of course! What else did you want me to do?"

"Did it ever occur to you that there were two women in this room?" Jenny asked. "Not just her."

She finished her beer and walked out of the house.

- 7 -

The settlement of George (The "Bug Guy") Tolliver's divorce case should have been easy. The law indicated each party—husband and wife—should get one-half of the marital estate. For example, if George ended up with assets worth $200,000 and debts of $100,000 then he would have received the net amount of $100,000. If his soon-to-be ex-wife ended up with assets of $100,000 and debts of $50,000 then she would have received the net amount of $50,000. So to equalize the division of the assets and debts, George would pay her $25,000 so they each ended up with $75,000. Case settled.

The arguments in a case like this normally were: who gets which assets and which debts, and what is the value of each of the assets.

"This is bullshit!" George yelled at me over the telephone on Monday morning. "Absolute bullshit!"

A settlement offer had been sent to our office by opposing counsel, which we forwarded to George. I sat at my desk, reviewing it. His spouse wanted the house, all of her retirement plans, her car, and fifty percent of all of the remaining assets: the bank accounts, mutual fund accounts, and George's retirement plans. Graciously, she offered to pay the house mortgage.

She also wanted $20,000 a month in alimony until either she or George died. Given their ages, that likely would be twenty-five to thirty years from now.

Opposing counsel argued in the settlement letter that the division of assets and debts was fair because the house was worth much less than the debt against it.

"It's the bugs," George complained. "She says having the bugs in the house destroyed the house's fair market value. It's bullshit.

She brought the bugs into the house and now she wants more of our marital estate because of it."

"It's blackmail, too," I reminded him. "Remember the photographs at your deposition?"

"Damn it," he said.

I waited.

"So what the hell are we going to do about this?"

Although he couldn't see it, I was smiling.

- 8 -

"I have a problem," Landscuda told me over the phone a little while later. "Mia screwed up and double-booked me for tomorrow morning. I've got two hearings at the same time, in two different courthouses."

This happened at every law firm in town. I knew it from experience. When Arnie had been double-booked he'd ask me to cover whichever court appearance would be the easiest to handle.

"Glad to help out," I said, wanting to do him a favor and get on his good side. "Just tell me what you want me to do."

"Thanks. Mia will be bringing you the file and give you the details."

She was in my office before I hung up the telephone, carrying a large binder filled with papers.

"I'll go with you tomorrow," she said. "If you want, I can give you the background on the hearing now, if you have the time."

"Great. Let's do it."

Mia put the binder on my desk.

It was for the Manyard case.

"Who wanted the hearing?" I asked. "The case was just filed a few weeks ago. Are we arguing over the amount of child support or maintenance that Mr. Manyard has to pay Mrs. Manyard?"

Mia smiled sweetly. "No. And we're the ones who asked for the hearing."

"Are we arguing about who has to move out of the house or about the parenting time schedule for Sean?"

"No."

"Hockey?"

Mia laughed. "Not really."

"Then what is it?"

"We are asking the Court to force Mrs. Manyard to tell us who she's been screwing around with during all of these hockey trips."

- 9 -

We waited for Judge Frailly. Mr. Manyard and I sat at one table with Mia on a bench behind us. Teri Manyard's attorney sat at another table. The court reporter fiddled with her machine, killing time.

David Smitherton was opposing counsel. He had a reputation for being a believer in the decades old concept of a two martini lunch. For him lunch began at eleven o'clock a.m. Thus, for this nine o'clock hearing there was a chance he was still sober.

Teri Manyard was not present in the courtroom. Mr. Manyard tugged at my jacket sleeve. "Where is she?" he asked.

"This isn't an evidentiary hearing," I explained. "It's just arguments by the lawyers. She doesn't need to be here; in fact, neither do you."

"She's worried the judge may order her to immediately provide the names of the bastards she's been fucking."

Me too, I thought, nodding my head in agreement. I was glad she was not in the courtroom. Smart move by her lawyer, I thought. Smitherton burped and chewed on breath mints.

I tried to sit still and stay calm but my nerves were jangled and my head buzzed from the coffee and energy drinks I had been guzzling since dawn. I hadn't slept, and had alternated between drinking whiskey and vomiting throughout most of the night.

How am I going to do this? I kept asking myself in The White Apartment. Maybe I should just surrender my bar license as soon as the hearing began and call it a career.

We called it the smell test, though calling it the 'sound' test made more sense. Treat a thought or an argument as if it were a smell. If it smelled bad avoid it even if you knew the thing that smelled bad was okay.

My arguing a motion requesting the Court force Teri Manyard to disclose the names of her lovers clearly failed the smell test. Even if I won I was doomed.

Mia wore a blue dress that hugged her like a mother holding a newborn child. I glanced back and she smiled at me.

"All rise!" announced the court reporter.

Judge Frailly stumbled into the courtroom and wearily climbed up to his seat on the bench. He called out the name of the case and the attorneys stated their appearances.

Frailly ignored the computer screen and file on his desk. "Why are we here?" he asked no one in particular.

I walked to the podium, half expecting a noose to be lowered from the ceiling to encircle my neck.

"This is my client's motion on a discovery issue," I said.

"What discovery?"

"When Mrs. Manyard received the Petition For Divorce she was also served with interrogatories. Her attorney filed objections to some of the questions and Mr. Manyard is asking the Court to overrule certain objections and require her to answer the questions."

Smitherton burped.

Frailly sighed. "What questions?"

I started to speak but Frailly cut me off with his booming voice. "Not you. Her attorney."

Smitherton stood, momentarily lost his balance but caught himself. "Sex questions," he said.

"Sex?"

"Yes."

"Is there a dispute as to the gender of Mrs. Manyard?"

"No. She's a woman."

"So what's the problem?"

"Mr. Manyard is asking my client to divulge the names of anyone she had sex with during the last three years."

Frailly cleared his throat. "I take it the true answers would involve person or persons other than Mr. Manyard."

Smitherton shrugged. "The questions on the topic are irrelevant and intended only for harassment. I didn't ask Mrs. Manyard for the answer and don't believe legally Mr. Manyard should ask it, either."

"Sex." Frailly looked at me. "Your client wants to know this stuff?"

"Yes."

"If she kissed someone does she have to disclose that person's identity?"

"If it was a romantic kiss, yes."

"What about a hand job?"

"Excuse me?"

"Never mind. Go ahead. Make your point."

"Mr. Manyard believes marital assets were spent by Mrs. Manyard in regard to her numerous affairs. We need to question her various partners in order to determine if there was any dissipation of the marital estate."

"You can't find out their names from other sources?"

"We do not believe so. We clearly do not want to start quizzing possible suspects. It may be awkward for Sean, the parties' son."

"Why?"

"It may involve his hockey team, or more precisely, one of the other team parents."

"Hockey team?"

"Yes."

"Don't tell me. Let me guess. Your hockey team?"

"Yes."

"You got one helluva interesting team."

"Thank you."

"Are you going to be a witness, because last time I checked a lawyer in a divorce case can't also be witness in the same case."

"I am aware of that. Mr. Manyard agreed not to ask me to testify when he retained our law firm. Mr. Landscuda will handle the case. I'm just filling in."

"What if Mrs. Manyard calls you to testify?" Judge Frailly asked. "If you have relevant information I think she can do that."

Not likely to happen, I thought. "I guess we'll deal with that situation if it arises."

"So on your hockey team you got some spouses fighting about whether their son should play hockey at all and you got other spouses sleeping with people to whom they're not married?"

"It is a contact sport."

Frailly glared at me. "Are you making fun of this Court?"

"No, sir."

Frailly turned his gaze to Smitherton. "What does Mrs. Manyard do for a living?"

"Nothing except live with Mr. Manyard."

"And Mr. Manyard?

"He owns some sporting good stores."

Frailly addressed me. "Is that correct?"

I turned and Mia nodded. "Yes, sir."

"Okay. Another easy case. This is a no fault divorce state. Mrs. Manyard could have sex with everyone in China but if she doesn't spend any marital funds on her lovers it doesn't matter. So if Mr. Manyard can prove some evidence of financial misconduct or missing monies I might make her disclose names. But if no money is missing, forget it. Anything else?"

"No, your honor," Smitherton said.

"Thank you. No," I replied.

"You know why Landscuda sent you?" Frailly asked me.

"Why?"

"Because this motion was a loser before it was written. And Mr. Manyard?"

"Yes?" my client responded.

"You might want to stock condoms near the hockey equipment in your stores. From what I'm hearing, sounds like it would be a gold mine."

I let Mia console our client and left the courtroom.

Smitherton caught up with me in the hallway. He checked his watch, a small Rolex. "It's almost ten," he said. "Can I buy you a drink?"

- 10 -

The regulars at *The Bar Association* knew the code words to use with the waitresses. Smitherton led me to a booth in the shadows, far from the front door and ordered two strong coffees to be served in Styrofoam cups with lids because 'we might not be able to stay long.'

He lit a cigarette and offered me the pack.

"Thought it was against the law to smoke in a public accommodation," I noted.

"A number of judges like coming here. So do some of the sheriff's deputies. A gentleman's agreement was reached with the proprietor."

"What agreement?"

"He lets us smoke and we keep coming to his bar."

"And what about the other customers who complain about the smoking?"

"They get a code word, which is changed every day, that lets them slide if they ever get a traffic ticket or a misdemeanor charge. Some of the judges really like to smoke in here. Most prosecutors, too."

Smitherton was a small man with a few long strands of hair laying atop his pink skull, thick glasses covering his eyes and a body that seemed to have avoided any attempts at physical activity for decades. He had a few good referral sources and managed to scrape by year after year. He had never married. He was generally liked by all but I didn't know any lawyer who considered him a friend.

That's going to be me soon, I thought.

As if he could read my mind, he asked, "You ever wonder if you made a mistake becoming a lawyer or working on family law cases?"

"Sometimes," I admitted.

"What would you have done if you had a second chance at it all?"

"Anything?"

"Sure."

I thought of the hours spent on the pond with my dad, the cold not bothering us, skating with the puck and passing it to him. The few times I saw him really smile, really be happy, were on that pond or after one of my hockey games when I had played well and the team had won. He never coached my youth teams although he knew more about the game and the skills involved than any of the other coaches. He preferred to teach me about the game on the pond or by watching me shooting pucks off a piece of plywood in the driveway or by watching professional games with me on the television. When I was on the ice with my youth teams he was selfish—he only wanted to focus on me. He didn't want to worry about any of the other kids.

He believed in The Holy Puck and told me stories of the frozen lake at the foot of the mountain, and of The Hockey Gods and The Mountain Palace. Every generation The Hockey Gods blessed several children to go on and become legends in professional hockey. Children from all over the world, in their deepest dreams, were brought to the frozen lake to play. Only a few would have the necessary skills. Only a few would be deemed worthy. Only a few every generation would be blessed with The Holy Puck, and afterwards when the time was right those children would skate like magic with every other puck in the world.

"Did I ever go to that frozen lake?" I had once asked him when I was just eleven years old.

"Every young hockey player goes there."

"Was I blessed?"

"It's too early to tell. Sometimes the blessing doesn't take hold until the later teenage years. There's still time for you."

"Were you blessed?"

"No. I never even played in the minors. I had the desire but not the talent. The Holy Puck was not granted to me."

In time I realized it was not granted to me, either.

Coffee was served. The coffee smelled and tasted like a martini. Olives bobbed against the cup's lid.

"Seriously. If you had another chance?"

My father died in a car crash after it became clear I was not destined to carry The Holy Puck. At the time I didn't believe the car accident killed him. I believed that he had died when he realized I was not good enough to experience glory on the ice.

"Ice," I said.

Smitherton nodded. "They don't put ice in the 'coffee.' They don't want it to melt and dilute the 'coffee's' potency."

"No," I said. "Ice. If I had to do it again I'd live my life on the ice."

- 11 -

I took the rest of the day off.

Sly's World numbered four volumes, each over three hundred pages long. I began writing them during law school when I imagined my life as a daring young lawyer, socializing with the rich and powerful of the city, winning important court cases and gathering newspaper headlines. At first Sly was outrageous but seemed to live in a world that resembled my own. As the years of actual work and life passed, that changed.

Each night, at The White Apartment or The Ranch Retreat, *Sly's World* grew. There were long handwritten, narrative sections; other written sections on computer discs accompanied by music; crude cartoon drawings of Sly's life in the form of a comic book; pictures and artwork swiped from the Internet that appeared to match portions of his life. *Sly's World* was a multimedia extravaganza of love, sex, fun and power. *Sly's World*, by the time I met Rebecca, had very little to do with my reality. *Sly's World* was reality as I wished it could be.

Jenny had seen most of *Sly's World*. Jenny knew the person hiding inside me.

The hockey team didn't have practice that night. No one would miss me until nine o'clock the next morning when I was due in the office for a family law section meeting.

I smoked a spicy cigar as the Porsche ate highway miles. I had changed to blue jeans, a blue sweater and my black leather jacket before leaving the city. Smoke poured from the cigar's lit end to be caught in the air rushing through the vehicle and blown up through the open sunroof. The day was cold, fall turning to winter but I didn't care, the wind roaring through open front windows. I wanted to feel the cold. I wanted my skin to feel alive.

Last weekend she was mad because I touched Rebecca instead of her. She was mad because I didn't take off her clothes, feel her skin, devour her private parts. She wanted me to do so. Enough already. No more wasting time. No more living in fantasies. No more. She wanted me. A part of me—a large part of me—wanted her, too.

It was time.

She lived in the state's capital some fifty miles away on the top floor of a luxury condominium building. I had been there on a few occasions; once, when I left her in her condo unit to purchase more alcohol she told me the code for the building's front door. I hoped it hadn't changed. I inputted the six digits and the loud click indicated the door was unlocked.

Her condo unit consisted of the entire top floor: eight thousand square feet some ten stories above the ground. The elevator doors opened on her floor to a small lobby decorated with photos on the walls of various serial killers. Nice touch, I thought.

I knocked on Jenny's door.

It opened.

I was greeted by a person wearing a bright pink terrycloth robe with the words 'Fuck Off And Die' embroidered in blood red letters. Jenny's robe, I knew, but Jenny wasn't wearing it.

"Good afternoon," Jaime Landscuda said.

- 12 -

I fled to The White Apartment. Deputy Wales was waiting for me in the parking lot.

"Thanksgiving's in a few weeks," he said. "You're not planning on leaving town, are you?"

"Just to my country ranch. Can I help you?"

"Your hockey sticks. I want them, for testing. Okay?"

"Sure."

"Okay." He walked up to the apartment with me.

"How do you live in a white place?" he asked from the doorway. "How do you keep it so clean?"

"By not killing anyone in it."

"Funny."

"Thanks."

He took the sticks and promised to return them soon and left.

The next day I had to get out of the office. I usually skipped lunch, working at my desk or just surfing the Internet to kill time, but that day I just needed to leave. I didn't want to see Landshark any more than necessary. The morning meeting had been hell. We went through the cases, Landshark making a few unkind comments about the result of the Manyard hearing, complimenting Mia or Mai as being a 'happy girl' at every opportunity and making an offhand remark about Satan when discussing a particularly troublesome client.

I had to escape. The very air inside the office seemed poisonous to me.

The Physics Guy was leaning against my Porsche in the parking lot, cleaning his fingernails with what looked like a pearl handled switchblade.

"Good afternoon," he said, smiling.

Fuck.

"I usually meet with clients in the office," I replied. "Did we have an appointment?"

"Nope."

"Good. Can you get away from my car? I wouldn't want to run you over."

"I thought we could chat for awhile."

"You thought wrong."

He pushed the knife against his belt, retracting the blade. "I don't think so." He held the knife up to his face, pushed the switch and three inches of steel sprang into sunlight. "I need some legal advice."

"You need a good psychiatrist."

"Oh? Did my wife file a motion for a mental examination of me?"

"Your wife hasn't filed anything with the Court. Neither have you. You guys may end up having the slowest divorce case in the history of this county."

"Some things take time, like making a good wine or scotch."

"Or a good mechanical wristwatch."

"A wristwatch?" The Physics Guy asked. "Why bother? You could go to any wholesale store and buy a Japanese digital watch more accurate than anything ever made in Switzerland."

"That's an interesting comment coming from you. I figured you'd say something profound about time and physics."

"There's better ways to spend money than on a fancy timepiece."

"Most mobsters I know like to flaunt expensive watches."

"Who said anything about mobsters?"

"Oh, sorry. I meant garbage haulers. Slip of the tongue."

"The bosses for my company like to buy expensive watches. Lawyers do, too. Guys like me, who do the actual dirty work, don't."

"So you're a button man?"

"Excuse me?"

"You know, a button man, the kind of guy who goes to the mattresses when things get violent between families. I've seen *The Godfather*. All three movies."

"The third one was really bad."

"I agree."

"Besides, that was all fiction," The Physics Guy said.

"And you're not?" I asked. "What do you want?"

"Athletes can change lives, Their own, and of the people around them."

"How are you connected to Joey Balton?"

Storm ignored the question. "You know this, of course. You're a coach, right?"

"Huh?"

"Rebecca is quiet a catch."

"Excuse me?"

"Do you think you'd be fucking her if you weren't coaching her son?"

He smiled at me.

Storm was investigating me?

"Go fuck yourself," I said.

"Donnie will make people's lives better. He's made your life better. And it can become even better, in the future."

"How do you know about Rebecca?"

"Don't ask Mr. Balton about his play during his deposition," Storm said. "Stick to questions about finances, money, possible mistresses. Don't talk about badly thrown balls. If you do as I ask, everything will be fine."

"And if I don't do as you ask?"

"Love blooms. Love dies. Take your pick."

He walked away from my Porsche, got into his own car and drove away.

- 13 -

I ran into Landscuda that afternoon in the men's bathroom. We stood side by side at the urinals. I expected a comment about the size of his member. What I got was worse.

"You ever wonder which one is better in bed?"

Speechless, I just shook my head. Is he asking me whether his penis or mine is better in bed?

"Happy Girl or The Satanist? Do you know? Wait, forget that. She told me. You don't know. So guess."

"She's a good friend of mine. This is somewhat awkward."

"I'm your boss. Guess."

Guess. Happy Girl or The Satanist. The prom queen or the dominatrix.

"Happy Girl," I answered.

"Ha! Wrong." He sauntered out of the bathroom.

Fuck.

- 14 -

It's not unusual to be sandbagged by your own client. George Tolliver hadn't confided in me about his unusual relationship with the bugs until it had been exposed at his deposition. There were some secrets a person did not want to tell anyone, even his or her divorce attorney.

Later that afternoon I met Susan Henderson at the gate to the Tolliver's neighborhood. We parked our cars in a decent sized asphalt lot outside the community's eight foot tall brick wall and waited by the iron gate.

"You ever been inside this place?" I asked opposing counsel.

"Never," Susan replied. "I'm actually excited about this appraisal. I can't wait to see what these houses look like."

A brick wall encircled the entire perimeter of the community and at various points cameras mounted on it surveyed the surrounding land, rotating a full circle every ten seconds. The pictures were relayed to the guardhouse inside the gate; supposedly, there was enough ground between the inner wall and the nearest homes that no one climbing the wall could avoid being caught on a camera's sweep either inside or outside the community. At night the cameras switched to infrared detection mode. The people inside the community, some of the richest in the nation via hard work or inheritances, paid a great deal for their privacy.

The gate swung open. A guard waited for us on a golf cart, a massive handgun holstered on his waist along with a pair of handcuffs, a can of mace and an electric prod. I took the back seat and Susan sat beside the driver, nervously eyeing his assorted weapons.

"Where's the appraiser?" she asked me.

"With George Tolliver, waiting outside the house for us."

By agreement the appraisal would occur in the presence of both parties and their attorneys. The appraiser would not step foot onto the property, not even on the driveway or front lawn, without all being present.

We rode through the community. The Tolliver's home was on the other side of the community, far from the entrance gate. At a glance, the houses were not unusual. They were mansions, of course, but no different than many of the other monstrous structures in the wealthier neighborhoods in the county. The land was flat; lawns manicured and pristine; flowerbeds and trees as pretty as anything in any botanical garden. No one moved about. The place could have been a ghost town except for the upkeep of the lawns and yards.

We drove towards a wall of multi-colored stone and another gate. George Tolliver and another man stood beside the gate.

The guard said, "About two years ago the Tollivers had this wall built around their property. It took a few payoffs to the homeowner's association, I'm told, to get approval. They might have the only gated house within a gated community in the state."

He stopped by the gate. We climbed off the cart and with a wave the guard drove away. George and I shook hands.

George smiled at Susan. "Would you mind calling your client now?" he asked. "So that I can get into my own fucking house?"

I started to voice the need for civility but there was an audible hum and the gate began to swing open.

"Sorry," George said to Susan in a whisper. He pointed to an intercom built into the wall by the gate. "My wife's been listening the whole time I've been standing out here. I couldn't resist."

"Understood," Susan replied politely.

She reached out her hand to the appraiser and introduced herself.

"Sam Melton," he replied. He was my height but was painfully thin, as if he hadn't eaten in weeks. He wore glasses that perched atop his nose and heightened the angular look of his face.

George led us onto the property. The house stood some hundred and fifty feet back from the stone fence, a gigantic Tudor structure of stone and wood with a four-car garage and a circular driveway.

Curtains covered every window. His wife waited on the front porch steps.

"This had better be quick," she said. "I have an appointment at the spa."

I smiled at her, not bothering to respond. We walked into a tremendous foyer of white marble flooring and a chandelier dangling above a winding staircase, the banisters made from cherry wood. Several modern paintings hung on the walls.

"Interesting perfume," Mrs. Tolliver said to Susan.

"I guess you'll do the outside last so my client can lock up the house and go to her appointment," Susan said to Melton.

"I'm not concerned about the outside of the house."

"Don't you have to measure it? All appraisers take measurements of the outside of the house."

"He's an appraiser," I said, "but not for the real estate."

"Excuse me?" Susan asked. "Then what is he doing here?"

"He's an entomologist from the Smithsonian Institute in Washington, D.C.," George explained. "He's here to value the bugs."

"What!" his wife shrieked.

"Explain this now!" Susan demanded.

I shrugged. "The bugs are a marital asset. We are going to value them."

"You son of a bitch!" Susan swore.

"Get them out of my house!" Mrs. Tolliver yelled.

"I'll get a court order to come back," I replied. "I'll demand you reimburse Mr. Melton for the costs of his trip from D.C. and for my attorney fees coming out here. We are going to take pictures, even if you try to throw us out, and if anything changes the next time we come here then we'll also file a motion to hold you in contempt of court for concealing assets."

"You son of a bitch," Susan said with a hint of admiration.

George was smiling, probably happier than anytime he had spent with the bugs. "They're in the basement," he said. "I'll show you."

"No need," Melton explained.

"Why not?"

Melton open his satchel and removed a heavy hammer with a thick head of steel.

"I apologize in advance," he said. He walked to an outer wall of the foyer, near the front door. "May I?"

"May you do what?" Susan asked.

"Do whatever you want to do," George replied. "I do have an ownership interest in this house."

Melton slammed the hammer into the drywall, leaving cracks radiating from the hole.

"What the fuck are you doing!" Mrs. Tolliver screamed.

He widened the hole. Susan looked as if she wanted to grab the hammer from him but was afraid he might hit her with it. She turned to me. "We are going to demand that the Court order your client to pay for this damage! We are going to ask the Court to hold you in contempt for destroying marital property!"

"We're just finding marital property," Melton said, stepping back.

A stream of bugs poured out from the hole in the wall into the foyer and some began flying about the room. Melton put his satchel in front of the hole, to keep more of the bugs from coming out.

"As I would expect," Melton said. "They're breeding, probably in every wall in the house."

I backed away towards the front door, my eyes darting from the entomologist's satchel to the bugs flying about the chandelier. Mrs. Tolliver and George showed nothing; Susan stared up at the circling bugs. It's not the chandelier that attracts them, I thought.

Melton calmly said, "There probably are certain perfumes that remind the males of a female's scent during mating season."

Like kamikaze pilots spotting an aircraft carrier, the escaped bugs dive bombed Susan.

- 15 -

We waited in the backyard after Mrs. Tolliver fired Susan, and while she and George toured the rest of the house with Melton. The hole in the wall had been covered with several layers of duct tape, which Melton assured them would be sufficient.

Mrs. Tolliver had shouted, "I paid you to fuck him over! I didn't pay you to fuck him!"

Susan puffed on a thin cigar I had given to her, wearing high heels and cloaked in one of Mrs. Tolliver's long fur coats. "This is relaxing," she said although her hand continued to tremble.

"Yes," I replied. "It's also a great excuse to stand around doing nothing."

"I'm glad I was fired by Mrs. Tolliver. Those bugs made me want to puke. If I woke up and found them living in my house I'd burn it to the ground."

"That's probably the only solution anyway."

According to Melton who spoke to me before I fled to the backyard, the bugs probably had infiltrated every wall in the house, feeding on each other, the creatures reproducing faster than they could cannibalize one another.

"You're different," Susan told me.

"Excuse me?"

"Just standing here, you're different."

"How?"

"I find you attractive."

"What the heck was I before?"

"Quiet. Meek. Afraid of girls."

"Afraid?"

"Whenever you spoke to me, before, it was like I was just an adversary. Sexless. You never engaged in any small talk or said anything unrelated to a case. Now, it seems as if you're trying to undress me with your eyes and you project an attitude that says you want to touch me all over like a blind person reading Braille."

"If I were blind it would be the only way to get a picture of your frame."

"See, that's what I mean. You never would have said that to me before. You know what that means?" She didn't wait for a response. "You're getting laid by someone you like. So now you think you can bed anyone."

Not Jenny, I thought. "I am seeing someone. Unfortunately, because of it I'm a suspect in a murder case."

She giggled and puffed. "Does that make the sex with her better?"

I pondered the question for a moment. "Probably," I answered.

"I remember how it felt to have sex with my husband, in the beginning. I miss it. The thrill. The newness of it all."

"I suppose that's just the way it usually is. I wasn't married for very long. I never got past that stage with my ex."

"Your new girlfriend, is it like that with her?"

I nodded.

Susan looked about. "I've always thought you were someone that a person could trust."

"I'm not sure that reputation has helped out my personal life."

"But is it true?"

"I hope so."

But I was no longer sure.

- 16 -

"Then what happened?" Cowboy Jake asked.

"The bugs got into Susan's clothing and George was the only one who reacted. He ran to her and helped her remove her blouse and skirt to try and find the bugs. She was screaming that they were biting her and somehow they ended up on the floor, with her naked and George on top of her. When he started to pull down his pants Mrs. Tolliver kicked him between the legs. He took it very well once he stopped sobbing."

"So George will screw anything. I can't blame him. Susan's pretty hot."

I left it at that. We were sitting in my office the next day, sipping coffee and killing time before the day's work began.

"So what will happen now with the case?" Cowboy Joke asked.

I shrugged. "Mrs. Tolliver will hire a new lawyer and we'll see what the new lawyer demands."

We turned our attention to the quarterback case. That afternoon, I was to depose the former MVP of the Professional Football League.

In my ear I could almost hear Arnie whisper, "Make sure you get his ring."

- 17 -

If I hadn't known better I would have thought the football team's general manager was a member of the Kansas City mafia. But from personal experience I knew he dressed too well, was too dashing, and loved publicity too much. He had turned one lucky draft pick—taking Joey Balton late in the fifth round when most teams thought he was too slight of frame to survive as a professional quarterback—and turned it into a career. Somehow he maintained a perpetual tan through the town's cold winters, usually pacing the sidelines before games in a fur coat or a jacket of gleaming black leather. His hair covered his head like a helmet and thick gold chains dangled from his neck. The man's suit probably cost more than any suit in George Tolliver's closet and his pinkie ring was encrusted with diamonds. He crushed my hand in greeting in our law firm's lobby.

"Anthony Toscana," he said, introducing himself although everyone in town knew him. "I'm the President, Chief Financial Officer and General Manager of the Mohawks of the Professional Football League."

"Yes, I know," I replied. "Sam Oliver. I am very pleased to meet you."

"You're Meredith Balton's attorney."

"Yes."

"A fine lady. She's done quite a lot for charities in town. Our organization has always had a good relationship with her."

"Thank you. I will tell her."

We stood looking at one another. He was a good six inches taller than me.

"Can I help you?" I finally asked.

"I'm here for a deposition."

"Are you being deposed?"

"Of course not."

"Then why are you here?"

"For a deposition."

I smiled at the pompous ass. The parties were already in the conference room for the deposition with Mia and the court reporter.

"I'm ready for the deposition," Toscana replied.

"Well, if you're not being deposed and you're not a party to the divorce case, then you're not allowed to attend the deposition."

"I don't think you understand, young man. You are deposing my quarterback."

"I will be, as soon as we finish this conversation."

"Then let's get started."

"You can wait in the lobby," I said.

"Excuse me?"

"You are not allowed to attend the deposition."

"Mr. Oliver, I am the President, Chief Financial Officer and General Manager of the Mohawks, a Professional Football League team."

"Impressive," I replied. I was The Lawyer. At the stadium and every place in town besides my law office, an ice rink and a courthouse, Toscana dwarfed me in power. But not here.

"I am going to attend the deposition."

I turned to the receptionist, who was watching with a smile on her face. "Can you get my paralegal?" I asked. She picked up the phone and buzzed him.

"Is he going to escort us into the conference room?" Toscana asked.

"I watched most of your team's games over the last two seasons," I said. "Don't you think you have more pressing matters than attending a deposition?"

"Excuse me?"

"You're team sucks. Maybe you should be talking to an employment search firm instead of me."

"Now hold on there," he said, his face turning red.

Cowboy Jake entered the lobby, his hands on the butts of the pistols holstered at his waist.

"Need me, boss?" he asked.

"Please escort Mr. Toscana to his vehicle," I said. "As a warning, he may not be cooperative."

"Some bison weren't very cooperative on the range," Cowboy Jake replied. "After I shot and gutted the bastards, they made a whole lot of good steaks."

I didn't bother to listen to the rest of the exchange. I turned and walked into the conference room.

Joey Balton wore a tailored blue suit and a red tie. Meredith chose a low cut dress with a necklace of rubies and a matching bracelet. Neither sported wedding rings.

I shook hands with Balton's attorney. Hugo Gerald was a portly man with a round face and, in general, an easy going manner. He sat next to his client and I took a seat across from the quarterback. Meredith sat between me and Mia.

The court reporter swore the quarterback to tell the truth. He didn't appear nervous, sitting upright in his chair, but relaxed.

I went through the preliminary questions such as his name and address and whether he'd been deposed before, and he answered the questions in a calm voice.

I was about to start the main questions when the door opened and Toscana entered the room.

"Let's go off the record," I said to the court reporter, who stopped typing. To Toscana, "Do we have to go thru our verbal dance again?"

"I'd like to speak to my quarterback."

"No."

"Excuse me? I'm the President, Chief Financial . . ."

"No," I interrupted. "Now get out."

Hugo Gerald spoke to his client. "Do you want to have a word with Mr. Toscana?"

Joey Balton looked at Toscana. "It's okay. Let's just get the deposition over and done. I'm ready."

We all looked to Toscana. He stood still for a moment and then walked to an empty seat at the table and sat down.

"No offense," I said. "But please get the fuck out of my conference room."

"I think not. This case may have an impact on my football team. As the President, Chief Financial Officer and General Manager, I have a right to attend."

"I am willing to call security, or the police."

"I promise to be very quiet."

Mia stood and stretched, her arms raised to the ceiling, her blouse grasping onto her upper body. She slowly walked to Toscana, the long way around the table, taking her time, and everyone stared at her body. She leaned behind his chair, brushing her hair back from her face, and began whispering in Toscana's ear.

The football executive nodded a number of times.

"Okay," he said. "Good day to you all." He left the room.

Mia smiled and retook her seat.

She met my eyes and then tilted her head to the court reporter.

"Let's go back on the record," I said and the court reporter's fingers hovered over her machine.

I had an outline for the deposition on nine sheets of paper but my gut told me to ignore the pages so I did.

"Who is Jason Storm?"

Balton shrugged. "Do I know him from football?"

"Just answer the question."

Balton rolled his eyes up slightly to the ceiling. "No idea," he said.

"Are you sure?"

"I think so."

I glanced at his attorney. He had written Storm's name on his legal pad but nothing else. He didn't look worried.

Mia handed me a note behind Meredith's chair. It read: 'Did you just breach an attorney-client privilege?'

I shrugged, not caring. I crumpled the paper and handed it back to Mia.

"In the last year have you had a sexual or romantic relationship with anyone other than your spouse?" I asked. It was a standard deposition question and Gerald didn't bother to object.

He again shook his head to the negative. "No."

"Why do you think Mr. Toscana wanted to be at your deposition so badly?"

Again, a shake of the head. "I don't know."

"Really? Are you sure?"

"I have no idea why he wanted to be here."

Fuck.

Gerald showed no concern via his body language nor did he write anything on his legal pad. I clearly wasn't striking a nerve like Susan Henderson did at George Tolliver's deposition. I glanced at Meredith and Mia. Their expressions were blank.

I looked at the list of questions on my legal pad. They covered the usual subjects: a discussion of his income, the assets and debts of the marriage, and questions to try and find any negative information he had about my client. But I wasn't looking for any answers to those subjects. I wanted to know about Jason Storm. I wanted to know what the hell was going on in this case.

Joey Balton had grown up in a small New Jersey town that had never been known as a football power. He didn't play football until ninth grade when, during gym class, the football coach noticed he could throw a spiral almost fifty yards, on target. He was a good student who mostly was in Honors classes and never hung out with the jocks. His sporting career consisted of recreational baseball where he mostly played in the outfield because of his arm. He couldn't hit though and his parents, engineers for a Fortune 500 chemical company, never stressed sports. He was of slight build and average height; looking at him, no one would have thought 'now there's a football player!'

He didn't play on the Junior Varsity team until the first and second team quarterbacks, both with politically connected fathers, were injured. By then he knew the entire playbook by heart and could diagram each play in his head so that when the ball was snapped he could just concentrate on the positioning of the defenders. He knew where his players would be on every play, without thinking or looking. He also had watched intently from the sidelines during the time he did not play, always thinking where he would have delivered the ball if he had been playing.

The team was winless when he jogged into the game in the middle of the season.

On the first play he called an audible from the line and while his coach screamed at him not to change the plays he connected with a wide receiver for a sixty yard touchdown bomb.

The team won all of its remaining games.

For the next three seasons he was the starting Varsity quarterback and the team boasted its best three-year record in school history.

He played smart, getting rid of the ball when necessary, always avoiding the big hit.

Due to his size he was not recruited by any football power and played his college ball at a second tier school, leading them to three league titles.

Again, due to his size and sleight build, the Professional Football League teams shied away from him, until Toscana took a chance and drafted him in the fifth round. Five playoff seasons and a world championship later, everyone agreed he had become one of the best quarterbacks in the league.

I leafed through my pages of questions, settling on the next line of attack.

"Are you intentionally throwing interceptions this season?"

Joey's head remained still. "Why would I do that?"

"Please answer the question."

Now Gerald appeared perturbed.

"I get paid to win games," Joey answered.

"You still have not answered my question."

"Every quarterback will throw some interceptions. I'm playing against the best defensive players in the world. They are trying the hardest to pick off every pass I throw."

"Are you intentionally throwing interceptions?"

"My receivers had a chance to catch almost every pass I have thrown this year. They're young and inexperienced. Just because the ball is picked off doesn't mean it's my fault."

"You still have not answered my question."

"I think he has," Hugo Gerald said. "Move on to the next subject."

"No. He needs to answer my question."

"He has. Move on."

"Should we get the judge on the line?"

In a deposition if there was a problem the judge assigned to the case, if available, normally would be willing to talk to the lawyers by telephone and settle the dispute.

"Move on," Gerald said.

I called his bluff. "Mia, please see if the judge is available to talk to us."

Mia walked to the phone in the room and dialed the courthouse number.

"Fine," the other lawyer said. "Okay."

Mia hung up the phone.

"The answer please," I said to the quarterback.

He sat quietly but his body gave him away: a bead of sweat rolling down his neck, the clenching of his hands.

"Answer, damn it!" Meredith barked at him.

I put my hand on her arm to calm her down.

"I am waiting," I said.

"I am not intentionally throwing interceptions," the quarterback said.

"You liar!" Meredith shrieked. "Do you know how much money you are costing me!"

Mia put her arm around Meredith's shoulder and whispered in her ear. Meredith relaxed.

What the hell is Mia saying to everyone? I wondered. Why won't she whisper those words to me?

"Can we move on to the next subject now?" Gerald asked.

I scanned my list of questions, killing time. Is that it? Nothing is going on? I remembered the words of the football expert, considered them and put down my notes.

"Okay. Then tell me this: are you throwing the ball so your receivers can make easy catches?"

"I don't understand," Gerald said. "We're talking about an extremely violent game. Do you want my client to run down the field and just hand the ball to some sprinting receiver?"

"He understands the question," I said. "He needs to answer it."

Joey Balton didn't look upward; he wasn't searching for the answer. He knew it. "No," he said softly.

"What?" his lawyer asked.

"Now we're getting somewhere," Meredith said and Mia hit her hand as if she was trying to sneak a cookie from a jar.

"Why?" I asked.

"Maybe we need to take a break," Gerald said. I knew what he was thinking: his client was manipulating the scores and outcomes of games, likely a Federal offense. To keep it quiet, Meredith was going to get one helluva divorce settlement.

"I don't need a break. Let's get on with it," the quarterback said.

A stand-up guy, I thought. No wonder he was beloved. But soon that would all end.

"Why are you making it hard for your receivers to catch the ball?" I asked again.

"Because I don't want them to catch the ball."

"Why not?"

"Because I don't want our team to do well this year."

Got him, I thought. Arnie would be so proud of me. Not only was I going to get his Professional Football League Championship ring and a tour of the team's locker room before a game, I could probably negotiate to get his seed and then sell it anonymously over the Internet. What football crazed man wouldn't pay to impregnate his spouse with the seed of Joey Balton?

"Why not?" I asked.

"The worse we do, the higher a draft pick we'll get. If we finish with just three or four wins, we should have a pick in the top five of this year's Professional Football League draft."

"And why is that important?"

Joey Balton breathed in deeply. "Because I want to help Tyre Erving become A Blessed One."

"Excuse me?"

"I am a very good quarterback. Our team's receivers are mediocre. If we do poorly and it's because the receivers are dropping balls or letting them be intercepted, then no one will complain when we draft Tyre Erving with our first round draft pick."

Balton's lawyer looked like he was either suffering a heart attack or a week long bout of constipation.

"Tyre Erving," I said. "You mean the receiver from Notre Dame?" I had watched him play on television. He was six-feet four and weighed 240 pounds and was supposed to be the best receiver to come out of college in decades.

"That's him," Balton said.

"And you're willing to lose games this year just to get a great receiver?"

"You don't understand," Balton said. "You have no idea of The Higher Powers involved. Don't you understand: most teams with high draft picks have lousy quarterbacks. That's why they lose. If Tyre Erving goes to one of those teams, he'll suffer. But with me, he can become A Blessed One."

"A Blessed One," I said. "What is that?"

"A Blessed One is an athlete who has attained the highest level. He becomes a Spokesperson For The Lord. Tyre is the youngest athlete ever to attain Level 11. He's a Warrior Of The Lord. With me guiding him on the field, his elevation to A Blessed One is assured."

Hugo Gerald held up his hand. "Off the record?" he asked. I nodded. The lawyer looked at his client. "What the fuck are you talking about?"

- 18 -

After thirty minutes of questioning, on the record, this is what we all learned. In a sense, he had become a disciple of a new religion.

The recruiters were high school and college coaches, other players and agents. They sought athletes of great physical prowess. From the ancient Greek Olympians to Roman gladiators to modern soccer and football players, the eyes of the world had been focused on sports and physical perfection. The masses placed athletes atop pedestals once reserved for prophets. Did millions of people the world over watch genius physicists write equations on blackboards? Did our world base its leisure activities on the bloody work of soldiers and armies? No. It was athletics.

There were 12 Levels. Levels 1-6 were for learners; Levels 7-10 were for teachers. Level 11 was reserved for The Warriors Of The Lord. Level 12 was for only a few: The Blessed Ones, the representatives of The Lord on Earth.

There was no physical places of worship like churches or mosques or temples. There were online sites protected by 64 key encryption codes for one-on-one prayer sessions with teachers. Contributions were made to *Training For Excellence*, a not-for-profit corporation under U.S. law supposedly working to increase athletic performance.

Levels 1-10 were achieved through contributions and scholarly work, as well as athletic accomplishments. Levels 11 and 12, however, were beyond the reach of a mere monetary contributor. These were the levels where a person became both a worshipper and a figure to be worshipped.

Balton was recruited in college. He now was a Level 10. By aiding Erving, he would attain Warrior Of The Lord status. His slight frame, however, forever precluded him from being A Blessed One.

He's talking about The Holy Puck, I thought as I listened to his answers. He's talking about being blessed by The Hockey Gods. Who am I to say that he's completely nuts?

Balton's lawyer sat through the session open mouthed, not even bothering to take notes. He sweated like a man who had just run a marathon in the summer's heat.

Meredith stared at her husband, her eyes glazed. "I thought all that late night Internet surfing was a pornography fixation," she said. "I thought those payments were for real professional training sessions during the offseason."

"Does Toscana know?" I asked.

"I cannot divulge the names of The Initiated," Balton said. "I've said enough to be banished forever from The Lord's Field."

"Have we had enough for today?" Balton's lawyer finally managed to croak.

"Yea," I said. "Enough."

- 19 -

I called Cowboy Jake into my office. He wandered in without the holsters.

"I thought I asked you to get rid of that football guy," I said. "What happened?"

"He offered me season tickets to a suite at the stadium," Cowboy Jake said. "I figured I'd sell them and split the money with you."

I decided not to respond. After the deposition, what the hell was there to say?

- 20 -

Rebecca and I agreed no one should mention her husband's death at the rink, to her or Donnie. The rink should be Donnie's place for fun and to forget. I sent an email out to the team parents asking them and their children to honor Rebecca's wishes.

Donnie hadn't practiced in two weeks but I didn't think the layoff would have much of an impact on him. He was a kid who usually was on the ice fifty two weeks a year. Taking off the last two weeks would probably be good for him physically. But mentally, how would he cope, his father murdered . . .

My team had weekend home games. I got to the Ice Kingdom Saturday afternoon and smoked a cigar and drank coffee in the rink's parking lot while waiting for my players to arrive. I wore jeans and a fur lined Harley motorcycle jacket with numerous zippers. I could have passed for a member of Hell's Angels except for the short hair, eyeglasses and generally meek look about my face.

Donnie and Rebecca were among the last to arrive. She sat in her car while Donnie retrieved his bags and stick from the trunk and lugged his gear into the rink. I waited a few minutes but Rebecca did not look in my direction or get out of her car. I tossed the remainder of the cigar onto the asphalt and went inside.

It was forty minutes before game time and most of our team's parents clustered in the rink lobby. I avoided them and headed towards the locker room.

Teri Manyard was standing in front of the bleachers halfway to the locker rooms, pretending to watch the youth game in progress. She caught my eye and turned to face me, forcing me to stop. She wore a heavy, full length coat buttoned to her throat as if she was trying to hide her body from the world. Except for her face, no one would be able to recognize her.

"Afternoon," I said. "Is Sean fired up to play today?"

She shrugged. "I guess." She glanced about as if to make sure no one was paying any attention to us. "I want to thank you for losing that court hearing the other day."

Is she wearing a wire? I thought.

"I tried my hardest to win it," I replied. "I really can't talk to you about the case since our firm represents your husband."

"Do you think that's a coincidence?" she asked.

"I don't know."

"Things could get complicated since your firm represents my husband and you're coaching Sean."

"I suppose. Maybe it would be better if we stayed away from each other for awhile. We don't want to give anyone the idea that we're talking about your divorce."

"Stay away from each other?"

"I'm just the coach when I'm at the rink," I replied.

"The coach?"

"That's all I'm going to do from now on," I said slowly. "Coach Sean."

She bit her lip, nodded and looked away. "Okay," she said.

"Okay."

I began to step away when she said, "I'm pregnant."

Is it possible for someone to freeze mid-step as if time had stopped flowing for the person while the rest of the world rushed by?

My foot hit the ground and I pivoted.

"Really?"

"Yes. Oh, yes."

"Really?"

"Yes."

"Do we need to talk about this?"

"What do you think?" she asked.

"Okay," I said. "Okay. Later?"

"Later," she agreed.

As I was walking away from her I thought I heard someone yell my name. Deputy Wales waved to me from the top of the nearby bleachers. I waved back.

He had watched Teri and me talk. Terrific. I hoped he couldn't read lips. And I sure as hell hoped nothing bad happened to Teri's husband after this weekend's games.

Deputy Wales gestured to Teri and gave me a 'thumbs up' sign.

He couldn't read lips, could he?

I smiled and tried very hard to ignore the last few minutes of my life.

At the last practice I had spoke to Herb Rooks about changing the lines for the game. Donnie no longer needed two enforcers and Andy Rooks deserved to have a powerful player with him. I was going to move either Steele Williams or Sean Manyard onto Andy's line.

"Have you decided which one you'll move?" Herb asked anxiously. He had been pacing before the locker room and taping the blade of Andy's stick. Just before he saw me, I could swear he had been giving the blade a kiss. "I think it should be Williams, don't you?"

What a choice, I thought. If I move Sean off Donnie's line it will look like I'm punishing the kid because of Teri's alleged transgressions. If I keep Sean with Donnie it will look like I'm favoring Sean because my law firm represented his father. Damn.

"Sure," I said. "Williams it is. And I'll tell you what: Andy's line can start today's game. He practiced hard this week."

"He'll be so excited!" Herb yelled.

I let Herb announce the line-up and our starting players. Donnie didn't seem to care. He was quiet, looking mostly at the floor. Steele Williams had a scowl on his face and Andy was beaming.

Our goalies led our team onto the ice. From the bench I saw Teri in the stands, sitting off to the side of most of the team mothers. Mr. and Mrs. Williams sat together and when the game started I could see her expression and I knew where Steele inherited the scowl. Rebecca stood in a corner, arms folded, her eyes glued to the game.

Deputy Wales had moved to sit with the other team's parents, where he had a better view of Rebecca.

During the first period Donnie moved as if he had lead weights attached to his skates. If he was a manual shift car it looked like he had lost gears three, four and five. The other team's players knocked the puck off his stick, crowding him and he could not break free. His reputation, however, preceded him. Even though he seemed like an average player the coaches for the other team kept putting their best players on the ice against him. The ice opened up for Andy. He moved fast, gaining confidence with each shift. He scored our first and second goals, and then our fourth goal. Late in the second period, Andy had an opportunity to make a pass and spring Steele Williams alone against the goalie but he tried to be fancy instead, challenging a defenseman instead of making the pass and he lost the puck.

"Be a team player!" Shari Williams screamed from the stands.

April Rooks started to rise but another team mom grabbed onto her arm and held her down. Michael Williams sat quietly, acting as if he hadn't heard anything.

Towards the end of the final period we trailed by a goal. Donnie's line was to go out next. I hadn't wanted to talk to him this game. I just wanted him to have fun and play but through the iron mask covering his face he looked miserable and our team was going to lose a league game against an inferior opponent. We didn't need the game; we were in first place, comfortably ahead of the second place team. We could lose this game and it would mean nothing.

But I didn't want to lose.

I leaned over as he sat on the bench and tapped his helmet. "You okay?" I asked quietly.

"Just tired," Donnie said.

"You want me to get you a cup of coffee?"

He managed a grin but it was forced. "I'll be okay."

"You sure?"

"Yea."

"Good. Look, don't try to do too much. Just get the puck near their net and fire it. Just fire it at the net. Sean will knock in any rebound. Okay?"

"Sure, coach."

I tapped Sean Manyard on the helmet. "Knock in any rebounds you see."

I backed away, standing behind the bench.

"Andy's hot," Herb said to me as the whistle blew and Donnie's line took the ice. There was a little over a minute left in the game. "Shouldn't we get Andy's line back on the ice?"

"Let's see what happens," I replied.

Rebecca hadn't moved more than a foot in either direction during the game. Deputy Wales remained in the stands, now talking on his cell phone. When I occasionally looked in his direction he seemed to be spending more time gazing at Rebecca than at the game.

The puck dropped. The opposing centerman knocked Donnie down and pushed the puck forward to his winger. In less than six seconds the puck was in our net. When the final horn sounded the other team celebrated like they had just won the Stanley Cup. Their coaches were high-fiving each other on the bench and some of their parents were hugging and crying.

"Should have put Andy on the ice," Herb muttered to me.

"Live and learn," I replied.

- 21 -

Deputy Wales leaned against my Porsche.

"Tough game," he said. "I heard your team was favored by twelve goals."

"You bet on it?"

"No, but I took the 'over' on the number of women you'd impregnate this month."

Fuck, he can read lips. "What's the line?"

"Two."

"If you told me that two months ago I'd say either the bookie was nuts or I was having the time of my life."

"Is the bookie nuts?"

I thought of Teri. "He's getting there," I said. "So you learn anything today?"

"That Shari Williams gal is a piece of work. In the lobby after the game she sounded like she wanted to cut off your balls. Is she one of your jilted paramours?"

"I moved her son off Donnie's line."

"Watch out. If you turn up dead I'm going to question her first."

"Anything else?"

"Hockey parents are crazier than soccer parents," Wales replied. "By the way, we finished with your hockey sticks. I put them in your car."

I peered in the Porsche's window. The sticks were there. The car had been locked.

Wales smiled. "I can do more than just read lips."

"Breaking into a vehicle must come in handy when you're planting evidence," I said.

Wales chuckled and began walking away. "See you around."

"Can't wait."

- 22 -

Rebecca came to The White Apartment at seven that night, carrying two large bags of groceries. She wore a tight fitting gray shirt with a high collar and sleeves covering her forearms. Black cotton slacks hugged her legs. I stood beside her in the narrow kitchen as she emptied the bags. I tried to help but she slapped my hands away.

"When was the last time you cooked here?"

I shrugged. "Do TV dinners and frozen pizza count?"

"No."

"Then, never."

"Men can be so lazy." She laughed when she opened the fridge and freezer: both were empty. "The way you live is really so sad."

"I like to live lean."

"Lazy," Rebecca said, smiling broadly, her face glowing. "Not lean. Lazy."

Her small, pudgy fingers arranged the groceries into four piles on the tiny counter, her fingernails cut short and polished. She kept smiling, her shirt showing a flat stomach and small breasts, the pants outlining the curves of hips and legs. I wanted to hold her. I wanted to hold her and never let go.

I was short and the top of her head barely reached my chin. "We're going to put some meat on you," she said, bustling about. "If you're only going to heat up dinner, then it's going to be a home cooked meal." I watched as she prepared four meals, three for this week and one for tonight, all with side dishes. Meatloaf and potatoes with gravy, pork chops with apple sauce and green beans, breaded chicken cutlets with rice, and for tonight spaghetti and meatballs. She moved about, hemmed in by the counter on one side and the appliances on the other, eyes sparkling, occasionally refilling her glass of wine from the bottle she brought with her. She talked non-stop about her job and where she learned the recipes and cooking with her mom, laughing, sipping wine. I listened to her voice and watched her move. She apparently wanted nothing from me, other than my presence. She didn't mention hockey or Donnie or Henry.

She made huge portions for the both of us, mounds of spaghetti and homemade red sauce and meatballs as big as my fist, spicy and hot.

"I try to do this on Sundays when we're not traveling that day for hockey," she said. "There's so little time after getting home from work and before getting Donnie to the rink. It's nice to have a home cooked meal ready to reheat instead of always going to a fast food drive thru."

She liked to talk with her hands, waving her fork at me, the tines sometime empty, sometimes wrapped with layers of spaghetti or harpooning a large chuck of meatball. She ate everything and so did I. We finished what was left of the first bottle of wine and then emptied the second.

She gestured to the kitchen and I opened the third, a rich merlot. We left the dishes in the sink, donned jackets and stood on the balcony with glasses of wine, to smoke.

"Is Donne with the nanny?" I finally asked.

"No. He's spending the night with Sean Manyard. Teri has them tonight. Terrible thing, about their divorce."

But you were getting a divorce, I thought but held my tongue.

"Teri said your law firm is representing her husband."

"That's true. Obviously, I can't talk about it."

"Sure. I understand." She drew on the cigarette and a light breeze played with her hair, slicking strands across her eyes. "She talked to me for awhile when I dropped Donnie off, asking about you and me, how long we'd been together, how serious things were between us."

"She knows?"

"I told her where I was going tonight."

Great, I thought to myself.

"Is that alright?" Rebecca asked.

I leaned down and kissed her cheek, soft and rosy and just a bit cold. "It's fine. So what did you tell her?"

"That outside the rink you're a mess but that you're good in bed and you have an amazing tongue."

"Really?"

"I go to bed dreaming about your tongue," Rebecca said, looking up at me, her eyes moist.

"Really?"

"I cannot tell a lie."

I bent down again and tasted the wine on her lips and on the tip of her tongue and she pressed her body against mine and I soared. Music played in my head. I soared.

- 23 -

The next day, Michael Williams intercepted me, grinning. "I did it!" he exclaimed.

You found a muzzle for your wife? I thought.

"I sent videos of our first line playing a few games to The Committee and we've been accepted!" Michael continued.

"To what?"

"The Turkey Feast!"

I stared at him blankly.

"It's the most prestigious tournament in North America during the Thanksgiving holiday! The Committee only selects the best twenty-four Under 10 teams in the country! And because of Donnie and Sean and Steele they accepted us!"

"Thanksgiving?"

"From Wednesday night to Sunday night."

"Where?"

"New Jersey."

"New Jersey?"

"This is an amazing tournament! The kids who play in it have gone on to play for major colleges and the NHL!"

S.S. Williams was drinking from a large plastic cup, wearing a University of North Dakota hockey jersey. She swayed slightly beside her husband and her eyes were bloodshot.

"We need to talk," she slurred to me. "Soon. Real soon."

"Not now," Michael whispered to her furiously.

"You want the team to spend Thanksgiving Day at a hotel?" I asked.

"The hotel is right by the rink. And they have a Thanksgiving holiday dinner for all guests that's free!"

"Thanksgiving?" I asked again.

"Yes! The future is ours!"

I'll need to call Jenny, I thought. I had found life's meaning. It was to eat a Thanksgiving meal at a hotel by a hockey rink and play in the Turkey Feast.

"Sounds expensive," I said.

"Less kids that go, more ice time for Steele," Shari mumbled.

"Excuse me?"

"It could be a burden on some people," Michael said. "But I already spoke to Rebecca Warren and Teri Manyard, and the Rooks, and they are all willing to go."

"We need more than four players."

"I'm sure we can round up ten or so," Michael said. "That will be enough."

I nodded, looking about. A lot of the other parents were glancing in our direction. "Everyone on the team know?" I asked.

"Pretty much."

"Okay," I said. "I'm in. Besides, it won't cost all the other parents that much."

"Why not?" Shari slurred, reddish brown liquid dribbling down her chin from the cup.

"Your husband's offer," I replied. I gave Michael a friendly slug on the shoulder. "That $10,000 you were going to donate to the team's coffers? Turns out we need it after all. That should help subsidize the costs of airfare and hotel rooms."

"You want us to pay $10,000 for Steele to play with that little prick, Andy Rooks!" Shari screeched.

"This is one great gesture," I said to Michael. "I am sure all of the other parents will appreciate it."

He opened his mouth to speak but I had already turned away.

I bought coffee and checked on the kids in the locker room and took my place outside the locker room door. Rebecca was nowhere in sight but Deputy Wales sat in the bleachers and waved at me. I waved back. Twenty minutes before game time Herb joined me.

"You hear the news? It's amazing! No team from our state has ever been invited to the Turkey Feast!"

"Never heard of it."

Herb looked shocked. "There are scouts there. Once, a kid was offered a scholarship to play for the University of Minnesota when the tournament ended."

"A 10 year old was offered a college scholarship?"

"Yes. It's an amazing tournament."

"What happened to that kid?"

Herb shrugged. "No idea."

"Families really want to fly to New Jersey on the day before Thanksgiving for a hockey tournament?"

"We have to fly," Herb said. "We'd have to leave on Monday if we drove there."

My father and The Hockey Gods. Maybe I should have told Jenny that life's meaning could only be found on the ice, with a stick and a puck.

- 24 -

Things were back to normal for the game. Donnie's line accounted for seven goals, Andy Rook scored another two and we crushed an Arkansas team. I did little during the game. My team was on cruise control. With Donnie playing up to his potential, winning was assured. Rebecca stood by herself in a corner of the rink, wearing loose black sweats, not even bothering to cheer when Donnie scored. It was too easy. It was almost unfair. What would my father have thought? Donnie had been blessed by The Hockey Gods to carry The Holy Puck. There was almost nothing that I could teach him.

He was 10 years old but he was light years past me. He was beyond everyone at the rink. I wondered if a teacher, say a piano teacher, felt the same way after giving lessons to children for decades, and then one day having a new student arrive who in just a few moments showed that he or she would soon be, or maybe already was, beyond anything the teacher could teach.

I wondered if Donnie was going to be a player on The Lord's Field.

- 25 -

Unlike television depictions, a divorce lawyer rarely went to new and interesting places while on the job. We would go to our offices; we would go to another lawyer's offices; we would go to Court. We did not go to interesting places to investigate our cases. Monday afternoon would be a treat: a new and hopefully interesting place to visit.

The building was in the same corporate park as our law firm, about half a mile away. I drove. It was a boring rectangle, four stories of black glass.

I took the elevator to the top floor. Professor Melton told us to meet him on the fourth floor in Suite 401. Mrs. Tolliver had yet to hire another attorney, so Susan would attend on her behalf. Susan had agreed to represent Mrs. Tolliver for a few more days, especially given that Melton said it was urgent we all met. Suite 401 hid behind a plain door with nothing but a number on it. The suite was at the end of a hallway and appeared to be just one of two office suites on the floor. The door opened to a small room without any furniture, bare walls and the floor covered with cheap industrial blue carpet. Three doors were cut into each of the other walls. Susan was already there.

"What business is this?" Susan asked.

"Melton didn't tell me, other than he could use their conference room."

On cue, the door to our right opened and Melton stuck his head into the foyer. "Good. You're on time. The Tollivers were early and are waiting for us. Come. Come, then."

We slipped into an even smaller room and Melton closed the door, paused for a few moments as he shook each of our hands and then led us through a door on the opposite wall directly into a conference room.

The Tollivers sat side-by-side at the rectangular table. Melton gestured to the seats across from them; Susan and I complied, each of us putting our briefcase by our feet. Melton's satchel was on the table, scarred and old. The seats were the stackable kind of chairs one normally found at a school assembly. Like the foyer, the walls were bare, painted white, and the same carpeting covered the floor. There was barely room between the back of our chairs and the walls. There were no windows and another door on the other side of the room led to other parts of the suite.

The air conditioner seemed to be on full blast. Susan shivered and I rubbed my hands together. The Tollivers sat upright, not looking at one another, both dressed exquisitely.

"Thank you all for coming," Melton said. "After the inspection of the home the other day, I thought it important we get together and talk."

I held up my hand, palm outward and facing Melton, like a police officer ordering traffic to stop. "Before you say anything else, please remember you have been retained by my law firm to lend your expertise on behalf of Mr. Tolliver. As we discussed on the telephone this morning, you first need to talk to Mr. Tolliver and myself, and then we can decide whether the information will be shared with opposing counsel."

"I normally would agree," Melton said. "But not today."

The far door opened and three soldiers entered the room, all dressed in camouflage jumpsuits and wearing blue berets. One held a tray, the others aimed short barrels of submachine guns at us. The soldier placed the tray beside Melton. On it rested four vials, each affixed with a typewritten label with one of our last names, along with four syringes, gauze pads and a number of rubber tourniquets.

"What the hell is going on here!" George Tolliver demanded loudly.

"In addition to my work for the Smithsonian Institute, I also do consulting work for the Center of Disease Control in Atlanta. It is in the latter role I address you, and please believe me when I tell you I have more authority in this role than the Court has in your divorce case."

"Disease?" Mrs. Tolliver gasped, turning pale. She reached out and grasped onto her husband's forearm. "What disease?"

"We must draw blood from each of you," Melton said. "I'll explain after we do so."

Susan stood. "No, you will explain now, and if I'm not satisfied then you'll do your explaining to members of the local police."

One of the armed soldiers walked around the table, letting go of the gun which hung from a strap about his neck. He stood beside her, hands clasped behind his back.

"Please sit down," Melton said.

"She's right," I began to say but the soldier kicked the metal toe of his boot into the back of Susan's knee. She cried out, tears in her eyes and spit on her lips, falling and the soldier grabbed her by the shoulders so that she landed in her chair. The soldier aimed his submachine gun at her skull.

"No more questions," Melton said. "Please."

Susan sobbed quietly, grasping the back of her leg. I felt my stomach lurch as if I was seasick and I felt the urgent need to vomit and piss and defecate, all at once. Sweat rolled off my skin, everywhere. I leaned back in the seat, closed my eyes for a few moments, trying to breathe normally and get hold of myself.

"Oh my god," Mrs. Tolliver kept muttering to herself. "Oh my god."

"What is going on?" George whispered to her.

"I don't know," she replied.

The soldier without a weapon quickly and efficiently drew blood from each of our arms, filling the four vials. The soldiers all left the room.

"The doors are locked," Melton said. "Nobody bother to think of leaving. No one is going anywhere for awhile. If it will calm anyone, you can smoke in here. I don't think they'll be any raid on these offices from the police. Ever."

I lit up with shaking hands. Susan reached out her hand. "I only have one."

"We'll share."

Melton waited until we were all looking at him, his elbows resting on the table and hands clasped together. "If you haven't guessed yet these offices are rented by the CDC. The soldiers are Navy Seals, part of a division assigned to the CDC on a full time basis. To do our work, we sometimes have to send teams of scientists to places unfriendly to the United States. Sometimes we go to friendly places, but without official permission. The Navy Seals help get us in and out of those places, safely."

"What's going on?" I asked. "Just get to the point."

"It's the beetles, obviously. They're banned from export out of the rain forest. The cover story is that they would pose a threat to any other ecological system, like the problem those barnacles are causing in the Great Lakes. But that's just the cover story. Truth is the beetles carry a parasite, another bug that's not visible to the human eye. This parasite is transmitted through the waste products of the beetles. They don't hurt the beetles and they actually feed on its waste before it leaves the insect's body. However, if they use a mammal as a host, they colonize in most of the mammal's organs, including the brain. An infected mammal can pass on this parasite through sexual contact. I hate to pry Mr. and Mrs. Tolliver, but since you both lived in the house with the beetles for years, I need to know if either of you have had sex with anyone else."

"Is there a cure?" Mrs. Tolliver asked.

"There's a treatment that's one hundred percent effective. But we don't want to have to start inoculating the entire population of this country, nor do I imagine you want to go to jail for bringing the damn things into this country. So again, Mr. Tolliver, have you had sex since the beetles came into your house with anyone other than your wife?"

"No," he replied. "No one."

"Are you sure?"

"Absolutely," he replied.

"Mrs. Tolliver?"

"No one. Just my husband."

"Okay then," Melton said.

"What about me and Susan?" I asked. How the hell can I tell Rebecca that I caused a microscopic insect to infest her body? What about Teri's baby?

"We doubt you've been infected, based upon what you've told us of your contact with the beetles. However, we just want to make sure, so we're testing you, too."

"What happens?" Mrs. Tolliver asked. "What happens if we're not treated?"

"Madness," Melton replied. "Psychopathic incidents and rages as the brain tissue is infected and destroyed. It takes years; that's why you wouldn't have shown symptoms yet. And there's a special agent that needs to be put into your blood to detect the critters. Your normal doctor would miss it at a physical. Ultimately, the end result is death."

"This is all a bad joke, right?" Susan asked.

"Anybody laughing?" Melton asked. His cell phone rang. He answered, listened for a moment and put it back into his pocket. He pointed to the four corners of the room. "Hidden cameras, each one trained on one of you. We have computers that can tell if a person is lying based on micro changes in the temperature of a person's face. Luckily, the Tollivers were telling the truth about their sexual partners. Otherwise, we probably would have had to work them over with cattle prods for the information."

"Now you are joking," I said.

Melton laughed. "You bet."

"When do we find out if we're infected?" Mrs. Tolliver asked.

"The test is quick. It will only be a few more minutes."

She began to cry. Her husband folded his arms, looking more pissed than scared and ignored her. Susan passed the cigar back to me. What if she's infected, I thought? I worried about if for a moment and then brushed aside the thought. There's a treatment, Melton said. This will all be okay.

"Bet you never figured you'd end up being part of a medical crisis, working divorce cases," Melton said.

"Beats sitting at my desk," I tried to joke.

"Let's talk about the house," Melton began, polishing his glasses with a cloth. "No one goes back there. Ever. Later today a few Navy Seals will drive over in a van bearing the name of a heating and cooling company. They'll drive into the garage and shut the door. They'll be wearing contamination suits, and they're going to plant a lot of thermite bombs and explosives throughout the house. They've studied the plans. Around midnight the entire house will implode in on itself and the temperature will reach over a thousand degrees at the time of ignition. Ain't nothing going to survive that. We've already spoken to the appropriate people. The fire company will say there was a problem with a furnace and that there was a gas leak as well. As a result, they'll be inspections of the other houses in the neighborhood, although we doubt the bugs have spread. Someone would have seen them, even if they were breeding in the walls. A few would have gotten out eventually to fly about the house. They are hard to miss. Your insurance company is going to cover 100% of your claim. For a disaster, it will be a pretty good one."

"Can I go back to get my jewelry and . . ."

"No," Melton cut Mrs. Tolliver off. "Nothing. It all goes up in flames."

"I told you not to bring the damn beetles into the country," George cursed.

"Look at it this way," Susan said. "Now you both get full value for the house. The divorce case should settle fairly easily now."

"We'll see about that," I said testily.

"Now, now children," Melton said. "Let's all be good little boys and girls. No fighting at the table."

The soldier/nurse returned with a tray and the lab results. "As expected," Melton said as he read the paper. "The lawyers are fine. The bugs obviously hate lawyers as much as the rest of the country. The Tollivers, however, are infected."

"So treat us!" Mrs. Tolliver shrieked.

"What if I want a second opinion?" George asked.

"Well, that's fine, but the second opinion is going to be given by one of the Navy Seals with his gun. Is that what you're looking for?"

"You can't pull this shit," George said. "This is America."

"And you broke one of our vital national security laws by bringing the damn things into the country. You're lucky we don't put you both on a helicopter and drop you back in that rain forest." Melton looked at the soldier. "I got things to do. Get this over with."

The soldier calmly swabbed each of their arms with alcohol and injected a brownish fluid into their veins.

Melton took two contracts from his satchel and slid them across the table to me and Susan. "Confidentiality agreements," he said. "You don't talk about anything that happened here today, to no one, ever. If you do, we can haul your asses into Court and then throw you in jail for a decade or so. And revisions are not acceptable, so keep your red pens in your briefcases. Sign them, please."

"What about us?" George asked.

"Oh, you don't need to sign them."

"Why not?"

Melton looked at his silver Rolex Submariner. "Cause when they pull your bodies from the ruins of the house, there ain't going to be any reason for us to need them."

"What!"

"This treatment is for the good of the rest of the country. There ain't nothing that can be done for you."

George tried to stand but his legs gave out. The Tollivers began shaking as if they were being shocked with electricity, eyes bulging and foam coming from their mouths as they bit apart their tongues. They flopped in their chairs like marionettes being handled by drunken puppeteers. After about ten seconds they collapsed, heads cracking against the wood of the table.

"Another day at the office," Melton said. He collected the signed contracts from Susan and I. "Well, I guess that ends the divorce case. Any questions?"

- 26 -

I retreated to The White Apartment for a cigar and a bottle of whiskey. I felt like an Eskimo, rocking from one foot to the other on the balcony, clothed in thermals and jeans, a heavy wool sweater and a blue parka bought just for smoking outside in the cold. Headphones from my MP3 player nestled in my ears. The Rolling Stones and *Wild Horses* floated across my mind.

I may not be the father, I thought. It could be Mr. Manyard. It could be anyone.

But for some reason I didn't want to believe it. The Manyards were getting divorced. She couldn't have been sleeping with him. I wanted to believe she was only sleeping with me.

She and Darla, in the locker room.

It could be anyone.

But if I was the father?

My ex-wife had spoken about raising a family but she wanted to wait a few years. Maybe that was just her excuse.

Alcohol molecules invaded my brain.

If I had a son we would skate in the winter on the pond. The puck would slide between hockey sticks, tape to tape. We would talk of his journey, one day in the future, to the frozen lake at the foot of the mountain, The Hockey Gods waiting, ready to judge him.

Would he fail?

Would I be happy if he didn't play as well as Donnie? I sucked down half of the whiskey in the tumbler, fumes in my nostrils.

Rebecca.

My pants vibrated.

The hard shell of the cell phone replaced the headphone's right ear bud.

"Sam?"

"Hello?"

"Come play with us!"

"Who is this?"

"Do you want to come out and play?" the voices came at me like a song, the lead singer's voice doubled, one voice a half beat behind the other.

"Who are you?"

"Mia and Mai," both voices said, repeating the same words.

"Well, I don't think so. Not tonight."

The sound of a sledgehammer smashing into the apartment's front door brought me staggering into the living room. A final gulp of whiskey and the door opened.

"You look like an Eskimo," Mia—or Mai—said.

"What do you want?"

"To play with you." They each grabbed one of my hands and dragged me away.

One drove the cramped subcompact car, the other sat in the back with me. I held the smoldering cigar, feeling nauseous and drunk. According to the Landslut driving the car we were headed to *The Lawyer's Lounge*, a bar supposedly in the heart of the midtown entertainment district. I had never heard of it.

"So how do I know what to call you?" I slurred. The woman beside me laughed.

"Most people ask us that immediately. It took you two months."

"I'm shy."

"You're socially comatose," the driver said.

I couldn't argue with her. The only evidence to dispute the point, Teri and Rebecca, probably would get me disbarred.

"There is a way to tell us apart,' the driver said. "But it's a secret."

"In college, we would take the same classes but in different semesters," the woman next to me said. "Mia, who is driving, was better at math and science. I was better at liberal arts-type courses and writing essays. So, Mia took all of the math and science courses. I took all of the courses that required essays and papers."

"What?" I asked, confused.

"Don't be dumb," the driver said. "Everyone knows you're very smart. It's simple. I would take a math class in one semester and Mai would take the same class in another semester. When it came time to take the tests I would show up in her place and take the tests for her. She'd do the same for me in classes that had essay exams. Sometimes it wasn't just for tests. Sometimes I would take a class as myself and the next year I'd take it as my sister. We did the same thing in high school."

"It also worked for college and law school entrance exams," the woman next to me said.

"So you're each living a lie? You gals play the same games with your boyfriends?"

"Finally, a good question from The Statue," the driver laughed.

"You'll never know," the woman beside me said.

Apparently, *The Lawyer's Lounge* did not have its own parking lot. We drove around, hunting for a space close to the building.

The chill of late fall had a huge impact on the midtown entertainment district. During the warmer evenings of summer the streets of midtown narrowed to bottlenecks as traffic competed with swarms of stoned teenagers too young to enter the taverns and inebriated young adults staggering from one drinking establishment to the other, along with a visible and aggressive police force trying to impose some order on the mind altered mess. The bars featured live bands and outdoor seating in the summer and only those deemed worthy by the bar owners were allowed to drink from glass. Most people received their beverages, from beers to martinis, in plastic cups. On Sunday mornings it was easier to throw out plastic cups than pick shards of glass off the floors and streets of the district.

But it was cold outside now and the crowds had thinned as snowfall approached. Still, parking was problematic and Mia had to squeeze the car into a spot several blocks away.

The Lawyer's Lounge was in the basement of a building situated between a Thai restaurant and a karate studio. Mia led us down a narrow alley and punched a code into an electronic keypad beside a steel door painted brick red like the building's outer walls. There was no signage or bouncer. I staggered down steel steps as Mia, or perhaps by this time Mai, punched a code into a second keypad. Behind another steel door came the deep pounding of drums and a bass beat and the scratchy singing of a heavy metal star.

The twins wore identical outfits: tight, faded blue jeans and leather coats.

"If someone had a match we could turn your breath into a flamethrower," one of the women said.

"How do people tell you apart?" I asked. "Really?"

They giggled.

The Lawyer's Lounge was a private club, not open to the public. A bar counter of polished wood with modernistic steel stools before it fronted an impressive collection of alcohol. A bartender in a tuxedo sans jacket patiently waited for the next order. Seating consisted of plush leather armchairs grouped in various numbers around coffee tables of metal and stone. Dark wood paneling covered the walls and rock music from the 1980's descended from hidden speakers. Exhaust fans pulled in smoke from cigars and cigarettes, blowing it out of the building. The crowd of some twenty people seemed happy, sipping cocktails and smiling and inhaling smoke, young adults and middle aged men and women.

"Have a cigar," Jaime Landscuda said, taking our coats and handing me an enormous stogie.

Jenny winked at me from across the room, slouched in a chair, fondling her cigar in ways she had never done with me. She took a deep draw and blew smoke in my direction.

"You own this place?" I asked.

"For years," Jaime Landscuda replied. "I got tired of the club scene. Too many teenagers sneaking in and there would always be a fight or alteration. When gang members began dressing up and carrying guns into the establishments I decided I needed a change of scenery. Go get yourself a drink. Everything's on the house."

The bartender poured a generous amount of whiskey into my glass as I cut and lit the cigar. Cuban, I noticed from the band. Impressive.

I recognized several attorneys from other firms, some court personnel and a few members of the sheriff's department. They made up the middle aged group. I assumed the younger set were friends of the Landsluts.

The chair next to Jenny was empty.

"May I?"

"Do you really think that you need to ask?"

I fell into the chair. The cushions and leather surrounded me. I could fall asleep here, I thought.

"Have you ever been here?" Jenny asked.

"No."

"My first time, too."

Landscuda stood next to the counter with the Landsluts and two young men who, if actors, would be cast as quarterbacks in a football movie. One had an arm around Mia—or Mai—and the other kept gently bumping into the other one. Like the girls they were identical twins. Like the girls, they dressed the same. Faded blue jeans and blue shirts.

I gulped my drink.

"Jaime has a loft on the top floor," Jenny said.

"That's a good way to avoid a DUI."

"I'm waiting to see if he and one of the female law students disappear for twenty minutes or so."

"Law students?"

"Friends of the twins." Jenny wore a short skirt and crossed her legs and smiled at me. Happy Girl, I thought. Later, would she transform into the Satanist when she and Landshark were alone in the loft?

"You can ask."

"About?"

"Jaime. You keep glancing from me to him."

"I'm looking at all of the twins."

"They're dating."

"The guys are law students, too?"

"No," Jenny said. "Male models."

"Figures."

"Feeling threatened or overmatched?"

"I wasn't going to hook up with either girl."

"Too bad. Jaime says one of them really likes you."

"Forget it," I said. "He knew you'd tell me. He's just trying to fuck with my mind."

"No. Really. One of them likes you."

"Fine. Which one?"

Jenny shrugged. "Who can tell? Jaime told me that when they first dated the models, they would switch off. One night Mia would be Mia, the next night Mia would be Mai. They had lots of laughs over it until they began to realize the boys were doing the same thing to them."

"Huh?"

"Okay, the boys are Jim and John. Mia dates Jim and Mai dates John. But for fun Mia and Mai would switch names so Mia would be with John on a date and Mai would be with Jim. But that's only what they thought because the boys switched, too. One of the girls would say she was Mai and go out to dinner with John but she was really with Jim because the boys switched, too."

I gestured to the bartender for a refill.

"How long did it take before they figured it out?"

"The girls figured it out when they were in bed. Each of the boys has a unique moan."

"And one of the twins likes me? Why?"

"Sometimes you really piss me off," Jenny said. "Lately, it's most of the time."

She stood and walked away.

I let the chair hold me. The cigar took small bites out of my brain with sharp teeth and a nutty breath and I thought about falling asleep and letting the cigar's burning tip fall onto the leather and the entire bar burst into flames and there was screaming and Mia—or was it Mai—decided to spend her last moments on Earth impaled on my . . .

"Here's your drink," Landshark said. He appropriated Jenny's seat so I tried to sit up straight and I reached for the glass of whiskey.

At the bar, the Landsluts seemed to be melting into the male models, tongues first. Jenny sat on one of the steel stools and flirted with the bartender.

"So why am I here?" I asked Landshark.

"You must be getting drunk. There's no other reason for the cowardly lion to find his balls."

"Huh?"

"Never mind." Landshark sipped from a martini glass filled with a clear liquid and four olives harpooned on a toothpick. "Though I'm not surprised. Men without courage normally find their dicks before they find their balls."

"If you're going to fire me then go ahead and do it. That's what you want to do, anyway. But I'm not going to quit."

"Exactly," Landshark said. "That's why you have no courage."

Enough alcohol and Cuban cigar smoke had invaded the blood vessels of my brain for me to start to rise, one fist clenched, but Landshark gently tapped me on my fist and said, "Relax. It's okay." I sat back down.

"I'm not going to fire you," Landshark said. "I need guys like you. You're smart and can help me when I'm in a jam at work and you'll handle the crap cases that I don't want to deal with. Since you don't generate a lot of business you're not a threat to my position at the firm. You're actually one of the reasons I agreed to join the firm. You'll keep everything running smoothly like a good Swiss watch but you'll never have enough power to challenge me."

"What about the twins, when they graduate from law school?"

"I love them for the image they project, both to and for me, but they're too ambitious to stay once they have degrees. Eventually they would try to oust me and take over. They've worked for me this long because I've promised them, in writing, a rather large, interest free loan when they graduate from law school, to help them start their own shop. A few years from now they'll probably be kicking both of our asses in court."

"Fuck you."

"You're almost forty, right? It can't be that hard to look in the mirror at your age and see who's really looking back. You're a worker ant. I'm a queen, so to speak. We'll get along just fine."

I should have brought a handgun to this party, I thought. The risk of shooting myself would have been worth it.

"Why did the Landsluts bring me here?"

"Be nice," Landshark said. "One of them, for reasons I don't understand, actually wants to sleep with you."

He stood, patted me on the head and walked away.

"Which one?" I called out.

I saw Jenny mutter her favorite obscenity.

I may have fallen asleep with my eyes open, somehow balancing the glass on my knee and sucking the cigar like a baby's pacifier when one of the Landsluts picked up my drink and sat on my lap.

I was wide awake.

"It lives," she giggled. She took the cigar, puffed on it a few times and handed it back. "Are you having a good time?"

"You're kidding, right?"

"Don't you trust anyone?"

"Everyone here seems to be talking in a language I don't understand."

"You're just out of practice, that's all."

"From what?"

"Socializing," she replied. "Assuming you ever knew how to do it." She adjusted, wiggling her bottom so the side of her hip pressed into my stomach, putting an arm around my neck, tiny hairs on the skin of her cheeks, her tongue sometimes slipping between lips, and she was warm, so warm.

"In the car one of you called me The Statue."

"It's your nickname at the law firm."

"No, it's not."

"It is," she said. "It really is. Even Arnie called you that, when he spoke to Jaime about joining the firm."

I thought she bit my neck.

Jenny watched, standing by Landshark. She had a look on her face that made me hope she hadn't brought a handgun to the party.

"I kind of got my client murdered this afternoon."

"I hope he doesn't owe the firm a lot of money," she replied.

"What are you doing with me?" I asked.

She took the cigar again and smoked it for awhile. The male models huddled with her twin sister and their hands seemed to be everywhere. Smoke from cigarettes and cigars overwhelmed the exhaust fans. If we were in Tokyo we'd be donning surgical masks.

"Are you the one who likes me?" My glass was empty and the room tilted for a moment.

"Does it matter?" she asked. She reached between her legs and pressed down on my crotch.

"No," I replied and passed out.

- 27 -

I awoke with a start.

Was it all a bad dream?

No, it was not. I was still at *The Lawyer's Lounge*. Muscles relaxed and I sank back into the chair alone in the bar room, my head throbbing. Someone had taped a piece of paper to my chest.

'Statue At Rest,' it read.

Funny. Very funny.

My coat lay draped on one of the bar stools and an envelope was propped up by a bottle of whiskey and a tumbler on the bar counter. At least no one stole my Omega watch, I thought. Ten o'clock, clearly not in the evening. Damn it, I had to be at work and my ride likely was long gone.

I wobbled to the counter.

Inside the envelope, written on pink stationary with purple ink the flowery note read: 'You have the day off. I cleared it with the boss in return for a favor. You owe me!' The signature proclaimed 'Your Semi-Secret Admirer.'

More whiskey? Forget it.

I called a cab and retreated to The White Apartment. The hangover began to diminish at noon. At one point, Landshark called my cell phone to express his sadness after learning of the fire at the Tolliver home and the death of both parties.

"They found the bodies in the ruins, both burned to a crisp," Landshark informed me.

"How surprising," I replied, sitting on my white couch in my white living room in boxer shorts.

"And the guy still owes us about three grand in legal fees," Landshark pointed out. "We'll have to sue his estate for the money.

Do you know if he had a will? Hell, maybe we can represent his estate."

He kept talking but I stopped listening. After awhile I terminated the call.

By four o'clock I began to feel normal. There was a half-full bottle of whiskey in the kitchen and several cigars in the humidor.

Another day, I thought. Another night lay ahead.

I waited for the assault of the sadness bubbles but they never came.

I was starting on my second cigar and my third tumbler of whiskey sometime after darkness replaced the light of day when she picked the door's lock and stormed into the living room. Not Happy Girl. Not The Satanist. It was The Insane One. I had heard rumors of its existence but had never seen any proof before.

"I think you may have walked in mud or something."

"Not mud," it snarled. "Black paint."

"Excuse me?"

"I coated my sneakers and legs and arms with black paint while I was outside your front door."

"Why?"

She began dancing, her legs pumping so furiously that black paint droplets flew onto white walls and white furniture.

"You need music?"

"Got the beat in my head!" she screamed.

I stood watching her until she finally stopped, panting and sweating, stains under her armpits and spreading on her stomach and ass. She wore one of those skintight bodysuits in gray from the Manyard store with Addidas high topped basketball shoes, perhaps once white but now black from the paint.

"Whiskey?" I asked.

"Yea."

"Cigar?"

"What you think?"

We went into my bedroom and sat on the floor, our backs against the bed. Reluctantly, she agreed to take off the sneakers but that did little considering her arms and legs were wet with paint.

"You ever think about your life?" she asked.

"In what way?"

"How fucking stupid can you be? Your life; your existence. The reason you keep breathing every few seconds instead of just smashing your head with a hammer and letting your face fall into a bucket of water."

Sadness bubbles. The reason I never would buy myself a gun.

"You left me at *The Lawyer's Lounge*," I replied. "You're supposed to be my friend."

"This isn't about me, you dumb ass."

"Excuse me?"

"Rebecca is a bitch who is using you."

"You're just pissed off at me," I replied. "Besides, you're in bed with Landshark. You're the last one who should be talking about a bedmate with me."

"Why haven't you thrown me out?"

"Huh?"

"I just trashed your apartment. I'm leaking paint all over your bedroom. Your response is to sip whiskey with me and smoke a cigar with me. Why?"

"I think I've had enough contact with the police."

"Bullshit. It's because I'm real."

"Huh?"

"Rebecca and that Manyard bitch. They're amusement park rides. I'm real."

"Huh?"

"Remember when we were at the mall and you chose the women you'd like to be with?"

"Yea."

"Do you know who you chose?" She began to cry. "No matter the age, they were all the same. Mannequins. You chose the same type every single fucking time. Short; somewhat flat-chested; round butts; athletic. They were just props. That's what a girl is to you. A prop. An amusement park ride. That's why you fail so often at getting a girl—because they all realize they are props to you and not people. I'm the only woman who really is a person to you. And you never look twice at me."

"Okay," I said. "Enough."

"Kiss me."

"What?"

"Kiss me."

I looked into her eyes and saw traces of madness and despair.

"You're drunk."

Jenny stood and walked to the bedroom door.

"I'm not drunk," she said. "I'm crazy and I'm unpredictable, but at least I'm alive."

I sat against the bed for a long time after she left, until the cigar was burnt to nothing and I shakily got to my feet, passed the ruins of the living room and found what was left of the whiskey bottle and finished it before dawn.

- 28 -

The town's newspaper broke the story of Rebecca and me. When I got to the office at nine-thirty, bleary eyed and nauseous, there were two television trucks by the main doors with telescoping antennas fully erect and on-site female reporters set to use them. Cameramen tracked my steps from my Porsche to the revolving doors.

"Can I have a moment?" a flat faced blonde asked, running towards me.

"Me, too!" cried a brunette whose cheeks seemed to be barely separated by her tongue.

Television isn't real, I thought, recognizing both women from evening news shows. They were pretty on the screen, transformed by the camera lens. In real life even I wouldn't date them.

"Are you really sleeping with Mrs. Warren?"

"What do you know of Henry's murder?"

"When did Donnie find out about the affair?"

"What did the police want with you?"

"Is there a connection between the deaths of Henry Warren and the Tollivers?"

I said nothing, trying not to make eye contact and hustled into the building.

The receptionist didn't bother to say anything to me either. She simply rolled her eyes and pointed upstairs. I turned for the elevator and waited for one going up. Somehow one of the Landsluts managed to join me as the elevator doors closed.

"Hey," she said. "You okay?"

"Peachy," I replied.

She reached out and hit the stop button and the elevator jerked on its cables before coming to rest.

"Really, how are you?"

She wore black slacks and a loose fitting blue blouse and her hair was tied into a ponytail.

"Which one are you?" I asked.

"From *The Lawyer's Lounge*. I sat on your lap."

"That's not helpful."

"Yes, it is. It's all that you need to know."

"I don't understand what you're doing."

"How old am I?" she asked.

"Excuse me?"

"Guess," she said.

I sighed, looked about the elevator, realizing there wasn't anywhere to go. "Twenty-four."

"No."

"Twenty-three."

"Try thirty-three," she said.

"Bullshit."

"My sister and I diet and workout most nights after school, and we go for runs most mornings. You see a short trim blonde and you assume twenties. You're looking at an image. You're not really looking at me."

I sighed and shrugged. "Fine. What do you want?"

Stepping forward, palms on my chest and on tiptoes she kissed me.

My hands stayed at my sides, one holding the briefcase.

She whispered, "You've never really looked at me. But I've been really looking at you."

She pulled back, licked her lips and kissed me again.

The briefcase fell to the floor. Her tongue sang a song inside my mouth.

"This is the building supervisor," a voice squawked from the elevator's cheap speaker. "Is everything okay in there?"

"He can see us," I whispered, tilting my head to a camera hanging in a corner.

"Then let's give him something to watch." She jumped and her legs wrapped around my waist and her arms locked behind my shoulders. "Hold me."

I reached down, gripping her bottom, supporting her.

"There is a way to tell us apart," she said, our noses almost touching.

"How?"

"When we were eighteen we went to a tattoo parlor. We had our names written in script on our bodies."

"Where?"

She whispered in my ear and found my lips and the world disappeared.

- 29 -

"You get lost?" Prickles asked. "The receptionist called fifteen minutes ago and said you were on your way up."

"You'll be okay," she had told me with a smile.

"But which one are you?" was my only response.

Unfortunately, my time in the elevator did not reveal the identity of my 'secret' admirer. Apparently, that would take a more thorough examination.

"I needed a few minutes alone," I said to Prickles. "It's been a long day."

"It's not yet ten in the morning."

"Feels like ten-thirty," I replied.

Prickles frowned and gestured to one of the leather chairs. He sat on the couch eating a children's breakfast from a fast food restaurant. A bright red fire truck adorned with the restaurant's logo sat by the food bag.

"One question," Prickles said, munching on a cinnamon roll. "Did the affair with Rebecca begin after our law firm withdrew from the case?"

"Yes."

"Are you sure?"

"Yes."

"Okay then." He fiddled with his ear. "I imagine the State Bar Association will have some questions for you but you should be able to handle them. It might be a good idea to take a few days off though, let the story die down a bit. Go home. Get some sleep. Take it easy for a few days or weeks."

"Is that a suggestion?"

"A very serious suggestion," Prickles said.

"Okay."

I stood and turned to the door.

"Oh, and there's another thing."

I waited.

"Jaime is going to be hiring a new associate. It's a good time. The market is full of law school graduates who can't find a job. Jaime wants to really focus on marketing and thinks he can generate a lot more business. He's hoping to fill the position in a few weeks. The person will be raw though; no real world experience. You'll probably have to train him, or her."

"Why not wait and hire Mia or Mai when they graduate from night school?"

"They've been working with Jaime for years," Prickles replied. "I think they've had their fill of him."

Fill of him?

"And can I give you some advice?" Prickles asked.

"Sure. Why not?"

"Arnie had it right. He paid an escort service to have a lovely woman on his arms for every social event. The rest of the time, he had the Internet. It kept him out of trouble for years."

"Excuse me?"

"Arnie's best friend was his right hand."

- 30 -

"So what have you found out?"

Unlike the other paralegals at the firm who worked from cubicles, Cowboy Jake had an office with a window. Jake tipped back his black cowboy hat and looked up from his computer screen. Heads of deer, antelope and bison gazed down at us from the walls. On his desk a fox lunged at a leaping squirrel. Astroturf covered the floor and Jake added areas covered with sand and several cacti.

"The entry fee to the web site was two grand. Meredith Balton authorized the firm to pay it."

"And?" I asked.

"It's an amazing set-up. *Training For Excellence* has separate religious sites for athletes, musicians, actors, painters, clowns, and unless I'm reading this wrong, freedom fighters."

"Terrorists?"

"Well, freedom fighters."

I sat down in a guest chair built of what supposedly were cattle bones but the firm didn't hire a specialist to confirm it.

"How did we miss *Training For Excellence* when we reviewed all of Joey Balton's financial information?"

Cowboy Jake dropped a hand below his desk, presumably to the butt of a revolver. "Think I missed something, boss?"

"No. No. Not at all. Just wondering."

His hand came back onto the desk top. "I spoke to Meredith about it when I looked over the account statements. She said Joey was into all kinds of fitness stuff. He had a private quarterback coach at one time, his own strength and conditioning coaches and ordered tons of fitness pills. She just figured *Training For Excellence* was connected to all of that."

"Okay."

I sat in the chair, gazing at the heads of dead animals.

"Did Arnie ever refer to me as The Statue?" I asked.

Cowboy Jake must have played a lot of poker with his buddies out on the western ranges. His expression didn't change, his eyes didn't blink.

"No," he lied.

"Okay," I replied, knowing he was lying. If he were telling the truth I would have got more than a simple 'no.'

I stood, hands in my pockets. "Did she want a divorce?" I asked absently.

"Who? Meredith?"

I wanted to take one of his guns and shoot either him or myself. "Yes. Meredith."

Cowboy Jake shook his head. "No. The money meant a lot to her but she really loves the guy."

I nodded. "And what about the Landsluts?"

"Huh?"

"Does one of them really like me?"

He shrugged. "There's no accounting for taste," he replied.

- 31 -

I figured there would be a news crew outside The White Apartment. I parked on the other side of the complex and walked through the backyards of the buildings, managing to reach the staircase for my building unseen. Before opening my front door I peeked out at my normal parking spot. A television news truck was blocking it.

Inside, the apartment resembled a Dalmatian's coat. The paint had dried, ruining most of the furniture and carpeting and the walls and ceiling needed a thorough repainting. There goes the security deposit, I thought.

A sadness bubble burst apart.

Fuck you, I told myself. Fuck everyone.

On the balcony, smoking a cigar, trying to catch my bearings, I held on to the railing and looked out at the complex's pool, covered by a black tarp for winter. At The Ranch Retreat the weather soon would leave a layer of ice atop the pond. I had skated on that pond when I was a boy. I had skated and smiled.

My cell phone rang.

Landscuda.

"I have a buddy at one of the local television stations. Turn on channel four at noon. Your girlfriend is making an appearance."

The pictures on the flat screen television were marred by black smudges.

At noon the station's local news program began. The Warren murder was the top story. The reporter with the pancake face stood before the courthouse, staring at the camera with a grim expression. "After weeks of investigation, our station is here to break the story of a possible motive in the brutal murder of a Kansas City businessman. Henry Warren was bludgeoned to death and now we may know why.

A review of the transcript of a hearing in the divorce between Henry Warren and his spouse revealed a violent disagreement between the couple involving their ten year old son, a disagreement that resulted in a contentious hearing."

Evelyn Baum appeared, sitting at a desk with shelves of law books behind her, with the caption 'Henry Warren's divorce lawyer' at the bottom of the screen. "Henry Warren was trying to save his family. His spouse, Rebecca, was determined to subject their ten year old son to her all consuming passion for ice hockey. She had the child practicing and playing constantly, putting the family into a serious financial crisis and acting against the wishes of Mr. Warren who wanted their son to be a well-rounded child. He wanted their son to be involved in chess and school activities. Ms. Warren only wanted him to play ice hockey, a needlessly violent game that results in concussions and other injuries to ten year old boys."

Rebecca Warren smashed her hands against the Plexiglas at the Saturday game when I first saw Donnie play, screaming obscenities and then a quick cut to her being escorted by the police from the ice rink.

The scene shifted to photos of various youth hockey players being carted off ice surfaces on stretchers and then to a medical office and a doctor in a white coat and stethoscope. "A brutal sport," he said, staring at a medical chart. "I've seen numerous injuries suffered by children being forced to play this game by mothers, and this sport results in many more injuries than have been caused by children playing chess, participating on school debating teams or acting in school plays."

The pancake face said, "It's a story told around this country and it may have resulted in this brutal murder."

A man identified as Dr. Phillip Koop sat in a wingback chair by a fireplace holding a pipe. "As a child psychiatrist, the tension between the Warrens probably was as palatable in their household as a thick smoke filling every room. Rebecca, in my opinion, clearly suffers from a need to dominate people and because of her small physical stature she cannot do so by engaging in such men's sports as ice hockey or football or rugby. Instead, she chose to live through her son. Henry Warren likely realized the danger this posed to their son as her need for physical violence became more pronounced, which likely would eventually lead to their son being forced to fight in mixed martial arts tournaments. This obsessive need would ultimately take root in their son and the ultimate destination would involve death. I have no doubt that if Rebecca is not stopped, their son likely will end up training pit bulls for dog fights or roosters for cock fights. This is a tragedy and Mr. Warren's death likely will only expedite the moral decline of that poor, innocent child."

Flat face appeared. "We tried to contact Rebecca Warren but she was unavailable for comment. However, if you know of any dog fighting or cock fighting rings in the area, we suggest you be on the lookout for this diminutive pit bull of a woman and her poor abused child."

A quick cut to the news anchor in the studio. "Tonight at six we'll have more on this story, including how Rebecca Warren's obsession led to her affair with her former divorce attorney and her son's hockey coach, all of which ultimately resulted in the vicious slaying of her husband."

Wow. I turned off the television.

At least they didn't mention my name, I thought.

And then: she looked awfully cute when mad. When will I sleep with her again?

- 32 -

Part of me dreaded going to the rink. I imagined all of my team's players having to walk through a gauntlet of reporters and photographers to get into the building; of parents horrified that their coach had slept with one of their own; and the association itself damaged by the negative publicity. I changed into my old coaching clothes, snuck back to my Porsche with stick and equipment bag in hand and headed to the Ice Kingdom.

They're going to fire me as The Coach, I thought. First I'm put on-leave as The Lawyer and now I'll be fired as The Coach. What's left?

Serving Your Needs, Inc. had a security division that ran more efficiently than most airport screeners. Wooden saw horses and ropes cut off most of the rink's parking lot and men bigger than Max the private investigator interrogated the passenger of each vehicle before allowing the vehicle to pull up close to the main entrance. Two news trucks were kept outside the closed-off area and the guards, wearing orange leather jackets and resembling gigantic pumpkins with arms and legs, kept the reporters and camera people at bay. I was waved through the checkpoint without much of a glance, and it appeared the guard by the checkpoint based the decision on my license plate.

Another guard waved me towards a parking spot apparently reserved for me, closest to the door. I parked and headed inside.

Michael Williams waited for me. "Good to see you, coach," he said. "How are you holding up?"

"Who hired the security people?"

"I did."

"Thanks, I guess."

"No problem." He stood right next to me, glancing about. The lobby was empty except for his wife, who drank from a large paper cup some dozen feet away. "The President of the Shooters is talking to our parents now. He's going to keep them in a back room until I give him the signal that you're in the locker room."

"Uh, thanks."

"We had a vote," Michael said. "It was done by telephone. Two families wanted you fired as the coach, but you have the support from the rest of the team, especially Rebecca. She was insistent about you staying on and coaching her son. And we can't have Donnie any more upset than he is, what with his father dead and all. And the Turkey Feast committee expects Donnie in New Jersey next week."

"Then I guess I'll stay on as coach," I said. "We need to act for the good of the team."

"That's what I told the other parents," Michael agreed. "And I shouldn't name the two dissenting families. Let's keep everything friendly."

"Fine," I said. "Where are the boys?"

"In the locker room."

"Okay. Thanks."

I started towards the doors to the rink but Shari intercepted me, wobbling over with liquid sloshing out of her cup onto the floor.

"Fuck the Manyards," she said.

I waited.

"Teri wanted you gone after she heard about Rebecca. It makes no sense since you left her son playing with Donnie."

"Religious convictions?" I suggested. "Morals, maybe?"

"That bitch? She lost her morals years ago when she started screwing anyone and anything that would touch her on road trips."

Anyone or anything that would touch her . . .

"Her son doesn't deserve to be playing with Donnie," Shari said.

"Understood," I replied. I tried to walk away but she grabbed my arm, reached into her pocket and pulled out a small USB computer hard drive.

"The Turkey Feast sometimes asks a coach for recommendations about players. I thought I could help you out. I prepared a brief letter, about three pages long, about Steele. I'm sure if they ask about your players you'd talk about him, but I wanted to save you the trouble of having to fill out any forms. I think I covered most of what scouts want: his height and weight, unofficial statistics over the last four years, his anticipated grades, and a number of referrals. Feel free to print it out and sign it. It will come in handy."

"Thanks. This will free up a lot of my time over the next few days."

"Michael and I are paying for the airfare for everyone. We're trying to be helpful. And we do want you to keep coaching. We know how much it means to you to coach Donnie. We worked real hard to make sure you'd still be coaching him."

And if I wasn't coaching and Donnie quit, I thought, the Turkey Feast invitation would be withdrawn and there would be no scouts watching Steele.

She stared at me, still holding onto my arm with a grip like a Doberman latching on to an intruder.

"We know how much enjoyment Rebecca Warren has on road trips. Please think about that. Michael and I are just happy to help out."

"Okay," I said. "Thanks."

She let go.

"You're welcome." She burped and downed a generous portion of the cup.

Deputy Wales stood inside the rink's doors.

"Quite a day," he said.

"If you'd catch the damn killer my life might become easier."

"That's our job," Deputy Wales replied. "The sheriff's department just wants you to know that we're still thinking of you."

Herb Rooks paced before the locker room. The stitching for the word "Assistant' had been removed from his coaching jacket, just leaving the word 'Coach' all by itself.

"I voted to fire you," he blurted out.

"I respect that. Good for you."

"No hard feelings?"

"My opinion of you won't change in the least."

He looked relieved.

I gave him a playful punch in the arm and we headed into the locker room to address the team.

- 33 -

The workmen waived at me as I pulled into the driveway at The Ranch Retreat later that night. They were laying some kind of cable underground, skirting the road along the front of the property. Jenny's Jaguar stood gleaming in the clearing by the front porch. Inside she swayed in the living room, listening to a raunchy punk rock band blasting from the stereo speakers, drinking a martini and smoking a cigar. Happy Girl wore a bright yellow dress with a neckline that reached down to her navel.

"Howdy," she smiled.

"What's the occasion?"

"I don't want to hurt you anymore."

"Sounds like a reason to celebrate."

She poured me a martini and lit a cigar for me.

"What's with the workers?"

"An electric fence," she replied.

"That only works if you put those special collars on the news reporters. Without the collars they won't get zapped."

"Not for the reporters." She pointed to the kitchen. Three large travel kennels lay on the floor and inside each kennel a monstrous pit bull gnawed on what hopefully was not a human femur bone. Each had a thick collar which I assumed would deliver an electric shock if the dog tried to get past the electric fence. "I thought you might need some company out here by your lonesome and some friends to keep the locals away from the house. Meet your new roommates."

One of the dogs stopped chewing on its bone and stared at my legs.

"Well. Thanks."

"I also bought an automatic feeding system," Jenny said. "It's on the patio. It automatically fills bowls with water and food every 12 hours. And the electric fence is being installed to cover all of the front yard and the back yard, including the pond."

"So they can play hockey when the pond freezes."

She looked concerned. "Can dogs play ice hockey? I didn't buy sticks."

"Are you serious?"

"You are not very smart," Jenny said, laughing. "You may be a great hockey coach for kids and a damn good lawyer but you are not very smart at all. You figure out how to tell which of the twins wants you?"

"Something about a tattoo, I've been told."

"So which one is she?"

"I haven't gotten to see the tattoo yet."

"Loser," Jenny laughed.

"Why does she want me?" I asked. The martini was ice cold and when the liquid slid down my throat I felt its coolness all the way to my stomach.

"Probably a masochist," Jenny answered. "Either that or she has a great need to help the poor and disenfranchised."

We sat down on the couch, shoulders touching, blowing smoke so it spiraled and intertwined on its way to the ceiling.

"I should be really pissed at you even with the gifts. You trashed my apartment. You left me alone at *The Lawyer's Lounge*. You could have waited and given me a ride home."

"Jaime is a prick," Jenny said. "He loves himself more than anything else. You could learn from him. But he is a monster in bed. I told him that I'd let you find your own way home if he'd fuck me again before he went to work."

I had no witty reply to her excuse. I finished the martini quickly and she went to the kitchen to make me another. The dogs barked, sounding together like an Indy race car screaming past the grandstands. I wondered if I would need ear plugs just to get some sleep.

"So what about Ms. Pit Bull?" she asked. "Are you going to get rid of her? One of the twins could take her place."

"What about Landshark?" I replied. "Are you going to get rid of him?"

"Not exactly."

"What does that mean?"

"I'm going to stop dating him soon. I don't need the aggravation of waiting by the phone for him to call me."

"Good," I said. "Smart move."

"We're getting married on Thanksgiving in Las Vegas."

"Married?"

"I'm going to keep my place but I'll keep some of my clothes at his house."

"Married?"

"A person only lives once," Jenny said. "And he's a monster in bed."

Married.

"Congratulations, I guess. Who proposed?"

"He did."

"Has he met The Insane One?"

"That's when he proposed," Jenny replied.

- 34 -

The airline wouldn't let me trade my ticket for another flight, so I just bought another ticket. I didn't want to fly out with the team. The team manager needed to be in New Jersey the night before the tournament began, to work out any registration issues and obtain the tournament rules from the tournament directors. As the head coach, I didn't need to be there until the first game started. I booked a flight to arrive sometime past midnight on the day of that game, and changed hotel reservations so I would stay at a different hotel than the rest of the team.

Missing Thanksgiving didn't bother me. The last few years I had spent the day with Jenny. But she was in an airplane flying in the opposite direction, with Landshark to Vegas. I found out the name of their hotel and as a gift had the concierge promise to have a bottle of champagne and a bottle of anti-depressants waiting for them.

Sleeping with Rebecca during this trip—if a possibility at all—would be more complicated since I was staying in another hotel. However, I didn't want to run into Teri Manyard or the Williams or the Rooks or anyone else during the tournament, other than at the rink.

Rebecca and I had spoken by cell phone, agreeing to take a break during the days before the tournament. She had the nanny bring Donnie to practices and the security personnel of *Serving Your Needs, Inc.* made sure 'unauthorized personnel' never came close to the Ice Kingdom.

If Landscuda was aware of his company's doings with my hockey team, he never called or emailed to let me know. Neither did my 'semi-secret admirer.' Cowboy Jake would send occasional emails to me for instructions on cases we had together while I was out of the office; other than his messages, the law firm went on with its business without me.

She's blowing you off, an Inner Voice said as I sat 35,000 feet above the ground. The murder is going to be a convenient excuse. She doesn't need you anymore. Donnie has never needed you.

Did she kill her husband?

- 35 -

I picked up the rental car and headed out of the airport. My smartphone indicated the hotel was 30 miles away in the northwest part of the state. I felt like I was driving back on the roads near The Ranch Retreat, except a two lane highway replaced the rural road. Most of the surrounding land consisted of dense woods, breaking up only at each exit ramp by gas stations and fast food restaurants.

At my exit I drove past such gas stations and restaurants and then into neighborhoods of small houses, many with 'For Sale' signs in the front yards. Most of the lawns looked unkempt and the houses were in need of painting. Many of the street lamps were broken and potholes marred the road. I drove into the business district. Large plywood panels covered many store windows. It appeared to be a ghost town.

How can the people afford ice hockey out here? I wondered.

In the distance I saw a hill that could almost qualify as a mountain, and lights dispersed among foliage. My navigation unit led me to that hill. I found myself in a corporate office park, not unlike the office park in which my law firm was based. Planted amidst the trees as the road climbed were new buildings of steel and glass surrounded by asphalt parking lots. Still the road climbed. Near the top of the hill I saw the rink, a large structure with a facade on the roof making it appear to be a castle, like the entrance to the Magic Kingdom at Disney World. A huge banner at the entrance to the parking lot of the rink welcomed players and parents to the Turkey Feast. A huge balloon figurine of a turkey floated nearby. One hundred yards further up the hill were the hotels. The team was staying at the inexpensive lodging, consisting only of rooms, a lobby and an outdoor pool. I, on the other hand, was staying at the ten-story Marriott with a restaurant and bar. With any luck, the team parents would bring their own beer to the lobby of their hotel and avoid mine.

Rebecca is in the cheaper hotel, I thought.

I wondered: what she is doing now?

Do I trust her? Is she alone? Is she thinking of me?

Do I love her?

Does she love me?

- 36 -

Our first game was at noon. As usual I had trouble sleeping. At about six in the morning I decided enough was enough, showered and dressed and went down to the lobby. There was free coffee. Outside the temperature hovered at fifty five degrees, unseasonably warm and I wore only my jeans, sweatshirt and a leather jacket. I lit up a cigar and paced by the revolving doors underneath the overhang by the hotel's front entrance, coffee in one hand and a cigar in the other. I thought of all the closed businesses and then of the massive corporate park climbing the hill. I saw how it worked. The businesses had sold tangible products: video cassettes to rent, compact discs of music to play on actual stereo systems, flower shops where people could actually smell the objects they were buying. But technology moved ever forward. Massive superstores opened and killed small shops. Digital content replaced items one would actually hold in one's hand. People no longer went to stores to buy flowers or cards or stationary, instead going online and clicking buttons and entering credit card data to be processed by all of the people sitting in cubicles in all of the surrounding office buildings.

Did they even still grow flowers or were they now just sprouted digitally?

What happened to all of the people who used to work in the boarded up stores who didn't have the skills to master the computer age?

Is that what replaced my ex-spouse? Were Teri Manyard and Rebecca no more than digital props? Were they real flesh and blood people or were they just amusement park rides, like Jenny said?

Was there any flesh and blood person in my life other than Jenny?

What the fuck was I doing here?

If the last few months had been an amusement park ride, was I the ride operator or the person who paid for his ticket—using what?—and boarded the mechanical contraption, not really caring about which seat I chose but merely using one while the ride lasted?

I spat at the ground.

Are you out of your fucking mind? What are you thinking about?

I am The Coach and I am at a hockey tournament and we are here to win.

Remember Sly. Sly lives for the moment. Sly doesn't care about details.

Except for The Holy Puck.

Enough nonsense, I thought, finishing the cigar.

Being a successful lawyer or coach required pre-planning.

After registering at the hotel and entering my room last night, the first step was ordering two full glasses of whiskey, not for the evening but to help kill the morning hours. I watched *Sportscenter*, a talk show featuring a short, perky brunette and then *Sportscenter* again. Eleven o'clock, all the whiskey down and gone, I was ready. I wandered down a hill of fallen leaves and massive tree trunks to the parking lot of the Ice Castle.

Rebecca was already by the entrance to the rink, smoking a cigarette. The parking lot was jammed with cars featuring license plates from as far away as California and Vancouver. Parents whose games had not yet started hurried into the rink while parents whose games had finished clustered in small groups by their cars, celebrating great deeds or bemoaning lost opportunities.

Fucking morons.

"You abandoned me," Rebecca said. "You left me alone on that plane and in that hotel with those people. I was about to get a razor blade and join my husband in the after-life."

"It couldn't have been that bad. The only reason we're here is because of Donnie. I would think everyone would be treating you like a queen."

"Being a queen is only good if you can kill your subjects," she replied. She moved closer to me, reached out a hand and touched my chest. "Can I come over tonight? Say eleven-thirty?"

"What about Donnie?"

"He'll be okay. He'll be asleep by then. Besides, the divorce is over. No judge is looking over our shoulders. We're free."

"Free? Have you been watching the news on television or reading the newspapers?"

She held my left arm, stood up on tip toes and kissed me. I was too surprised to even kiss back.

"This is New Jersey. Why would anyone care us about us here?"

- 37 -

"So you're the coach who is sleeping with the star player's mother?"

"She is single," I said.

"Oh, yes. That's right. Someone murdered her husband a few weeks ago?"

I stood by the tournament director, waiting to get my coaching badge for the tournament.

"A horrible tragedy," I replied.

"But what does Dick think?"

"Excuse me?"

The tournament director pointed to my pants. "The Boss Man. Dick."

"Excuse me?

"We love The Boss here in New Jersey. I bet you got a *Hungry Heart*. Her husband's dead, right? Sounds like you're looking at *The Promised Land*. You can *Prove It All Night* now."

He was large and fat with a thick mustache and he laughed at me.

We stood by the 'Team Sign-In' table in the rink's lobby, staffed by two hockey moms wearing jackets that proclaimed the name of the rink's home team and that the team had won The Turkey Feast last year. Banners hung below other tables for the Press, Scouts and Sponsors.

The press? For ten year olds?

Songs by Bruce Springsteen filled the three ice rinks and all of the other spaces in the building, pausing only in the ice rinks when the games were in play. A large case by the pro shop contained a live turkey that must have been pumped with growth hormones since birth.

The 'Sign-In' ladies told me the winning coach was awarded The Golden Hatchet, to be used to chop off the turkey's head after the championship game. The winning team—which was expected to stay in New Jersey an extra day—would be served that turkey at a championship luncheon in the rink's meeting room.

"Can I have my coaching pass?"

The director held it up to me. "Don't bring your messy soap opera to our tournament."

I looked at the caged turkey as Bruce Springsteen sang *Roll of the Dice* and a number of sports reporters passed a flask between them.

Rebecca walked into the lobby, saw an official from USA Hockey rush towards her, turned and walked back outside.

The tournament director handed me a large plastic cord with an attached lanyard and pointed to a door. "Go to the second floor," he said. "The Scouting Lounge is there and some guys will be wanting to talk to you."

Upstairs, the Scouting Lounge was a large room with a buffet that rivaled the Sunday brunch at a five star restaurant. As I walked in, a man wearing a jacket for the University of Wisconsin was wedged into a corner, trapped by Herb Rooks.

"Watch this," Herb was saying, holding a tablet computer inches from the man's face. "Notice how he barely moves his head to the left before passing to his right. Amazing, isn't it?"

The scout's eyes sought me out as if I was a cop stumbling onto an assault.

"Andy's a good player," I said, taking Rooks by the arm. "And his dad's a great coach. If you offered a scholarship to Andy it would be a two for one deal."

"You're Donnie Warren's head coach?"

"Yes."

"Andy's, too," Herb said.

The scout stepped around Herb and grabbed my hand. "Can you talk to me about Donnie?"

"And Andy," Herb said.

"Sure."

We left Herb in the lounge, stalking other college scouts who ran about the room like sheep being herded by a dog, pausing only long enough to grab another rib or chicken leg from the buffet.

Glass windows ran the length of the enormous room that comprised most of the second floor, offering a view of the two rinks below. Glass also lined the far wall for a view of the third ice rink and a concession stand sprouted from the room's center, selling food, hot drinks, beer and mixed cocktails. Several adults lay on the floor, sleeping, while other crazed, drunken parents and battle tested scouts stood by the windows overlooking the rinks, watching the games.

"Henry Warren is dead," the scout told me.

"He was yesterday."

"He was short."

"I guess."

"Wisconsin hates short players."

"You forming a basketball team?" I asked.

"No."

"Then forget about size. Donnie Warren can play." I fished the computer disk Shari Williams gave me from my pocket. "You want size, look at this."

"This isn't another proposition from a hockey mom, is it?"

I shrugged. "Some would say her gender is in dispute."

I'm drunk, I thought, one whiskey too many. And I'll be coaching ten year old kids soon.

Fuck.

Downstairs, I entered one of the ice rinks, hoping the cold air would clear my head. The game in progress featured a AAA team from California against a AAA team from Detroit. I found a place to watch behind one of the nets.

I could see the faces of anxious parents and impassive young men, the latter scouts, watching from the upper windows. The rink was cold and quiet except for the sounds of the game: the puck smacking against sticks or booming off the boards, the referee's whistle, the yelling of coaches and players. A number of parents stood by the boards watching thru the Plexiglas. All were quiet, watching intently, showing emotions only via facial expressions or the tensing of bodies.

My team's parents jumped and screamed at every play. But my team wasn't on the ice. My team, I realized, shouldn't be on this ice, in this city, at this time.

I could be standing at the lake with The Mountain Palace looming above, watching The Hockey Gods. The players were all as big as Steele Williams, almost as fast as Donnie, playing with precision and coordination like the movement of a quality Swiss watch.

Michael Williams joined me. His face was flush and his eyes bloodshot.

"I hope you're not going to ask me for the score," I said.

"No," Williams said softly. "I got here an hour ago and had to ask the tournament director if I was at the right rink. I thought I was looking at 15 year olds."

I said nothing.

"Will our games even be close?" he asked.

I didn't bother to answer.

"That letter my wife gave you on Steele. Delete it. I'm thinking that if anyone asks, we'll deny we know any of our kids. We'll deny we know anyone on our team in fact. Maybe we can get kicked out so the kids won't have to play."

I nodded, walked away and found a men's room, locked myself in a toilet stall and vomited.

I'm going to be on the bench as The Coach, I thought. I'm going to be responsible for my team's massacre.

Herb Rooks waited by our looker room, one of many located in the halls beneath the massive viewing area on the second floor.

"The kids are nervous," he said. "But I think we're going to shock the world."

"Forget it," I replied, chewing on breath mints.

"What?"

"Just forget it."

The boys had watched the games before getting dressed. There was silence in the locker room. A few of them looked scared; the rest nervous. I had a team of good kids, who played hard and did well in our region of the country. But we were just a good team and my players knew it. We were not one of the best teams in the nation that practiced five days a week and who chose players based on a talent pool of hundreds instead of dozens.

One of my defenseman asked, "Why are we here?"

An email popped onto my smartphone.

'Any good elevators in New Jersey?' the subject line of the text message read. It had been sent from a Google account and I didn't recognize the sender's email address. Attached was a Word document. entitled 'Who Am I?'

I thought of the great inspirational speeches in movie history: Gene Hackman in *Hoosiers*, Kurt Russell in *Miracle*, Billy Bob Thornton in *Friday Night Lights*; John Belushi in *Animal House*.

But their teams—and fraternity—had a chance.

Mine was dead meat.

Herb brushed by me to stand in the middle of the square room.

"Let me tell you a story," he began. "In the 1940's wicked men took over Europe and they raped and tortured and killed everyone. People were brought to death camps and starved and burned to death. The world had gone to hell. But boys like you, from the middle of our great country, decided to stop them. Those boys traveled across an ocean and stormed the beaches of Europe, many of them dying in sprays of machine gun fire, but a few managed to survive and they took over those beaches and slowly retook Europe, killing all of those wicked men. Those boys faced hardships and lost limbs but bloody and weary they saved the world. They watched their friends die but they did not quit. They fought and fought until they either won or they were dead."

Herb pointed to me. "They had a great leader." He pounded his chest. "They had a great assistant leader. They saved the world."

I took a deep breath but he cut me off before I could speak.

"We're playing a team from Pennsylvania in a few minutes. Most of their parents are descendants from people who came from that country of wicked men. They were defeated in the 1940's by your descendants and now it is your turn. Some of you will struggle; some may not make it through this game. You have flown across a great distance. You have entered this rink, the territory of the enemy. You made it to this locker room. The ice surface, the beaches, await you. And you have your leaders. And you have Donnie and Andy. Follow them on the ice. Follow them and you will prevail!"

One of the players began to cry.

Herb turned to me. "Coach," he said. "It's your turn."

Seventeen little heads in helmets swiveled towards me.

I stared back at them.

My mind went blank.

Long seconds passed, maybe a half-minute.

Donnie stood up. "It's just a hockey game," he said to his teammates. "Let's go kick some ass."

"Right," I mumbled, then louder "Right! Everyone to the center of the room! Hands together! Count to three: It's just a hockey game and let's go kick some ass!"

"Fuck 'em," the defenseman from New Jersey said, standing. "We survive tornadoes. This is nothing."

"Yea!" Sean Manyard yelled.

The boys slammed together, surrounding Donnie who shouted, "One, two and three!" and then all together they yelled, "It's just a hockey game and let's go kick some ass!"

They rushed by me, heading for the ice.

"My speech worked," Herb said happily.

"You're one in a million," I replied and followed the boys to the rink.

- 38 -

The document attached to the email was entitled 'Who Am I?' It looked like a standardized test with two columns running down each page, consisting of a series of questions. One column was headlined <u>Mai</u>; the other <u>Mia</u>. It began:

Mai	Mia
My favorite color sometimes is: 　　Red 　　Blue 　　Yellow	My favorite color sometimes is: 　　Red 　　Blue 　　Yellow
For a few years my favorite movie was: 　　Titanic 　　The Notebook 　　Aliens	For a few years my favorite movie was: 　　Titanic 　　The Notebook 　　Aliens
I lost my virginity _____ before my sister lost her virginity. Fill in the blank: 　　Three days 　　Five hours 　　Not Applicable [we did it at the same time]	I lost my virginity _____ before my sister lost her virginity. Fill in the blank: 　　Three days 　　Five hours 　　Not Applicable [we did it at the same time]

She wants me to figure out her identity by answering questions about her personality; her wants and needs. I guess I won't be seeing that tattoo until I do, I thought. I turned the power off the smartphone and pushed it away.

331

Fuck.

I sat at the bar in my hotel, away from the parents and the scouts and my players. Three fingers of whiskey, a television tuned to *Sportscenter* and my identity unknown to everyone else in the bar. Perfect.

I was anonymous.

I am anonymous.

I am no one.

Waiting, because the sadness bubbles would be coming soon and I didn't want to be alone in a hotel room when they arrived.

Whiskey scorched my throat, bringing tears to my eyes and I choked back vomit.

The first bubble flowered. Just one, but it did not stop growing. It expanded, consuming me, enveloping me, crushing me.

I'm not The Lawyer. I'm the office boy for Landscuda. Before, I had been the office boy for Arnie. For both of them, a statue. At rest.

I'm not The Coach. My team lost 14 to 2. We were outhustled and outplayed and worst of all, outcoached. We were amateurs playing against pros.

Both Teri Manyard and Rebecca Warren found me convenient and in a position to help their kids. Even if Rebecca felt something, she would be following Donnie to Minnesota or Boston or Canada. She wouldn't be staying with me.

And the Landslut? Why could she possibly want me? I had nothing to offer her. Nothing.

I am alone.

The glass empty, I signaled to the bartender for a refill.

The years stretched before me into the future.

I began to have trouble breathing. Waves of sadness broke against my heart. Hands trembling, I sipped amber fluid, seeking self-medication, trying to turn off my mind and deaden negative emotions.

Silence and peace: the sleep of the dead. Is that my future pleasure? Is that all there would be?

I drank.

A penny for no thoughts.

A penny for release.

- 39 -

Rebecca knocked on my hotel room door at eleven-thirty and only wanted to speak of Donnie. She paced in the narrow lane between the dresser and the bed, hands in jean pockets, frowning,

"He played well," I told her again and again, showered and fortified by three cups of coffee. "He was just without any help, that's all. The rest of our team was completely overmatched. In a sense, he was on the ice without teammates and he still looked really good."

"The other parents are fuming," she replied, staring at the carpeting. "They're all either totally pissed off because we came here in the first place or because they think their sons are being coached badly or because they aren't playing with Donnie. Most of them are sitting in their hotel lobby drinking heavily and bitching."

"Coached badly?"

"Can't you do anything?" Rebecca asked. "Do I really have to watch Donnie suffer thru another three games?"

"He could fake an injury."

"Be serious!" she shouted and standing before me was the woman who furiously pounded on the Plexiglas at that first game I attended, eyes blazing, muscles tensing, wanting satisfaction by some act of physical violence.

I sat at the end of the bed a foot away from her. "There's nothing I can do. Our team doesn't belong here. No matter how good Donnie plays, one player can't make up for the lack of talent of the other sixteen players if we are playing against the top teams in the country."

She covered her face with her hands and began to cry.

"Hey." I stood and touched her shoulder and she recoiled as if shocked by a taser.

"He doesn't look like a superstar!" she yelled. "You have to do something!"

"I didn't book this trip. There's nothing I can do."

"Then what the hell good are you?"

Stunned, I mumbled, "That's out of line."

"Is it?"

"Yes."

She slapped me across the face. "He can't look bad here!" she shouted. "There are scouts from colleges and private high schools watching!"

My face throbbed, tears in my eyes.

"Haven't I been good to you?" Rebecca shrieked. "Do something!"

Sly's World

- 40 -

The Blondeshell walks in a halo of bright sunlight by the frozen pond at the courthouse. Lawyers and clients hurry up and down the courthouse steps while children play hockey on the ice. Sly takes off his suit jacket, shirt and pants amidst flurries of snow. He wears a skin tight red bodysuit that covers him from his neck to his toes.

"Very flattering," The Blondeshell says, her body showcased in a blue bikini. "Your clients will be impressed."

"Why are you here?" Sly asks.

"I'm not," she replies. "I've never been here." Sly sits on a bench and laces up his skates.

"I've spent years with you. You've always been with me."

He stands and puts on hockey gloves and grabs his stick. The children skate wobbly, feet far apart and leaning on their sticks for balance. They slap at the puck, unable to control it, just trying to advance it closer to the waiting net. Most fall down, laughing, only to pick themselves up and move in jerking motions after the puck. Around the lake their parents yell encouragement, cheering when their son or daughter's stick touches the puck, jumping up and down.

"How old am I?" Fay Blondeshell asks. "What's my favorite color? What movie do I hate to watch? Where was I born? Who was my favorite teacher in school?"

"Why does it matter?"

"I've never been here," she says.

A moment of confusion for him and then a shrug. Sly skates onto the ice and falls. Shakily, he gets to his feet, a boy of ten, long hair and skinny arms and legs. His father watches among the jumping bean parents. He looks back and Fay is gone.

"Go!" his father's voice calls to him. "Go and play!"

With jerking strides he moves towards the puck, no different than the other kids. A slap of the puck and it bounces over the chipped and uneven ice surface. Straining, reaching out, it bangs against Sly's stick blade and stops. The kids wobble towards him and he pushes the puck, skating away from them, towards a goalie wearing a baseball catcher's equipment: chest protector, shin guards, face mask and glove. I'm going to score, Sly thinks. He tries to speed up and loses his balance, almost falling . . .

"Be calm," his father whispers into his ear.

Sly stays on his skates, the puck near his stick, the other kids but a few yards behind. The goalie crouches, a kid like him, unsure of what to do. Shy raises his stick, eyes looking down, his father watching, other parents yelling, the other kids almost on him, and he brings the stick down and the blade meets the puck and it flies forward, spinning . . .

Sam

- 41 -

"Do something!" she had yelled at me.

The other team had showed mercy by only scoring 14 goals. By the middle of the second period they were just killing time, passing the puck around, playing keep away. My players chased after the puck but except for Donnie they could never intercept it.

Once a shift Donnie would manage to get his stick on the puck and he would make an outstanding pass to a teammate or stickhandle around three opponents only to be foiled by the fourth. He did get off a number of shots and scored twice. However, for most of the game the other team just kept the puck away from him, rendering him harmless.

"Okay," I said to Rebecca, hands by my side, experiencing my first sadness bubble in her company since I had slept with her. "Okay. Let me think about it. I'll try to find him open ice. But he did look good today. He scored two goals against a really good team. He looked good. He really did."

"You think so?" she asked in a small voice.

"I do. And I checked the online score sheets for all of the tournament games. The most goals scored today by any player was three. For Donnie to score two goals without any help from his teammates was really good."

"Will you really think of something?" she asked. "Will you be able to help him?"

"We have until tomorrow at two. I'll figure something out."

"Really? You care about me and Donnie that much?"

"Yes."

She moved to me, fingers on my cheek. "I'm sorry." With a smooth motion she pulled the hoodie over her head, nipples dazzling like headlights in my eyes. "Okay?"

"Yea," I said, not sure if I meant it. "Sure."

You are kidding, right? I asked myself. She's been fucking with me the whole time, in more than one way.

She removed her sweat pants and thong and stood on tiptoes to kiss me.

Am I this shallow? Do all of these women think that after a few times in bed I would become their personal genie, willing to grant any of their wishes?

Are they all so desperate to think there was something of value I actually could provide to them?

I let her kiss me, my hands on soft skin.

Someone banged on the door.

Reporters, I thought. I could see the lead on the local news show. 'Hockey coach continues to sleep with widow, story at midnight.'

"No," Rebecca said. "Don't answer it. I want your tongue."

She probably doesn't even like your tongue, an Inner Voice said. While you pleasure her, she's probably thinking of someone else.

The question popped out of my mouth. "Do you love me?"

She looked stunned. "What?"

Still dressed I answered the door.

"Howdy," Max greeted me in his Harley Davidson jacket, his body wider than the door frame. "We need you for a few minutes."

"We?"

"Me and Darla." He looked past me to Rebecca, naked and staring at him. "I wish my hotel room came with a view."

"What do you want?"

"We're working on a case and we need you."

"I'm on leave," I said.

"Still, you have to come with me."

I realized their mission. "Manyard."

"Perhaps."

"I'm not working the Manyard case. Call Landshark."

Max grinned. "We did and he said you needed to come with us. Do I need to use physical force? I get paid extra for that."

Fuck.

"Stay here," I told Rebecca. "I'll be right back."

We took the elevator to the lobby and went through the revolving door. Below the parking lot shared by the Marriott and my team's hotel, the Ice Castle shimmered in a sea of pale blue light. I shivered in the cold air, following Max. My team's hotel had exterior walkways and I could see Darla waiting outside one of the rooms on the second floor.

Max said, "Landscuda wanted you to be with us, so later we could say you were as surprised as everyone."

"There was a hearing on this issue already. The judge doesn't care if Teri Manyard is sleeping around. Besides, after that hearing she would be crazy to be fucking someone during a hockey trip."

"Maybe Landscuda wanted us to find you first, just to make sure her bedmate wasn't you this time."

This time.

"Prove I slept with her," I said.

"We're private investigators," Max replied. "Do you even know when we were hired to work on the Manyard case? Do you know how long we've been following her?"

"Did Landscuda send me to a court hearing on the case knowing I had sex with Teri Manyard?"

"The Lord works in mysterious ways," Max replied.

We climbed the staircase to the second floor.

"He sent me to a hearing to get me disbarred?" I asked.

Darla wore a black leather cat suit so tight that she probably could activate saliva glands in a corpse, male or female. She pointed to the hotel room's door. Curtains covered the room's window, concealing the interior.

"Herb," I suddenly realized, remembering how much he said he despised Teri Manyard and her sleeping around, and that Andy and Sean had been teammates for years. *He protests too much.* "It's Herb Rooks, right?"

Oh fuck, I thought. My dick had been in the same place as his dick.

I wanted to vomit.

"Let's do it," Darla said.

From across the parking lot, Rebecca screamed, "No!"

Max kicked in the door.

Teri Manyard groaned and writhed on the bed as he pumped furiously between her legs.

Darla began taking pictures with her infrared camera.

"Hi coach," Donnie said.

Overtime

THE LAST SHOT

- 1 -

And we all lived happily ever after.

Well, not exactly.

My team was disqualified from The Turkey Feast. No one believed I wasn't in on the fix since I had been sleeping with Rebecca. How could I not know Donnie was seventeen years old and shaved most of his body each morning to conceal the passing of puberty? My days of coaching youth hockey were probably over because of the controversy. In retrospect, it was no great loss.

Mr. Manyard was awarded sole legal custody and sole physical custody of Sean at the divorce trial. Mrs. Manyard was granted supervised visitation rights. Apparently the Court was concerned she might try to have sex with Sean once he attained the age of sixteen.

It turned out she was pregnant. Donnie's child support was set at a fairly high amount.

Herb Rooks took over the hockey team the next season. The team finished with a dismal record, in last place. Andy went on to become a golfer. He was home schooled by Herb to allow for more practice time during the day and he's now on psychiatric medication.

Herb and April Rooks were divorced.

Shari Williams served ninety days in jail due to an altercation at one of Steele's high school football games. She went on a hunger strike to protest her incarceration and most of the prisoners and jailors rooted for her to die. I have been told by informed sources that Michael Williams bribed the jailors to not feed her.

Surprisingly, the marriage of Jenny and Landshark has worked out just fine. They live apart and see each other a few times a week. The Insane One hasn't made an appearance for quite a long time.

Cowboy Jake retired and went back to the range. I hope the bison are safe.

After being disqualified from the Turkey Feast, I returned to The Ranch Retreat. I found Deputy Wales trapped in his car while the pit bulls used their heads as battering rams to smash dents into his vehicle. On Jenny's advice I had stopped at a market on the drive home. I tossed the raw steaks into the yard as I got out of the Porsche and the dogs raced after them.

"Nice pets," Wales said.

"They appear to be a good judge of character," I replied as we went into my house. "Whiskey? Cigar?"

"No," he replied. "I'm on duty."

"I'm not." In the kitchen I poured myself a generous amount of whiskey and sat at the table, lighting up a cigar.

"Heard your team was kicked out of New Jersey."

"Just an ice rink. I think we're still allowed to travel on the Turnpike."

"How old is Donnie?"

"Who knows?" I replied.

"How did Rebecca get away with it?"

"It's the digital age. A good computer and printer can create fake documents, like a birth certificate. No one really checks. He's small for his age, obviously."

"What was the end game?"

"Do you have kids?" I asked.

"No. Not even married."

I drank. My father had believed in The Hockey Gods. He believed sports glory to be a gift bestowed by a higher power. Hard work and perseverance and ambition were important but in the end the player either had superior talent or didn't. Only a few were to be blessed. The rest were spectators, even the coaches.

"I imagine you deal with all kinds of delusional people, as well as people trying to find an easier way to succeed," I began. "They think it's easier to rob a bank instead of building a factory and making money by selling products, or going to graduate school to obtain expertise and sell services. But where the delusional and the

ones trying to find an easier way to succeed intersect is at any youth
sports event in this country. Parents will stab each other in the back
to help their kids but almost all of them do it in vain because their
kids don't have the talent. Rebecca took it to an extreme. Maybe she
hoped by the time Donnie got to college he would have grown and
developed his ability to the point where he could continue to succeed.
Either that or she was just another fucking lunatic parent."

"Henry tried to stop her."

"Look where that got him."

"I think I will have that drink," Wales said. He sat at the table
with me. "So was she good in bed?"

I wondered if I should be offended.

"Yea," I said after awhile. "She was."

"How about that cigar?" He lit up, leaned back and blew smoke.
"Teri Manyard was sleeping with the kid?"

"He's seventeen, too old for Teri to be charged with statutory
rape under New Jersey law."

"And she claimed she did it to help her own son?"

"Maybe she thought it would be easier to advance his career
by hanging onto a teammate's coattails as opposed to paying off a
college coach."

"I imagine it wasn't the coattails that she was hanging onto,"
Wales said.

We clinked glasses and drank.

The story filled the newspapers and television stations for a few
days and then died away. There were other scandals to cover.

Henry Warren's murder was never solved. It turned out that Mr.
Ginskofsky was Donnie's biological father and agreed to participate
in Henry Warren's chess deception in the hope of spending more
time with Donnie. I never found out why Rebecca slept with
Ginskofsky when she was a teenager or why Ginskofsky allowed
Henry to adopt his son. No one could connect Ginskofsky with the
murder. After several months, with no solid evidence the prosecutor
lost interest in the case. I hear Donnie and Rebecca live together in
Maine. Somehow Donnie became the hockey coach for a team of

eight year olds girls and has applied to the National Hockey League to serve as a player agent.

Donnie also works as a masseuse at a Maine resort hotel.

Joey Balton received a revelation from *Training For Excellence* shortly after Thanksgiving. He and Meredith reconciled and dismissed their pending divorce case. After the football season he signed a one year contract with the Mohawks for three million dollars and the Mohawks drafted Tyre Erving with the fourth pick of the Professional Football League draft. The next season, Joey Balton set Professional Football League records for completions, passing yardage and touchdowns and led the Mohawks to the Professional Football League Championship. Tyre Erving was named Rookie of the Year.

Balton then signed a new contract with the Mohawks for six years and ninety-six million dollars, making him the highest paid player in the league. Meredith divorced him a year later.

I never spoke or saw The Physics Guy again, although I heard through my 'youth betting contacts' that he expected to fully recover from his broken legs.

As for me, I left the firm and joined the twins after they graduated from night school. I mostly work in their office preparing briefs, pleadings, settlement documents, and talking points for court hearings and trials. The twins win most of their divorce cases. They even beat Landshark the few times they were on opposing sides.

I try to avoid clients. I spend most of my work day in front of a computer in the quiet of my office. I am very good at what I do. The Hockey Gods did not bless me but everyone has a chance at their version of The Holy Puck. It is not always athletic grace. Sometimes it is just trying to find out who you are and learning to appreciate the people—the actual people—around you.

It took me three months to come up with an answer to the quiz entitled 'Who Am I?' That night the tattoo confirmed my conclusion. The pit bulls have grown fonder of me as the years pass. They always liked Mia. I'm still not exactly sure what she sees in me, but no longer worry about it.

It's okay. We all have to make choices and live with the choices of others. We all have to accept ourselves.

RICHARD L. BECKER

As the our nation reels from terrorist attacks and our soldiers fight a war of attrition in the Mideast, the President of the United States seeks help from a supernatural source: a powerful witch he encountered years ago. At his urging the witch, her serial killer boyfriend and a mercenary battle the enemies of America. But to do so they must become allies with demons of pure energy known as Ravagers—and all the while the murderous needs of the witch's boyfriend must be met.

Fast paced, careening between scenes of violence and lust, *Hell Beckons* shifts from the Jersey shore to the tunnels beneath Manhattan, from a war in the Mideast to a supernatural world of energy and evil. As the pages turn, we begin to realize the true enemies of America may not be readily apparent. Who are the good guys and gals of our world, and what true evil confronts our nation? Until the violent conclusion, the reader is left guessing.

Hell Beckons by Richard L. Becker is available for purchase at iuniverse.com.

The first three chapters follow.

- 1 -

The first bomb exploded in New Jersey. The minivan had been one of many in a line of vehicles stretching away from the elementary school, and the detonation occurred just as the van reached the main entrance, at dismissal time. The blast wave tore through students and teachers and parents. Above, an American flag fluttered in the warm breeze as metal and glass sliced open flesh.

Pain.

She grasped at her stomach, staggering.

The plate glass windows of the diner shattered inward, becoming daggers. Blood streaked the walls and people lay sprawled among the tables, bleeding and butchered.

She blinked.

"Sandy?" One of the other waitresses took hold of her arm.

The vision faded. Wincing, she straightened. "I'm okay, really." She forced a smile at the older woman. "That time of the month for me. A cramp. I'm fine."

A customer beckoned from a booth with an empty cup and the older woman hurried for a pot of coffee.

The pain built. She knew it was not a pain that one could survive.

She didn't bother to remove the apron or nametag. The diner's manager chased her into the parking lot, threatening her job. She gave him the finger.

Fire trucks and ambulances raced past her car.

She parked several blocks from the elementary school on a neighborhood side street. A few persons stood on front porches, crying. Many others rushed towards the sirens. She hurried with them onto school grounds.

A wall of air shimmered and she stepped through it. The line of vehicles stretched away from the main entrance. The van slowed. Children with backpacks emptied from the school, some holding art projects. Parents milled about on a warm spring day. She studied the license plate and walked up to the driver. He was young and thin with dark hair and the trace of a mustache.

She could watch, but not intervene, in the past.

"We will meet someday," she told him as he reached to the seat beside him and threw a switch.

The van buckled and inflated like a balloon, rose off the ground and then popped. The driver's face melted as he was incinerated. She watched each piece of metal and plastic and glass as it tore free of the van and hurtled through space.

The kindergarten teacher had been up the path, leading a few of her tiny charges to a waiting bus. The shock wave flung her backward and she had slammed into the brick wall of the school building. Metal shards drove into her guts.

The air shimmered. Paramedics hunched over children and adults, tending to grievous wounds. A man sat on the grass by the flagpole, most of his left arm and leg gone. Blood flowed onto wet grass. He held a woman's severed hand.

The screaming did not stop.

Sandy knelt beside the kindergarten teacher.

"I thought of you," her friend whispered, blood spraying from her lips and coating her teeth. "In my mind, I called out for you. My kids?"

Sandy looked at the tiny bodies, broken on the grass. "They are gone," she said. "I'm sorry." Her friend began to cry.

A rescue worker examined the wounds and caught Sandy's eyes. A shake of the head, to the negative, and he moved to aid another victim.

"Can you help me?" her friend asked, time so short. "Please, so that I can see him again. Help me. Please."

The blade sprung from the handle. Sandy leaned forward as if to listen to last words, and no one saw the blade passing between ribs and finding her friend's heart.

The pain faded from the schoolteacher as final tears rolled down her cheeks. "Thank you," she whispered, and died.

Sandy palmed the blade. Around her, confusion and sorrow and death.

- 2 -

He left the others in the Situation Room, debating options.

Everyone had something to say. None of it made a damn bit of difference.

Upstairs, the President of the United States hunched over the toilet in his private bathroom off the Oval Office and vomited. He clutched his sides and continued to puke until he was coughing up just spittle and air, and tears blurred his eyes.

When he was sitting at the conference table in the Situation Room, listening to the most powerful officials in the country babble, he had been thinking of her.

On the computer screen that dominated one wall of the Situation Room, blinking white lights pinpointed the bombing sites. Next to each blinking light were two numbers: the number of dead in red, the number of wounded in yellow. Each time the President had looked at the screen, the red and yellow numbers increased at each site.

The President wondered if she was still pretty.

He rinsed out his mouth and rubbed water on his face and left the bathroom.

The Oval Office was empty. He sat at his massive desk and turned on one of the flat panel televisions with the remote control. CNN, reporting on the attacks. He watched the coverage, his hands folded before him on the desk.

Facing him on the desk were photographs of his wife and daughters, a pen set adorned with the seal of his Ivy League alma mater, and a telephone. There were no papers, nor a computer of any sort; he had no calendar—his aides directed him from appointment to appointment, place to place.

He had been in office for three years; unlike his predecessors, the office had not yet aged him.

CNN continued to report from the scenes, but there was no new information. Instead, just the ghastly images, endlessly repeating. The suicide bombers had struck in seven different States; all of the bombs detonating within a span of a few minutes, in front of seven elementary schools, as the pupils were let out, hurrying to their homes.

Over two hundred dead and the toll mounting with each passing second. Hundreds more in hospitals, many beyond hope. Some were adults—teachers and parents waiting to pick-up their children. Most were students, all younger than twelve.

The television crews were at each of the scenes, in some cases even before the ambulances. There were not enough ambulances. One or two cameras at each site fed the carnage to the nation. Medical personal had to be rushed in from surrounding communities, and there still wasn't enough to help the wounded. Minivans clustered about emergency room entrances, leather seats splattered with blood and skin, people screaming for help, and there weren't enough stretchers to bring all of the wounded inside, or doctors to treat the maimed.

So scary, he thought. CNN had as much information as the professionals in the Situation Room.

Since the Second Mideast War began, hundreds of suspected terrorists had been questioned in overseas detention facilities. According to his legal experts, the interrogations conducted by U.S. armed forces and intelligence personnel bordered on torture.

But the terrorist attacks continued.

Maybe we've tortured the wrong people, the President thought. Maybe we haven't tortured enough people.

I have to make hard decisions, he thought. I have to stop the slaughter. This is for our national defense.

It had been a month to the day since the fatalities on the Golden Gate Bridge. Three months since the hospital bombings.

All eyes in the nation would soon turn from the carnage, to him.

What the hell can I tell them?

353

Bruce Davidson entered the Oval Office. He had gained almost a hundred pounds over the years, a marathon runner's frame bloating into a middle age life of long days and nights, bad food and little sleep, and no exercise.

"The words of wisdom from my advisers?" the President asked.

His Chief of Staff took a deep breath and looked through the patio doors to the wide expanse of lawn. "We have the license plates of five of the vehicles used by the bombers. Most were bought for cash above their blue book value within the last few weeks. They were all older vans with lots of miles on them. It's early. Our people are working on it."

"What about the schools?"

"No connection found yet, other than they are elementary schools on the east coast, with dismissal times at 3:20. We're going to ask all public and private schools to remain closed for the rest of the week, while we come up with guidelines to protect them. How far to keep cars from the buildings, establishing a minimum police or National Guard presence for a few weeks, things like that."

"We can't protect them," the President said. "This is a nation of targets. Schools, hospitals, office buildings, apartment complexes. Nuclear and chemical power plants. We can't defend everything."

Last May, a factory worker had walked into a one-room schoolhouse in rural Kentucky and shot eleven students to death. Last October, a teenager brought an AK-47 assault rifle to his high school and opened fire in the hallways. Two teachers and six students were buried a few days later.

Those were not terrorist attacks. That was just daily life in America. No one expected the President of the United States to stop that kind of violence. But one foreigner detonates a car bomb and the entire country would demand action, from him.

The fucking press makes fun of me; calls me a simpleton, an idiot. They think I'm dumb. They think I started the Second Mideast War without justification, and that all of the dead and dying, on foreign shores and at home, are my sole responsibility. My fault. All my fault.

He resisted the urge to bring his hands to his head and kept them folded on the desk, with no expression on his face.

All my fucking fault, they say.

What would they say if they knew what I am about to do, to try and stop it?

The enemy is evil.

Good cannot wait for evil to strike. Good must seek out and destroy evil. It is the only way.

He thought of her, and felt his stomach roll again, and he swallowed hard to hold back another surge of vomit.

I am the President of the United States. The decision is mine.

"We can't protect them," the President said. "We can't defend all of the schools. We can't defend every hospital, and every building."

"I agree. But we have to make it look like we are trying."

"I don't want to defend. I want to attack."

"The Joint Chiefs are going to be presenting military options in a few hours."

"We've done that. We've hit the nations that sponsor these bastards. That's not enough. This isn't about nations. It's about good and evil. We need to fight this another way, with other means."

Davidson's face turned white.

"Find that bitch," the President ordered.

The decision was made. He felt suddenly calm, and turned off the television.

"You'll bring down this government," Davidson said. "Do you understand?"

"Find her," the President ordered. "Find her, now."

- 3 -

Gunfire erupted a few blocks away and black smoke spiraled in the air from another explosion. Gorman understood the smoke: the town was littered with improvised explosive devices, and half a dozen men had been wounded from them in just a few hours of operations. The gunfire was a mystery. He guessed an inexperienced soldier had fired at his own shadow, or at a rat darting from one room to another. It was doubtful any human being had been a target. There didn't seem to be any human beings left alive in the town, other than the U.S. soldiers crawling like ants through the ruins.

Gorman crouched beside an abandoned sedan. He peered through the shattered passenger and driver's side windows, down the block towards the temple. The inside of the vehicle was peppered with bullet holes, and dried blood smeared the windshield and dashboard.

What happened to the driver? Gorman thought. Are the rumors true? Have the insurgents resorted to cannibalism? Do they eat their enemies, to steal their souls?

Two soldiers ran from the cover of a nearly store and joined him by the car.

"No contacts," one said, a pimply faced kid. "Nothing."

They looked to him for leadership, although he was a civilian, with no official connection to their unit or the U.S. armed forces.

Gorman keyed the satellite phone on his belt, pressing a button on the earpiece, making the call. "This is Gorman. We're within sight of the target. Status update."

The response came in a whisper. "We need a few more minutes. We're sweeping through the last of the buildings around the square."

"Anything?"

"Just dried blood."

He pushed the earpiece button, ending the call. A hot wind blew sand into his face and he ducked his head and tied the bandana tighter about his neck. But it was no use. The sand was everywhere. He felt the grit in his pants and between his legs, in his hair and in his mouth. His eyes itched but he fought the impulse to rub them: he would just grind away his corneas with the sand.

Damn country, he thought.

Sweat rolled down his face and drops trickled onto the sunglasses. It was almost sundown and it was still too damn hot, and the sun was always too damn bright.

For some reason, he suddenly thought of Beth, lounging by the swimming pool in the backyard of her house, raven black hair about her face and dark sunglasses covering her eyes. She wore a black bikini and he knew she was watching him as he mowed the backyard lawn . . . .

Laughter.

He looked about, but only saw the two soldiers nervously kneeling next to him. Neither had the trace of a smile on his face.

But somewhere, it sounded as if an old man was laughing.

Fucking heat, he thought, wiping his forehead.

The last of the patrols swept through the square. The units had begun at the edges of the town, checking each structure, one at a time, converging on the central square. Like most of the other small towns dotting the land, hundreds of miles from the country's capital, a temple dominated the square.

Seven days ago, the town of Basghar had been home to over three hundred residents. The U.S. satellites that constantly monitored every town in the Mideast country had transmitted pictures of everyday life, with no sign of civil war, or insurgent activity.

Six days ago, the satellite photos depicted burning buildings, abandoned vehicles and no signs of life. Overnight, the town had been decimated.

Army personnel began entering the town within the last twelve hours, once it became clear there was no biological or germ warfare agent at work. As of yet, none of the townspeople had been found.

What the hell happened here? Gorman thought.

He had been ordered to join the investigating units by his employer, with the approval of the U.S. military. To the American public, he did not exist. To most of the military, he was an observer outside the chain of command. To the soldiers in Basghar, he was in charge.

Three soldiers emerged from a squat building to the east, which once housed a grocery store. Now, the food inside was rotting, and a cloud of flies bigger than Gorman's thumb swarmed through its interior. Maggots crawled on the shelves.

The floor by the counter had been slick with blood.

Three helicopters moved into position, forming a triangle with the temple in its center. The swirling air blew more sand down his back and Gorman grimaced.

More laughter?

The earpiece buzzed.

"It's all clear, sir."

"Understood. We're going to proceed."

Gorman gave a hand signal to the soldiers and they rounded the vehicle and sprinted up to the temple. The building had a domed roof and columns guarded the entrance. The soldiers ran up the steps and flanked the door. The temple, like the others in the area, had no windows.

Gorman moved forward. He wore a bulletproof vest beneath the camouflage pattern shirt and loose pants that tightened about his boots.

The temple door was cracked open and he could hear the buzzing of thousands of flies.

Gorman stepped inside.

There was no furniture in the room. A prayer mat covered most of the floor. He could not tell its original color; it was now stained a dark crimson red, and was still wet. One of the soldiers vomited onto his own boots.

The decapitated heads were arranged in rows, all looking to the west and the man tied to the chair in the front of the prayer room.

Three hundred residents, Gorman thought. He keyed the earpiece. "Form a perimeter around the temple. No one else comes in. No one. I'll report soon."

All of their eyes were open, aimed at the man in the chair.

Gorman stepped over them and knelt by the man. He was naked, with his ankles and wrists chained to the chair's arms and legs. His lips were cracked and dry and his face sallow. It didn't appear as if he had anything to eat, or even drink, in days.

"You've come," he whispered. His eyes focused on Gorman for a moment and then went glassy.

"Who are you?"

"I have a message. I have to give it to you. They are watching me, to make sure I give you the message. If I fail, they will persecute me, forever, in hell. They will kill my child."

The man began to weep and as he sobbed, his ribs tried to split open his skin.

"What message?" Gorman asked. "Who did this?"

The man said, "A hall and a court. Thousands will die. It is the last warning. You must leave our country. All of you. Leave here or your very cities will burn. You will know I am telling the truth, because of the hall and the court."

"Who gave you this message?" Gorman touched the man's shoulder, feeling bone, and the man screamed. His body convulsed, causing the chair's legs to dance on the floor and Gorman stumbled backwards as blood flew from the man's ears and nose and mouth.

"Get a medic!" he yelled as the man's body tightened as if electricity burned through his muscles, and then he went slack. Piss flowed down his legs.

The two soldiers in the room retreated towards the doors.

Gorman followed, careful not to disturb any of the decapitated heads.

From somewhere in the distance, he could hear the laughter.

What the hell happened here?